PASSION UNLEASHED

"What really bothers you, Mr. McKean? Is it that my father trusts me enough to help him, or that you have to take orders from a woman?"

"I don't mind taking orders from a woman. I guess, maybe, I don't like being put in one of your categories."

"You don't mind doing the same thing, though. Who are you to judge me? Just what little niche do you put me in?"

He reached out and took hold of her shoulders, dragging her against him. She gasped in shock; for a moment she was too dumbfounded to fight. Her lips were parted in protest and when his mouth crashed down on hers, she could make only a soft sound before she was silenced.

Rachel had been kissed before, but never with this rage or this hot passion. She felt something coil tightly within her as his mouth plundered hers. Sensation after sensation rippled through her, and she felt as if she were falling from a great height. She could only cling to him as the very breath seemed to be drawn from her.

Sylvie SOMMERFIELD

FOREVER

LEISURE BOOKS NEW YORK CITY

To a wonderful and caring
sister-in-law, Jennie June Fusco

A LEISURE BOOK®

April 1999

Published by

Dorchester Publishing Co., Inc.
276 Fifth Avenue
New York, NY 10001

ISBN 0-8439-4491-9

The name "Leisure Books" and the stylized "L" with design are trademarks of Dorchester Publishing Co., Inc.

Printed in the United States of America.

FOREVER

Prologue

Yuma Territorial Prison, 1878

The hot Arizona sun poured down on the harsh landscape like molten lava. It touched the faces of the three men who had just disembarked from the train, washing them in its glistening white heat.

The tallest of the three squinted his eyes against the glare and raised both hands to remove his hat and wipe the perspiration from his face with the crook of his elbow. He had to raise both hands because they were manacled together. As the trio moved forward, his shuffling gait and the rattle of chains bore witness that his ankles were also manacled.

The silver badges on the chests of the other two and the guns worn low on their hips were enough to explain the situation to any onlookers, and there were a number of them.

It wasn't that the people of the town had not seen this situation before: they had. They paused to watch because there was something about the prisoner that drew every eye.

He was tall and lean, and moved with the grace of a predatory panther. His hair was midnight black and hung to his shoulders in a thick, unruly mass. His firm jaw was darkened by a few days' growth of beard. It was a handsome face, yet cold and full of an untamed and very dangerous strength.

But it was his eyes that drew shivers from the fainthearted and wary respect from others. They were hard, cold, and the same steel gray as the barrels of the guns his guards carried.

He had paused too long to suit one of the guards, who gave him a rough shove that made him stumble forward a step or so. He turned his head, and the cold fury in his eyes made the man's smile fade.

"Let him be, Jeffords," the second man said, "or I might take a notion to let him loose and see if you still want to push."

"You gonna baby this killer all the way to the prison?" Jeffords responded, but he kept his distance from the prisoner nonetheless.

"Baby him?" The sheriff chuckled humorlessly. "If you think he's going to be babied in that hellhole he's headed for, maybe you ought to change places with him."

This brought a bitter half smile from the prisoner, and a curse from Jeffords. But before he could answer, a wagon stopped beside them. The driver spat a stream of tobacco juice, then drawled "Y'all the boys for the prison?"

"Yes, I'm Sheriff Douglas, and this is my deputy, Jeffords. The prisoner is one Steven McKean. I have his papers here." Douglas reached for his pocket, but another stream of tobacco cut him short.

"Y'all don't need to give me any papers. I cain't read nohow. Jes bring 'im along for the warden to see."

"All right," the sheriff answered. He took hold of his prisoner's arm and led him to the back of the wagon. For the first time the prisoner spoke. His voice was deep, and just as hard as his appearance promised.

"You expect me to climb in with these irons on?"

"You don't think I'm going to take them off, do you? Turn around with your back to the wagon, I'll heft you in."

"You sure are a trusting man," Steve said with sneer.

"No, not trusting. But I'm still alive, and I intend to stay that way. Now, turn around."

Steve grunted as he was unceremoniously dumped into the back of the wagon. He had to struggle to a sitting position. The deputy and the sheriff climbed in also, but it was only Steve who remained on the floor. The two took a seat on each side of him on a wooden shelf that ran the length of the wagon, and in minutes they were in motion.

The wagon rumbled out of town along a rutted road, and Steve was sure he had personal contact with every rut and bump in it. He grimaced, but adamantly refused to utter a sound. He could see the laughter in the deputy's eyes, and he would be damned if he would give him the satisfaction of complaining.

He had a pretty good idea he was heading toward worse, and that the deputy had a longing to tell him just how bad it would be. He was already struggling to hold on to his nerve; he sure didn't need to be reminded of the years facing him.

To Steve the ride seemed interminable, and he was a

mass of aching muscles by the time they pulled through the gates of Yuma Prison. Dirty, and longing for a cool drink of water, he was dragged from the wagon with the same care with which he had been thrust inside. When his eyes adjusted to the blazing sun, he immediately wished they hadn't.

Yuma Prison had been built only two years before. Situated on a bluff on the south side of the Colorado River, it had walls eight feet thick at the bottom and four feet at the top. The Gatling gun on the watchtower that exploded with three hundred rounds per minute dissuaded any man from attempting to escape.

Hell. The sheriff had been right. He had just walked into hell. He didn't mean to make a sound, but he realized he must have, for both the deputy and the sheriff turned to look at him.

"This is where murder gets you, boy," Sheriff Douglas said quietly. "You should have thought of this before you shot a man."

"I shot a man . . . but it wasn't murder," Steve said coldly.

"Sure, that's what they all say." The deputy laughed.

Again Steve turned his head to look at Jeffords, and the murderous look in his eyes wiped the smile from Jeffords's face.

"Get me where I'm going, Sheriff, and get this bastard out of my sight before I rip his tongue out."

Jeffords's face blanched, for he had the distinct feeling that, manacled or not, Steve McKean might just carry out his threat. In fact, to the sheriff's amusement, Jeffords backed a step or two away. His face flushed as Steve laughed softly and derisively.

Hauled roughly between them, Steve was dragged to the warden's office. Martin Swope was a tall and extremely spare man, with a face like a hatchet, and the eyes of a rattler who dared anyone or anything to disturb him. He took the proffered papers and slowly read them, leaving the three to stand in silence until he finished. When he spoke, his voice was dusty and hoarse, as if he had spent his life in the heat of the desert.

"Seems you're a violent man, Mr. McKean." Steve remained silent. It was a statement of fact and not a question. "Well," he added quietly and looked up at Steve, "we'll take care of that. We have a way of taming down violence. So if you just decide to behave, there won't be any problem, but if you don't see things our way . . . well, we'll just have to do the taming."

His gaze held Steve's and a cold silence filled the room.

"You didn't answer me, Mr. McKean."

"I don't intend to give you any trouble," Steve said reluctantly, giving the answer he knew the warden wanted to hear. The warden actually smiled, but the smile wasn't pleasant.

"Oh, I'm sure you don't." He turned to look at the sheriff. "You can leave him here with me, Sheriff. I'll take responsibility from now on."

When the sheriff and the deputy got back into the wagon for the trip back to the train, Douglas voiced his thoughts.

"I got a feeling it's going to be the longest ten years of McKean's life."

"That be a fact," the driver said. "That be a pure, honest fact. That boy ain't been to hell until now. But he's gonna learn. You can count on that. He'll learn, or they'll bury him here."

11

The deputy smiled to himself and wished he could be around to see McKean brought down. The sheriff began to think he had seen enough of the law, and to wish he had never seen Steven McKean at all.

The cell door slammed shut behind Steve, who stood still and looked slowly about him at the three men with whom he was to share this hole for the next ten years. Ten years, here in this furnace peopled by the dregs of the earth. If he had been of weaker character, he would have wept like a child. But Steve McKean had no thought of tears . . . all his thoughts were on the near impossibility of surviving here for ten years.

Chapter One

Three Years Later

Steve stretched out his long legs and shifted his position slightly so his line of vision encompassed the warden's office. He sat against the hard adobe wall. It was the first time he had been allowed to stop work long enough to take a deep breath and wipe the dirt and grime from his face. If there was anything he missed, it was the luxury of a hot bath with soap that smelled of something besides lye.

He was watching the warden's office for a purpose. He had seen the stranger arrive, and he, like all the others, was curious. There was little of interest in Yuma Prison and the arrival of a U.S. marshal without a prisoner was a unique thing.

Steve took no part in the general speculation about the marshal. He was known as a loner. There were those who had tried to push him after his arrival, and the battles were short and sweet. The word spread: Leave Steve McKean alone or suffer the consequences.

The three men who were walking toward him were the only three he trusted. They shared his cell, and they had been the first to test him. One was a tall and heavily muscled black man named Mikah. Steve had seen some large men in his day, but Mikah was not only the largest, but the strongest. He and Steve had fought to a standstill, until the only thing left to do was to agree not to kill each other. Over the next three years they had become friends.

The second man was a full-blooded Apache with a name he refused to reveal, so they called him Apach. He had a deadly reputation that Steve had learned was more a defense than the truth. He was as graceful as a gazelle, and handy with a knife.

The third man was a Spaniard named Carlos Ortega. Steve had always thought Ortega had been born to better things, for there was a gallantry about him that made him seem out of place anywhere but in a drawing room. Yet he coldly faced any aggressor with a fury that had won him respect long before.

Steve had not asked the reasons for their incarceration, and he had told them none of his past. For these sorts of men, today might be the last and they did not confide in one another easily.

The three squatted down near Steve. Apach spoke first.

"The lawman, does he look for someone?"

"What's the matter, Apach?" Mikah laughed softly. "Afraid of gettin' arrested? Hell, you might get tossed in prison."

Apach grinned, and the smile was so rare that it changed

his countenance completely. "Like all my people, I don't trust the white man's law. He's after something, and it means trouble for someone, my brothers."

"It's Steve's pretty face," Carlos said. "The marshal's wife, she is lonely."

"I haven't been with a woman for five years," Mikah said. "If she's lonely, I could sure be convinced to accommodate her."

This was one time when Steve did not respond as they had expected. "There's not a woman alive I'd walk across this place to touch. They're all alike, and none of them have an honest bone in their bodies. The marshal is after something, though, and I'd sure like to know what. I agree with Apach, you can't trust the law."

The three exchanged glances, but none remarked on Steve's words.

"What do you think, Steve?" Apach asked.

"I don't know. But when the law comes around, it pays to be real careful."

"*Hermano,* do you think he's here to talk to one of the prisoners?" Carlos asked thoughtfully. "I wonder who."

"And I wonder why," Mikah added.

"Well, it doesn't concern me," Steve said, rising to his feet. "I don't have anybody outside of here that gives a damn if I live or die, and there sure isn't anyone outside of here that I give a damn for either, so there's nothing they can say to me." He walked away, and for a minute the three were silent.

"That boy sure carrying a heavy load of hate for one man," Mikah said. "He's hurtin'."

"He ever tell you why he's in here, Mikah?" Carlos questioned.

"He don't talk about nothing before last night's supper. I think he don't want the past in his mind. He's workin' like hell to get rid of something. It's eating him alive. But he don't talk about it and I don't think he ever will. No sir, I don't think he's ever going to let someone that close again."

"Again?" Apach said.

"Yeah, again. I got a sneaking suspicion he opened up and let someone real close, and he got burned bad."

"A woman?" Carlos suggested.

"I don't know, but I wouldn't doubt it. You seen how he was when you mentioned the marshal's wife. Yeah, a woman. He isn't going to trust anyone, but he sure ain't going to trust a woman . . . no, sir, he just ain't."

"Take a look," Apach said softly. The three returned their attention to the warden's office, where the door had opened and the warden and the marshal had walked out onto the porch. They stood and talked for another fifteen minutes, then the marshal walked to his horse, mounted and rode away. The warden stood alone for a minute, then went inside and closed the door.

Steve lay in the darkness of their cell that night and listened to the assorted noises about him. Men confined and uncomfortable. Men full of hate and guilt. Men with no future. He pushed these thoughts aside, for they only increased his anguish.

Instead he searched out the other sounds that permeated the night. In the distance a coyote cried and it was answered by another. There was the rustle of a soft breeze through sycamore trees. The scent of mesquite and a sweeter scent of some kind of flower was in the air. Poignant sounds and scents that made him wish for the freedom he had lost.

God, how he hated this place with its perpetual thirst, and its burning heat, and its confinement. There were times when he was tempted to try to escape; being shot in the attempt was better than this.

For three years he had kept old memories at bay, and he didn't intend to admit them to his thoughts now. It was the marshal's visit that had almost undone him; for the first time since his arrival, he had hoped. Hoped that the truth had been found and his freedom would be restored. But when the marshal had ridden away, he had cursed himself for believing there was hope. There was nothing in life to believe in.

He thought of the three men who made up his life now and wished he could tell them, but even after three years, the wounds were too painful to probe. Still, if there were any he could trust, it would be the ill-assorted companions who slept nearby.

He found it hard to think that there were seven more years to serve on his sentence. Seven more years in the gentle care of warden Martin Swope, who had come to hate him with the same passion that Steve hated where he was.

Swope was waiting patiently for Steve to provide him with an excuse to practice his particular kind of brutality, and Steve had just as patiently refused to break, or even to bend a rule and give him the chance. He had swallowed his pride more than once, but seven years was a long time to take Swope, and Steve wasn't too sure who was going to have the patience.

He wondered if Mikah, Apach and Carlos had the same feelings. They had been here longer than him. It was Apach who cautioned patience and Mikah who talked down

Steve's fury occasionally. The three had stood between him and foolish mistakes more than once. He meant to find out just how much longer they were to be here, because without them he was not going to last under Swope's gentle care very long.

"Mikah, you asleep?" he whispered cautiously. This life was too hard to disturb what little rest a man got.

"No."

"Mind if I ask you something?"

"What's on your mind?"

"How much longer do you have in here?"

"Two more years. But I'm not the lucky one. Carlos only has six months."

"And Apach?"

"I don't know."

"I have three more months." Apach's voice came from the darkness.

Great, Steve thought, in two years all three would be gone. If his life was desolate now, it would be hell when he was alone.

The morning dawned just as hot and dry as the day before. Steve had thrown himself into as much strenuous activity as he could, hoping he would be able to sleep from sheer exhaustion. Mikah's hand on his arm drew his attention.

"That marshal is back," Mikah said softly.

Steve turned to follow the marshal's progress as he rode through the gates and up to the warden's office.

"I wonder what the hell that man's after."

"I don't know, but he sure looks persistent."

"He must be pretty set on what he wants, to come back. Old Swope isn't too easy to deal with, and if that marshal wants something from him, he'll have to beg for it.''

"He don't look like the begging type," Steve replied.

Apach and Carlos approached slowly. It was not wise to look as if they were congregating.

"You two see that the marshal is back?" Carlos asked.

"Yeah," Mikah said. "He's pushing Swope for something."

"I'd like to hear what's going on in there," Carlos added.

"So would I," Steve said thoughtfully. He was forcing hope from his mind. He couldn't afford it.

They stood and watched the closed door until a guard forced them to separate. Even then they remained within sight of the warden's office. The door remained closed for what seemed like hours.

When the door finally opened, it was to reveal an orderly, who trotted across the compound directly toward Steve. His heart in his throat, Steve fought against hope. He couldn't stand the disappointment of another defeat. From nearby, Carlos, Mikah and Apach watched with the unselfish hope that this might mean some good news for a man none of the three thought belonged where he was.

"McKean?"

"Yeah?"

"Warden wants you in his office, quick."

"What's going on?"

"That's for the warden to say. I can tell you he ain't real happy."

"Damn," Steve muttered. He hated the fact that he was dirty and wiped his hands on the tail of his shirt as he walked across the compound. Could it be? Could the truth have been discovered? Could he be free? He could feel his heart pounding fiercely against his ribs. He had not allowed himself to hope before, and it was painful to try to contain it now. God, how he wanted to be free of this place and the grasp of Swope.

It gave him a bit of satisfaction when he was chained before he was led to the office door. For some reason, Warden Swope was afraid of him.

When he opened the door, his gaze met Swope's and for the first time he felt a tingle of real pleasure. Swope was furious. It could be seen in the coldness of his eyes, and Steve could feel his antagonism from across the room.

"You wanted to see me?" he asked quietly, but he was well aware of the intense gaze of the marshal, who was studying him.

"On the end of a rope perhaps," came the Warden's dry and brittle voice. "It's not me who wants to see you. The marshal has something to talk to you about." He rose and walked from the room, closing the door none too gently behind him. There was a long moment of silence.

"I take it the warden doesn't care too much for you." The marshal's voice was soft, and a bit amused.

"What do you want with me, Marshal?"

The marshal walked to the door and opened it a bit to speak softly to the guard outside and take something from him. Then he returned to stand near Steve.

"Sit down, McKean."

"I'll stand, thanks."

"Real hard case?"

"No, just not as trusting as I used to be."

"I want to do you a favor."

"Yeah, sure"—Steve laughed harshly—"a favor. What's in it for you? Besides, I can't do much like this."

He rattled the chains harshly. It surprised him when the marshal took the key from his pocket and unlocked the chains.

"Get the chip off your shoulder."

"Either tell me what you want from me, or let me get about my work. I have a lot to do."

"If I know anything about this place, and I do, there's too much time on your hands . . . maybe too many memories too."

"You didn't come here to discuss my memories."

"No, I didn't. I had a long talk with Sheriff Charles from your home town. Colorado is a nice place. Anyhow, the sheriff seems to think your claim to innocence is justified."

Steve narrowed his eyes and studied the marshal carefully. "I always said it wasn't murder, but none of that means much now, does it?"

"Maybe it does."

"Who the hell are you?"

"Marshal Thomas P. Wade, Marshal of Montana Territory."

"I've never been to Montana, so what does this have to do with me?"

"I know you've never been to Montana. But I think I can be of help to you."

"Like I said, Marshal Wade, what's in it for you?"

"How would you like to have the rest of your sentence commuted? It's seven years, I think."

"You know damn well it's seven years, and I'd lick somebody's boots to get out of this hole. Now, what's in it for you?"

"You're one stubborn man, aren't you?"

"I just don't trust gifts. If you have something on your mind, why don't you just spit it out?"

"All right, there is something I want you to do for me . . . but you'll be doing yourself a favor too." Wade walked to the warden's desk and opened a drawer to remove a bottle of whiskey. He crossed the room to get two glasses from a small cupboard, and then poured two liberal drinks. "Have a drink. It's Swope's best, and he'd be livid if he knew I had offered you one."

Steve smiled for the first time, a tight, seldom used smile. He wanted a drink. He took the glass and tossed the drink down, grimacing as it burned its way to his belly. But the warmth spread through him and almost made him sigh in pleasure as it cut through the dust in his throat.

"Now, sit down and listen."

Steve sat and waited while Wade thought for a minute. "I've got a problem in my territory that puts me up against some hard rock. I need an undercover man, someone no one in the territory knows. I won't say it's not dangerous, because it is."

"That doesn't come as much of a surprise. What's the story?"

"An old one with a new twist. There's a lot of good ranchers there, but only two really large ones. Someone is driving off the small ranchers and trying to swallow up the whole territory. There have been a few murders. A rancher named Macquen was found in his own barn. It seems he hanged himself. Another named Travors died in a suspicious fire. Two others, Gibson and Niles, left a little too fast for me to believe it was of their own free will. I can't prove anything, and no one has the courage to talk, but I have to protect those small ranchers. There's a big and very slick group at work here, but I can't figure out who's behind it. I need help.''

''What made you pick me?''

''I'll tell you the truth, I didn't pick you. In fact, I didn't have this idea in the first place. It seems you've got a friend in Sheriff Charles. He thinks our plan is a good way to lift that sentence from you. He also thinks,'' Wade added softly, ''that you can be trusted . . . that you won't run.''

''You went to see him?''

''No, he came to see me.''

''Then you never met the judge?''

''No. But from what Sheriff Charles says, you were fighting odds you couldn't beat.''

''And how does the sheriff think Judge Graham feels about this?''

''He—'' Wade began.

''No, let me tell you. He'd like to see me hanged but since he can't, he wants me to rot. He's against this and promises I'll betray you the first chance I get.''

''That's about right.''

''And you still want me?''

''Yes. Should I tell you why?''

''I wish you would.''

''I like and trust Sheriff Charles. I don't happen to know the judge, but the sheriff has little respect for him. He and I would like to prove Judge Graham wrong.''

''I didn't know there was anyone who saw through Judge Graham but me.''

''Sheriff Charles says the judge hates you. But if you run . . . if you betray us, I can promise you one thing. I'll find you and there will be five years attached to your sentence . . . that is, if I bring you back alive.''

23

"How much do you think I'm worth?"

"Money?"

"Hell no. Support."

"Just about whatever you want."

"You said there were two big ranchers, either of which could be behind this group that's causing the trouble."

"Yes."

"You know it's impossible for one man to be in two places at the same time."

"I can offer you all the help you need."

"I pick my own friends."

"To be truthful, I didn't know you still had any."

"There are three men in here I'd like to ride with me."

"You mean you want me to get three more men pardoned?"

"Exactly."

"The warden will have a nervous fit."

"Yeah"—Steve grinned—"he just might."

"I'll do my best, but—"

"No buts. They go . . . or I stay."

"That's your final word?"

"It sure is. They don't have as much time to serve as I do, and they're men I would trust at my back. Four are better than one, aren't they?"

"Do you always ask impossible things?"

"If you can get me out of here, you've already done the impossible. The judge does hate me, so you don't have to tell me how much pull it took to get past him. Who did you see?"

"A few influential people in Washington. Graham has influence, and you're sure right, he hates you. Care to tell me why?"

"You don't know?"

"I know what he says; I'd like to hear your side."

"Is it part of the deal?"

"No, there are no strings attached. You don't have to tell me anything."

"Then if you don't mind, I'll take care of Judge Graham my own way."

"You talking revenge?"

"Not to a territorial marshal." Steve smiled a tight smile. "Don't worry, I don't mean to kill him, just to find my own answers . . . after I take care of this little problem."

"You think you can 'take care of this little problem'?"

"I'll give it my best . . . if I have my friends behind me."

"Damn . . . I'm going to have to find some strong strings to pull."

"So, find them. Believe me, I'm not going anywhere."

"Have another drink. Then I'm going out to find my strings. In the meantime, take a piece of advice from me."

"Yeah?"

"Keep on the good side of the warden. I have a feeling if you died in here it would satisfy a lot of people."

"He doesn't have a good side. Besides, if they were going to kill me, they would have done it a long time ago."

"No, you're still a story back home, still in everyone's mind. A little more time and I think your days would be numbered. Just be careful and stay out of his way. Don't give him cause."

"He wants cause, he'll find it."

"Just don't provoke him. He's afraid of you."

"He ought to be afraid of something. The men here are living in hell. Swope thrives on his prisoners' pain."

"Steve, you can get free and maybe help your friends

too. Don't let him push you into something foolish.''

"How long is it going to take you to find out about my friends?''

"A week at least.''

"Does the warden know why you're here?''

"Not everything. I want to make my move before he can get word to the judge and stop me.''

"The judge will know as soon as Swope is certain. You'd better make that a fast week or forget it. I have a feeling your plans for me and Swope's don't match.''

Wade nodded and poured two more drinks. Steve drank, and silently hoped he would be alive when Wade got back. He knew Judge Graham better than anyone else.

Apach, Carlos and Mikah had watched the office carefully, while keeping an eye on the guards. They saw the warden leave and walk toward a group of three guards they knew to be his personal bloodhounds.

"Keep an eye on them," Apach said. "I'll see if I can get around back and hear anything. Signal if they come sniffing."

Apach could move with the silence and swiftness of a coiled snake. In seconds he disappeared behind the warden's office. Mikah and Carlos kept an eye on the guards and wished they could hear the words the warden was saying so rapidly and intently.

Apach appeared at their side just as the office door opened and the marshal came out. Beside him stood Steve, in chains. The warden and the three guards went over to them.

"What went on in there, Apach? Did you hear anything?''

"Let's wait until we hear what Steve has to say."

They looked at him with puzzled looks, but asked no more questions. The three guards pushed and shoved Steve back to the group and ordered them to go on with their work. Swope stood on the porch and gazed across at Steve with a malevolent look.

"Steve, what the hell did that marshal want with you?" Mikah asked.

"They know I'm a fast gun. They want me to help them catch a few skunks."

"Got a hell of a lot of nerve, don't they," Carlos said mildly. "What's in it for you?"

"Knock off a little time, they said," Steve answered, but he had become aware that Apach was regarding him with a deep and unfathomable look. "What's on your mind, Apach?"

"You said they were going to knock off a little time. Perhaps there is more you would ask for if they want help."

"What are you talking about, Apach?" Mikah questioned. Steve was caught by surprise. He had no idea Apach had heard enough of what went on in the office to understand what Steve meant to sacrifice for them.

"Our friend had a chance to get free, and to have his sentence erased. He refused unless we were freed with him." Apach said the words quietly, his gaze holding Steve's. All three were momentarily silenced. No one had ever sacrificed anything for their benefit before.

"Look, it was just a gamble. They could say no," Steve protested.

"It's not the gamble, amigo," Carlos said. "It is that you chose to try. Such a thing is very rare."

"Rare, hell," Mikah said. "Ain't no one ever gone out

27

on a limb for me. You telling me he could have agreed and gone alone?''

''That is what Apach is saying,'' Carlos replied. ''I'll not forget this, compadre, even if it doesn't work.''

''Well, if that just don't beat all,'' Mikah said as if awestruck. ''If that don't beat all.''

''Look, it was a chance and I need help. I don't think one man can do what they want done. Besides, I'd like to know I have a friend or two somewhere if the going gets rough, and I think it will. Any of you ever been involved in a land battle?''

''It was purely a selfish request then?'' Carlos grinned. ''You could get no help from the marshal and his men?''

''It was offered,'' Apach said. ''Steve refused. Said he wanted men at his back he could trust.''

''Apach, where the hell were you, in the marshal's pocket?'' Steve said peevishly.

''Close,'' Apach chuckled. ''I heard everything . . . and I am grateful. I do not hope too much, but if it does happen, I would have you know my life is yours. If I can do anything for you, I will be beside you. I have never known such a friend . . . and I do not forget.''

''Don't count on anything,'' Steve protested. He would not have told them until he knew for sure. Now they might all be disappointed.

''I ain't had anything to count on for years,'' Mikah said. ''At least this is something to think on. A man givin' up his freedom to fight for mine. Hell, I'll be your shadow for as long as you need me.''

''I think you speak for us all,'' Carlos said.

''Break it up.'' The guard's snarling voice came from

close by, and they obeyed quickly. All four knew the penalty for not moving fast when an order was given.

Within his office Martin Swope raged. He had been ready to move, to carry out the orders he had been given when McKean had been brought to him: See that he doesn't survive, but don't do it right away; give him a few years of torment first.

Now he'd lost his opportunity, as well as a sum of money that could still make his mouth water in anticipation.

How could he go against the force of a U.S. Marshal? The interfering do-gooder was going to thwart not only his wishes, but also those of the man who was paying him.

He considered writing to his employer, but he had no way of knowing what had been said in his office. No, he needed orders from someone who could take the blame if anything went wrong. He was afraid the man he had mistreated just might get his freedom. The idea made him sweat.

For three days Swope watched Steve McKean, who seemed to be giving no thought to the marshal's visit at all. Then he had Steve dragged, in ankle shackles and wrist irons, to his office.

It infuriated him when he could see the derisive amusement in McKean's eyes as he shuffled his way across the office to stand before his desk.

As if he were unafraid, Swope sent the guards from the room, and returned Steve's gaze as steadily as he could. The damned man had a look of such leashed power that Swope felt nervous despite the chains.

"There something on your mind, Warden?"

"Shut up until I tell you different."

Steve shrugged with such an arrogant gesture that Swope clenched his teeth.

"I have a few questions, and I want answers." Steve remained silent. "Did you hear what I said?" His voice grated across Steve's nerves like a saw blade.

"Sure."

"Well?"

"You told me to shut up until you said different. Do you want me to comment on your statement or what?"

"You son of a bitch. Don't you get clever with me."

"I'm afraid you're wrong."

"Wrong?"

"I knew my mother, and she was a lady. I have a suspicion you can't say the same . . . that is, if you knew who she was at all." Steve knew he was playing with fire, but the chains and the cowardice of the man got under his skin. It did him good to see Swope's face turn so red it looked as if he were about to explode. "You want me to answer questions, maybe you ought to ask some, instead of showing off your power."

Swope fought an obvious battle for self-control, but finally his face cleared and he smiled a vicious smile.

"I want to know what Marshal Wade wanted with you."

"You mean he didn't tell you?" Steve asked so innocently that Swope felt the urge to shoot him where he stood.

"No, he did not, and I want to know."

"I don't think it's anything I can tell you. Why don't you ask the marshal . . . or did he decide he didn't want you to know?"

"You're pushing your luck, McKean."

"No, sir, just making sure I don't make any mistakes. I

wouldn't want Marshal Wade angry with me. Yes, I think you should ask him.''

"Do you think a couple of days in the box will change your mind?" Swope asked softly. Even softened, the voice was like a file rasping over a piece of splintered wood.

Steve felt the bottom drop from his stomach, but his gaze held the warden's. The box had drained the life from more than one man. Steve had no intention of letting Swope know he was scared to death. He remained quiet.

"I asked you a question."

"No," Steve said as firmly as he could. "I don't think the box will change my mind."

"That your last word?"

"I can't think of anything else I'd like to say . . . to you."

"Guard!" The guard opened the door at once and stepped inside. "What's the longest time anyone has held out in the box?"

"We dragged Thompson out after three days, and he was blubbering like a baby."

"Three days. Do you want to talk to me," he asked Steve quietly, "or shall we try for four?"

Steve swallowed hard. He was more scared than he thought he could ever be. "I don't have anything to tell you." His voice sounded hoarse to him. There were other lives that depended on his silence, and he was not going to betray his friends no matter what happened.

"Take him to the box," Swope said coldly, "and call me after four days. McKean, if you have something you want to say to me, just call the guard." Swope smiled smugly, certain his prisoner would be begging in no time.

31

Steve remained silent. He didn't think he had enough spit to make a sound. Instead, he smiled.

"Get him out of here. Four days, remember that."

The guard took Steve's arm and he did not resist. There was no use in resistance. He only prayed that Wade would be back before he was dead.

The box. One of the worst forms of torture ever devised by a sick mind. It was a box of iron, buried just below the ground, with only a small pipe for air.

It was too short to stand in and too narrow to lie in: all a man of Steve's proportions could do was crouch or sit with his knees drawn up. It was also an oven that quickly made a man agreeable to anything that would relieve his agony.

All eyes watched as he was dragged to the box, and thrust down into the darkness.

"What the hell did he do to get the box?" Mikah whispered.

"I have a feeling there's something Swope wants from him," Apach said.

"Mother of God, if he gets more than a day or two, he'll die in there," Carlos said.

"Hey!" Mikah called out to one of the guards. "How long does he have in there?"

"Four days . . . or until the warden lets him out."

"Four days," Mikah said. "That's a death sentence."

"No!" Apach said fervently. "We will call on all the gods we know. He will not die . . . we won't let him."

Steve sought every ounce of will he possessed, and when the first day of his entombment ended, he shivered with the fear that he did not have enough will to make it. He thirsted with an unbearable thirst, and his body had sweated away what moisture he had. He had vomited until there was nothing left of the little food he had eaten.

The next day the smell of his own body, and the filth in which he had to remain, made his world spin out of control.

How long had it been? He didn't know anymore. Every muscle and bone in his body felt as if it were on fire. Reality began to fade, and old memories crowded his mind until he was lost.

Three days after Steve had been thrown in the box, Swope rode into town and returned more than satisfied. He had received a telegram in response to one he had sent. He needed to know how much freedom he had, to what lengths he could go. The telegram contained only two words: Kill him. He knew just how to accomplish that. He meant to leave McKean where it would take him a long time to die.

But he had only been back in the prison half an hour before the gates swung open to admit Marshal Wade, the last person Swope wanted to see. Now he could only hope Steve McKean was dead already.

"I have permission to take Steve McKean and three other inmates from the prison," Wade said as he handed the appropriate papers to Swope.

"I'm afraid you might just be too late. McKean was . . . disturbing the peace and safety of the prison, and needed to be disciplined."

"Disciplined?" Wade was angry. "I suggest you take me to him right now, and for your sake, he had better be alive."

Swope led Wade to the box, and stood with him as Steve was resurrected. He was dragged up from the pit of hell more dead than alive. He never knew when he was laid on a bunk, and water was trickled down his throat.

He also never knew that his life was saved by the combined efforts of Wade, Mikah, Carlos and Apach, who knew a great deal about Indian methods of healing. The four fought for his life, but it was a week before they knew they had succeeded.

When Steve opened his eyes and rationality gleamed there, all his friends breathed a sigh of relief.

When they rode from the prison, Steve vowed one thing. He would carry out the mission Wade had given him, because he would die before he would go back to the place that had almost taken both his life and his sanity.

When they rode across the border into Montana, Steve was dedicated to the purpose that had freed him, and his three friends were just as dedicated to him. They felt he had almost given up his life for them. They meant to follow him into hell if the need arose.

Chapter Two

Montana, One Month Later

Rachel Walker folded the letter she had been reading, and smiled at the message it brought. She rose from the bed where she had been sitting. Walking to her bedroom door, she opened it and half ran down the steps and into the kitchen where her mother was busy making dinner plans.

Lori Walker, the opposite of her daughter in most ways, was a petite woman of forty-two, who carried her years so well she looked less than thirty-five. Her hair was deep auburn, and she had a shy, melting smile that endeared her to just about everyone who lived on the Walker ranch.

Servants followed her every whim with utter devotion, and would have stood between her and anything that could ruffle her equanimity. And what ruffled her equanimity the most was her wayward daughter, who did not seem to know what the words "no" and "propriety" meant.

This was why the people of the Rocking W took it upon themselves to be Rachel's protector. Rachel took after her father, the volatile and handsome Carter Walker. He was a flame-haired man with a grand sense of humor and a temper to match. Rachel received her height from him, for she was five foot seven, and slender, with a lush body that could, and did, drive men to distraction. Her skin was peach and gold accentuated by her fiery hair.

When Rachel burst into the kitchen, Lori smiled resignedly. She would never tame the enthusiasm of her daughter and force her into the gentler ladylike actions she favored.

"Rachel, must you explode into a room?"

"Mother! Guess who I just received a letter from?"

"I can't imagine."

"Yvonne! Yvonne is on her way here to visit me for a few weeks."

"Yvonne?"

"You remember. She was the best friend I had at school."

"Ah, yes. Yvonne Avery. Lovely young lady, if I remember well."

"She was wonderful, and a dear friend. We shall have to have a party."

"Of course. When does she come?"

"If she left on schedule, she should be here in less than a week."

"Then I shall make some plans . . . and you shall have a new gown made."

"Oh, Mother, my old gown is good enough. I've only worn it once. You will love Yvonne," Rachel laughed.

"She wears ruffles and lace, and acts like a lady all the time."

"Perhaps it will rub off. You will never catch a husband the way you act."

"If you mean I don't flirt and flatter, then you are right. Anyway, I don't want a man I have to 'catch.' As a matter of fact, I'm completely happy and I don't want a man at all. I haven't seen one I'd cross the street for."

"What about Cal Davis?"

"Cal? Mother, Cal is a friend."

"I don't think he has the same idea."

"What makes you say that? Has he been talking to Dad?"

"He has . . . suggested that a marriage between the two of you would make these two ranches the largest in the territory when you inherit."

"How utterly romantic," Rachel said dryly. "More of a merger than a wedding."

"There are times to be practical too."

"Cal has said nothing to me, and if he does, don't expect me to say yes."

"Just what is it you're looking for, Rachel?"

"Someone like Dad. And I don't think his kind is too easy to find. I'm just not going to settle for less, so let's stop talking about it before we fight. I don't want to argue with you. I have enough trouble with Dad."

Lori knew Rachel was right. She shook her head and sighed. Rachel grinned and snatched an apple from the bowl on the table before she left the kitchen.

Walking out on the porch, she shielded her eyes against the sun and studied an approaching rider. She knew who it was. She stuffed the folded letter in the pocket of her pants, and continued to munch the apple as she waited for him to arrive.

She considered her mother's words, and wondered mildly why she could not find it in herself to fall in love with one of the most eligible bachelors in the territory. She didn't know what she wanted, but it wasn't marriage and it wasn't doubling the size of the ranch either.

As far as she was concerned, there was enough to the Rocking W for her to be more than satisfied. She was no fool, and she knew what was happening to some of the small ranchers, but her father had said "a man shouldn't have what he can't hold" and she leaned toward this philosophy as well.

Her father had fought for and developed the land they had, and she would fight as hard as anyone to hold it. Like everyone else, she wondered who was buying up all the small ranchers, but since it didn't affect her, she put the question from her mind as Cal rode up to the porch and dismounted.

There was no doubt about it, Cal Davis was one of the handsomest men around. He was tall and huskily built, with an easy smile, a witty and intelligent mind. He had sandy brown hair, and a neatly trimmed moustache to match. His eyes were sky blue, and always warm and friendly. Rachel knew quite well that most of the single women around had set their caps for him. Maybe there was something wrong with her, but she just couldn't see spending the rest of her life with a man whom she thought of as an older brother.

"Morning, Rachel."

"Good morning, Cal. What are you doing out here so early?"

"Actually, I came to talk to your father. I heard some

news in town last night that he might be interested in.''

''News? What?''

''The Parker place. It seems they signed away their ranch a couple days ago to some organization.''

''I never thought they would sell out. I always heard Ellie say she and Fred had put all their dreams and their money in that ranch. They were small, but they could have made it.''

''Well, what makes it even more strange is that there wasn't any money exchanged that the bank knows about. It was either a cash deal, or Parker left with nothing.''

''You mean they were forced out, without anything?''

''That's the way it looks. I thought your father would want to know.''

''Why? I mean, why would Dad be particularly interested?''

''Because he's asked me to let him know which of the ranchers in the area are selling.''

''If you wait until I get my horse, I'll ride out with you. I know exactly where Dad is.''

''I kind of hoped you'd suggest that,'' Cal said, grinning. ''That's why I came here first. I want to talk to you about something.''

''All right. I'll just be a few minutes.''

''Why don't I walk to the stable with you?''

''Fine.'' Rachel walked down the four steps, and Cal moved to walk beside her as they made their way to the stable. A short time later Lori watched from a window as they rode away together. She was sober-faced, for she knew her daughter well, and knew Cal was in for a disappointment. She just wished she knew what would change her daughter's mind.

Carter, the man she loved to distraction for twenty-four years, wanted this marriage. Did he want it enough to convince Rachel to marry a man he knew she didn't love? There was no doubt that Rachel adored her father. The question was, would she marry to satisfy him? Lori was suddenly afraid.

Rachel rode well and Cal always enjoyed riding with her. He could watch her, and that was one of his favorite pastimes. He fantasized about making love to her in as many assorted circumstances as he could. Always he seduced her and always she came to him willingly. It would soon be time to put his fantasies away, and bring reality to life. His father, Joseph Davis, had been pushing the relationship for the past few years. Joseph knew quite well that the two ranches, joined, would be a power no one could defeat.

"I've been meaning to ask you something," Cal began.

"Why haven't you?"

"Because you're hard to pin down," he laughed. "It's like trying to catch my own shadow."

"Well, I'm here"—Rachel smiled mischievously—"and I will be pleased to go to the dance with you. I always thought that we had an understanding."

"Speaking of understandings—" Cal's eyes sparkled, and Rachel realized she'd walked into it.

"Oh no, we were speaking of dances, and since that's settled . . . come on, I'll race you." She kicked her horse into a run and Cal shook his head, then followed. One day he would pin Rachel down, but it sure didn't look like that would be today . . . perhaps at the dance.

They found Carter at the camp where branding was going on. Carter had never been an absentee boss, but had governed every move that was made on his ranch. Rachel waved when he spotted her, and he stood up slowly and waved back.

As they approached, Rachel again felt the wave of pride and love she felt for her father. He was the model she held every man up to. So far no one had measured up.

"Hey! What are you two doing out here?" Carter called out to them.

Cal was well aware of how Rachel felt about her father. She could never see anything he did as wrong. Cal didn't think the man had been born that could live up to her image of Carter Walker. He just had to convince Rachel that he was at least second best.

Carter was a huge man, without an ounce of fat on his six-foot-two body. He had gold red hair, grass green eyes, and a booming voice that could make a strong man tremble, yet could turn deep and warm to melt a woman's heart. He had given his own heart to Lori, and had never strayed from that day on. The only other woman who had a place in his affections was Rachel.

"Dad, we were just coming out to bring some news."

"Don't tell me you two have something to announce?"

Cal didn't look at Rachel, because he was afraid to see anger. Instead, he heard her laugh.

"Stop matchmaking like an old gypsy. Cal and I have not decided to do anything but go to the dance next week. Cal has some other news for you. I didn't know you were interested in the Parker ranch."

"The Parker ranch?" Carter cast a quick, scowling look at Cal. "What's happened?"

"To tell the truth, nobody seems to know the facts," Cal said.

41

"What the hell does that mean?"

"Dad."

"A man sells or he doesn't," Carter said.

"The bank says he deposited no money, and no one withdrew enough to pay for it. Still, it's changed hands."

"Another one? They were supposed—" He stopped and glanced at Rachel's curious face. "I guess there's nothing to do about it. I suppose they'll be after the others too."

It was clear that Carter didn't want the matter discussed any further. "I need a few more hands," he said, changing the subject. "There are more calves this roundup than I thought there would be. I'm going into town today to see what I can find. I suppose your dad might need some help too."

"He has mentioned it," Cal replied. Again he didn't look at Rachel. She had the sense that he and her father shared some knowledge that they wished to keep from her.

"Cal," she said abruptly, "would you mind leaving me and my father alone for a while?"

"Rachel—"

"Please, Cal."

"All right, but I'll wait back at the house for you. I need to talk to you."

"All right," Rachel replied, but she had never taken her eyes from her father, who stood very still and returned her gaze. Rachel waited until the sound of Cal's horse faded away.

"Dad . . . I intended to go into town. I knew we needed more hands. Is there something you're not telling me? Something that Cal knows?"

"Like what?" He looked at her blankly.

"I can handle the ranch, Dad. I love it. Don't give Cal the impression it might be his one day."

"Rachel, that's not fair. You know I would never take a thing from you."

"But you would put me in the position of handing it to him with your blessing."

"No!"

"Dad, will this ranch be mine one day?"

"You know it will. You're my only child."

"Then let me learn to run it, all the way, not just from the kitchen. I can handle it. I'm as good a judge of hands as you or Cal. I need to know everything there is to know about this ranch."

"Step down from that horse, girl."

Rachel dismounted and walked to her father, who opened his arms to embrace her. "I'm sorry. I stepped out of line. I know what you are capable of. You go and hire the new hands, and we'll forget this happened."

"Dad . . . I'm not going to marry Cal Davis."

"Has he asked you?"

"No, but I know he's going to, just as I know you and mother wish it was true."

"Can I help it if I want what's best for you?"

"It's okay if you *want* it, but not to buy it."

"You have to admit, the two ranches together would make us strong enough that we would never have to fear anything."

"Enough is enough, and I don't believe you have ever been afraid of anything in your life."

"Rachel, if I thought enough was enough, I never would have gained what I have now. Don't sneer at having bigger and better."

"But you see, I'm happy with what I have, and I know Mom is too. We have you and the Rocking W. That's enough to make life perfect. Let's just forget merging for now."

"For now? Is there hope?"

"Who knows?" She laughed. "If Cal were more like you, I would agree right away. Besides, I'm the best foreman you have, and Cal is not you."

"Why, sweetheart," Carter boomed. He put his arm about her waist and walked to her horse with her. "There is only one me, so you're going to have to settle for second best."

"Nope. I'm my father's daughter. I never settle for second best."

He watched her mount, then reached up to put his hand over hers on the saddle horn. "Cal is a good man, Rachel. I don't think he's second best to any man."

"I know he's a good man. It's just . . ."

"Just?"

"I don't know, and that's the truth. You and Mother have always been so happy together. I want what you have."

"Marriage takes growing into."

"Just remember, Rocking W goes with me. Consider whose hands you want it in."

"I have no doubt that whoever you marry, the Rocking W will always be in your hands." Carter laughed. "So when are you going to look up some help?"

"First thing in the morning. Right now, I have to wiggle out of hearing a proposal from Cal."

"You're impossible. I don't think Cal will be held off too long."

"I'll worry about tomorrow, tomorrow. I have the ranch to think of now. See you at home for dinner."

"Sure." Carter watched her ride away, and stood there, quite still, for a long time after she had disappeared.

Rachel rode slowly now. She liked being alone, and riding across the land she loved. Lately she had felt a restlessness, and a longing for something she did not understand. She didn't like the way everything in her life seemed . . . ordered, as if she were just following a pattern, slipping into a mold . . . doing what was expected of her.

So what if she agreed to marry Cal? Of course, they would have the largest acreage in the territory, and it would make them powerful. But what of their life together? Could she pin herself down and be what Cal wanted? No, it was not in her nature. She would be fighting him within a month, and hating him within a year. She had been her own master for too long, and she could not give that part of herself to a man . . . any man.

When the ranch house came into view, she reined in her horse to admire the spread, as she had done for most of her life. It had started out as a small cabin, when her parents had first come here, and together they had added to it over the years until it contained nine rooms and was as close to luxurious as it could be.

She could see Cal's horse tied to the rail before the house. Slowly she rode down the hill toward home.

Steve and Mikah rode into Chambersburg slowly, looking closely about them to commit everything and everyone to memory. Carlos and Apach had come into town from a different direction. Plans had been discussed and solidified, and places of meeting and methods to send messages arranged. They would have little contact with Marshal Wade unless they found something. Only then, or in case of emergency, were they to contact him. It was up to them now to find jobs with the right people, to keep their eyes open, and to uncover any clue as to who was behind the threat against the ranchers.

Freedom . . . freedom was the dominant thought in Steve's mind now. He could taste the pleasure of it, breathe in the scent of clean, sweet air, and savor the ability to ride where he chose without someone with a gun and a belly full of hate hovering over him. He had his freedom, and he meant to keep it. He would find who they wanted found if he had to die trying. He would not go back to Yuma.

"Right nice looking little town," Mikah said.

"Yeah, quiet."

"I guess the saloon is the best place to get a start. Any man looking for hands, or any hand looking for a job, generally ends up there."

"I won't argue. I could use a drink and a good thick steak as well. I don't think I'm ever going to get over being hungry."

"Yeah, Yuma has that effect on a man. Me, I don't think I'll ever get enough of just riding around. Freedom tastes good, doesn't it?"

"Too good to lose. Here's the saloon. Let's eat and ask some questions. Find out who has the biggest ranches around. They're the best bet to be needing help."

"Think we're going to cause any problems?" Mikah asked quietly.

"Who, you and me?"

"No, me and Apach."

"I don't think everyone is going to be receptive. But Apach is the best man with a horse to be found. All Apaches are. Any smart rancher is going to know that. If he gets hired, he'll just have to battle it out with the hands. I think Apach will be all right. As far as you're concerned"—Steve grinned—"I don't think there's a man alive who's going to give you any trouble. I tried it and all I got was a couple broken ribs and a bad headache. You'll be fine. Anyone who doesn't like it will just have to find out how stupid it is to argue with us."

"Us?"

"We're in this together, Mikah. I don't think it can be done alone, and I know none of us wants to go back. We don't have any choice . . . we work together and we're all free. We don't and we'll fail. I don't know about you, but I don't intend to fail. I don't care who's responsible, I intend to find him and dump him in Wade's hands and get on with my life."

"You got your own scores to settle, don't you?"

"Yeah, I do."

"It could send you back to Yuma, if you mess with the same people who put you there in the first place."

"No, it won't. I was a fool once, I don't intend to be one again. I learned about trust the hard way."

"I take it she was beautiful."

"Yeah, she was beautiful. Let it go at that, Mikah."

"Sure . . . at least until you can believe that you really can trust me and the others. We're grateful to you, Steve, and we'd go along with helping you if you needed us."

"I won't drag you into it, Mikah. Let's settle for one job at a time."

"Fine . . . just don't forget."

"I won't."

The pair were aware of the curious gazes that followed them as they dismounted and walked into the saloon. Steve had been right, and Mikah was amused. It was obvious that some would have liked to throw Mikah out, but his size, his dangerous look, and Steve at his side with the gun that hung low on his hip dissuaded their ugly thoughts. The bartender tried for some courage by ignoring Mikah.

"What'll you have?" He directed his question to Steve, who smiled a tight and aggressive smile.

"I'll have what my friend is having. Why don't you ask him?"

The bartender swallowed and looked at Mikah, who was smiling benignly. "We'll take two of the biggest steaks you've got and all the trimmings. And get us a bottle of your best and two glasses."

"Sure, sure," the man mumbled and left as quickly as he could. Steve grinned at Mikah, who laughed softly in return. When the bartender returned with the bottle and glasses, he set them on the table and turned to leave without another word, but Steve stopped him. He turned to Steve, hoping there would be no confrontation.

"Who are the biggest and best ranchers around here?"

"There are a lot of ranches in this territory, but if you want the biggest and the best, that would be the Davis place or the Walkers'."

"Either of them looking for help?"

"You boys looking for work?"

"If we find the right place."

"This is branding time. I guess just about every rancher is looking for more help."

"Who would you say would be our best bet?"

"You mean pay wise?"

"There any other reason for work?"

"No, I guess not. I think they're all about the same. Davis and Walker, they pay about thirty a month. Some of the smaller places pay a little less. I guess that's why those two get the best help most of the time."

"How do the smaller places compete?" Steve asked casually.

"How the hell should I know? I don't like ranching, that's why I opened this saloon. You can make a hell of a lot more without breaking your back and your heart." He moved away quickly.

"Kind of touchy, ain't he?" Mikah said. "Especially about the small ranches."

"Looks like," Steve agreed. He took the bottle and poured two drinks, and he and Mikah silently observed who came and went while they waited for their meal. Neither were surprised when someone else brought the food. They ate and drifted from the saloon.

"Where do we go from here?" Mikah questioned.

"We find out as much as we can about those two and make a choice. Then we go asking for work."

It took very little time to learn more about Davis and Walker, but in the end they used a flip of the coin to make their decision.

"You call it," Steve said to Mikah.

"Heads it's Davis," Mikah said at once. Steve tossed the coin in the air and caught it, slapping it on the back of his hand.

"Tails. Looks like we try the Walker place first. I wonder what their brand is." He stopped a passerby. "Can you tell me the brand of the Walker ranch?"

"You must really be new in this part of the country, if you don't know the Rocking W."

"Pretty important are they?"

"Important! You bet your bottom dollar they are. Big and carry a lot of weight. I wouldn't be surprised to see old Carter Walker get into politics one day. He likes to grow."

"You think they're hiring?"

"Wouldn't doubt it. Size of them, and it being branding time, I just wouldn't doubt it. You might ask Carter's kid, though. She came into town this morning."

"She?"

"Yeah, Carter's daughter. She takes after her daddy, that's for sure. She's second only to the old man, and she's just as stubborn and ambitious."

"Thanks. Oh, by the way, where can I find this . . . lady?"

"She'd be down to the town hall, that's where most go to check out folks needing work."

"Thanks again."

"Steve," Mikah said as soon as they were out of earshot of the stranger. "You think this . . . ambition has both father and daughter making a grab for the whole territory?"

"I wouldn't be surprised. Greed, ambition and larceny aren't just a man's way. A pretty face can cover a black heart and no conscience without any trouble. Let's go see if we can find her."

Rachel had not had much luck finding the new hands she knew her father would need. There were a lot of layabouts around, but she knew they could not be depended upon to work any longer than it took to get enough money to move

50

on or find a bottle. She wanted men she could count on for an honest day's work. She also wanted a man who did not believe she might come with the job.

So far, the few she had talked to had been drifters or shrewd-eyed men who looked at her as if to convey the thought that they didn't think much of a woman doing man's work. She had not hired any of them.

The hall in which she stood was the place where most of the activities of the town were held, from dances to trials, when a traveling territorial judge came by about once every two or three months. At that time, anyone the sheriff had arrested on any charge was brought to the town hall, tried and sentenced.

At the moment the hall was nearly empty, with the exceptions of a gathering of ladies of the sewing circle, and several of the town council men who were deciding how the hall would be decorated for the annual dance given by the local church.

Rachel stood in one corner of the room and discussed her situation with a friend.

"You ain't had much luck today, Rachel," William Price was saying, "but you need to be patient. I guess Joe Davis got hold of a couple of good boys. One's a real Apache, but Brace Miller says he ain't never seen a man who can handle horses like that boy can."

"Nobody knows horses better than Brace does. Where did he find them?"

"Says they just rode in and asked for work. Brace says the other one is quite a character. He talks like an educated man, but he's Spanish. Brace's sister says he's a real handsome fella."

"Well, a handsome face is not a requirement. I just need

51

some hard workers. I'll come back tomorrow. If you run across any likely prospects, hang onto them.''

"I sure will, Rachel. You give my best to your ma and your pa.''

"I will, Mr. Price.''

Rachel had just turned from him toward the door when it opened and two men walked in. For a moment they were just shadowy forms in the doorway, and she continued in their direction. Then the door closed and Rachel stopped in mid stride. She had seen handsome men before, but never had she seen a man such as the one before her. It was not just that he was handsome. It was an aura of . . . danger was the only word she could think of. Then his gaze met hers and for a moment she sensed . . . lush jungles, forbidden places, excitement. His gaze was silver heat and it pierced her, stopping her breath somewhere within her and leaving her uncertain if she could catch the next.

His gaze remained on her and she felt it sweep over her. It was as if he had reached out to touch her. The sensation was unnerving. Slowly and deliberately she continued to walk toward him.

She knew in those moments what it must be like to be the prey of a violent predator. She didn't like it. Worse yet, she didn't like the sudden realization that she wouldn't struggle too hard to escape.

Steve was as caught off guard as Rachel. He had seen pretty women before, but few with the absolute magnetism of this one . . . and in pants! He'd not seen many women with enough poise to carry off wearing pants. They hugged her body like a second skin, and he admired the picture she made with the sunlight melting over her.

She regarded him with a straightforward look, and for a

second he lost track of why he was there. Her green eyes met his, and in their depths he read mystery and a kind of reserve that left him wondering. He hoped she was Rachel Walker, for he felt an interest in the kind of woman who wore men's pants and handled men's work with aplomb.

Rachel drew close enough to pass before he spoke.

"Miss Rachel Walker?"

His voice was deep and low, as if he meant to caress her with it, or to share some deep and vibrant secret.

"Yes, I'm Rachel Walker."

"We heard you were looking for riders."

"You're looking for work?" Somehow, the idea surprised her. She had the impression that he should be in command, not commanded. She wondered if a man such as this would be easy to control. She meant to say no . . . she knew it would be smart to say no.

"Well, the Rocking W needs a few riders now. It's branding time. Have you done this kind of work before?" She felt foolish when he smiled. It was stupid. Of course he was experienced; it showed. In fact, she wondered how far the experience went.

"Yes, ma'am," he said quietly. "We'll take whatever you offer."

"You're accepting a job and not even asking what it pays?"

"Beggars can't be choosers. We need work." The voice left little room for questions.

"The pay is thirty dollars a month and board."

"Good enough."

"The job is rounding up and branding . . . among other things."

"Oh?" he said. There was a look in his eyes, and a faint

touch of laughter in the set of his mouth that brought a tinge of color to her cheeks. "That's fine, we'll handle branding . . . or any other things you feel necessary."

"You can come out to the ranch any time before tomorrow noon. If you don't show up then, you don't have a job. Is that clear?"

"This is Mikah, and my name is Steve McKean."

"Hello, Mikah."

"Ma'am."

"We thought, if you were done hiring and were going back to the ranch now, we might ride out with you. We don't know how to get there."

She smiled. "You leave town by the east road, and follow it to Coral Canyon; you can't miss it because of the color. You turn west there, and in ten minutes you'll be on Rocking W land."

"I take it the Rocking W covers a lot of acres."

"Over seventy-five hundred acres," she said proudly. "My father came here and built it from practically nothing." She had no idea why his eyes grew cold, but it was as if he had closed something between them.

"It must have been quite a job to . . . gather that much land. Are you still growing?"

"Dad grew because he knew how to develop what he had. I hope we keep growing," she said, her eyes flashing.

Steve didn't want to push her any further and chance losing the job. "Will your father go along with your hiring us?"

Again he saw the anger leap into her eyes, yet she smiled. "If you're worried, ask around. If I hire you, Dad will see you get all the work you can handle."

"We'll be there," Steve added.

"Then I'll see you later."

"Yes, ma'am."

Rachel brushed past him and left the hall. It was only then that Mikah spoke.

"You think the Rocking W is the one?"

"I don't know."

"Then why did you push her like that? Were you trying to make her fire us before she hired us?"

"No, it's just—"

"Just what?"

"Never mind. Come on, let's see how this Rocking W is run. I think we need to meet Carter Walker, and see just how he 'gathered' all this land. Could be he has a connection to what's going on."

"She looked like a really nice lady to me. Such a pretty face."

"Mikah, don't let a pretty face fool you. There's usually a diabolical mind with some pretty surprising motives behind it. Let's get going."

Mikah followed Steve outside and they walked to their horses. From the window of a dress shop, Rachel watched them pass. Again she was aware of too much about this stranger. He walked with a lazy grace, like the easy walk of a panther. A million questions filled her mind. Where did he come from, and why would a man like him be looking for work like this instead of trying to build something for himself? Besides that, she had the distinct feeling he knew quite well how to use the gun he wore, for it seemed to be an intrinsic part of him. She wondered if she had made a drastic mistake.

She had nothing more to do in town, and was annoyed with herself that she had refused to ride back to the ranch with him. She prided herself on being afraid of nothing, but now she began to wonder if that was true.

Chapter Three

Rachel left the shop and rode rapidly from town. It was not long before she saw them in the distance. Mikah and Steve reined their horses to a halt when they heard her call. They turned to watch her approach.

"Well, well." Mikah grinned. "It seems the lady changed her mind."

"Or she's suspicious."

"You sure are a mistrusting soul."

"She's the kind of trouble that could land us back in Yuma, and I, for one, don't intend to let it happen. Her kind look for what can profit them, and they don't mind who pays the price."

"Man, you don't know her. Maybe you're wrong about 'her kind.' She might just be what she looks like."

"Right, and she looks like a pretty trap. You heard her. What's wrong with growing? Her kind don't think there's any boundaries to their world. They reach out and take what they can. I'd be willing to bet her father has got a real hunger for more."

Mikah didn't answer, because Rachel had drawn up beside them. He could see what Steve refused to see, that the girl had her eyes on him and didn't care if Mikah was there at all.

"I'm sorry to have been so rude. I'll ride with you to the ranch. Dad ought to be there now, and I'll introduce you to him and the men."

"Thanks." It was Mikah who replied. Rachel moved her horse forward, and both men made room for her between them. For a few minutes they rode in silence. A silence that made the gregarious Mikah uncomfortable.

He was grateful when Rachel broke it first. He had no way of knowing she was just as uncomfortable as he. She was annoyed that Steve was acting as if she were something he was putting up with.

Steve was shaken by the thought that his anger was having little effect on his awareness of her. An awareness that made him struggle to keep from looking at her. She was a danger he couldn't afford. She had everything a woman could want, and wasn't that the kind of woman who always sought more? The kind of woman who thought it a game to play with a man's mind and senses until . . . He shook the thought aside. This was mental quicksand he couldn't afford to get caught in.

"You're not from around these parts." It took Steve a couple of seconds to realize she was talking directly to him, and that Mikah didn't intend to answer.

"No, ma'am."

"Where are you from?"

"A few years back, from Colorado. Lately from Arizona."

"You did ranching there?"

"Is talking about my past part of the job?" He turned to look at her, and again she was mesmerized by the silvered heat of his eyes. He was a mystery, and she had the distinct feeling that he contained a violent kind of anger. She wondered what had put that anger in him.

"No . . . no. I was just curious. You don't seem like a drifter."

"I pretty much am, if your idea of a drifter is a man who chooses not to have anything to tie him down."

"You don't have any family anywhere?"

"No." The reply was flat and final . . . and Rachel didn't believe it.

"How about you, Mikah?"

"I ain't got family to speak of . . . and I come from Arizona too. In fact, that's where I met Steve. You might say we was kinda thrown together." Mikah was amused at his reply; he refused to acknowledge Steve's scowl.

"How about you, Miss Walker?" Steve said. "Were you born here?"

"Yes, on the Rocking W."

"And I'll bet you went East to school."

"Yes, I did." She looked at him. "My father has given me the best of everything, and no one could be more grateful for it than I am. I try to pull my weight on the ranch. I do most of the bookkeeping, and I handle the payroll and do a lot of supply buying. Did you think I just lie about waiting for a rich husband? There's not one around that has enough money to tempt me." There, she thought, put that in your pipe and smoke it.

Mikah grinned, but said nothing. These two were like oil and water, but he had a feeling . . . yes sir, he had a feeling that if they didn't kill each other, Steve was going to get a little lesson in the fact that all females were not alike.

"Look." Rachel pointed. "There's Coral Canyon. We go down that way, and do you see that rise there in the distance?"

"Yes."

"That's our boundary. In a few minutes we'll be on my land." She said the words with satisfaction. Steve could feel her immense pride like a sour taste on his tongue. How many people shared that single-minded ambition, which seemed to force them to reach for what someone else had? He remembered . . . He forced those thoughts from his mind. He had no time for them. He had a job to do and he didn't intend to let another pretty face distract him.

"What about the smaller places around here?"

"What about them?"

"Word has it that some of them are having a real tough time."

"I guess most of the smaller places do have a hard time. They can't afford to hire at our wages and they can't sell at our prices. But if they work as hard at their ranches as Dad did, there's no reason they can't make a living."

"And, of course, there's someone ready to buy them out if they choose to sell."

"Are you talking about my father?"

"I don't know." Steve smiled. "You tell me."

"Let me tell you something, Mr. McKean. My father would never take advantage of someone's misfortune, but, yes, if another rancher wanted to let his land go, why shouldn't he buy it?" Before Steve could reply, she spoke again and her voice was far from gentle. "You have a job on the Rocking W, and that means you work, you don't question the boss's ambition or his methods. If you don't like them . . . then quit now."

Steve had to bite his tongue, because he knew he had pushed too far. But she seemed to have a way of bringing out the worst in him. "All right . . . boss. I'm sorry. No more questions. I want the job."

Mikah would have laughed aloud if he hadn't thought Steve would pounce on him later. From the corner of his eye he could see Steve's stony countenance.

They continued to the ranch in silence, each caught up in his own thoughts. When they crested the hill from which they could see the ranch house, Rachel stopped and both men stopped with her. Steve had to admit it gave the appearance of a place tended with loving care. It also displayed the wealth of the owner. He became more and more curious both about the man who had built it, and the people who had parented the woman who sat her horse beside him.

"It's beautiful," Steve said almost to himself. But Rachel turned to look at him. She smiled for the first time, and Steve felt the first tug of guilt. He accepted the fact of her beauty, without letting it draw his mind from what he had to do . . . but her unaffected smile of pleasure suddenly flowed through him like warm wine. It took him totally off guard, and created a strange and unwelcome sensation that he had to struggle to control.

She had a perfect body and a face that could charm any red-blooded man. But it wasn't that that drew him. It was . . . he found it hard to put his finger on. A vulnerability, a sense that she needed protection. What she would need protection from was beyond him to understand. The one needing protection was any man who fell under that mystic spell of hers. Abruptly her smile was gone, and they rode down the slight grade toward the ranch house.

Carter Walker stood on the broad front porch of the house and watched his daughter ride toward him. He didn't recognize the two men who rode with her, so he was pretty certain she had hired the extra hands he would need.

He studied them as they drew closer. His eyes missed nothing, and he knew men. Probably better than most. His gaze fell on Mikah, who returned it levelly. Carter didn't judge by looks. It was too easy to make a bad mistake like that. But when he turned his gaze on Steve, he found it hard to refrain from passing judgment. The stranger looked like a real hard case. There was an untamed and dangerous look about him that made Carter pause.

Lori walked out onto the porch and watched with Carter as Rachel and the two strangers dismounted and climbed the steps to the porch. Lori wasn't expected to judge or to hire men, but there were not many, including her daughter, who did not know that her word carried a lot of weight.

"Mom, Dad, this is Mikah and Steve McKean. I just hired them." She turned to Steve and Mikah. "This is my mother and father, Lori and Carter Walker, owners of the Rocking W."

Steve tipped his hat. "Mrs. Walker."

Lori smiled and acknowledged his polite greeting.

"How do you do, Mr. Walker." Steve held out his hand, and Carter took it in a firm grip.

"Steve, welcome to the Rocking W. Mikah, you look like you could handle your share of work and more."

"I'll give you my best," Mikah replied.

"I'll take you to the bunkhouse and introduce you to the rest of the boys."

"No questions?" Steve said quietly.

"Did my daughter hire you?"

"Yes."

"Then there's nothing I have to ask. If she hired you, she thinks you'll work out. If you don't, trust me, she'll fire you just as quick. Her decision has always been good enough for me."

Lori was watching her daughter, for she had seen a fleeting look in her eyes that she had never seen before . . . interest. As quickly as she read Rachel, her gaze went to Steve, and she watched him as he looked at Rachel. His face was closed and expressionless.

"Then I guess we'd better find out what the . . . boss wants us to do," Steve said.

"Don't get carried away." Carter chuckled. "I go on Rachel's instincts, but I'm the boss of this place. I have the last word."

Steve nodded, and Carter turned his gaze toward Mikah. "You've done this work before?"

"This work and just about anything else a man can dream up, from wrangler to blacksmith."

"I could use a good smith. Suppose you give two days a week to the smith and the rest to roundup?"

"Anything you say."

"Rachel tell you what we pay?"

"Yes sir."

"Then come on, we'll get you settled. You have dinner in the back kitchen with the rest of the hands. I expect you to be up and on the job by five thirty."

Rachel didn't move, and Steve and Mikah followed Carter across the wide stretch of lawn, then the well-worn area before the large bunkhouse. They stepped inside and closed the door before Rachel became aware that her mother was watching her.

"He's quite a handsome man."

"I'm afraid I didn't notice. Dad needed more riders, so I hired them. I think they look strong enough to handle anything Dad might throw at them."

"I shouldn't be surprised." Lori smiled. "They look quite . . . capable. Do you think they'll stay after branding?"

"I . . . I don't know. He told me he was kind of a drifter."

"He?"

"I mean they. Mom, why do men do that?"

"Do what?"

"Drift through life with no roots, no anchors to hold them?"

"I guess they all have different reasons. Some have things they're running away from, and some think they have to keep running to find what they want."

"Which way do you think it is with him?" Rachel asked softly.

"I don't guess it's any of our business . . . is it?"

Rachel flushed, and didn't look at her mother. "No, I suppose it isn't."

"But he certainly is an interesting man. He kind of reminds me of your father when he was much younger."

"Mother! He's nothing like Dad at all. Look at him. He's like . . . He's . . ."

"Untamed? Maybe that's what reminds me of your father. He had that same wild and hungry kind of look when

64

I first met him. Maybe that's why my parents were so set on me not having anything to do with him.''

"You never told me such a thing before.''

"You never asked me.'' Her mother smiled.

"You mean your mother didn't want you to marry Dad?''

"Not so much my mother as my father. He said Carter would never amount to anything, and that we'd end up hungry.''

"I don't think he was much of a judge of men.'' Rachel laughed.

"Neither do I. I knew as soon as I met your dad that he was . . . different.''

"Mom, you and Dad have tried to marry me off to Cal. Are you telling me now that this man is the kind of husband you'd want to see me with? I doubt it.''

"Rachel, I never implied that at all. I was just making an observation that he was the kind of man most girls find challenging.''

"Not this girl. He looks like an outlaw. Dad would have a fit.''

"You could be right.''

"You bet your life I am. I can't believe you think this . . . stranger is so special.''

"Good heavens, child, I didn't say he was special. I said he was handsome. I'm old, but I'm not blind.''

"I'm going for a ride. I'll be back in plenty of time for dinner.''

Lori stood and watched Rachel mount and ride away. She glanced toward the bunkhouse. It had been clear to her, even if it hadn't been clear to anyone else, that her daughter had looked at Steve McKean in a way she had never looked at another man. With a smile on her lips, Lori walked into the house. Yes, Steve McKean did remind her of Carter . . .

Inside the bunkhouse, Steve and Mikah were being introduced to the men who were there, and promised introductions to the others when they returned.

Men who rode the Rocking W were a special breed, chosen by Carter for their honesty and their proven devotion to him and the ranch. Within days they would either accept the newcomers, or Carter would let them go. He had no trouble among his men. He expected to treat them fairly, and expected a fair day's work in return.

"This is Tom Bordon." Carter introduced a tall, rangy man with a shock of wheat-colored hair and a smile that sliced his face and made him look younger than the age revealed by his eyes. "Tom will ride with the two of you tomorrow and show you around. You'll be given your orders every morning by him or me."

"Tom." Steve extended his hand, and was relieved that as foreman, Tom looked as if he meant to accept them without any trouble.

"McKean . . . Mikah, good to have you. We been needing help. Supper's at dark, and we get on the move at dawn. Any problem with that?

"Not from me," Steve said. "I don't have anyplace to go and no money to spend if I did."

"Me either. You have to tell me what days I work smithing," Mikah said.

Tom looked at Carter, who hastily explained. "He said he'd been a smith before. I thought we could use him a few days to shoe any horses that might need to be shod."

"We're lucky. We were going to hand that job to Martin,

and I'm not too sure he would have been good at it. Why don't you work the first three days of the week smithing, then you and McKean can partner. I guess you might want it that way."

"We'd be grateful. Mikah and I have been together for three years now. We should manage pretty well."

"Okay, boys," Carter said. "I'll see you in the morning. Get some supper and some sleep. Dawn will be here before you know it."

Left to their own devices, both Mikah and Steve set about making as many friends among the men there as they could. By nightfall, more men came and went, and by suppertime all were gathered.

The bunkhouse was large and now Steve could see why. At one time or another over twenty-five men slept there. When it came time for supper, they followed the group to a back kitchen attached to the main house. They all seated themselves at a long table, and the cook, Steve was soon to find out, was very good. Not only that, but the food was served in ample supply. No one left the table hungry. For Steve and Mikah, this alone was a novelty, and they exchanged an appreciative look.

Rachel had ridden for some time trying to erase the image of Steve's penetrating silver gaze, and the fluttery sensation she felt every time he looked at her.

She returned in time for dinner, and even though her mother never brought Steve's name up again, Rachel feared she would, and it spoiled her meal. She even had to be spoken to by her father twice before she realized he was talking to her.

"Rachel?"

"Huh . . . oh, what?"

"I asked you what Cal had to say this morning."

"Well . . . I didn't give him a chance to propose, if that's what you mean. I simply said I would be happy to go to the dance with him, and I didn't feel like company when I went to town."

"Rachel, really!" Lori said.

"He took it like a man, Mother," Rachel teased. "I know he plans on making the dance a special occasion."

"Just like I said," her mother laughed, "you need a new gown."

"I give in. I'll go into town and find something."

"And I'll go with you," Lori said with a chuckle. "Just to make sure you do."

"You're exasperating."

"So are you," Lori replied complacently. "You get it from your father."

"Lori," Carter laughed. "Why is it she gets all her flaws from me?"

"Because you're the only one who has any." Lori exchanged a look with Carter that was filled with love and tolerance.

That was it! That was what she wanted to share with someone. That special way her parents looked at each other that closed everyone else out. She couldn't name it . . . but she did know it was the thing that kept her from accepting Cal's proposal.

When supper was over, Carter went to his office to go over some checks Rachel had left for him to sign, and Lori occupied herself with some sewing she had begun. Rachel took the time to walk outside and enjoy the warm night air.

This was one of the times when she loved her home the

most. These quiet nights with their warm breezes and the soft night sounds. She walked past the bunkhouse and toward a thin stand of trees that bordered a stream. She used to play there as a child.

She stood beneath a tree, leaning her shoulder against it, and closed her eyes. She had never felt so content.

"Beautiful night, isn't it?" His voice came from so close that she was startled. She spun around to find Steve less than two feet behind her.

"I didn't know you were here."

"Sorry, I didn't mean to frighten you."

"You didn't frighten me. I was just surprised. What are you doing out here anyway? If you don't get some sleep, you'll regret it in the morning."

How could he tell her that the bunkhouse walls closed in on him and he felt confined and slightly panicked? How could he tell her that four walls and closed doors had been too much to bear, and he had had to open the door and come out, just to prove to himself that he could? That he could turn the knob on a door and actually have it open?

"I never did need much sleep. I like the night, and this is a particularly nice one. In Arizona the moon looks . . . different." She laughed softly and he had to smile. It was a foolish statement to make, but he didn't want to explain that the moon looked different from between bars. "What are you doing wandering around at night?"

"I was having a little trouble sleeping myself."

Suddenly there seemed to be nothing else to say, and the silence grew. But it was a calm and easy silence. He stood with the moon behind him, and was little more than a shadow to her. But its mellow light bathed her in a soft glow. In fact she looked a little unreal, as if she might vanish if he spoke harshly or said something she didn't like.

"Who are you, Steve McKean?" The question was asked so softly that he wasn't sure she had really spoken.

"Nobody."

"Everyone is somebody."

"You really believe that?" She could hear laughter in his voice . . . derisive laughter.

"Everyone has his place in life, and the chance to make what he can of it."

"Do you do that all the time?"

"Do what?"

"Put people in nice little categories . . . in their proper places. I'll bet it annoys you when someone steps out of his 'proper place.' "

"You sound . . . angry. Why take out your anger on me? You don't know anything about me."

"I'm not angry, I'm realistic. And I'm not taking anything out on you. I'm observing a fact. You like things neat and controlled. Do you always have to be in control of yourself and everything around you?"

"I have to be in control of my own life. I don't want to control anyone else's."

"But you like being 'the boss.' "

"What really bothers you, Mr. McKean? Is it that my father trusts me enough to help him, or that you have to take orders from a woman?"

"I don't mind taking orders from a woman. I guess, maybe, I don't like being put in one of your categories."

"You don't mind doing the same thing, though. Who are you to judge me? Just what little niche do you put me in?"

The tables were neatly turned on him and he wasn't exactly comfortable with the truth. "I don't."

"Sure you do. I'm the spoiled little rich girl who doesn't care how others live as long as my life is good. You set yourself up as some kind of a judge. Who gave you the right?" She walked close to him, and he was suddenly aware of her scent and her warmth and her beauty in the moonlight. "Or is it because someone else upset your thoughts on the order of things? Who was she?" Rachel added softly.

The control he had on his thoughts and his tongue deserted him. The old anger he'd held in control for so long bubbled through him like molten lava. He felt the old pain, and wanted to lash out against it.

He reached out and took hold of her shoulders, dragging her against him. She gasped in shock; for a moment she was too dumbfounded to fight. Her lips were parted in protest, and when his mouth crashed down on hers, she could only make a soft sound before she was silenced.

Rachel had been kissed before, but never with this rage or this hot passion. She felt something coil tightly within her as his mouth plundered hers. Sensation after sensation rippled through her, and she felt as if she were falling from a great height. She could only cling to him as the very breath seemed to be drawn from her.

But if she was caught in a maelstrom, it was nothing compared to the shock that shuddered through Steve. He had expected outrage, and would have laughed . . . and conquered. He did not expect her to feel so warm and soft in his arms, or to respond to his kiss with a mouth that had grown pliable . . . and deliciously sweet.

He broke the kiss before he lost all control. For a minute neither said anything. He could see the look in her eyes,

and it was not what he expected . . . not what he wanted
. . . and not what he needed.

He relaxed his hold on her and half expected her to run
or to slap him . . . maybe even to fire him. Instead she continued to look up at him. He found it impossible to read
her thoughts in the brilliance of her eyes. Then she spoke
softly.

"I'm sorry."

Before he could recover his thoughts and ask her what
she meant, she left his arms and was walking into the darkness.

He remained still, for he sensed he had been defeated in
some way. He just didn't know how. Most likely her father
would hear of this, and by morning he and Mikah would
be out of a job. He had made a drastic mistake, and had
only his foul temper and ugly memories to blame. Now he
and Mikah would have a harder time finding their answers.

Slowly he walked back to the bunkhouse. No one heard
him come in and lie down on his bunk. He let the silence
enfold him and fought the memory of that momentary
sweet response. It seemed impossible to find sleep. He lay
awake wondering why in the hell he had pulled such a
dumb stunt, and why he'd let her get under his skin. There
was something about her that made him defensive, as if she
could penetrate the shields he wore and find a vulnerable
place.

The next morning the sun was just a thin band of light
across the horizon when they were awakened. He didn't
want to tell Mikah what had happened the night before, but
he knew there would be both surprise and plenty of questions from his partner when they were summarily fired from

a job they had barely started. There was no doubt Mikah would be angry, but the truth had to be told.

They had to gather in front of the main house to receive orders for the day, and before he had a chance to tell Mikah, Tom was herding them outside. Steve sighed deeply. It looked like the lynching was going to be in front of the whole group.

It got worse when they had gathered by the front porch and Carter walked out. Worse because Rachel walked out behind him. For a minute their gazes met and held, and he was puzzled that there was no look of satisfaction or revenge in hers.

"Boys, I'm making a few changes. I want Jones and Roberts to partner and hit the south range. I've been told some of the fence is down. Get it repaired. Stone and four others are to ride with me. Tom, you take Mikah and three others to the north and drive the cattle down to us." He continued to give orders, and Rachel and Steve continued to try to read the thoughts in each other's minds. When all the orders were given, Steve realized that Rachel had told her father nothing about the night before.

He knew he should just let it go, but his curiosity was growing. Why? He had his orders, and started away to get his horse and gear. After a few steps he turned to look back and found she was still standing on the porch watching him.

Her last words still echoed in his mind. "I'm sorry." He wondered what she was sorry for; she knew nothing about him. The thought came to him that he should enlighten her. Maybe if she knew where he came from . . . He stopped his thoughts as quickly as they came. What was he thinking of? It was necessary that she know nothing about him at all, and that he find out about her and her father. He gathered his things and started about his day's duties.

Rachel stood and watched him until he disappeared from sight. She could not get the previous night's incident out of her mind. His kiss had been shattering, because she sensed a need in him to push her away, to hurt her somehow. After thinking about it all night, she had come to the conclusion that he was reacting to a fear he could not face. Another woman. Had he been hurt so badly that he had put every woman into the same mold? She knew she should fear his anger, but she didn't. Instead she felt a kind of pity for him, and she was sure that was one thing that would infuriate him.

She had looked into his eyes this morning and known that he had expected her to run to her father with some tale of his "attack" on her. He'd thought he would be fired. It gave her a sense of satisfaction to see his eyes change from certainty to surprise and then to puzzlement.

She meant to prove to this defiant and angry man that she hid behind no one's protection, least of all her father's. She had stood on her own two feet for a long time, and he was not the man to knock them from under her.

For the next three days she did not see Steve at all, and it thoroughly annoyed her that he had probably chosen to sleep out on the range rather than take the chance of crossing her path again.

She was not wrong in her supposition, though Steve blinded himself to the real reason behind his choice. He told himself he needed to talk to the men, without the presence of Carter or his daughter.

Steve knew that Tom was watching both his progress and Mikah's and most likely reporting to Carter. He wanted that report to be a good one.

He realized it gave him a great deal of pleasure to be working again at something he loved to do. He had been ranching all of his life, first for his father and then for himself. He fought the memories of the small ranch he had called his own. It did little good to think of what he had lost.

He worked with a singular devotion that was not missed by the men who worked with him or by Tom. He knew what was needed before Tom could give the order, and after a while Tom stopped watching him and accepted the fact that not only did Steve know what he was doing, he knew how to do it well.

The fourth night Tom was talking to Carter about the new hands.

"They're both damn good. If I didn't know better, I'd say that McKean had a place of his own and maybe lost it for some reason. He's used to giving orders, and he's smart."

"Used to giving orders?"

"Yeah, I'd say so. He knows what I'm going to say before I say it. Most of the time I go out to give an order and I find the boys already working on what I wanted."

"Then what's a man like that doing begging jobs like an ordinary drifter?"

"Damned if I know, but I sure don't think that boy's a drifter . . . no sir. He's too quick and too experienced."

"It's a puzzle, isn't it? Maybe," Carter said thoughtfully, "I should watch him a bit closer and ask him a few questions."

"I don't advise that, boss."

"Why not?"

"He don't take well to people asking questions about him. He's already made that clear."

"You don't say. Tom, do you think he's hiding something?"

"I don't know. You know it ain't our way to ask about a man's private business."

"No, it isn't. I'm sorry, I guess I was just too curious. If he's working out and he's good enough to suit you, he's good enough for me. See if you can convince him that he should stay on after roundup."

"I will. And I don't think you'll regret it."

"What about his friend?"

"Good man. He works like a horse, and he's a good smith too."

"Then present him with the same offer."

"Sure will, boss."

"Oh, by the way, Tom. Rachel has to go into town and pick up a friend of hers who's going to be visiting for a few weeks. Get Steve to ride in with her. He can see to the luggage for them, and he can pick up that crate of new rifles I ordered. Tell him not to forget the ammunition."

"When?"

"I'll check with Rachel, but I think she said day after tomorrow. Wait here."

Tom waited while Carter asked Lori if she knew for sure when Rachel's friend Yvonne was coming. He returned with the news that it was as he had said, the day after tomorrow.

"I'll see it's taken care of."

The next day passed before Tom could ride out to the

camp and inform Steve. He rode up at sunset, and the men were gathered around the fire to eat the evening meal.

"Steve, I want to talk to you," Tom said. Steve walked over to stand beside Tom's horse and look up at him. They were far enough away from the others that their words were unheard.

"I want you to go back to the ranch tonight."

"What for?"

"You need to take the buggy into town tomorrow. Miss Rachel is meeting a guest from the East, and Mr. Walker said you was to drive her."

"Why me?"

This was the first time Steve had questioned an order given by Tom, and it surprised him. "Because I said so. Besides, there's a crate of rifles at the rail station you're to pick up. Be ready by first light tomorrow."

"All right, I'll leave now."

"Fine."

Steve saddled his horse and rode toward the ranch, but all the way he cursed Rachel . . . he didn't want to come face to face with her again . . . and he didn't want to face the reason why.

He arrived at the ranch late, and made his way to bed. By the time the sun was a red rim on the horizon the next morning, he was harnessing the buggy and leading the horse toward the front porch of the ranch. The door opened and Rachel came out.

Chapter Four

It took Steve only a moment to realize that Rachel had had no idea he would be accompanying her into town. For some reason the realization gave him a bit of satisfaction.

Rachel continued down the steps toward him and got up into the buggy without saying anything. He tied his horse behind, and climbed in beside her.

"Good morning, Miss Walker."

"Good morning, McKean," she replied stiffly.

Steve picked up the reins and was about to get moving when another rider appeared. He paused when he saw Rachel's attention drawn toward the rider.

"It's Cal."

"Cal?"

"Cal Davis. His parents own the Bar D."

Steve was more than glad to wait. The name Cal Davis was a familiar one. The Bar D was the other big ranch in the area. When Cal rode up beside them his smile wavered for just a second, and his gaze went from Rachel to Steve and back to Rachel quickly. Steve contained his smile. It was pretty obvious there was something between Rachel and Cal Davis, and his curiosity was stirred.

"Morning. You on the way somewhere, Rachel?"

"Into town to pick up a friend who's visiting. Yvonne and I went to school together." It was obvious to Rachel that Cal was putting Steve in his place silently, by ignoring him. "This is Steve McKean, one of our new hands." She had no idea why Cal's treatment of Steve annoyed her, but it did. Cal was forced now to acknowledge Steve's presence, which he did with a short nod.

"McKean."

"Mr. Davis." Steve's nod was just as short and cold. "I've heard of your ranch."

"Thanks. Dad's taken all his life to build it." Cal was pleased, first that Steve considered the ranch as much his as his father's, and second that Steve was no more than a hired hand. It renewed his sense of superiority.

Again Steve smiled to himself. Cal Davis was easy to read, and his purpose was just as easy. He had the desire to join two ranches and have the prettiest girl in the territory as well.

Steve glanced quickly at Rachel, who was looking at Cal with a look Steve could not read. This surprised him, for if she was of the same mind, why didn't she display it?

"I can't seem to pin you down, can I, Rachel?" Cal laughed. "Do you mind if I ride along?"

"No, of course not. I would like you to meet Yvonne anyway. We have to supply her with an escort to the dance, and I might just need your help."

"Be glad to. Is she as pretty as you?"

"Yvonne is . . . different from me, and she is much prettier."

"I doubt that." Steve spoke before he thought, and both Rachel and Cal turned to look at him. He grinned. "Sorry. I spoke out of line . . . but I meant it. You're just saying she's prettier than you to get the boys to fight over who will take her to the dance."

Now Rachel laughed softly. "No, I'm not; but to prove it to you, why don't you take her? Then there won't be any problem. In fact . . . the four of us can go together."

Both Steve and Cal stared at her in shock. Cal didn't like the idea of the four of them together. Steve didn't like it either, for a thousand different reasons, one of which was that he would have to be near Rachel. But the challenging look in her eyes and the smile on her lips forced an agreement from him.

"Sure, why not?"

Rachel's smile wavered, but only for a second. Then Cal spoke again. "What time is the train due?"

"In about two hours, so we'd better get going."

Steve didn't wait for Cal's reaction. He whistled to the horses and slapped the reins, and they were moving forward. Cal fell in beside them. But Cal's horse must have sensed his master's tension, for it skittered sideways and danced with nervous energy, effectively keeping Cal out of earshot of Steve and Rachel.

"Thanks," Rachel said.

"For what?"

"For the compliment. Yvonne really is prettier than I. She captured every male in the city while we were at school."

"You said 'different.' What did you mean by that?"

"She's just what my mother planned on when she had me. I don't fit Mother's mold. Yvonne is all ruffles and lace, and she's . . . well, charming is not a strong enough word."

"A flirt," Steve chuckled.

"No! . . . Well, yes. But she's sweet and honest."

"Honest . . . very rare today."

"You mean for everyone or for women?"

Steve shrugged. He didn't mean to answer that one. Instead he sought an answer for himself. "When you left me the other night you said you were sorry. What do you have to be sorry about?"

"Maybe you should answer a question for me first."

"Like what?"

"Like why were you so angry with me? That kiss was meant to scare me, or to . . . threaten somehow. Did you consider me some kind of a threat? If so, forget it. You can trust in this, Steve McKean. I don't interfere in the lives of the men who work for us, and you're no exception."

"I wasn't angry."

Rachel was silent for so long, he didn't think she meant to answer. "I said I was sorry . . . but for you, not for me."

"For me? Sorry for me?" He laughed. "Do I look like I need sympathy from you?"

"If you go around with all that anger inside and fight every sign of friendship anyone offers, you sure do."

Steve was shaken. She had a way of upsetting his thought processes that disturbed him. Most likely he would have to be the one to bring the law down on her and her father. He drew the buggy to a halt, which surprised both Rachel and

Cal. When he climbed out, he untied his horse and mounted. Then he spoke to Cal.

"Miss Walker would like you to drive the buggy."

Rachel said nothing, and Cal was obviously pleased. He tied his horse behind and got into the buggy.

Rachel watched Steve as he rode a few feet ahead. It was a surprising thing to see a man as strong and as tough as Steve run from the truth . . . and from her. Somehow she had hit a very raw nerve. It stirred her curiosity. Steve had secrets . . . shadows that were troubling him, and she felt a sudden and very unwelcome desire to know what could have been so bad in his past that he couldn't allow anyone close.

They arrived in town and Cal drove straight to the train station. But when Steve dismounted and walked to the ticket window to inquire if the train would be in soon, he was told the train was behind schedule and wouldn't be in for at least an hour. He returned to the buggy to tell Rachel.

"Well, there's nothing to do but wait," Rachel said.

"If you don't mind," Steve replied, "I think I'll go over to the saloon. That is, if you don't have something you want me to do?"

He hoped she wouldn't suggest that he wait with her. First, he had already had enough of Cal's close and annoying scrutiny, and second, if he was not mistaken, he was sure he had seen Carlos and Apach go into the saloon minutes before.

"No, of course not. Go ahead. Just be back here in an hour. I don't want to keep you from your work any longer than necessary."

"Thanks, boss." He smiled to ease the words, and was satisfied with the way her mouth tightened. He told the station master to have the rifles loaded in the wagon when the train came, then walked away.

"He's pretty arrogant for a hired drifter, isn't he?" Cal complained mildly.

"Oh, he's all right. Some men find it hard to be ordered around by a woman." She said it, but she knew that was not Steve's problem.

"Did you have to invite him to the dance?"

"Cal! The dance is for everyone. He could have gone whether I had invited him or not. I just thought it would be nice if I arranged Yvonne's escort."

"I could have done that."

"I don't think I need guidance on how to treat my best friend." The coolness in her tone prompted him to rein in his anger and his jealousy.

"Sorry, I didn't mean to interfere."

"You didn't interfere. I'm sorry too. I didn't mean to be so short-tempered. I can't wait for you and Yvonne to meet. You'll like her."

"I suspect I will. But I don't think it's going to change my mind."

"Change your mind?"

"Rachel, I've been trying to talk to you about something important for weeks. I know this is not the best of times, but you're hard to catch up with, so I have to grab the only opportunity I might get for a while."

"Cal, you're right, this is not the place for—"

"Just hear me out for a minute, please."

She could do little other than agree . . . or jump from the buggy and run, which was what she felt like doing. "All right."

"Rachel, we've known each other for a long time. I'm

not an unstable man, and I will own the Bar D one day. I think you know by now how I feel about you. I have grown to care for you a great deal. I mean . . . I more than care for you . . . Hell, this is not coming out the way I planned.''

''Are you by any chance asking me to marry you, Cal?''

Cal looked at her as if he were shocked. ''Yes, I am.''

''You think the Rocking W and the Bar D would make a great combination. We'd be the strongest and biggest in the territory.''

''Rachel, we would. Just think of it! Together we would practically rule this territory.''

''That has never been my life's dream,'' she said quietly. Cal recognized his mistake at once.

''Rachel, that wasn't what I had in mind. I don't think of you as the Rocking W. I think of you as a lovely woman I desire for my wife. I do love you. You just haven't given me the chance to prove how much. Don't answer me now, not in haste. Think about it. Let's share more time together. Let me show you how much you have come to mean to me.''

''I . . . I don't think I'm ready for marriage, Cal. I don't want to settle down and have babies. I want to help run the Rocking W awhile longer.''

Cal was about to make another mistake. ''But your dad is the power and he doesn't need . . . I mean . . . Damn it, Rachel, ranching is a man's job.''

Rachel didn't speak for a minute, because she was suddenly gripped by anger. When she did speak, her voice was calm and controlled. ''All right, Cal. I'll think your offer over.''

''That's all I ask. Just look at this thing from the proper

perspective, and you'll see what a combination we would be."

"I don't doubt it. I'll think about it."

"You won't regret marrying me, Rachel. I'll do everything in my power to make you happy."

"I'll consider it, Cal, honestly. I'll consider it."

Cal seemed content for the moment, but Rachel was in turmoil. Cal was a good man, and he was handsome and strong. He was also right: the two ranches together would become a power. Her father knew a lot of influential people—judges and senators and men of wealth. It would do him a lot of good as well. The marriage would be profitable and it would be wise and it would be a way to help her father. Yes, it would be a good move . . . Why then, did she feel both like crying and running away?

Steve pushed open the swinging doors of the saloon and glanced around. He had been right. Carlos and Apach were sitting at a table near the back, in a corner where they would be out of earshot of anyone who came in.

Steve crossed the room and stopped by the table.

"Morning, gents. You both new in the territory too?"

"Sí," Carlos replied. "We just hired on at the Bar D."

"Then it looks like we're neighbors. I just started at the Rocking W."

"Well, sit awhile and let us buy you a drink," Carlos said. Steve dragged a chair out and sat down. When the bartender came over, they were discussing the two ranches and their new jobs for his benefit. But when he left a bottle and walked away, Steve leaned closer to his two friends.

"Did you have any trouble?"

"No," Apach said. "It seems everyone is looking for

riders. But I do not know if what we are doing is wise. We may be making a mistake.''

''What kind of a mistake?''

''If the big ranches are doing the pushing, they'd be too smart to have any evidence show up at their places. If we worked for one of the smaller ranches, we might just be hanging around at the right time for someone to show up and do some pushing.''

''You could be right,'' Steve said, ''but it's sure hard to quit.''

''Especially when we have just begun,'' Carlos added.

''Maybe it would be wise if we could find a way to get fired,'' Apach suggested.

''I'd like to stay at the Rocking W and keep an eye on the old man. I have a feeling there's a lot going on there.''

''He's the biggest around, so he can pretty much do as he pleases.''

Steve considered their words. ''Do you boys know the lay of the land?''

Apach spoke quickly. ''I took most of last night and rode around a bit with some of the hands. They pointed out all the ranches in the area. Look.'' The bottle and glasses had left rings of moisture on the table, and Apach used his finger to draw a rough map. ''Here's the Rocking W . . . here's the Morrisons, that's the Circle M . . . and here's the Bar D. Now, here's where the other ranches are located.'' He continued to trace an outline until Steve knew where every place could be found. ''Quantrell, Bradley, Holmes, Jessup, and a woman named Jane Crenshaw. She's south of the Rocking W. Parker, the one just north of the Davis place, has already sold out. Niles, Macquen, Gibson and

Travers, who are also north of Davis, have given up or been driven out.''

"Okay, so if these others would sell to Walker, the Rocking W and the Bar D would make a hell of a combination.''

"Yeah, looks like it," Carlos said.

"What do you think we should do, Steve? You're the boss.''

"I need time to think. Your idea about working for one of the smaller places is a good one. If we can't do it now, at least we can get to know those ranchers. In our free time, let's make a point of stopping around or giving a helping hand now and then. In short, gentlemen . . . let's make friends.''

"All right," Carlos said. "That sounds good to me.''

"What are you two doing in town anyway?''

"Sent in for supplies." Apach laughed. "We're the new men, so we get all the go-fors.''

"Well, I'm glad you did. By the way, there's a dance soon.''

"Yeah, we know.''

"It would be a good place to mingle and talk. Boys get drunk at these things, and they can get carried away with having fun. It's a good place for questions.''

"Steve," Apach laughed. "You don't really think I'm going to be welcome there, do you?''

"Maybe not," Steve said honestly. "It might be better for you not to go looking for trouble.''

"Right. Let me do some looking around in my own way.''

"Anything you want, just so we find who we came after.''

"Carlos can go to this dance. I have some plans. Besides, we have to set up a camp somewhere, where we can go and get together in case something goes wrong."

Before Steve could answer, a train whistle sounded in the distance. "I'd better get a move on. I have to meet that train. The boss's daughter is having a friend from the East for a visit."

"She as pretty as everybody says?" Carlos grinned.

"Who says?" Steve countered.

"Just about every vaquero around."

"Yeah, I guess you'd say she was pretty . . . and maybe just as guilty as her father, so don't let a pretty face fool you. I'll contact you soon." He walked away, and Apach and Carlos exchanged silent glances.

Rachel had looked over her shoulder several times to see if Steve was coming, and was thoroughly annoyed with herself for doing so. Still, the sound of the approaching train was a relief. When she glanced back at the saloon again, Steve was just coming out and starting across the street.

The train chugged to a halt as Rachel left the buggy and walked out on the platform. Both Cal and Steve came up beside her.

Yvonne Avery stepped down from the train, and she and Rachel caught sight of each other at the same time. They called out to each other, then ran to share an enthusiastic embrace. Yvonne stepped back and appraised Rachel with a sparkle in her eyes.

"Good heavens. If you had worn that outfit at school, you would have caused quite a stir."

"Pants are more functional here. Can you see me riding in a dress?"

"You ride astride?"

"Of course."

"I'll bet you cause quite a stir here too."

"No, I think everyone is used to seeing me in them."

"They are intriguing. I like the look. Perhaps I can purchase a pair."

"I'll make a rancher out of you yet, if you give me half a chance," Rachel laughed.

"For the freedom of wearing an outfit like that, I might just let you."

"Come on, let me introduce you." Rachel motioned toward Steve and Cal.

"Well," Yvonne said quietly, "maybe I can see why you wear pants. I shall definitely have to go shopping."

Steve watched, and thought that Rachel had been right. She and Yvonne were entirely different. Where Rachel was all brilliance and color, Yvonne was ebony-haired, with a complexion like a white rose. She was not as tall as Rachel, but she was slender. Yes, Steve thought, Yvonne was different . . . but Rachel was wrong, she definitely was not prettier.

"Cal, Steve, let me introduce my very best friend, Yvonne Avery. Yvonne, this is Cal Davis and Steve McKean."

Yvonne extended her hand to each man in turn, and smiled a devastating smile. Both smiled back, and Steve could see that Yvonne Avery was used to conquering men wherever she found them. He could see the light of mischievous laughter in her deep blue eyes, and decided he liked her.

She was a girl who liked fun and being admired, and there was a lot to admire in her.

"Welcome to Montana Territory, Miss Avery," Cal said.

"Thank you, but please, both of you, call me Yvonne."

"I'll get your baggage," Steve said. Yvonne picked out the pieces of luggage that belonged to her, and Steve stored them and the rifles in the back of the buggy. Within minutes, Rachel was guiding the buggy out of town, and Cal and Steve were following close behind.

"I'm so glad to see you again, Rachel," Yvonne said. "And this place, it's lovely."

"It is beautiful. I can't wait to show you around."

"The man who is escorting us . . . who is he?"

"Cal? He owns the ranch next to ours."

"And . . . the other one . . . the dark one?"

"Steve? He works for Dad."

"What a beautiful animal he is."

"Yvonne!"

"Well, unless you are blind, you'll have to agree with me. He looks like . . . like a hungry panther."

"You are as incorrigible as you always were. You haven't changed a bit."

"And I don't intend to. A handsome man is still as intriguing to me as ever."

"Well then, it will please you to know Steve will be your escort to a dance we're having in a few days."

"Delightful. Are you going with the other one . . . Cal?"

"Yes, I am."

"My dear friend, is this serious? Do I detect a romance here? I never thought I would see the day, my practical and rather shy companion." Yvonne laughed.

"I'm not shy, I'm just careful. And no, you don't see a romance here, but, ah . . . he has asked me to marry him."

"Now the plot thickens. I sense a dilemma."

"And as always, you thrive on dilemmas."

"I do not."

"You certainly do. Remember, I went to school with you for four years. I don't want you to take me on as your personal problem. I can handle my life, thank you. You just decide on having the time of your life. Because the men outnumber the women around here by about five to one. You should be in your element."

"Are you calling me a flirt?"

"You're not?"

"Well . . . maybe a little." Yvonne laughed.

The laugh carried on the breeze to the men who rode behind, and Steve smiled. It was a pleasant sound, and Yvonne seemed harmless to him. She was the kind of girl a man could laugh with and not be in danger of taking her more seriously than she meant to be taken. He had a feeling she shied away from commitment as much as any man did.

"You planning on staying after roundup?" Cal asked, without looking in Steve's direction.

"I hadn't planned on a long stay," Steve replied. "But . . . if Rachel or her father needs help, I might hang around." He didn't like Cal's attitude or his arrogant manner. Besides . . . he might need a reason to stay if success didn't come as quickly as he planned.

"Generally, after roundup, the . . . drifters just drift along."

"You call me a drifter, but you don't know a damn thing about me. Maybe . . . you feel a threat or something."

"You're no threat to me, Steve McKean. Rachel and I

will soon be getting married. When we tie the knot, I think it would be wise of you to consider finding another place to work . . . preferably in another territory.''

"Planning on getting married, are you? Does Rachel know anything about it, or did you just decide for yourself?'' Steve enjoyed the look of fury in Cal's eyes. "I got the impression Rachel was the kind of person who made her own decisions.''

"She does. You're not her kind, McKean. Don't get any ideas. No one around here will tolerate Rachel getting hurt. There's a lot of respect for the Walkers.''

"Don't get in an uproar, Mr. Davis. Rachel and me don't get along too well, and I'm not the marrying kind.''

"Oh, I'm not in an uproar. If Rachel doesn't like you, I can only compliment her on her good taste. She always did have a good head on her shoulders. Drifters are seldom the marrying kind. That's why they end up with nothing to show for their lives. Rachel needs someone with the same ambitions she has.''

"Sometimes there's such a thing as too much ambition.''

"You're crazy. Ask Carter if he'd tolerate a man in Rachel's life who didn't have the drive to make the ranch he worked for so hard bigger and better than it is.''

"Don't you think Carter is the last one to ask what Rachel wants?''

"She wants what her dad wants. She adores the man.''

"I don't doubt that one bit.''

"What's that supposed to mean?''

"Nothing.''

"Take my advice, move along. Before you find you have more trouble than you bargained on.'' With this, Cal nudged his horse forward to draw up beside the buggy. He began a conversation with Rachel. Steve rode up on the other side and was welcomed by Yvonne's inviting smile.

When they arrived at the ranch, Yvonne thanked Steve for bringing in her luggage and watched him thoughtfully as he walked away. She had a good idea she was going to enjoy her stay at the Rocking W . . . very much.

When Steve left the main house, he crossed to the blacksmith's shed, where he found Mikah hard at work.

"Steve, what's going on?"

"Nothing much. Brought back the guest. I'm going back out to the camp. Mikah, I talked to Apach and Carlos. They were in town to pick up supplies. They seem to think I made a mistake in getting us onto the big ranches." He went on to explain how the other two thought. "What do you think?"

"They got a point there. I suppose you know where all the small places are?"

"Yeah. You know how Apach is. He knows all the territory around him within hours of getting there."

"How can we make any changes now?"

"I don't know. I'll think about it. In the meantime, keep your eyes open for anyone who doesn't belong to the ranch. Whoever is behind this has a lot of men working for him. If it's Walker, sometime or other we should see some strange faces around here."

"I'll be on the lookout."

"I'll see you later."

"You coming back tonight?"

"Not unless I'm ordered to."

"You sure are keeping your distance. Any reason for that?"

"Walker's men are getting talkative. I want them to trust

me. I need time, and I don't need to dance attendance on the lady of the place.''

"Yeah . . . okay.'' Mikah watched as Steve mounted and rode away. "You sure got a burr under your saddle and I wonder if she doesn't have a name,'' he murmured to himself and went back to work.

Yvonne was fascinated by the size and luxury of the ranch.

"I had not expected such . . .''

"Civilization?'' Rachel laughed. "Yvonne, we are not so provincial, really. Father has worked long and hard to make this place as comfortable . . . and luxurious as he can. You are in for a lot of surprises. We actually stopped eating with our fingers a long time ago. We cook our meat, and eat with knives and forks.''

"I'm sorry, Rachel. I didn't mean to sound snobbish. I think most people back East have the same misconception. I think I am truly going to like staying here for a while.''

"Good, now let's find my mother. She is excited about your coming. I think she hopes you'll get me out of pants and off my horse and turn me into a lady.''

"You are a lady.''

"I'm afraid Mother equates femininity with silk, lace and giggles.''

"Really? She should see all the hearts you broke when we were at school.''

"Me? Yvonne, be serious.''

"I am. The problem is you had your heart set on coming back here and you never noticed. But I can see why you wanted to come home . . . five to one are great odds. Do the other four look like this Steve McKean?''

"Yvonne . . . I don't want you to misunderstand, but

men like Steve McKean . . . well, out here they're called drifters and they won't be around the morning after. That's just the way they are, unstable.''

"Unstable . . . and handsome and dangerous and exciting. Good heavens, what a challenge.''

"They're the kind that leave you when you need them.''

"Maybe they're the kind that leave when nobody can hold them.''

"Yvonne . . .''

"What's the line in Shakespeare? 'Methinks the lady doth protest too much.' I know one thing, he finds it pretty hard to keep his eyes off of you.''

"Now you're getting carried away. We don't really like each other.''

"Then, if you're truly not interested, I think I'll see just how long Steve McKean wants to hang around.''

"I'm just giving you fair warning.''

"Consider it taken.''

"Come on, let's go.''

They found Lori in the garden she loved. Lori had a green thumb, and flowers bloomed for her when they would bloom for no one else.

She greeted Yvonne warmly, and soon Yvonne found herself being fed and regaled with questions about the East. She thought Rachel's mother was warm and interesting.

"Rachel has told me so much about you that I feel I know you. Please consider this your home while you are here. If there is anything you want or need, don't hesitate to ask. Has Rachel told you we have planned a party to welcome you? Everyone will be here. I'm sure they are anxious to meet you.''

"You are so kind. I shall look forward to the party, and thank you so much."

"Rachel was going to go and find a new gown for the dance in town. I was to accompany her, but since you're here, I'm sure your taste is more up-to-date than mine."

"Mother," Rachel laughed. "You won't get away with it. I have already warned Yvonne."

"Warned her? Good heavens, whatever for?"

"Your little attempts at conspiracy won't work. Yvonne knows me too well to try to change me."

"The fact is, I like you just the way you are," Yvonne said firmly. "And I wouldn't be caught dead trying to make any changes."

"Then that settles it. Mother, you've been outdone, so let's just make the best of it."

"I suppose I must surrender gracefully." Lori smiled fondly at her daughter. "But I do insist on a new gown."

"I would not mind a little shopping," Yvonne agreed.

"Then we'll plan on it tomorrow. For today, I want to show you my world and introduce you to my father and the rest of the boys."

They spent the rest of the afternoon riding across the land Rachel was so proud of. Yvonne could see both her pride and the reason for it.

Rachel told her of the Bitterroot Mountains and the basin below them in which the ranch lay. She led her to a meadow filled with plumy bluegrass, and to another colorfully blanketed in yellow bells, daisies and buttercups. They walked along a stream lined with cottonwoods, aspens and birch trees.

The clear warm air would turn cool at night, Rachel said,

and it would be filled with the scent of mariposa lilies and dogtooth violets.

"Is it cold here in the winter?"

"Is it ever, and we get a lot of snow, but mostly between January and March. I've seen times when we get hail big enough to kill chickens."

"What do you do in the winter?"

"Snuggle in front of a fire, or just enjoy the snow."

"I can see that the East was no temptation to you."

"No, it really wasn't. I would not have gone to school at all if Mother hadn't insisted. Actually, Dad did too. he said if I was going to run the ranch, I'd better get all the education that I could. He said he couldn't leave it to a woman who wouldn't have brains enough to handle it."

"Doesn't it scare you sometimes?"

"What?"

"Running this place after your parents are gone. It's an immense job. I can tell you that it would scare me silly."

"No, I'm not afraid. This ranch has some of the most dependable men around. I would have all the help I'd need."

"It's a lot of responsibility. I should think, in this case, a husband would be more than welcome."

"I don't intend to hand the ranch to any man . . . at least not until I know I'm going to fall. I wouldn't let it go so easily."

"I didn't say let it go. Rachel, why do you see marriage as giving up something?"

"Isn't it?"

"It shouldn't be. If you find the right man, it should be a partnership."

"That's the way it's been for my parents, but they came

out here with nothing and she helped him build it. I suppose it's as much her work as his. But I'm just taking over something that's already built. I had nothing to do with it."

"So you feel you have to live up to something?"

"No, of course not, unless it's my own expectations."

"I don't think your parents are pushing you to marry. I don't think either of them would want you to marry unless you were in love."

Rachel stood silently for a minute. "I was considering marrying Cal."

"Just make sure it's for the right reasons," Yvonne said. "You're very important to me, too, and I don't want to see you hurt by anything."

"Thanks, Yvonne."

The two embraced, then remounted their horses and continued their ride.

Chapter Five

The trip into town to shop was successful enough to satisfy Lori, for Yvonne helped Rachel choose a lovely gown that complemented her brilliant coloring.

"It is beautiful and, Rachel, the color is perfect for you," Lori said.

"I must admit you're right, Mother. It is very pretty."

"And I found a new gown as well," Yvonne said. "I had not expected to find anything so perfect here, and I'm sorry again that I underestimated your town."

"Frankly, I was not really expecting to find anything that would please your cosmopolitan taste," Rachel laughed. "But I'm glad we went. I would never have chosen this gown if you had not been with me. It is a bit daring."

"Trust me that when you come in with that creation on, there won't be a man in the room who won't swarm about you."

"Great, I might get another proposal from Cal, and that is the last thing I want."

"Rachel"—Lori shook her head—"I don't know what you find wrong with Cal."

"Nothing. There's nothing wrong with Cal. It's just that I don't intend to marry him. So you and Dad will just have to combine our ranches some other way." She chuckled mischievously. "Why not buy him out, like all the little ranches are being bought out?"

"Rachel!" Lori did not seem to be amused by her words. Rachel looked at her in surprise. "Your father is not the one trying to buy up all the smaller ranches. He is quite satisfied with what we have."

Rachel looked at her mother. "Mother, don't you think that Dad has some political aspirations?"

"No. I've told you, he is satisfied with what we have."

"And what about Montana's statehood? He's all for that."

"Rachel, I want to hear no more about it. Montana is far from statehood, and your father is not involved in that anyway." She turned her attention to Yvonne, as if determined to change the subject. "Yvonne, I had not thought of a new gown for myself, but you have such good taste, perhaps you would be willing to help me choose one."

"Of course," Yvonne replied. But she decided to question Rachel about her mother at the first opportunity. It seemed Lori was trying to ignore anything that might upset her life.

But there was little time to get Rachel alone long enough for any discussion. The dance was two nights away, and it seemed Rachel was not in the mood to discuss it.

The night of the dance they were getting ready together

in Rachel's room, dressing each other's hair and considering perfume and accessories. Yvonne, who had insisted on doing something special with Rachel's hair, stood behind her and brushed it.

"Rachel, your hair is wonderful, so thick and silky."

"And unmanageable."

"No, not really. All you need to do is this." She gathered the tresses on the top of Rachel's head in a mass of tangled curls and pinned it. "Look, it's perfect."

"It looks like I just got out of bed . . . or . . ."

"Or like you're ready to climb into one."

"You are getting out of hand. I don't want to be a walking invitation." Rachel laughed, but she examined herself closely and fought the idea that she wanted Steve to see her this way.

"No?"

"No. So get your imagination tamed down and let's find something else."

"All right, all right. I'll find another way. But I assure you—"

"Don't assure me of attracting every man in the room. I get enough of that from my mother."

"How is this?"

Yvonne had coiled the heavy weight of Rachel's hair in a crown about her head. It suddenly gave Rachel a regal look that she liked.

"Wonderful. Now, help me into this creation of yours, and we'll be ready to go."

"I suspect your Cal will be along soon."

"He's not *my* Cal, and yes, he's always on time."

"Dependable."

"You say that as if it's a criticism. I like dependable and steady men."

"Oh, then I guess you'll come around to saying yes to his proposal one of these days. As for me . . . I am more than curious about Steve. I have a feeling . . ."

"What kind of feeling?"

"I don't know yet, but I expect I'll have my answers soon. Do you think he'll be on time?"

"I told you the kind of man he is. If he's on time it will surprise me."

"You don't like him at all, do you? Why? What has he done?"

"He hasn't done anything. I just don't think he will be around long."

"Would you like to make a small wager?"

"A wager?"

"Yes. I say he'll be here longer than you think, and with your blessings. You say he won't be here after the roundup is over. Let's bet on it."

"All right. What do you want to bet?"

"I don't know. Give me some time to think about it."

"Make it good, I like to win."

"Don't be so sure of yourself."

"I'm not, I'm sure of him."

"Come on, it's time for them to come."

The two left Rachel's room and started down the steps. There was a knock on the door. Rachel continued down and went to the door and opened it.

Steve was still not too pleased with the idea that he had to escort a girl to a dance he'd meant to attend only to meet the other ranchers. He'd wanted to listen to conversations, not spend time with a near stranger.

He had bathed, shaved and dressed carefully in clothes he had bought on credit. All the while, he was constantly being reminded by the other men of how lucky he was. He wished he did not have to be in the company of Rachel and Cal for the evening, though. Cal rubbed him the wrong way, and he knew he did the same to Rachel.

He also had a feeling that dances were not Rachel's forte. She was the lady in pants who wore spurs, and he was pretty certain she wouldn't mind digging them into a man if she didn't get her way about something.

He crossed the clearing between the bunkhouse and the main house, noticing that Cal Davis had not arrived yet. When he knocked he expected to see Lori. He had not expected the vision that met him.

In the glow of the light, she looked like a hungry man's dream. This was not the woman who had hired him: this was a princess from some long-ago romance. His body instantly reminded him that it had not tasted the pleasures of a warm and willing woman for a long, long time.

Her gown was a color of green he hadn't known existed, and it was cut low enough to leave little to his imagination . . . and his imagination was working at full speed. Her hair looked . . . he sought the word . . . glorious was the only one that came to mind. She was close enough that the scent of her perfume came to him, and if he hadn't been overwhelmed by the vision she made, her fragile and delicate scent would have done the trick.

Almost desperately he struggled for control. He had been caught in this scented trap once before, and he was not fool enough to let it happen again. Besides, prison loomed in the back of his mind, and if he let Rachel Walker get to him, she might just be the one to turn the key in the lock. He fought for the right tone of voice.

"Good evening, boss. You sure look different in a dress."

"Thank you," Rachel said, but her smile was less than friendly.

"Hello, Mr. McKean," Yvonne said, smiling her welcome. "Come in. I'm afraid we might have to wait for a while. Cal Davis isn't here yet. It's nice to see you're on time, though. I hate a man who isn't . . . dependable." She ignored Rachel's dark look. "Can I get you something while you wait? A drink?"

"No, thank you."

"My parents have gone on ahead," Rachel said. "Since Mother was in charge of the food, she wanted to make sure everything was ready. As soon as Cal comes we can go."

Steve followed them into the parlor, fighting his awareness of Rachel and cursing it. He concentrated on Yvonne . . . she was less of a danger.

"You do look pretty, Miss Avery."

"I thought I told you to call me Yvonne." She pretended to frown, but her eyes sparkled with humor.

"Yvonne," he repeated. "It's a real pleasure to escort you tonight."

"How gallant," Yvonne laughed. "But I have a suspicion you didn't have much choice about it."

"Had I a choice"—Steve grinned—"I would have asked you anyway."

Rachel was annoyed and she fought to hide it. Steve and Yvonne seemed to understand one another for some reason.

They were smiling at each other as if they shared a wonderful secret.

"Thank you. I intend to have some fun tonight. Do you dance?"

"I'm a bit out of practice, but if you don't mind my clumsy feet, I'm willing to give it a try."

Rachel just knew she was going to say something snappish, when the sound of an approaching carriage came to them.

"Cal's here," she said in relief. She had to stop herself from running to the door.

Cal seemed to be as stunned as Steve had been when he caught sight of Rachel. Steve got the impression she did not wear dresses often . . . but then the sight of her in those snug pants was a treat also. He would have to debate with himself just which way was more enticing . . . and he had to remind himself that it meant nothing to him anyway.

They left together, and Steve was soon grateful for Yvonne's presence, for she was an amusing and interesting person. They chatted and laughed all the way to town.

The hall was gaily decorated, and there were long tables laden with food along the wall. The group that played the music were six men strong, and what they lacked in talent, they made up for in enthusiasm.

There was laughter, and the hum of the voices of people who did not get this opportunity often and intended to make the most of it.

Rachel introduced Steve and Yvonne to a large number of people. Among them were Cal's parents. Joseph Davis, a tall, burly and jovial man, seemed well matched to Rose, the friendly-eyed woman beside him. In fact it annoyed

Steve a bit, because he would rather not have liked them. He would have welcomed a reason to suspect them . . . and Cal . . . more.

Steve also met the owners of some of the smaller ranches in the area. Steve studied their faces, watching for any sign of anger toward those from the Rocking W. But if there was animosity, it was carefully concealed.

As the evening grew longer, Steve identified two small ranchers whom he would subtly question. He relinquished Yvonne to another man, and watched the pair dance away. Then he walked to the table where the punch, laced by now with potent ingredients, was being enjoyed by a gathering of men.

The group consisted of a few hands from assorted ranches, and two of the owners he sought. He stopped close, and slowly let himself become involved in the conversations. What drew his attention right away was that one of the older men had a few bruises on his face, and carried himself as if he were not exactly comfortable.

It didn't take long for Steve to recognize the animosity in the older man's eyes as he gazed at an arrogantly smiling man who stood a short distance away.

Steve was about to go and talk to the older man when he paused. The man had closed the distance between himself and the second man, and from his posture and the aura of anger around him, Steve wondered if he wasn't intent on violence.

There were a few words exchanged that Steve couldn't hear, but the rage on the rancher's face made hearing unnecessary. Steve moved closer. He wanted to find out what he could.

He was too late. The angry rancher was drawn away by

two obviously worried friends. After they forced a drink on him and detained him long enough to be sure his anger was under control, they finally left his side. Steve walked over nonchalantly, and stood for a few minutes before he struck up a conversation.

He was quick to find out the rancher was Otis Quantrell, and that his ranch was not doing well.

"You're not far from the Rocking W?" Steve questioned.

"No, I'm just the other side of Skyrock Canyon. We're neighbors . . . at least for the time being."

"For the time being? You planning on a vacation?" Steve smiled as he spoke.

"Right now . . . no. I'll be damned if I will 'vacation.' "

Steve had no doubt that Quantrell was being forced off his land by someone. He knew the signs of violence better than most.

"You thinking of selling?"

"I don't know yet." Steve could hear the anger and the fear in his voice. "I might."

"Been offered anything yet?"

The man was silent long enough to let Steve know he had hit home. The hesitation spoke of the man's fear as well, for he glanced suspiciously at Steve, who tried to keep his face bland and mildly curious.

"No . . . no, I ain't. And I ain't decided to sell yet. You work for the Rocking W, don't you?"

"Just got hired on a few days ago. It's a fine ranch."

"Yeah, it is."

"Carter Walker is a pretty good boss."

"And his daughter don't take no back seat to anyone either. Not only does she give every buck in the county a run for his money, she's right good at handling her dad's place. Man who gets her is going to be pretty lucky.''

"I guess she's interested in Cal Davis."

"Well, money gets money, don't it? I know Cal's interested, but I'm not too sure about her. She's pretty independent."

"Those two ranches would make a nice property."

"Maybe you and Cal are thinking on the same lines. Maybe that's why the girl shies away from all the fellas howling after her. Maybe she ain't so sure it's her they're after."

Steve had never thought of it that way, but the words made him wonder. Maybe Rachel Walker had a good reason for not trusting too much.

"Has the Rocking W made any offers for your place?"

"Why should they, they got enough."

"I was just wondering."

"Selling would be pretty hard. I got a lot of work tied up there."

"You had an accident lately?"

"No, why?"

"I noticed the bruises, and you look a little stiff."

"It's nothing, just a cantankerous horse."

"You look like you might need a little help at your place."

Otis looked at Steve with such an unguarded look of surprise that Steve felt he'd surely discovered the next rancher in line to lose his land. Now all he had to find out was who was pushing him.

"I do, but I can't pay the wages the big places can. You know anyone looking?"

"Not right off hand, but you never know. A lot of riders pass through Rocking W land."

There was a lull in their conversation, and Steve did not want to push his questioning. He took the time to study the crowd again . . . and his gaze fell on Rachel. At that moment the musicians stopped for a breather, and he watched Rachel smile at her partner, say something, then leave the fellow to cross the room toward the door. Why Steve followed he didn't know, but he found himself stepping out into the cool night air and looking around for her.

She was walking some distance away from him, at the edge of the long porch that wound around the entire building. He followed as she turned the corner.

This side of the porch was empty except for her, standing with her back to him and looking out into the night, which was brightened by a large, full, yellow moon. He came up behind her, and he sensed that she knew he was there.

"We used to call them harvest moons," he said quietly. She didn't turn around.

"Why did you leave home, Steve?"

"I was kind of forced to."

This statement made her turn. The moon glazed him in its light, and left her in shadow. He could feel her gaze.

"I was talking to Tom today, and he says you're an exceptional hand."

"Good. Does that mean you've no intention of firing me?"

She ignored his humorous question. "He says he had a feeling you were used to ranching and to giving orders . . . as if you'd had a place of your own at one time."

"It could be just his imagination."

"No, I think not. He doesn't have a fanciful imagination.

If there is anyone solid in this world, it's Tom Bordon."

"He's just solid enough to appreciate a hard worker, and I'm working hard to keep my job."

"You don't ever answer a question directly, do you?"

"What did you ask?"

"You're not just a drifting worker, are you? You've really had a place of your own."

"I'll answer a question for you, if you agree to answer one for me."

"Agreed."

"You first."

"I asked you once before, who are you, Steve McKean?"

"I'm a man who likes the kind of work he does and the kind of people he works for. I like to have my freedom and I like to watch things grow. I just don't have roots of my own right now. Maybe I plan on it . . . someday."

"I guess it's your turn."

"How big do you think the Rocking W should be?"

"That's an odd question."

"Answer it."

"As big and as profitable as Dad wants it to be. He has a lot of plans for this territory."

"I don't doubt it one bit."

"You don't understand. It's not for himself alone. The ranchers here will appreciate what he has planned."

"All of them?"

"You're talking in riddles."

"I just wonder about people like Otis Quantrell."

"What about Otis?"

"He's going to lose his place, if I'm not mistaken."

"How would you know?"

"Just talked to him for a bit. He's a worried man . . . and a frightened one."

"Frightened? Of whom?"

"You tell me."

"You don't think Dad would force another man out? You're wrong, Steve, wrong."

"I didn't say that."

"Of course you did. Is that what happened to you? Did you have a small place of your own that you couldn't hold? Is that why you're so angry?"

"My past has nothing to do with the situation around here. Whether or not I had a place of my own is immaterial."

"Why should the situation around here be of any concern to you? You'll be on your way one day, and no one here in this basin will know what you thought."

"Suppose I'm just an interested person who doesn't like injustice."

"Then stay here and do something about it." She said the last words without thought, and she could tell by his sudden silence that he was wondering whether her words meant anything besides a challenge. She wondered too.

"Maybe I will," he replied. "Can I ask another question?"

"I thought we agreed on one apiece."

"Then I'll let you ask another."

"All right."

"Would you marry Cal Davis just to give your father what he wanted?"

"No." She said the word so bluntly and so firmly that he didn't doubt that she spoke the truth. It surprised him that she had said no.

"I guess it's your turn," he said.

"Did you own a place of your own?"

"Yes." His answer was as abrupt and as firm as hers, and she knew he was not going to add anything to it. She laughed softly, and he had to smile. "I haven't had a chance to dance with you."

"What's wrong with right now?"

"Out here?" He was totally taken off guard by her challenge. A large room full of people was much . . . safer than a moonlit, star-kissed night, alone. But he could not let her believe the thought shook him.

"Why not? It's a lot cooler."

It might have started out a lot cooler, but when he put his arms about her and she moved so easily into them, he was not so certain. She seemed to fit against him so easily, and the slow waltz the musicians were playing seemed to match the rhythm of the night.

In his arms she felt soft and warm. The scent of her was intoxicating. She moved against him with a sensual grace and he unconsciously drew her closer.

Rachel was amazed at herself, first for enjoying the embrace of a man whose way of life was everything she rejected. But the arms that held her felt strong and protective. She could feel the strength of his body pressed against her, and feelings she had never experienced before flooded her.

He moved with the same smooth grace that had intrigued her before. His hand, pressed against the curve of her waist, felt warm. The pressure was just enough that she knew she could break it if she chose, but she did not choose.

They did not speak until the music came to a halt, and even then he held her longer than both knew was proper. He looked down into her eyes and recognized not only her vulnerability, but his own as well. He wanted her, and the heat of desire licked through him like a wild fire.

Rachel did not try to deny that something huge and powerful was uncoiling within her. She had never felt this way in her life, and the new and sudden taste of desire shook all her resolve.

She knew so little about him, and was filled with questions she knew he did not mean to answer. He was all wrong for her . . . but she felt the heat swirl up from the depths of her, and she could not do battle with her wayward body. It was demanding something more . . . something she had never tasted before, but something she knew she wanted.

"When the summer is full near the river in Colorado where I was born," he said softly, "the scent of something wonderful and sweet can come to you on the breeze, and you know you will never forget it if you travel a million miles. It makes you understand just how important small things can be. Rachel you have all that any man or woman could ever dream of. It would be a shame not to savor and hold it. Life is such a fragile thing. You can lose something precious if you don't have the courage to grasp what is valuable and forget what is not."

She looked up at him, and was almost mesmerized by the silver glow of his eyes and the soft, mellow sound of his voice. What was he trying to tell her? Was he warning her in some way . . . about what?

"You are different from any man I have ever known. I don't know why, I only know you make me feel things I don't want to feel."

He was falling into the depths of her green eyes. Against everything he knew was right, he felt he had to kiss her . . .

and he knew that kissing her was the worst thing for both of them.

He blamed it on the fact that he had not held a woman for three years, and that his body was hungry for the taste and feel of her. He lied to himself that it would be nothing more than just a kiss on a moonlit night. He promised himself it would harm no one . . . no one.

His mouth touched hers lightly at first, tentatively. But the jolt of the contact echoed through him like a searing fire. He heard her soft intake of breath; then her mouth softened and parted beneath his, and he lost the control he had bargained on.

Passion swept through them like wildfire, and he let it carry them both away with its heat. She did not fight him, in fact could not find the strength or the desire to fight him. Her body was pressed so close to his lean, hard form that she didn't know if she could catch her next breath.

For a long moment her lips were smothered beneath his passionate kiss, and he seemed to be drowning in the sweet taste of her, and in the feel of her soft curves pressed so intimately to him. Every fiber of his body wanted her, wanted to find the completion of this magical thing . . . he was losing himself.

Suddenly alarms began to go off, shrieking through him like sirens. He put his hands on her shoulders and held her away from him. He recognized the heavy-lidded, misty look, and knew he had touched a place he had never intended to touch.

Guilt was followed quickly by self-protection. There was no doubt in his mind that he wanted her; his body was as hot as a live flame. But he named it lust . . . pure and simple lust. She was beautiful and much too willing, and he knew a hunger such as he had never known. But the hunger was a silken trap, and one he had no intention of falling into again.

"I'm sorry, Rachel." His voice was thick with the desire he was struggling to control. "I didn't mean to do that."

"I think that I am to blame as much as you, and I'm not sorry."

This only made his guilt worse. He needed her resistance, but it seemed she would not fit into the mold he had provided for her.

"I think you'd better go in."

"Steve . . ." There was both surprise and hurt in her voice. She had practically told him she would not resist him if he wanted to kiss her again.

He could not defend himself with any kind of honesty, so he resorted to sarcasm.

"I don't think it's wise for the boss to play games with the hired help, do you? Your daddy might get angry." He struggled to keep mocking laughter in his voice and was pleased with her soft gasp of shock.

She could feel her face flame. He was accusing her of throwing herself at him.

"I don't mind being accommodating, but don't you think we could find a safer place?"

"Accommodating!" she gasped. "You arrogant oaf! Do you think . . . Oh, you really are a . . . a beast." When she struck, he had half expected it, and knew he well deserved it. The sting of the slap lingered long after she had reentered the hall.

Yvonne and Cal were dancing together. She tilted her head and smiled up at him. He was a handsome man, and

Yvonne intended to find out more about him. There had to be a reason Rachel didn't want to grab him up.

"Are you enjoying your stay so far?" Cal asked.

"Very much. This is such a huge and exciting place. I find Montana . . . and the people here all so . . ."

"Large?" he offered with a laugh.

"Yes. Large. It seems the people match the place. You were born here?"

"Yes."

"You've never wanted to leave?"

"Oh, I'd like to travel sometime, but leave, permanently, no. I wouldn't."

"You sound like Rachel. I shall have to find out about the magic this place has. But first, I would like to know it . . . and you . . . better."

"I would be happy to show you around. Our ranch is a pretty special place."

"I imagine you have your own favorite spots."

"I do. Great Falls. I'll show it to you. It used to be my hiding place as a boy." Cal was a bit surprised at how much he was enjoying Yvonne's company, and that he had extended the invitation. Still, he realized he would enjoy showing her Great Falls.

Yvonne was finding her interest growing and wondering why Rachel would let this charming and interesting man slip out of her life. She liked the way his eyes crinkled at the corners when he smiled and the direct way he looked at her. She could feel the warmth of his hand on her back and the tingling sensation his touch gave her. Yes . . . this Cal Davis was interesting . . . very, very interesting.

* * *

116

Steve stood where he was, angry with himself for being a fool and letting himself get caught up as he had, and guilty for treating Rachel as if she were a woman of loose morals. He took a pouch of tobacco from his pocket and rolled a cigarette. When he struck a match and bent his head to light it, he became aware that he was no longer alone. He turned to see Yvonne standing near the corner of the porch.

He'd not exactly been the best of escorts, leaving her to wonder where he had gone. "Yvonne, sorry, I just came out for a smoke and some air."

Yvonne didn't speak at once, but she walked toward him and stopped inches away. "I just saw Rachel come back into the hall. She didn't look very happy. What in heaven's name happened?"

"Nothing, it's just that we get along about like a cat and a dog."

"Must be you, cowboy. Rachel gets along with everyone."

"Yeah, must be."

"Steve, may I ask you something?"

"This seems to be the night for questions. Why not?"

"If you don't like Rachel, why do you go on working for her?"

"I don't work for her, I work for her father," Steve replied, but his gaze shifted from her to look out over the town. He heard her soft laugh, and she came to stand close beside him.

"Rachel and I met in school," Yvonne began as if she were ruminating. "She was such a shy girl when she first arrived. I think she had never been so far from home before. She didn't change one bit all the time she was there. I was really pleased that we became such good friends, and I always promised myself if I could ever help her, I would.''

"You know, I don't have any idea what you're talking about."

"Don't you? I'll make it clear. If you're a friend and loyal to her and to the ranch she loves, wonderful. If you're not . . . why don't you just drift on and leave her to go on with what she loves without interference?''

Now Steve turned to look at her. His eyes were like molten silver, and she stood still and let her senses react.

"I can't do that."

"Why?" Her question was soft, and probing. Suddenly she got the idea that Steve McKean was not as hard as he appeared.

As for Steve, her intense gaze made him uncomfortable. He felt another twinge of guilt. "There's a lot more going on in this territory than a visitor like you would know about. I don't know what would disturb Rachel about me, but something does. Maybe because, as I said, everything is not as it seems. Let us work our own problems out."

"Rachel is a person who feels deeply about things. She's also the kind who can get hurt easily."

"I have no intention of hurting her."

"Good," Yvonne said. "Now, I believe you owe me a dance or two. The party is almost over."

"Sure," Steve replied. They returned inside and shared the last two dances. But Steve did not take Yvonne's words lightly, for behind her bright and vivacious smile he saw a woman with a very clever mind. She and Rachel were close, Yvonne had said. Maybe Yvonne's friendship was worth developing. Not only for what she might confide, but for what she could carry to Rachel. He needed Rachel's anger, and . . . perhaps her jealousy.

"Don't you think it would be better if we found our own transportation home?" he asked.

"That sounds like a delightful idea. I shall go and tell Rachel and Cal. I'm sure they will be glad to have some time to spend alone. I think we will soon be hearing wedding bells."

"Really?" Steve grinned. "Maybe you don't know Rachel as well as you thought. Go and tell them. I'll go and round up a ride home."

Yvonne wasn't too sure if the grin was a promise, or if he had a secret she really should know about. She watched him walk away, then turned to find Cal and Rachel. When she did, Cal received the news with a warm smile, but Rachel's face revealed nothing. Yvonne decided she had to give this situation a lot of thought.

Chapter Six

Cal stood on the front porch of the Bar D and looked out with pride on what he had helped his father build. He had worked his fingers to the bone to make the place grow, and he was even more pleased that his father recognized and gave him most of the credit for doing so.

He had his dreams—making the Bar D the best in the territory and having Rachel Walker mistress here were the two foremost. That thought led him to Steve McKean. He knew already that Steve attracted Rachel. Men like him always attracted women.

He guessed there was something mysterious about them, something that spoke of adventure and excitement. But as far as he was concerned, there was no mystery at all. They were men who built nothing, remained nowhere, and accepted no responsibility. Men who seemed to be a challenge to every woman who came near them; men who were nothing but promising illusions, and did their level best to take what belonged to others.

The ride home with Rachel the night before had been disappointing. He couldn't seem to pin her down, and she kept telling him she wasn't ready for marriage yet. He tried to fight the idea that if Steve McKean hadn't come along, she might have been more receptive.

The sun had just come up, and this was one of Cal's favorite times of day. He watched the door to the bunkhouse open and the men come out one by one. Among them were the two hands recently hired.

The difference between the two drew his attention. The Indian wore his black hair shoulder length with a band of red cotton tied about his head. He was a graceful man, and Cal had watched his dark eyes gleam with pleasure after he had brought a particularly wild horse under control. He would laugh and the laughter would be triumphant. Cal wondered if there was a horse alive that could get the better of him.

The Spaniard came from a completely different background, smiled more easily, and yet had the same air of independence. No one seemed to care to move past the cool warning that appeared in his eyes when curiosity brought someone too close. Dark hazel, they would turn a strange shade of green gold that was chilling.

The two men were so different, yet alike in ways no one could name. They worked hard, and as far as Cal was concerned, that was all that mattered.

He had been surprised when his foreman had taken a dislike to the Indian. He was better with a horse than any man he had ever met . . . maybe that was it.

However, if the situation went on as it was, the Indian

would have to go. Fighting was not conducive to getting good work done. He watched as the two newcomers stopped to talk together for a minute.

"You're doing pretty well with everyone else," Carlos was saying, "but I don't think there's any love lost between you and the foreman."

"He abuses his animals," Apach said with a frigid expression. "I have already crossed him twice because of that. Getting me fired is all he can do, but I wouldn't mind that, to be truthful. It might just be the only way. There wouldn't be any trouble getting word to Steve to ask where I should go next."

"I know what you would like, amigo, but don't push it too far or you might find yourself getting hanged."

"There is no doubt in my mind about that. It seems Apaches are not held high in the foreman's regard."

Carlos laughed. "He would spit you and roast you if he had the chance."

"Then," Apach said, "perhaps I should give him the chance."

"Apach, be careful. He doesn't just want to see the last of you, he'd like to hurt you bad."

Apach's smile was quick and satisfied. "If he begins it . . . I will see it to an end. Do not fear. My ancestors would sleep better among the spirits if his kind suffered some." Apach began to walk again and Carlos moved beside him as they made their way to the corral, where they would cut out their horses and get on with the day's work.

They were just approaching the corral when the sound of furious activity came to them. They hurried forward, and as they drew near the corral, Apach muttered a curse, along with a few words in Apache that Carlos felt it was just as well he didn't understand.

Inside the corral the foreman, Doug Briden, had a firm hold on the reins of the bridle that he had just put on a horse. The horse was struggling to be free, its eyes filled with terror. His sleek body trembled and Doug was using the end of the bridle to strike the horse about the head. He was cursing the animal, who was growing more afraid by the moment.

Apach was over the rail of the corral before Carlos could stop him. He raced to Doug and gripped him, spinning him around. Then he struck a blow that drove Doug to his knees. Quickly Apach took a small leather whip he wore on his belt and began to strike Doug.

"How do you like it?" he snarled. "How does it feel to be whipped when you can't defend yourself?"

Doug was taken by surprise, and for a while he did not grasp what was happening. The attack had come too fast. Then he realized the hands were already gathering. He could not lose face among them. He gathered himself and threw his body at Apach's knees, bringing him down. Then the two were exchanging blows, and rolling in the dirt until it was a mist of brown dust that hung about them in a cloud.

But it wasn't long before it became obvious that Apach, wiry and lean, was getting the upper hand. The men gathered at the fence to watch. Carlos kept one eye on the fight going on and the other on Cal, who had been standing on the porch but was now walking toward them.

In the short while they had been at the Bar D, Carlos had formed his own opinion of Cal and his father. They were good ranchers, and outside of joining with the Walker ranch, they seemed to have no goals other than to be good at what they were doing.

Carlos believed it would be a good thing if this fight led to Apach being fired. Being Apach's friend, he wouldn't be criticized if he decided to go with him. It was the way of the hands that worked a ranch. Partners worked through rain, storms and blizzards together, forming powerful bonds. Their relationship would give him just the excuse he needed.

"What's going on here?" Cal said as he reached the fence.

"A disagreement on how to treat horses," Carlos said.

"That's Doug and Apach, isn't it?"

"Sí."

"Who started it?"

"Take that up with them. I'm not getting in the middle."

"Damn," Cal muttered. "Go in there and break 'em up," he called out to several of the nearby hands.

It took four of them to separate Apach and Doug, and the two glared at each other even while they were being held apart.

"You're fired!" Doug panted as he pointed a firm finger at Apach. "Get your gear and clear out right now."

"What's going on, Doug?" Cal asked.

"He jumped me! He's fired," Doug replied. He knew Cal would be forced by unwritten law to stand behind him or to show good reason why Apach should not be fired. Doug had been with the Bar D for a long time and knew there was no question whom the boss would support. He smiled when Cal turned to Apach.

"Sorry, Apach. Get your gear and move on. You're a

damn fine wrangler, but I can't have this kind of thing going on."

"I'm going with him," Carlos said at once.

"You don't need to do that, Carlos," Doug said. "You're a good hand. He's nothing more than—"

"My friend," Carlos finished. "C'mon, Apach. Let's get our things."

Apach nodded, then turned to Cal. "You ought to take better care of your stock. Mistreating an animal is stupid. It is worse when that animal works his heart out for you. It is going to cost you if it has not already." He turned away and followed Carlos to the bunkhouse.

"You really were mad," Carlos laughed. "But it has worked out all right."

"There is something about a man who will be cruel to an animal. He is not to be trusted. Cal Davis may feel Doug is his best, but if it were me, I would watch Doug Briden." He grinned. "But you are right, we have just lost our jobs."

"So what's our next step?" Carlos asked.

"Get word to Steve and see what he wants us to do. I would like to find work at one of the smaller places and see what we can find out there."

"And how do we let Steve know, just ride up to him and say we got conveniently fired?"

"We could ride past the Rocking W and tell Mikah to ask Steve to meet us."

"Good idea. If we don't let him know, he'll be wasting a lot of time figuring out where we went. Do you think we ought to find work at one of the smaller places ourselves?"

"Maybe we should take different trails here, Carlos. You go and speak to Mikah, or Steve if you can find him. We can meet at the crossing of the twin canyons. I will make camp there and wait for you."

"Good idea, but it will most likely be late before I can meet you. And, Apach . . . since we've got no cook shack to go to"—Carlos grinned—"I expect some supper."

"I'll see what I can do to keep hunger from your door."

Carlos laughed, and Apach chuckled in response as the two separated and went on their different missions.

Mikah was naked to the waist, his huge body slicked with sweat. He held the red hot horseshoe over the anvil and his strong arm wielded the hammer that struck sparks from it. Then he immersed it in a tub of water and it sizzled as a cloud of steam arose.

Through the steam he looked out past the open doors and saw a rider approaching. It did not take him long to recognize Carlos. Who else rode with the easy grace of a conquistador . . . with such arrogance and pride?

Mikah smiled as he stepped outside and waited for Carlos to ride up to him.

"Carlos, what're you doin' here?"

"Looking for Steve. Do you know where he is?"

"Last I heard, he was up at the river camp. He hasn't been here for a couple of days. Is something wrong?"

"Apach and I were thinking of a way to get off the Bar D and sign on with one of the smaller ones. Today Apach got into it with the foreman and he was fired."

"Fired for what?"

"Jumping the foreman for mistreating a horse. You know how he is."

"Yeah. So what now?"

"I'll meet Apach later, but we think we should separate.

126

I'm going to try the C Bar C. It's small and it's run by a widow with a couple of young sons. Good place for whoever it is to apply some pressure.''

''Good idea, except I don't expect Steve to be back here for a few days yet. You ought to get word to him.''

''Maybe I should go on up and see him. He has to meet with me and Apach so we can discuss our plans.''

''If he should happen by, I'll tell him where you and Apach are campin'. If you don't find him at the river camp, maybe you two better just wait until he comes to meet you.''

''You could be right, Mikah, but I'll try the river camp anyway, just in case.'' He explained quickly where he and Apach could be found.

Mikah nodded and Carlos rode slowly away. Mikah watched him, and after a few minutes had the uncomfortable feeling that he, himself, was being watched. He scanned the area and the house, then saw Rachel standing in the shadows of the front porch. He turned back to his work.

Rachel had seen Carlos ride up to the stable door and she was curious. Visitors came to the house and did not usually stop to speak with the blacksmith.

She knew quite well that Steve and their new blacksmith were friends, and she had wanted to talk to Mikah to see what information she could glean from him. This seemed to present the best chance. She left the porch and crossed to the stable.

Mikah knew she was coming—he had a peripheral glimpse of her—and began to think of answers that might satisfy her.

''Mikah?''

"Yes'm?"

"I haven't seen your visitor around here before."

"No, ma'am. He's just someone I've run across a couple of times. He heard I was working here and dropped by to say a word or two."

"Does he work around here?"

"I don't rightly know, Miss Rachel. I had to get this job finished and he was in kind of a hurry, so we didn't talk long."

Rachel couldn't understand why she had the feeling that Mikah was deliberately lying to her. But she smiled as if his words were enough explanation. She started to carry her saddle to her horse, and Mikah laid aside his tools and went to do it for her.

"You goin' to town, Miss Rachel?"

"No, I'm just going for a ride while Yvonne is occupied with my mother and her recipes and fashion ideas. My mother is in her glory with all those ruffles and petticoats."

"She's sure one pretty woman. 'Course you're prettier."

"Come on, Mikah."

Mikah looked at her as if he were a bit surprised. "You sure are. Ain't a man on this ranch don't believe that's true. You're pretty down deep. It comes glowin' out of your eyes and bubblin' in your smile. I just can't understand why that Cal Davis has been waitin' so long."

"Cal's not to blame, Mikah. It's me."

"Well . . . I guess bein' careful is good. Your daddy got a fine place here to hand down, and you're gonna choose who's gonna run it."

Rachel looked directly at him. "The man I choose is not going to run it. Either it will be me and him together . . . or I'll do it alone."

Before Mikah could say any more, Rachel mounted and rode away. Once out of sight of the ranch, she turned her horse toward the river camp. She was going to talk to her father, she decided . . . but she knew she lied to herself about that too.

She was curious about the man who'd stopped to talk to Mikah, then ridden toward the river camp as if he had a definite destination in mind.

She knew every stream and gully of the ranch, and every ridge and valley, so she reached the camp before Carlos did. She sat on a ridge lined with trees and looked out over the camp, knowing she could not be seen from where she was.

Carlos had ridden slowly, simply because he did not know the area well. He was not surprised that Steve was not in the camp at the moment. Camps were usually empty during the day except for the cook or the hands who came in and out for coffee or food.

When Carlos rode up he was met by the irascible cook, who spat a stream of tobacco juice, then informed Carlos that he had no idea where the riders were. He said they had ridden out that morning and he didn't know when they'd be back.

"Climb down and help yourself to coffee," the cook offered.

Carlos dismounted and took the coffee as politely as he could. It had probably been brewed sometime before dawn and was strong enough to drop a mule in its tracks.

Carlos engaged the cook in conversation and prepared himself to wait.

Rachel, too, dismounted. She tied her horse nearby and

made herself comfortable on an outcropping of rock. Her instincts told her that riding down into that camp now would be the wrong thing for her to do.

She had loosened her canteen from the saddle horn when she dismounted, and carried it with her. Now, as the sun passed midday, she drank . . . and waited.

She knew Steve was keeping as much distance between them as possible, but the more distance he kept, the more curious she became. There was some mystery here and it involved more than just Steve McKean. If it concerned her family and her ranch, she felt she had a right to know. She knew that many of the ranchers had sold out to some large group of investors, but she did not feel that fact had any connection to her or the Rocking W. But when a man she had recently hired seemed to be involved in mysterious goings on, she felt she had some rights in the matter.

Two riders came and went, each stopping for a short time, then leaving. Then a third rider approached, and Rachel knew him even at a distance. Steve.

He reined in his horse, and even from where she was, Rachel sensed that he knew Carlos. He entered the camp and stood in conversation with Carlos. He spoke to the cook, and Carlos mounted and rode away. Then, after a short while, Steve rode away too. But she could see they took the same route.

It was not difficult to follow them. Barely keeping the men in sight, Rachel held her horse back so as not to be seen. She knew that her mother and Yvonne would be wondering where she was, but she subdued her guilt quickly under a layer of avid curiosity. There were a great many problems brewing here on the Montana range and Steve McKean could very well be at the center of them.

Her curiosity aroused, Rachel continued to trail the men until they crossed onto Widow Crenshaw's property. She drew rein at the border.

What reason did Steve McKean have to go to Jane Crenshaw's ranch? she wondered.

Steve suggested that he wait while Carlos spoke with Mrs. Crenshaw, and Carlos agreed. Steve took his horse to the watering trough, then walked slowly to the barn and entered it. He meant to give Carlos time, but he also wanted to hear what Jane Crenshaw said.

Carlos dismounted before the house and stood for a minute looking at it. An expert eye such as his could see in an instant that this house and everything around it needed work.

He remembered what he had already heard about Jane Crenshaw when he'd seen her at the dance. He knew from asking subtle questions that she had come to the territory with her husband, James, and their two young sons five years before. Two years after they had arrived, James had been killed in an accident and Jane had been left with the ranch and two sons who were now fourteen and twelve.

Everyone said she seemed to be handling it well enough. But still, Carlos could see that two young boys and a woman could not build up the ranch; they could only subsist.

He walked up the three steps, crossed the porch and raised his hand to knock. But before he could make a sound, the door was opened by a wary-eyed boy. For a second the two simply looked at each other.

The boy was slim, as fourteen-year-olds tended to be, all arms and legs, with hands and feet he hadn't grown into yet. His hair was a thick shock of wheat-colored strands and his eyes were a deep blue.

He was regarding Carlos as closely as Carlos was regarding him, and it took a minute for Carlos to realize that the boy's eyes were not warm and welcoming. At his side he carried a shotgun. Although it hung in what looked like a relaxed hand, Carlos had the distinct feeling that both boy and gun were dangerous.

"I'm look for Senora Crenshaw."

"Who are you? Who sent you here?"

"My name is Carlos Ortega, and I have just recently come from the Bar D. I was told that perhaps Senora Crenshaw was hiring men for the spring roundup."

The boy started to answer, then grew silent as a woman stepped up beside him. She regarded Carlos, and he could have sworn she could read clear to the depths of his soul.

"Senora Crenshaw?"

"Yes. Who are you?"

"I am Carlos Ortega. I am seeking work."

"I heard you tell my son. Why would a man leave the Bar D, which pays more wages, to come to a small ranch for less?" Her voice dripped suspicion, and Carlos wondered what had put the suspicion in her eyes. He instinctively knew this woman would accept no lies . . . and that she just might know if he was lying. He decided the truth was the best way. The truth as far as expediency would permit.

"I did not leave the Bar D. I am afraid the truth is, I was fired."

Jane was taken aback by his words because she had hardly expected them. Carlos went on to explain the circumstances under which he had lost his job.

132

"So you see, Senora, I need a place to work. I have been told your husband died some time ago. I had hoped that an extra pair of hands might be of some help."

"And what happened to your friend?"

"He will be seeking work elsewhere too. I . . . I do not want to insult you in any way, but I do not know if you can afford to hire both of us. If you can, I could get word to him. If you can't, perhaps it is better if he looks elsewhere."

"I will consider that and let you know later. How long have you been in the territory?"

"Not very long."

"And where did you come from?"

"Arizona."

"You're a long way from home."

"Sí, Senora, I am. Just the same, I need to work because I need to eat and to live. Are you willing to hire me?"

Jane stood in deep thought for several minutes, and Carlos began to think she was going to say no. He felt resistance, and it took him some time to realize that her eyes were shadowed with what he read as fear.

He continued to watch her, and his respect grew when he saw her mouth firm up with determination and her shoulders straighten. She was not a weak woman.

"Yes, I'll hire you. I no longer have a bunkhouse, but you can stow your gear in the barn. You'll find it comfortable."

"What happened to the bunkhouse?"

"It burned down," the boy answered angrily.

"Joey . . . be quiet," Jane said; then she looked at Carlos again. "Go and get yourself settled. We can talk about what your job is later."

"Sí, Senora." Carlos smiled. But he promised himself he would get Joey Crenshaw alone at the first opportunity. The boy was angry, and angry people had a way of talking.

Carlos led his horse to the barn and tied it outside. He entered and looked about the barn. Steve was waiting for him. There was a loft, and he was grateful for that. It was filled with hay, so he would have no trouble finding a comfortable place to sleep.

"Barn looks comfortable, Carlos," Steve said.

"It will be good enough," Carlos said with a smile. "Better than some places I've been forced to sleep."

"You have the job then?"

"Sí . . . she does need help."

Steve was about to question Carlos some more when they heard a noise coming from above them. They looked up again to see a young boy's face. The same wheat-colored hair and blue eyes told Carlos that he and Joey were brothers. His innocent eyes had a knowing look that held Steve silent for a moment. The boy continued to gaze down at them for some time before he spoke.

"Who are you, and what are you doing in Ma's barn?"

"My name is Carlos, and your mother has hired me to help her. This is a friend of mine who is just . . . visiting."

"Unh-uh . . . Ma didn't."

"Sí, she did. Why don't you believe that?"

Carlos could see that the boy realized he was talking too much to a stranger.

"Cause Ma ain't got too much money until the roundup is over. Me and Joey been doin' real good," he continued as he started to climb down. "We don't need any help."

"Maybe you don't . . . but I do."

134

This stopped the boy in his tracks and he paused to look up at Carlos. "You do?"

"Sure. A man cannot live unless he works. It seems to me you work pretty hard. Maybe . . . you do need some help. What's your name?"

"David."

"Well, David, suppose you give me a chance. Maybe we can learn to be a big help to each other and work together to help your ma."

Steve tried not to smile as he watched David give this matter deep thought. Finally the boy nodded his head, and Carlos, his face serious, extended his hand to David, who took it. Then the boy's wide grin told Carlos he had been accepted.

"Suppose we go to the house now? Your mother has to give me my orders, and tell me all about where your boundaries are. If we're going to round up all the cattle that belong to the C Bar C, I think we'll have our work cut out for us."

The boy said nothing, but Carlos did not miss the pain, nor the hunger in his eyes. He couldn't be much more than twelve and he very obviously missed the father he had lost. Silently, he walked from the barn with Carlos and Steve.

But they had hardly gotten halfway across the yard when Jane and Joey came from the house with alarmed looks on their faces.

"What are you doing on my land, Steve McKean?" Jane said. When Steve displayed some surprise, she smiled. "I know you. I saw you at the dance with Rachel Walker. You ride for the Rocking W."

"Yes."

"Then I repeat, what are you doing on my land?"

"If you'll give me a chance, Mrs. Crenshaw, I'll do my best to explain."

Jane looked doubtful and both boys watched their mother closely to see how to react.

"Why should I trust a man who rides for the Rocking W?"

"Why shouldn't you?"

Again Jane was still, studying Steve, whose gaze held hers steadily.

"All right. I don't know what business you have with me, but come on in."

Chapter Seven

Rachel had been shocked when she'd seen Steve cross onto C Bar C land and ride directly to the ranch. She remained still, watching, and eventually saw Carlos go into the house. But it was not long after that she saw Carlos leave the house, go into the barn, then return to the house, this time accompanied by Steve and the youngest Crenshaw boy.

She waited, but time dragged on and on. Finally she reached the end of her patience, and besides, she was hungry and thirsty, and it would soon be dark. She started toward the house. She would find her answers herself.

Inside the house Steve and Jane were again facing each other.

"You said you didn't trust the men who rode for the Rocking W. Do you mind telling me why?"

"I don't see any need to tell you what you must already

137

know,'' Jane said, her anger under control yet visible. ''Haven't the men you ride with bragged about burning my bunkhouse, threatening my children, and running off the few men who tried to be loyal to me?''

''Well, Mrs. Crenshaw, I've only been on the Rocking W for a few weeks, but the men I've been with seem to be good, honest, hard-working men, and none of them ever boasted of such a thing. I just can't believe it. There's no reason for such actions.''

''No? Maybe you should ask Carter Walker.''

''He has all the land he wants and he has a reputation that seems clean.''

''I suppose he told you that.''

''No . . . not exactly. But you have to have more than supposition to condemn a man.''

''The men who attacked—'' she inhaled a ragged breath as if the memory was too much. ''They wore masks . . . but Joey was smart. He saw the brand on one of the horses. It was the Rocking W.''

Again Steve was struck with a strong doubt. It was not a very smart man who attacked an almost unprotected woman with men riding horses branded with his brand. Joey saw his doubt, and belligerence was visible in his entire body.

''I saw the brand and I don't get mixed up about brands. I know every one in this territory.''

''Joey, I didn't think you were mixed up. I only thought the situation might be different from what you assumed. Maybe the horse was stolen to throw suspicion on the Rocking W. Mrs. Crenshaw, have you heard any word since? I mean—''

''Have I been threatened anymore? Oh yes, a man came

. . . very late one night. He called to me from outside. When I came out with a gun, he laughed. He said there was no need for that, he'd only come to give advice.''

"Advice?"

"Yes . . . to sell out. He said someone would be making me an offer soon, and I would be a lot safer if I took it. I would be safer, and so would my boys. He said it was possible that the next fire could be my home, and maybe the boys and I might not be lucky enough to escape. He also said it was possible a lot worse things could happen if I wasn't reasonable.'' Her gaze held Steve's, and he knew what the promise of something worse was.

He felt an explosive anger well up in him. These men were so greedy they would threaten a woman and two children. He was aware that Carlos's face had grown dark with barely contained anger.

"Will you trust me far enough to let me try to find out what the truth is?" Steve asked.

"I don't see any reason why I should. You might have been sent by them to see what I'll do." She turned to Carlos. "It seems you know him. Maybe asking for a job here was all part of a plan."

"Senora, if you want to find out for sure, you need only contact Cal Davis. He will tell you I was working for him until this morning. What I told you was the truth."

"I'll do that. Until I do, stay away from the house."

"I will. You can send Joey to tell me your orders for the day."

"And me," David said.

"You are a vaquero too?" Carlos asked with a smile.

"What's a vaquero?"

"A cowboy from my country. If you like, I will tell you about the vaqueros."

"Oh, yes." The boy's eyes glowed with enthusiasm, which soon died when he received a cold look from his older brother. Carlos had a feeling that winning Joey Crenshaw over might not be an easy project.

Joey was at an age when honor and nobility of cause were important. His mother and his way of life had been threatened, and he was not going to give his trust to a stranger until that stranger proved himself.

"Mrs. Crenshaw, if anyone should come back, try to send one of the boys for me. I'll help if I can," Steve said.

"You might be making a mistake that will cost you your job."

"Or I might prove the Rocking W is not behind all this. Still, if you're right . . . I'll quit and come help you."

Jane was silenced. She could only nod, while Joey and David gazed at him in disbelief.

"I have to get back on the job or I might not have the chance to quit. Remember, if you need help, let me know."

"I will see that you are called," Carlos said. "Until then, you must know that I will be very cautious."

Steve nodded. He walked to the door, opened it, stepped out onto the porch . . . and came face to face with Rachel, who sat on her horse in the yard, gazing at him in silence. For a minute Steve was too shocked to speak. This was certainly the last place he expected to see her . . . or for her to see him.

"Well," Steve said softly, "afternoon, boss. What are you doing around these parts?"

"I might ask you the same question, Mr. McKean."

"I just stopped by to be neighborly. I always like to find

out about the people who live close by." Steve could see that she didn't believe a word he said.

Jane came out behind Steve with Carlos and the boys close behind her. She and Rachel exchanged glances. It was Rachel who spoke first.

"Hello, Jane . . . boys. How are you?"

"About as well as can be expected under the circumstances. Rachel, I wish you would carry my final word back to your father."

"Final word?"

"I don't intend to sell."

"Dad has never mentioned to me that he wanted to buy your land."

"Maybe your father doesn't tell you everything. I don't intend to sell . . . no matter what they try to do."

Rachel's face flushed at the vague accusation. "Dad has always been straight with me and with everyone else in this territory. If you think he's behind—" Her gaze leapt toward Steve. "I think it's time you and I have a private talk," she said to Steve, growing increasingly annoyed at his relaxed attitude.

In actuality, Steve was far from relaxed. His mind was searching for ways to pacify both women.

"I'll be right with you, boss." He saw her irritation and wanted to smile, but he wasn't too sure that would do him much good. He turned to Jane. "Remember what I said."

"I will." Steve started to walk away. "Mr. McKean?"

"Yes."

"I'm sorry if I judged too quickly."

"It's not the first time I've been misjudged, Mrs. Crenshaw, and I doubt if it will be the last." Steve walked to the barn to retrieve his horse and mounted. Without a word he and Rachel rode away from the ranch. Carlos stood on the porch and watched until they disappeared.

Steve and Rachel rode some distance in silence. He could see that she was deep in thought, and had no intention of interrupting her musings at the moment. He was too busy trying to figure out how to get out of the situation without doing any accusing of his own. He wanted her to be on his side, even though she didn't know what his "side" actually was.

He wished he could ask her questions without trespassing on her loyalty to her father. It blinded her to any faults the man might have.

"It's never been the policy of the Rocking W for riders to go 'visiting' on our time," Rachel said coldy.

"I wasn't just visiting."

"Oh?"

Steve glanced heavenward and sighed. The "oh" was the coldest word he'd ever heard. He looked at her again. In the pale glow of the setting sun, she made a picture that would be hard to forget.

"Boss, I told you at Mrs. Crenshaw's, I thought it was a good idea to know who's who in this territory and—"

"And since your friend was riding this way, you thought you might ride along."

"Friend?"

"The man who came with you . . . the one who stayed behind. What's going on?"

"I don't know what you're talking about."

"The man at the river camp. He was also at the ranch talking to Mikah. I think he was searching for you."

"Shows how wrong you can be." Steve smiled an infuriatingly condescending smile.

"How wrong?"

"He came by our camp looking for directions to Mrs. Crenshaw's place. It seems your friend Cal Davis fired him today and he was looking for work. I don't see anything so wrong in that."

Rachel flushed at the accent on the word *friend* when Steve referred to Cal.

"If Cal fired him, he most likely deserved it."

"I have to give you credit, Miss Walker. You sure give a hundred-percent blind loyalty when you trust a man."

"Blind?"

"I can understand your father, but such loyalty to a man you can't make up your mind whether to marry or not seems a bit overdone."

Now Rachel's anger slipped beyond her control. She was about to strike back with a sharp retort when a shot rang out, ricocheting off the ground between Rachel's horse's feet. The horse reared in fear, throwing a surprised Rachel to the ground so hard the breath was forced from her lungs.

Steve swore, thinking at first she might have been hit. He started to dismount when the second shot rang out. Drawing his rifle from his saddle sheath, he leapt from the saddle. He raced to Rachel and gathered her up, then rolled with her over a small embankment.

He lay still, cradling her in his arms, relieved when he could hear her breathing and feel the strong beat of her heart against his chest. Now he wondered how he was going to get the two of them out of this situation. He had a good idea what would happen to him if Rachel was hurt while she was out here alone with him.

Rachel moaned and opened her eyes to find herself pinned firmly to the ground. She inhaled deeply and was about to do battle when both the memory of the shot and the reality of her position came to her.

"What happened? Who was shooting at you?" she asked.

"How do you know they were shooting at me?"

"For God's sake," Rachel said angrily as she struggled to sit up, "why would someone be shooting at me?"

"I wish I knew not only who our shooter was, but which of us he was aiming at. Or if he was aiming at all. This might just be a threat or a warning." He pushed her back to the ground. "Don't get too brave. We don't have any answers, and he might still be out there."

"Oh God!"

"What? Are you hurt?"

"Our horses, where are they?"

"Halfway home I'd say."

Rachel groaned, lay back and closed her eyes, disgust written so plainly on her face Steve had to laugh.

"It might be a good thing, you know," he said.

"Good? I doubt it. I don't see how being out here for hours with you and someone who's trying to kill you could be considered good."

"Well, we have one consolation."

"I don't see it."

"The sun is almost down; it'll be dark soon."

"That's heartening."

"Nobody makes a target in the dark. Our shooter will give up. In fact, I'd be willing to bet he's gone already."

"I'm not sure I want to test that. What do we do if he just waits us out?"

"Like I said, when it's dark, we slip away."

"Slip away? We're miles from home."

"Okay, so it's a long walk. Want to stay here?"

"No."

"Then we walk."

"Great."

Steve smiled, cocked the rifle and cautiously raised his head over the lip of the embankment. Nothing happened. He searched the area around them but saw and heard no sign of life.

He couldn't see well enough to satisfy him, for evening shadows were slowly filling the crevices of the hills surrounding them. He stood a little higher, hoping the assailant was gone. Again there was no sign of another attack.

"What do you see?"

"Nothing, but that doesn't mean he's not still out there somewhere," Steve said as he slid down beside her. "I guess we wait a little longer."

Rachel sighed and squirmed into a more comfortable position, then studied Steve's profile for a moment. The shadows were falling across his face, and while he wasn't regarding her, she took the opportunity to consider him without letting her suspicions and anger interfere.

She fought a losing battle, finally admitting to herself that Yvonne was right. He was unbearably handsome. His face seemed to have softened now while he was caught up in his own thoughts.

She swallowed heavily. Very well, she thought, admit it. Go ahead. He is virile and magnetic. His dark hair, and for heaven's sake, those eyes, silver against his teak brown skin. Every other man she had known looked like a schoolboy in comparison. A pale, piddling schoolboy.

Another realization struck her. She was alone with him for God knew how long . . . and she didn't mind. In fact, it stirred an excitement within her that surprised her with its warmth and intensity.

She watched as he took some extra shells from his pocket and snapped them into the rifle. A shimmer of fire and ice brushed across Rachel's flesh as she watched him. How beautiful and graceful his big hands were. She wondered, scarcely breathing, how those long, dark fingers would feel stroking and caressing her.

It might have shaken her even more if she had known how aware Steve was of her. Aware of the scent of her and the unwanted way his senses responded to her presence. Aware and angry at the awareness.

"No one would be shooting at me, Steve."

"Then it's someone who's angry at the riders from the Rocking W, and wanted to take a pot shot at me. Know any reason why they might feel that way?"

"You're still implying my father is behind the trouble with the small ranches."

"I didn't exactly say that. I like Carter. I even defended him to Jane Crenshaw. But . . . sometimes unqualified loyalty can blind you to things that can hurt you."

"That sounds like experience," she replied softly. "Have you found loyalty so painful?"

Steve didn't answer; he simply returned his concentration to the rifle and let the silence grow between them.

"Steve?"

"What?"

"Is there some enemy from your past who might have caught up with you and taken a shot at you?"

Again this drew his attention, but when he turned to look

at Rachel, the last of the dying sun was behind her and her face was in shadows.

"I suppose that's a possibility," he admitted.

"Then why can't we call a temporary truce, at least until we're out of this? I'd like a truce and some honest answers."

"I'll agree to the truce, but I have no idea what you mean by honest answers," he said evasively.

She moved closer to him . . . too close. The scent of her was a physical shock. It brought to mind the fact that it had been a long, long time since he had tasted the warmth of a woman. She was close enough that he had to do battle with himself to keep from touching her.

"I once asked you who you were. I know you're not just an ordinary, roaming ranch hand."

"I don't see how you can know that."

"Because . . . you're too good at what you do. As everyone on the ranch says, you're used to giving the orders, not taking them. Why can't you tell me what changed your life? Maybe it's not too late to change it back again."

"Trust me, Rachel, it's too late. Don't waste your time. One day, I will ride away from here as easily as I rode in." Steve knew he lied, and Rachel could hear it in his voice, no matter how hard he tried to disguise it. Riding away from here toward a bleak and empty future would indeed be difficult.

He felt a longing for what had been, a need for something he now thought was a dream out of his reach. That longing only made Rachel feel the same mysterious pull toward him she had felt before. It was as if he were wounded and needed comfort.

147

Rachel reached out a hesitant hand to rest against his chest.

"I don't believe you really want to do that. I think you are a man who needs strong roots like a plant needs water." She could feel the increased beat of his heart, the warmth of his flesh beneath his shirt. "Somehow I think that is what you've lost."

Steve caught her hand with his, meaning to force her away, but instead he found himself holding its delicate softness in his.

He bent down to kiss her, his mouth covering hers. His long fingers slipped around her neck, thumbs gently touching her jaw, then her cheeks. She felt a swift, delicious sensation spread out from her center to every inch of her. He seemed to be cradling her within his hands. Chills were followed by flowing heat coursing through her.

He kissed her again and again as if a hunger was growing in him he could no longer deny. She knew she was clinging to him, and she could hear the soft sound she made as his arms came about her and he crushed her to him.

Gently she was pressed to the ground, but she cared little for where she was, only for the wondrous sensations that were filling her. She had never felt this flowing, hungry heat before.

Slowly the kiss grew fiercer and deeper and still she did not resist. She felt as if she were melting around him, within him, and the strength of him filled her. She wanted him, she would not lie to herself or deny it.

The ecstasy surging through Rachel was nothing compared to the fierce explosion of passion that filled Steve.

A long-repressed hunger burst into flame and he was lost. He wanted her with every sense he possessed, and he knew from her response that she wanted him. Need overwhelmed the common sense that he'd always had and left him bereft of all thought. He was only conscious of the sweet, warm and surrendering woman in his arms.

Rachel closed her eyes and gave in to pure sensation when his mouth touched the corners of hers and teased along her cheek to the soft flesh of her throat. His hand roamed up her waist to cup one breast. Through the material of her blouse, she could feel the heat of his palm.

Buttons were expertly undone and she sighed as the warmth of his lips caressed the soft, half-exposed rise of her breasts.

"Steve . . . Steve," she whispered, and her hands tangled in his hair, pressing him closer.

It was the sighing sound of his name being called out in passion that brought Steve back to reality.

He released Rachel so abruptly that she was unable to react for a minute.

He sat up and turned his back to her, struggling for control.

"Damn," he muttered, "I'm sorry, Rachel, I didn't mean for this to happen. We'd better get going." As he said these words, he stood, still refusing to look at her. If he did, he didn't know if he'd be able to control the hungry beast that was ripping at him.

Trembling and unable to think clearly, Rachel sat immobile for a minute. Then, cheeks flushed with a combination of thwarted desire and anger, she fumbled with the buttons of her blouse. She couldn't form the words she wanted to say.

She could feel his withdrawal like a physical force, but she refused to allow the tears that threatened.

Finally, as she stood, he turned to look at her. He'd regained his cool impassiveness and meant to cling to it . . . for her sake more than his. He knew the anger and resentment bottled up in him; he could only hurt her. He did not have a whole heart to give any woman . . . and he did not trust any woman with the shattered remains of his spirit. It had been trod upon once, and he couldn't face such betrayal again.

"I'm sorry . . . boss," he fought to sound detached.

"Sorry?" she said, then smiled an icy smile. "I don't know who you're sorry for, me . . . or yourself. If it's me, don't bother. I don't need sympathy from you, Steve McKean. As your boss, I suggest you do your visiting on your own time. And now, you're right, it's time we get going."

She brushed past him and started to walk away. Steve stood for a moment digesting her changed manner and words. Then he bent and picked up his rifle and followed her.

Carlos dismounted and walked toward the fire near which Apach was kneeling. The scent of meat roasting and beans bubbling in a pot hung over the fire was welcome to Carlos, whose stomach was rumbling. He knelt near the fire and poured a steaming cup of coffee.

"Damn, that smells good. Is it done?"

"It is done . . . eat . . . and tell me what has happened."

Carlos tore off a piece of meat and took some beans on a tin plate. When he was settled he began to explain what had happened.

"So . . . you will work for this woman?" Apach asked.

"Yes. She needs a lot of help and I think Steve wants it that way. If she is attacked again, maybe I can learn something. Either way I can be some protection for her and those boys. We can also make sure that whoever is behind this doesn't get his hands on her place.''

''And Steve, what did he do?''

''He had small choice, he went back to the Rocking W with a very annoyed boss.''

''Soon it will be time to meet the marshal. Does Steve have plans we should carry out?''

''Yes, and I think as he does. It would be wise for you to find work on another ranch . . . say, Quantrell's. This way there are two ranches we can keep an eye on. Mikah is at the Rocking W, and he does not miss anything. It will give Steve a chance to roam a bit and to watch for the movements of the other ranchers.''

''Quantrell . . . yes, that is a good idea. I will go there first thing tomorrow.''

''Apach?''

''What?''

''I've got a feeling there's more going on between Steve and his boss than he'll admit.''

''You think that is bad? Steve is a good man.''

''Sí, I know that. But Steve has been stung, and maybe he'll do her more harm than good.''

''Maybe . . . or maybe she will change his mind.'' Apach grinned. ''I have seen women change many a man's life.''

''Too good and too easy to be true.''

''Maybe. The gods do strange things when they decide which trail we should walk. Did you ever believe the four of us would be free and working for the law that put us in Yuma?''

''I guess you could be right.'' Carlos laid aside his empty plate and relaxed for a minute.

151

"You will stay here tonight?"

"No, I'm going to ride back. There is no way to be sure someone won't attack tonight. Her bunkhouse was burned and her men run off. She's already had some snake ride by and give her a warning. Either someone will come to give her another offer . . . or to burn her out for good."

"That is wise. I will sleep here. Quantrell's Lazy 8 is a long ride."

"It's been rumored old Quantrell does not like Indians too much," Carlos chuckled.

Apach grinned in response. "That is a trail I have walked many times before. I guess I must change his mind."

"Good luck, my friend." Carlos rose and stretched. "I guess I'd better get back. The hay in the barn is much more inviting than this hard ground. Buenas noches, hermano. Sleep well."

"Walk in peace, Carlos."

Apach watched as Carlos mounted his horse and disappeared into the darkness. Then he sat by his fire and pondered the most effective way to handle Otis Quantrell. By the time the fire died, he had solidified his plans and rolled up in his blanket to sleep.

Chapter Eight

Mikah wiped the sweat from his face and washed himself off in a bucket of water, grateful that the day was over. He was surprised that Rachel had not returned yet. After having been questioned several times by both Carter and Lori, who were beginning to worry, Mikah walked toward the house, intending to ask if they wanted him to go and look for her. The sun was just beginning to disappear and he was certain Carter would soon be riding out to find her.

Before he had put one foot on the first step, the door opened and Carter came out, shrugging into his jacket.

"Mikah?"

"I just thought you might want someone to ride with you."

"Thanks, Mikah. Saddle my horse, will you?"

"Yes, sir, right away."

Mikah took little time to saddle both horses and lead

them from the barn. They rode a short distance before Carter spoke again.

"This is not like Rachel, to worry us like this. She can take care of herself, I know, and she'll probably laugh, but her mother and her friend are worried to death."

"Maybe Miss Rachel is visiting someone and just forgot about the time."

"I hope you're right. It's getting dark. Anything can happen."

"You think Miss Rachel got thrown?"

"Now, that I doubt. She's too good a rider. She—" Before Carter could finish his sentence the sound of approaching horses came to them. They reined in, waiting, expecting to see Rachel riding toward them.

But they were in for a surprise.

"It's two horses," Mikah said with a frown.

Carter was silent, for the horses had come into view . . . and they were riderless.

"Good God," Carter muttered. "Who's the other horse belong to?"

"Steve McKean."

"Then . . . either one of them is hurt, or the two of them are out there walking. He'd better be taking good care of her."

"Steve wouldn't harm a hair on her head. If she's in need of help, he'll be helping her."

"Let's get a move on."

They caught the horses and led them. Kicking their mounts into motion, the men rode on in silence, each with his own troublesome thoughts.

Carter was worried about Rachel, and wondering about Steve. Mikah was wondering where Rachel had run across

Steve, and just what their being together meant. Also, if one of them had been thrown or otherwise unhorsed, why was the other one on foot too?

The night was lit by a large white moon, making it easy to see. Mikah kept his silence, for the last thing he wanted was for Carter to begin asking him questions. Mikah had never considered himself a good liar and he knew Carter was an astute man who missed little. Time seemed to drag, and Mikah was beginning to get as tense as Carter obviously was. They had to ride slowly to make sure they didn't miss anything, and this only made the tension worse.

To Mikah it seemed like hours before they saw the two figures walking toward them. Carter expelled a sigh of relief and Mikah seconded it. Steve and Rachel were both walking easy, so no one had been hurt.

Carter sped up until he was nearly beside them; then he dismounted.

"Rachel, girl, are you all right?"

"I'm fine, Dad. A little dirty and maybe bruised a bit, but I'm fine."

"What happened? When we saw the horses, it scared the hell out of us. Did you get yourself thrown?"

"No . . . not exactly."

"What exactly did happen, and where were you all day?"

"I . . . ah—"

"She rode over to the Crenshaw ranch with me," Steve said. "I had meant to find out just how all our boundaries lay and to meet the neighbors. Rachel was kind enough to offer to take me around. If you want to know why you found us both on foot, it's because someone took a pot shot at me. It scared Rachel's horse and he dumped her. When

I dismounted to help, a few more shots sent the horses running for home.''

"Someone shot at you? Who? Why?"

"I thought maybe you could tell me. I only ride for the Rocking W. Maybe someone has taken a dislike to us."

For a minute Carter was silent, and all three knew he was fighting anger. "I don't know if you have any enemies, but nobody in this territory would attack one of my riders, and sure as hell, no one would consider raising a gun against Rachel."

"You're saying you have no enemies. Maybe you should talk to Jane Crenshaw. She has a different point of view."

"Jane? I don't understand."

"Dad," Rachel interrupted, "I'm tired and maybe this is something you and I should talk over at home . . . in private."

Steve turned to look at her, for the words she had said appeared to be words of warning.

"Come on, Rachel. Let's go home. Your horses are a bit winded, so we'll ride slow. But they'll get you back."

Steve nodded and walked to his horse without saying any more. Rachel was just as silent. Both Mikah and Carter were nursing a lot of questions.

The ride back to the ranch was pregnant with silent tension.

At the sound of approaching horses, both Lori and Yvonne walked out onto the porch. Relief flooded their faces when they saw Rachel safe and sound.

Rachel was embraced by her mother, who propelled her inside at once, and would not be interrupted until she had assured herself Rachel was not harmed in any way.

Steve and Mikah turned and started for the bunkhouse. Steve was anxious to talk to Mikah, and Mikah just as anxious to do the same.

"McKean," Carter called out. Steve turned to face him. "What did you mean about Jane Crenshaw?"

"You'd better let your daughter explain. If the truth comes from her, you're more likely to believe it."

"All right. I'll listen to her. But I want to talk to you about this too."

"All right."

Carter watched Steve walk away, certain that a great deal had passed between him and Rachel. He wasn't sure he liked that idea at all.

Inside, Rachel had finally convinced her mother that she was perfectly fine. But Yvonne was well aware that Rachel had avoided meeting her gaze directly. Like Carter, Yvonne had the feeling that more had happened between Rachel and Steve than Rachel intended to admit.

Later, in the guest room Yvonne had occupied since her arrival, Rachel came face to face with Yvonne's curiosity.

"So, what happened out there? Where have you and your handsome cowboy been all these hours?"

"He's not *my* cowboy, and stop imagining things. Nothing happened except our horses ran off."

"Yeah," Yvonne chuckled. "I've never seen a horse run off when you were riding it. How did it manage that?"

"Yvonne, please. Don't create anything. Someone took a shot at Steve and my horse dumped me. When he dismounted to help, there was another shot and both our horses ran off. That's all there is to it."

"How did the two of you come to be together anyway?

I thought you were going out by yourself, and that was early today.''

Rachel's cheeks flushed. She didn't want to admit she had been following first a stranger, and then Steve. How could she explain her motivation to Yvonne when she couldn't explain it to herself?

"I ran across him out there and we were riding back."

"Umm."

"Yvonne, for heaven's sake!"

"I didn't say anything. I'm just telling you that if you didn't take advantage of the opportunity, you sure missed a good one."

"I've told you before. Steve McKean is not the kind of man I'm interested in knowing."

"What is it you want, Rachel?"

"I . . . I don't know. A man who's stable and wants . . . I don't know."

"You don't know what you want, you only know what you don't want."

Rachel spun around to face Yvonne, who was silenced by the new look in Rachel's eyes.

"All right, Yvonne. You won't stop until you know the truth. Well, here's the truth.'' She went on to tell her what had happened, how she felt, and how close she had been to surrendering. "And it wasn't me that ran away, it was him! He's the one who pushed me away! He apologized and told me he never meant for it to happen. What should I have done, Yvonne, beg?"

"Rachel . . . I'm sorry. I didn't mean . . . oh, hell, I was only teasing. No, you should never beg. I don't understand him. The way he was looking at you the night of the dance, he could have eaten you alive. I thought . . . I guess I was wrong. I don't want to see you hurt.''

"Don't worry, I won't be.''

"But . . .''

"But what?''

"You told me how he made you feel. Are you sure he didn't feel the same and was doing his best to hide it?''

"Why?''

"Maybe . . . maybe he's afraid of something. Men can be afraid too, Rachel. Who knows? Maybe he was hurt before and is shying away from the possibility of being hurt again.'' Yvonne laughed. "Maybe he's a little scared of your dad too.''

"I don't think Steve McKean has ever been afraid of anything in his life, much less a woman.''

"You don't think . . . but you don't know.''

"Are you trying to say he was running away from me out there? Thanks, Yvonne, I didn't know I was such a threat.''

"I didn't mean he was running from you. I meant he was running away from himself, from an emotion he can't handle. That tells me he's more than attracted. Maybe he's so attracted that he thinks running is best.''

"Well, I don't have the time nor the inclination to sympathize. What could he be running away from?''

"A woman,'' Yvonne said softly.

Rachel was silenced by these words, and considered them seriously for the first time. When she spoke again her voice was just as soft as Yvonne's.

"Perhaps you're right, Yvonne. But there is little that I can do about it. Steve made his decision out there and I won't go to him again . . . I won't.''

Sylvie Sommerfield

*   *   *

Mikah and Steve cared for their horses, then walked onto the porch of the bunkhouse, but before they entered, Mikah reached out a hand to stop Steve.

"Before we go in where there are too many ears, you oughta tell me what's going on."

"I went with Carlos to visit Mrs. Crenshaw. We wanted to see if anything was going on at her place and what she knew."

"Good idea . . . so?"

"How was I to know Rachel was following me? I came out of Mrs. Crenshaw's and she was there waiting."

"I bet you did some fancy jigging and jogging to get out of that one."

"I don't think I did get out of it. I have a feeling Miss Rachel Walker is not too pleased with me."

"About your visitin' . . . or is there more for her to be displeased about? Maybe her daddy needs to drag out his shotgun."

"You're very funny, Mikah . . . very funny. Now let me tell you what else happened."

"This gets more interesting by the minute."

Steve laughed with him, then went on to explain what had transpired at Jane Crenshaw's. "So, Carlos is going to get settled there. He'll meet up with Apach. Apach will find a place with one of the other small ranchers and we'll keep our eyes open."

"You know we have to meet Marshal Wade in a couple of days. I hope we'll have something to tell him. A one-way trip back to Yuma don't excite this boy much, no sir."

"It doesn't exactly excite me either. I would have more time left to serve than the three of you put together."

"Time you had no business servin' in the first place."

"That doesn't really matter much now, does it, Mikah? I can't prove what happened, and there's no use butting my head against a stone wall. It's time to start over again . . . once we get this business cleared up."

"You have anyone in mind who might be behind this?"

"Well, here's the way I see it. Jane Crenshaw's certainly not the one. Fred Parker from the Lazy P has already sold, along with the others who have disappeared or had 'accidents.' Quantrell has been attacked a couple of times already. I don't think the Davis place is up to any tricks because Cal Davis would like to merge with the Rocking W. That narrows it down to Walker, Jessup, Morrison and Holmes."

"What about Bradley?"

"He's already had his barn burned."

"Steve . . . you think it really could be Walker?"

"God, I hope not," Steve said half angrily. "It would sure destroy Rachel. She thinks her father walks on water."

"Carter Walker could swallow up this whole territory if he is behind this."

"I just don't think he is."

"You don't think so, or you don't want to think so?"

"A little of both, I guess. I think Carter Walker has dreams for his place and his town, and getting caught up in something like this could only get in his way. I also think Montana is going to be a state before long, and Carter wants a hand in running it."

"Well, what's our next move?"

"We'll talk to Wade first. Maybe Carlos and Apach can get a handle on something. I'm going to stay close to home for the next couple of days. Rachel and her father are both suspicious of me and I need to get back in their good graces.''

''Might be a good idea.''

''When you get some time off, ride over to see if Carlos is doing okay and what he knows. If Apach gets hired on with one of the others, I'm sure he'll find a way to get word to us. For now, let's get some sleep.''

''Sounds good.'' Mikah opened the bunkhouse door and the two went inside. It was dark and they didn't want to disturb the group of very tired men, so they found their way to their bunks in the darkness.

Tired as he was, Steve found it very hard to get to sleep. Despite his grim determination to get some rest, the memory of those moments he had shared with Rachel were too vivid to ignore.

It was as though he could still taste the softness of her mouth and feel the moment of surrender when she had clung to him.

He fought it with a kind of desperation, for he refused to be caught again with a promise that was beyond his reach . . . and Rachel Walker was beyond his reach.

Fight as he might when he was awake, sleep lowered all the mental barriers and Rachel walked in his dreams with a freedom he would never allow had he been awake.

She walked through his dreams like a misty vision, disturbing and exciting. In the small hours of the morning he woke in a cold sweat and lay for a long time before he found elusive sleep again.

For Rachel it was not much different, except that the dreams were welcomed and savored. She battled the enigma that was Steve McKean, sensing that he, too, had faced that moment of ultimate surrender and fought it. She wanted to understand him, to reach him somehow. But there was a wall between them. A wall he had built from old memories, and Rachel sensed it was the kind of wall that would be hard to break through.

As they had planned, both Steve and Mikah remained near the ranch for the next few days. Mikah had his hands full with his smithing duties, and Steve found enough work to keep him busy. Conveniently, Carter fell in with Steve's plans by ordering fences to be repaired and horses to be broken.

Rachel occupied herself with as much work as she could handle. Steve came to believe that she was involved in every sphere of the Rocking W's operation. He knew for certain she was the one who handled the payroll, for he stood in line with the others before the table she had set on the porch and received his pay. The small stacks of coins sat before her, and as she checked off each name she slid one forward.

"Steve McKean."

"Right here, boss," he said.

She looked up and saw the humor reflected in his eyes and the half-smile on his lips. She slid his stack of coins toward him.

"Going to spend a night in town?"

"No, ma'am." He put the coins in his pocket. "Town doesn't have anything special for me. Beside, I'm saving my money."

"For what?"

"My own place. Man never gets rich working for someone else."

"Good luck," she replied. "Mac Taylor."

Steve moved away, unaware that Rachel still watched him thoughtfully.

Rachel seemed to be always on the periphery of Steve's vision. He would see her laughing with Yvonne, riding away from the ranch, or sitting on the porch in the warm evenings, and he fought the urge to go to her. It was better for her peace of mind if he left her alone and stayed as far away as he possibly could.

One warm evening when Rachel and Yvonne were seated on the porch swing, conversation had died into a comfortable silence when they saw Steve leave the barn and walk toward the bunkhouse.

"Have you told Steve about the barbecue party?"

"The barbecue Mother is having to welcome you here?" Rachel asked innocently, dodging Yvonne's question.

"You mean there's another one planned?" Yvonne asked in dry amusement.

"No, I haven't said anything."

"Are you going to?"

"I don't know."

"My, my. Scared, are we?"

"No, but I do have some pride. I practically threw myself into his arms before. Rejection is not exactly my cup of tea."

"From what you told me, it didn't really sound like rejection. Maybe he was worried about his job. After all, you are the boss's daughter."

"It was more than that, Yvonne. I've had this . . . feeling since the day I hired him that there's more to him than anyone knows. He's full of secrets. You don't think he's running from the law, do you?"

"He doesn't strike me as a man who would run from much of anything."

"No . . . I suppose not. But there is some kind of shadow in his past."

"Maybe just some bad memories."

"Maybe. But whatever it is, it's a sensitive spot and one he won't let anyone near."

"Sounds like he's the one that's afraid."

"Yes, doesn't it? But you've said that before and it doesn't change anything. If Steve wants to hang on to his secrets, that's fine with me." Rachel stood up. "If you don't mind, Yvonne, I think I'll go to bed. It's been a long day."

After the door closed behind Rachel, Yvonne sat in silent contemplation. She knew Rachel, perhaps better than Rachel knew herself, and she had an instinctive feeling about Steve McKean. He was not the hard, cool man he pretended to be. Often, she thought, when one ran from something it was because that something had touched a vulnerable spot. In this case both Rachel and Steve were running. She smiled to herself. Perhaps in all their frantic running, they were going to collide, and she wanted to be around when they did.

Apach had ridden up to the Quantrell ranch, knowing he would have a battle of sorts on his hands. Yet he knew Otis Quantrell had the reputation of being an honest, straight man.

As he approached the ranch with the morning sun behind him, he saw the door open and a man step out onto the porch. A rifle was cradled in one arm. The way he stood told Apach, without words, that he could and would use it if he felt the need. He was tall and lean as a scarecrow, with sandy hair and a stubble of beard. But his hazel eyes, filled with calm intelligence, missed nothing.

He appraised Apach carefully, old memories fermenting in his mind. Indian. He had little love for Indians. Yet this young one met his eyes directly and Otis sensed a difference.

Apach drew his horse to a halt before the porch, and for one long moment the two men contemplated each other in silence. It was Apach who spoke first.

"Good morning, Mr. Quantrell."

"Morning. You wantin' something?"

"Yes, sir. I need a job. Before you say anything, I have to tell you I was a wrangler for Joe Davis before I got fired."

"Why'd you get fired?"

"Me and the foreman got into a little battle. If you ask Mr. Davis, he'll tell you I'm the best wrangler around here . . . and I need work." Apach continued to hold Quantrell's gaze. "I'm also good with a gun . . . in case there's any trouble."

"What makes you think I got trouble?"

"I've been hearing a lot. The Double B had their barn burned and Mrs. Crenshaw had her bunkhouse burned. Seems like somebody is trying to do some pushing around here. Maybe . . . I could help."

"You say you was working for Cal Davis?"

"Yes."

"Maybe you oughta know first off, I don't put much confidence in Injuns. Don't trust 'em. They wiped me out once when I first come out here."

"Well," Apach said calmly, "it was white men who

burned my whole village and killed half my family. I don't think I trust whites either. But I guess we have to learn to trust one at a time. Red or white, there are those who can be trusted and those who can't.''

Quantrell contemplated Apach's words for a long moment. Apach continued to hold his gaze and remained silent.

''Right clever.''

''No, sir, just straight. I need work and from what I see, you need some help. That's a good place to start. Trust can come later.''

''Where you from?''

''Arizona.''

''Quite a way from home. You runnin'?''

''You mean is the law after me? No. I'm not running.''

''Step down, we'll talk. You say you're good with horses. I got one that might change your mind about workin' here. He's a devil. You settle him and you got a job.'' Apach smiled and dismounted. ''I wouldn't smile if I was you. He's dumped more men than I can count.''

''Maybe,'' Apach chuckled, ''he has not met a man he respects enough to let ride him.''

''Respect?'' Otis looked at him with a frown. ''You don't use no whips? I can't abide a man who beats the will out of an animal.''

''No, I don't use a whip. And that's why I lost my job. Because I used a whip and my fists on a man who was abusing his horse.''

''Come on. I'll take you out to see Widowmaker. He's a full-blown tornado, but damn, he's one hell of a horse.''

''You don't expect me to break him in one day?''

"Hell, no! Fact is I don't expect you to break him at all. But it sure will be fun watchin'."

"Yes . . . fun," Apach said dryly, and Quantrell chuckled.

When they stopped beside the split rail fence, Apach was silent . . . in fact, he was awestruck. He had seen and tamed many a powerful horse in his time, but he was sure he had never seen a more magnificent animal than the huge black that stood before him.

The horse stood deceptively immobile, but Apach was acutely aware of the powerful muscles beneath the gleaming ebony hide and the damage the animal could do with hooves and teeth. There were enough scars on Apach's body to prove this. He had immense respect for the horse and meant to prove to the intelligent animal that he was worthy of the same.

"Some critter, ain't he?"

"He sure is. I think maybe he and I need to become friends."

"Good luck."

"It's not a matter of luck."

"Well, whatever you call it, I hope it works."

"It will."

"Sure of yourself, are you?"

"No, in this case I think I'm sure of him."

"Well, you can go ahead and store your gear in the barn. Come on up to the house after that. There's some food and you can sit on the porch and eat. Then we'll see what you can do."

"Fair enough."

Quantrell walked away, but Apach remained to gaze again on the black that would determine his future.

After a while he went to his own horse, unsaddled it and led it into the compound where the black was. His horse carried not only his own scent, but Apach's scent as well, for Apach had taken the time to run his hands over his horse. In time the scent would become a familiar one to the black.

Apach closed the gate and carried his bedroll, saddle, canteen and rifle to the barn, where he created a comfortable place to sleep. Then he walked to the house. It was time to begin a new strategy, for it was not only the trust of the big black he wanted . . . he wanted Quantrell's as well.

Chapter Nine

Listening . . . watching, absorbing, and forcing his mind away from those few minutes in Rachel's arms kept Steve busy for the next two weeks. He only had contact with Mikah now, but Mikah seemed to have more freedom than Steve to meet Apach and Carlos. He would slip away from the ranch at night to rendezvous with them.

Steve's work had attracted Carter's attention, and he found himself working closely with him. To his surprise, Carter not only listened to his ideas but responded to him with a new respect. Steve began to worry that Rachel might have had a hand in this, and that only made his guilt grow deeper and more annoying.

It was just after dawn and Steve was walking from the main house to the barn. He'd received his daily orders and was about to get started with the work when he saw Mikah approaching.

"Mikah."

"Mornin'. Thought I'd get a minute to talk to you."

"What's wrong?"

"Nothing. Just wanted to remind you that we've got to meet Wade before long."

"Yeah, I know. I'm going into town day after tomorrow to send a message."

"How you going to tell Carlos and Apach?"

"I'll do that myself. Carter just sent me out to ride the line. I can see Carlos and Apach then."

"Good enough."

"How they getting along?"

"Apach is doing great. Seems Quantrell thinks he's something. He tamed his horse, I heard."

"Leave it to Apach. When it comes to horses, there's none better. And Carlos?"

"Seen him in town yesterday while I was getting supplies. He brought in Mrs. Crenshaw's oldest boy. It seems they're getting to be friends."

"Any evidence to report?" Steve asked.

Mikah shook his head. He was silent for a moment. He looked around as if he was uncomfortable with his thoughts.

"Mikah, something on your mind?"

Mikah turned back and his gaze met Steve's. "What's between you and Miss Rachel?"

Now it was Steve who grew silent. His mouth pressed into a hard line.

"Nothing. Just let it go, Mikah."

"Me? Sure. What about you?"

"It's not something I can ever consider."

"Why the hell not?"

"Because, A, Carter wouldn't stand for it. He has her life planned pretty well. And B, Rachel doesn't need an ex-convict as part of her life."

"Boy, you're wrong on all counts. Carter Walker isn't the kind of man to push his daughter into something she doesn't want to do, and Rachel is the kind to listen first and judge later."

"That's easy to say. But I wouldn't put her in that position."

"Steve—"

"Let it go."

Mikah was about to speak again when the door to the house opened and Rachel and her father stepped out onto the porch.

Carter spotted them at once, and he and Rachel walked toward them. Rachel smiled pleasantly, but both Steve and Mikah were aware that she did not meet their direct gazes.

"I'm leaving right now, Mr. Walker," Steve said. "I just stopped to have a word with Mikah."

"Well, don't rush off. Rachel is going over to Mrs. Crenshaw's and I'm not going to let her go alone. Steve, you have to go that way anyhow. I want you to ride with her."

"Dad, I told you, I've gone to Jane's a million times. I can go alone. Besides"—her gaze flew to Steve—"I still don't think anyone was shooting at me."

"Your dad's right, Miss Rachel," Mikah said, avoiding Steve's glare. "Pretty girl like you shouldn't be out there alone when there's trouble brewin'."

"This 'trouble' could be greatly exaggerated, Mikah," Carter said. "Some of the folks around here just don't have the courage to build. They sold out and left. That's nothing unusual. There will be others moving in."

"If there's land for them," Steve said quietly. "If the land being 'sold' isn't being gobbled up by one group. If that's the way it is, then the way I see it, you might be next."

"There's no man or group around here that has the guts to go against me, and nothing I have is up for grabs."

"What about others . . . the little places?" Steve was getting angry and ignoring Mikah's warning looks.

"The 'little places' as you call them, can do what I did." Carter's face had grown cold. "I held my place with my guts, my rifle and my own two hands. I didn't call on nobody when I was cutting my place out of the wilderness."

Steve struggled for control. He knew he'd gone too far, and the last thing he wanted was to have an open conflict with Carter Walker.

Mikah breathed a sigh of relief when he saw Steve regain his equilibrium and smile.

"Sorry, Mr. Walker. I know how hard it must have been to accomplish what you did. I stepped out of line and I had no business shooting off my mouth." He turned to Rachel. "If you're ready, I'd be honored to ride along."

Rachel was surprised into momentary silence. Then she gathered herself together. If Steve could ignore all that had happened, so could she. Besides . . . she was fighting the memory of what Yvonne had said to her before they went down to breakfast.

"Rachel, are all the hands coming to the barbecue?" Yvonne had asked.

Rachel had been brushing her hair and braiding it, and took advantage of the task to keep from looking at Yvonne.

"Yes, of course."

"Who keeps an eye on all your property . . . and your cows?"

"Cows." Rachel had laughed. "I'll never take the city out of you. They aren't 'cows,' they're referred to as cattle. We raise beef."

"Oh well, so, who's on guard?"

"No one. Who needs to be for one day?"

"Then I guess Steve will be coming. I'm sure that interests you."

"Look . . . I'm not going to make a fool of myself twice. I told you. He pushed me away with both hands. He's . . . he's a man who doesn't want a future, hides his past and his todays—"

"His todays?"

"I don't know. He's got too much buried behind those eyes and he won't let anyone close enough to find a key to it."

"Well, I think you might personally invite him."

Rachel had laughed. "I think you're more interested than I am."

"Boy, are you wrong. I could tell right away that Steve might be someone I could have fun with, but I'm not the type he'd get serious about. Now, your friend Cal Davis is another cup of tea."

"Yvonne, you're always the same. You're like a hummingbird. You pop from one flower to another so fast no one can even see your wings move. I like Cal, truly, but I know I don't love him. Marrying him wouldn't be fair to either of us. As for you and Cal . . . maybe you could make him happy. He deserves that."

"Maybe I could. I do enjoy myself, but so what? You're

not the same as me, Rachel. I think you're a one-man woman.''

"You could be right."

"Maybe Steve is the man."

"I don't think so."

"Why, because he shied away? He's just afraid of the boss's daughter."

"Come on, Yvonne."

"What? You think a big, tough man can't be afraid?"

Rachel had become quiet, somewhat annoyed that Yvonne was always so accurate. She had sensed some deep, abiding fear in Steve. Maybe . . . maybe Yvonne was right. Maybe she should try to find out the truth for herself.

Now Rachel looked at Steve and saw the resistance in his eyes. He had built a wall around his emotions. Maybe it was time to find out what was on the other side.

"Thank you," Rachel said softly, and her quiet response came as a surprise to all three men. It left Steve with little to do but follow behind her as she walked toward her horse.

Silas Holmes eased back in his soft leather chair and smiled across his desk at Charles Morrison. Charles's discomfort was obvious by the way he held the whiskey glass in both hands and sat on the edge of his chair with his elbows resting on his knees.

"Silas, you said . . . you promised there wouldn't be any violence. You said this would be as easy as taking candy from a baby."

"I wish you'd stop whining, Charles. A few bruises here and there for some that are stubborn. A burning of a barn or bunkhouse isn't exactly violence. No one is going to be hurt any worse."

"We've only gotten hold of five ranches that way. Why not try just paying a fair price?"

"Because you have stubborn people like Jane Crenshaw and Carter Walker. They don't seem to have a price. The men involved in this don't usually take no for an answer."

"Carter Walker . . . damn it, that's impossible. He'll never sell. You know he wants that kid of his to take over when he's gone."

"Sure, sure. But women are easier to deal with."

"God. Are you saying . . . not Carter Walker!"

"We're not moving that fast yet. In time. Carter has ambitions. There's more than one way to skin a cat. Right now we're concentrating on the Crenshaw place. We've warned her. I don't think it will take much longer to run her off." Silas took a deep drink, set his glass on the desk and rose to walk to the window. He drew aside the curtain to look out.

Charles watched him closely. He wished with all his heart he had not become a part of this situation. It was just that Silas could be so persuasive . . . and the promises . . .

Silas was a man who looked the part of a successful rancher. He was strong of build and tall enough to give that strength the appearance of lithe grace. He was tanned deeply because he loved the outdoor life and worked his ranch hard.

His hair had been gold brown, but now it was silvered with gray. It didn't age him, it only made him look distinguished. He smiled almost all the time, yet it was seldom that the smile reached the ice blue of his eyes.

Actually, Charles had always been a little afraid of him, for in almost all ways he was Silas's opposite.

Charles was not the kind of man to bear confrontations

of any kind. Consequently he was one to take the easy way out, to accept the promises of others and to be malleable to a stronger will.

He was a slender man of average height, with mouse brown hair and brown eyes. He had a nervous habit of chewing his bottom lip before he spoke. It came from his constant worry about the way his remarks would be taken. Charles had never had a new or creative idea in his life. Charles was a follower . . . a follower who usually chose the wrong people to follow.

"Silas . . . who's really behind all this and what do they have to gain by running all these ranchers out? I don't see any benefit. I have all the land I can handle."

Silas turned from the window only after he had control of his expression. His dislike of Charles was intense. Silas had little respect for men he could dominate, and less for those of such meager intelligence that they could not focus on the ultimate goal of any plan. He smiled at Charles.

"Think, Charles. Montana is going to become a state one day soon. Who do you think will wield the power around here, a group of penny-ante ranchers or one man who holds the largest piece of the territory? I'll tell you. It will be our group. Play our cards right and we can be the biggest power in the new state of Montana."

The magnitude of this idea was difficult for a man like Charles to digest. He wasn't too sure he could handle such power. Silas was certain that he never would be able to.

Charles was the weak link in their chain, and Silas knew that, one day soon, he would have to be eliminated. There was room at the top only for men who understood power and knew how to use it.

"Then one of our group will end up being the governor of this new state."

"Absolutely . . . maybe you. After all," Silas lied, "you're one of the ones we have depended upon for so long. I wouldn't be surprised if you were chosen for bigger and better things than running that place you have."

Charles was naively impressed, as Silas had known he would be. It amused Silas to know how well he could handle Charles. He considered how he was going to go about handling the others in his group.

He intended to be the first governor of the state of Montana and to eventually hold all the reins of power in his own two hands. But the men he dealt with were not as easily used as Charles. He knew he would have to outwit them in some unique way. He'd been giving the method a lot of thought lately . . . a lot of thought.

Of course, one of his first thoughts was that Carter Walker carried much too much influence throughout the territory. Slowly and subtly he'd been doing his best to undermine Carter's credibility. It was not enough to have drawn notice yet. Using horses marked with Carter's brand had not yet had the effect he wanted it to have, but there was still plenty of time. If all his plans worked, Carter would be suspect soon, and suspect right up until the last moment. By then it would be too late to stop Silas's plans.

"It is almost too . . . too large to believe," Charles said, awestruck as he considered Silas's words. The picture they drew in his mind was one of a future he never could have believed.

"You must learn to think and believe larger than you ever have before. Why should we let these minuscule land grubbers divide up what could be whole and magnificent?"

"Yes . . . yes, I guess . . . I mean . . . this is just going to take getting used to. I'll get hold of it, trust me. I'll be an asset, Silas. I promise."

"I'm sure you will be. Haven't I trusted you all along? There is only one thing . . ."

"What?"

"Don't do another stupid thing like hiring someone to take a shot at Rachel Walker."

"I didn't hire him to do that."

"Then what happened?"

"He was aiming at Carter's rider. I've been having him watched."

"Oh? Why?"

"He's been nosing around."

"What do you mean, nosing around?"

"He's been asking questions that no hired puncher has any business asking. I thought it better to put a stop to it."

"That wasn't too clever."

"Why not?"

"Because your man missed, and because if he was asking questions before, he'll be asking more now. Charles, for God's sake, he's one stupid hired hand. Don't let someone like him spoil this. He'll get no answers, and one day he'll just ride on and never be the wiser."

"All right, all right. So it was a mistake. I just had a feeling—"

"Forget your feelings and remember what's at stake. If it will make you feel any better, I'll alert everyone and we'll all keep an eye on him."

"I just think—"

"You just worry," Silas said. "So stop. There's nothing

to worry about. I have it under control and I'll take care of the worrying. All right?''

''All right.''

''Good. By the way, have you been invited to the Walkers'?''

''Of course. Hasn't all the territory?''

''Well, a lot of very important people are going to be there too. Important to us. It's time you had an understanding with the other people in this with us.''

''I'm going to look forward to it.''

''Then let's have another drink and forget about this nosey puncher. He can't do us any harm. He's only one man and he's going to be no problem ... no problem at all.''

Steve and Rachel rode in silence for a while. It would have surprised each to know the other was struggling for words.

''Steve?'' Rachel said as she drew her horse to a halt. Steve had no choice but to stop as well.

''What?'' They had stopped side by side and he turned to look at her, resting one hand on the pommel of his saddle and the other on the back of it.

She paused before she spoke again. It did her equilibrium no good to react the way she did, but she couldn't seem to control it. It annoyed her that he looked so calm and cool.

It also annoyed her that he was so invitingly handsome and that suddenly the memory of the moments she had spent in his arms was so vivid that she could still feel him pressed close to her.

''You've ... you've been working pretty long hours lately.'' She wanted to bite her tongue for uttering what sounded like an immature girl's hero worship.

"I'm sure nobody knows better than you how much work it takes. You're not exactly lazy."

"There has to be time for other things."

"Like what?"

"Like the barbecue my parents are having," she said in a rush. "You are coming, aren't you?"

"Well, I think somebody has to keep the store running, and since I'm the most recently hired, I'll probably have to work."

"I hate to tell you this, but when Dad throws a barbecue everybody comes. He stops all work. He's not one to leave anyone out."

Steve turned his head to look off in the distance. "I just think it's better for me not to go."

"Why?"

"We'd better get a move on. I have a longer ride than you do."

"Why, Steve?" she repeated. His gaze returned to her, but she was aware that he was retreating from her as fast as he could. "I want you to come. Will you consider this my personal invitation?"

Now it was his turn to ask the same question she had. "Why?"

"Because I can't see any reason for us not to be friends. You work for my father and it's silly for us to dance around each other like we're some kind of enemies."

"We're not enemies." He tried to laugh at this but failed. "But I don't think we'll be employer and employee for very long if I don't get moving."

Rachel had begun to crack the shell around him and had no intention of riding on until she could see behind his guard. She dismounted slowly and led her horse to the shade of a tree. Reluctantly, but knowing he could not ride away and leave her standing alone, Steve dismounted and joined her. Running was not in his nature.

He tied his horse near hers and went to stand beside her. It was the worst thing he could have done. He was emotionally off balance to begin with, and close proximity to her only made it worse.

Rachel turned to face him. "Don't you think it's rather foolish for us to think of ourselves as employer and employee?"

"Don't you think," he replied quietly, "that it would be foolish of me to think of us in any other way?"

"No, I don't."

"Rachel, don't make a mistake. Like you've said, I'm a roamer. One day I'll be gone. I'm no good for any woman, but especially not for you."

She was stung by his words, but she refused to let him see her hurt. "Why especially me?"

Because I'm vulnerable with you, he thought. *Because for some damn reason I can't get you out of my mind.*

"Because you're Rachel Walker, and one day you'll own the biggest chunk of Montana Territory around. Me, I'm nothing more than a footloose cowboy, who hasn't anything to offer you."

"I don't think I asked anything of you. Is being friends too much for you? To me it looks like you have a habit of running from any situation that doesn't please you. I know who and what I am, and what the Walker name means in this territory. What I don't know or understand is who and what you are."

"Rachel—"

"Let me finish," she interrupted. "You claim to be a

182

footloose and fancy-free cowboy, a wanderer. But you know more about ranching than all our hands put together. You don't want the responsibilities of sinking roots. But it's obvious to everyone that you used to have a lot of responsibility. Consequently,'' she concluded, ''you're running. Don't you think it's time you told someone what you're running from?''

''Are you finished?''

''Yes, I am.''

''Then suppose you listen for a change.'' The corners of her mouth lifted in a tentative smile, and Steve fought the urge to kiss her.

''You're right about a lot of things. Especially the part about running. What I'm putting behind me is a hell you would never understand. I had roots, and they were torn up and can't be replanted. I don't intend to try here. You're trouble I can't afford . . . and I don't want to see you hurt.''

''I asked you to come to a barbecue, not to spend the rest of your life with me. I'm not afraid of you and your wandering ways, Steve McKean. What makes you think I should be?''

She had moved a step or two closer as she spoke and it seemed as if she stole into his senses like a wraith. Without touching her, he could feel the softness of her skin. It was almost as though she was in his arms and he was tasting her mouth with a need that was near torture.

He had to fight his own longing, and that could only be done by fighting her. He knew only one way that might work. He had to make her afraid.

''I *know* you should be afraid. You think you understand me, Rachel, but you don't. I'm not one of the boys who'd like to sleep with you and maybe grab a ranch in the process.'' He ignored her intake of breath. ''I'd like very much to make love to you, if that's all you're looking for. But I don't need to grab a ranch by sleeping with the boss's daughter. I'll leave that for your friend Cal.''

''Damn you,'' she gasped at the insult. She struck so hard and so quickly that he felt the sting of her slap before he realized she meant to do it.

But the sting was what he wanted . . . no, needed. Grimly he held onto the fury he saw in her eyes. One step more to make that fury enough to keep her safe.

He reached out and gripped her shoulders, dragging her to him. He ignored the way her eyes widened in surprise and the sound she made as his mouth covered hers.

Her struggle was ineffectual, and he savored the honey taste of her, storing it in that deep, empty spot within him. Desperately he struggled not to sink into her warmth, to build a barrier of anger that would be a wall between them. He didn't count on Rachel's own self-control.

In a blinding flash she realized what his words and actions meant. He was driving her away from him with the weapon of anger, and she knew also that he was both vulnerable and afraid. She fought him in a way he hadn't counted on. With the instincts bred into women from the days of Eve, she slipped around his well-built walls like a wisp of mist.

She slid her arms about his waist and melted against him, causing his resistance to tumble like the famed walls of Jericho.

A wave of intense desire washed over him so strongly that he was drowned in it. All he could do was sink into the fiery kiss.

Hunger! Wild and overpowering hunger ate at him,

weakening his resolve to protect either her or himself. He wanted her, God how badly he wanted her.

Both were panting softly, hardly able to catch the next ragged breath. His arms were binding her to him now and his mouth had traced a path of heat down the column of her throat to the pulse that beat furiously at its base.

Rachel knew that she would soon be lost, and she also knew that if she lost herself to him now she would lose him forever. She wanted to give all to him, but she didn't want to lose him. Reluctantly she moved from his arms and backed away from him a few steps, fighting for her breath and her equilibrium.

Steve released her, not because he wanted to but because he knew he had to before he took this situation beyond his control.

Rachel could see clearly that for once she had pierced his shield. Her heart was pounding furiously and she wanted nothing more than to go back into his arms and find the magic she was sure was there. She had her answers, and she knew why she had waited and what she had been looking for. Now, she had to wait until he found the same answer.

Neither spoke. For a long moment they simply stood and looked at each other. Then Rachel slowly turned, walked to her horse and mounted. She turned to look at Steve, who remained still.

"Come to the barbecue," she said softly, "for me." She kicked her horse into motion and rode away without waiting for an answer.

Steve stood immobile, watching her until she was out of sight. He couldn't believe it. His will had crumbled before the overwhelming desire he felt for Rachel.

He fought for control, but it was a long time coming. He knew there was no way to close a door between them again. He must not go to the barbecue . . . he wouldn't . . . but he knew he lied to himself.

Chapter Ten

Brandt, Colorado

Judge Nathan Graham smiled, then reread the letter to renew the satisfaction he had felt at its contents. He folded the letter and laid it back on his desk. After a few minutes of deep thought, he sent for his secretary, a young man who, after several years of working for the judge, was still in awe of him.

"Yes, Your Honor?"

"Call for my buggy, and send a message to my home, Hiram. Tell my daughter to pack our bags for an extended time. I'm going on a trip and I want her to come along. Please tell her I'll explain in more detail when I get home."

"Yes, Your Honor." Hiram turned to leave. He was a tall, gangly young man—an Ichabod Crane of the law business, as Nathan liked to describe him.

When the door closed behind Hiram, Nathan again picked up the letter. It was the second piece of good news he'd had in the past twenty-four hours.

The first letter had been from the Pinkerton detective Nathan had hired some weeks before. It amused him that the letters had come at almost the same time, with such similar information.

"So, Mr. McKean," he murmured to himself, "You've finally turned up, and under such suspicious circumstances. Like the proverbial cat, you seem to have landed on your feet. I wonder . . . yes, I wonder."

He took the letter up again, rereading words he had already committed to memory. He knew that Martin Swope was sweating over the fact that he had let Steve McKean out of prison without completing Nathan's orders to see to his demise.

Swope had relayed as many answers as he could to Nathan. That the marshal who had come for Steve was a Thomas P. Wade; that he wielded a great deal of power, for he had taken three of Steve's cell mates as well.

His nose to the scent, Nathan soon learned a great deal about the marshal and his possible motivation for doing what he had. But every question led to another question. The Pinkertons were called in, and now he had much better answers.

It seemed that what was going on in Montana was much the same as the scheme that he had plotted himself, a scheme that had cost Steve McKean his freedom. It amused him to think he could defeat Steve at the same game again, and perhaps make a large profit for himself.

He could feel greed well up within him. Greed, and a desire to put an end to Steve's freedom and his life before

Steve could put an end to his. Yes, he had to find Steve and put him out of commission before he made a decision to try to come home.

He knew Steve McKean, knew his tenacity too well to let the matter lie. He had too many dark secrets that would not bear the light of discovery.

He rose from behind his desk. Nathan Graham was a strikingly imposing man. Tall and lean, he had a mane of silver hair and a politician's wide and often disarming smile. He was a man who had a rare ability to make use of people, and who did not hesitate to do so.

He manipulated and coerced and seduced until he bent other people's wills to his own. He had been a phenomenal success . . . until he had run across Steve McKean. Oh, he had punished McKean for standing in his way, but the punishment had not had the conclusion he desired. Now, perhaps, a second opportunity was presenting itself.

He left his office and stepped outside onto the busy street. As he walked to his waiting buggy, he accepted the warm smiles and tipped hats of passersby as his just due.

The ride to his home was given over to deep and calculated thought. He was now, as he had always been, a spider who could spin a web of treachery and betrayal to gain monetary success.

In his mind his success was measured by his possessions, the money in his bank account, and by the elaborate house where his buggy pulled up. He looked at it with the same sense of satisfaction he always felt.

It was a large structure, two stories high with ten rooms within. The double entranceway was brilliant with leaded glass he'd imported from the East. There was a wide front porch that extended across the front of the house and circled both sides. A walk led to the front porch, and on each side of it was a garden, profuse with multicolored flowers. Encircling all of this was a three-foot-high stone wall with a gate.

He opened the gate and went up the walk and onto the front porch. When he opened the first door, he stepped into an enclosed area that reflected the prisms of light from the sun piercing the glass. He opened the second door and stepped inside a cool entranceway. Polished wood and gleaming floors were complemented by crystal chandelier that hung from the high ceiling. From the entranceway he could see the huge parlor and beyond that a formal dining room. His study lay off to the opposite side. Beyond, out of sight, was the kitchen and another airy dining area where he shared more informal meals with his daughter.

Directly before him was a large circular stairway that led to the five bedrooms above. He went up the stairs and stopped before a door and rapped.

"Come in." The voice that called to him was mellow and sweet. He smiled and opened the door. Nathan stood in the doorway for a minute gazing at the woman who stood across the room from him. She was folding clothes and placing them in a satchel.

Ann Graham was a vision that could always make him pause and wonder. She was small-boned and fragile looking, and so remarkably beautiful that he never ceased to enjoy just looking at her.

That she was his daughter there was no doubt. But what amazed him was that she was the daughter of the woman he had made the mistake of marrying. She had been a gentle and sensitive person, usually afraid to open her mouth or form an opinion, or even to defend herself. In truth,

Nathan was glad when she had given up the struggle of living and died.

Ann was nothing like her mother, and completely like her father. She was strong and unaffected by senseless emotions. Nothing stood in her way. In this she was just like him. He enjoyed the fact that they worked so well together.

"So"—she smiled at him—"just where are we going so abruptly?" There was no question that she would accompany him. She trusted his motives always, for they usually coincided with hers.

"I have had word of a friend I thought you would like to see again. I know I would. We seem to have left some business unfinished."

"And just who is this friend?"

"Steve McKean."

Her eyes widened, and for a minute she didn't respond. "Where? I thought that he was safely ensconced in Yuma Prison?"

"So did I. It seems he has acquired some friends with more influence than I realized. I received a telegram from Swope."

"I don't understand."

As quickly as he could, he explained all he knew. "I think it wise that we go and take care of our unfinished business. We can't afford to leave such loose ends as Steve McKean."

"No, I don't think that would be wise. Where is he?"

"Chambersburg, Montana Territory."

"What is he doing there?"

"That's a question we have to find an answer to. How long before you are ready to go?"

"I'm nearly ready now. I can't understand how he managed this, but if you remember, I told you that if you didn't eliminate him he would eventually cause you trouble.''

"I should have listened to you. I underestimated him. I also overestimated Martin Swope. I have sent him men before to take care of. He never failed me until now.''

"Steve was not your usual weak vessel. He was the kind of man we weren't used to handling.''

"That sounds like a wee bit of admiration.''

"Actually it is. He was . . . unique. I really missed him for a while. He was . . . satisfying.''

Nathan chuckled. "He was a handsome fellow, I will give you that. But he stood between us and what we wanted.''

"And that is not a safe place for anyone,'' she said with a smile. "Not even the unique Steve McKean.''

"Then let's go and clean up this little mess. From what I have been able to find out, he is doing something for this marshal, and if, by chance, he should decide to run . . . well, the price would be incarceration.''

"And we intend to see that he runs.''

"Of course.''

"And I don't doubt there is a profit in this somewhere for us?''

"Don't doubt that for a minute. Taking care of our one loose end is only part of the plan. There is much more going on up there, and I just happen to know a few of the people involved. I'm sure, with a little persuasion, they'll be more than happy to cut us in. There's a great deal of money to be made, my girl, so let's get going and find our share.''

Her cornflower blue eyes lit with the gleam of avarice he knew so well, and her smile was brilliant. "Let's.''

A Special Offer For Leisure Historical Romance Readers Only!

Get Four FREE* Romance Novels

A $21.96 Value!

Thrill to the most sensual, adventure-filled Historical Romances on the market today...

FROM  LEISURE BOOKS

As a home subscriber to the Leisure Historical Romance Book Club, you'll enjoy the best in today's BRAND-NEW Historical Romance fiction. For over twenty-five years, Leisure Books has brought you the award-winning, high-quality authors you know and love to read. Each Leisure Historical Romance will sweep you away to a world of high adventure...and intimate romance. Discover for yourself all the passion and excitement millions of readers thrill to each and every month.

SAVE AT LEAST $5.00 EACH TIME YOU BUY!

Each month, the Leisure Historical Romance Book Club brings you four brand-new titles from Leisure Books, America's foremost publisher of Historical Romances. EACH PACKAGE WILL SAVE YOU AT LEAST $5.00 FROM THE BOOKSTORE PRICE! And you'll never miss a new title with our convenient home delivery service.

Here's how we do it. Each package will carry a 10-DAY EXAMINATION privilege. At the end of that time, if you decide to keep your books, simply pay the low invoice price of $16.96 ($19.98 CANADA), no shipping or handling charges added.* HOME DELIVERY IS ALWAYS FREE.* With today's top Historical Romance novels selling for $5.99 and higher, our price SAVES YOU AT LEAST $5.00 with each shipment.

AND YOUR FIRST FOUR-BOOK SHIPMENT IS TOTALLY FREE!*

IT'S A BARGAIN YOU CAN'T BEAT! A Super $21.96 Value!

GET YOUR 4 FREE* BOOKS NOW—
A $21.96 VALUE!

Mail the Free* Books
Certificate
Today!

4 FREE* BOOKS 🌹 A $21.96 VALUE

*Free * Books Certificate*

YES! I want to subscribe to the Leisure Historical Romance Book Club. Please send me my 4 FREE* BOOKS. Then, each month I'll receive the four newest Leisure Historical Romance selections to preview for 10 days. If I decide to keep them, I will pay the Special Member's Only discounted price of just $4.24 each, a total of $16.96 ($19.98 in Canada). This is a SAVINGS OF AT LEAST $5.00 off the bookstore price. There are no shipping, handling, or other charges.* There is no minimum number of books I must buy and I may cancel the program at any time. In any case, the 4 FREE* BOOKS are mine to keep—A BIG $21.96 Value!

*In Canada, add $7.95 US shipping and handling per order for first shipment. For all subsequent shipments to Canada the cost of membership in the Book Club is $19.98 US plus $7.95 US shipping and handling per order. All payments must be made in US dollars.

Name _____

Address _____

City _____

State _____ Zip _____

Telephone _____

Signature _____

If under 18, Parent or Guardian must sign. Terms, prices and conditions subject to change. Subscription subject to acceptance. Leisure Books reserves the right to reject any order or cancel any subscription.

(Tear Here and Mail Your FREE Book Card Today!)*

Get Four Books Totally
F R E E* —
A $21.96 Value!

(Tear Here and Mail Your FREE* Book Card Today!)

PLEASE RUSH
MY FOUR FREE*
BOOKS TO ME
RIGHT AWAY!

Leisure Historical Romance Book Club
P.O. Box 6613
Edison, NJ 08818-6613

AFFIX
STAMP
HERE

She returned to her packing, and in a few minutes the last bag was filled and she closed all the satchels. Nathan had taken the time to appraise her while she did so.

It was her rare and almost perfect beauty that had first captured Steve, and Nathan could see that the three years since then had only enhanced her looks. If it were possible, she was more beautiful than before. Her skin was rose-petal soft, and her wheat-colored hair was thick and luxurious. Her figure would have made any man lust for her, and all who met her usually did, to their eventual distress.

"The buggy is outside. Are you ready? I have already sent someone for our tickets, they'll be at the station. The train leaves in less than an hour."

"I'm ready."

"Good. Let's go. I will send Henry up for the bags."

Nathan had paid little attention to Ann's unusual quietness. She had thoughts of her own that did not include him . . . but did include Steve McKean. She remembered with a slow, pervading heat every moment they had shared together. Steve had been the only man to awaken any emotion in the usually cool and controlled Ann. Already she was calculating whether she could convince him that she was an innocent pawn in her father's schemes. It would give her immense satisfaction to have Steve in her arms and in her bed again.

They left the house, and within two hours were on the train for Montana. Nathan was looking forward to profit, and Ann was looking forward to renewing a passion she could not put from her mind.

Cal rode slowly toward the Rocking W. He was utterly confused. He knew he loved Rachel . . . he knew it! But why, for God's sake, did Yvonne Avery's face continually appear in his thoughts and dreams?

He had seen a great deal of her, for it seemed that each time he rode to the ranch it was to find Rachel already gone somewhere or involved in something that took her time, and Yvonne with time on her hands and a smile on her face. They had amused themselves with afternoon rides and long, satisfying talks.

He discovered that under her laughing manner lay a clever and interesting mind. He enjoyed talking with her, being with her. She questioned him about his ranch and listened to his hopes and plans for it. He reflected that this was something Rachel had never done. Rachel was so engrossed with the Rocking W, she had not considered his own love for his place.

For several days and nights he had wrestled with this dilemma, and now he intended to find some answer to it. If he could corner Rachel, which was a problem in itself, he would ask her to be direct and to tell him just what she wanted. It occurred to him only now that he had never asked Rachel what she thought, or what her dreams were. Perhaps that was why she seemed to fade away from him every time he wanted to talk about joining their ranches.

Joining their ranches . . .

God, was that what he had said to her? Was that what he truly wanted? Slowly questions found answers in his mind, and he didn't flinch before them. Yes, he had wanted to put the two ranches together, and yes, that was exactly what he had said to Rachel. No wonder she held him at arm's length.

Now he considered his own true feelings, and again recognized the truth. In actuality, he was a little afraid of Rachel. She was a woman who had to hold the reins, and to be in control. He wanted a wife, one to grace his home and let him provide for her.

He reached the Rocking W before the thoughts forming had solidified. When he dismounted near the house, the door opened, and Yvonne stepped out onto the porch. She was dressed for riding. For a second he was struck dumb, for her slim body was displayed to perfection in a blouse and pants . . . pants! He smiled. Rachel's influence on Yvonne was a charming and delightful one. Yvonne's soft curves did things for the pants that were remarkably sensual. He expected Rachel to come out too, and remained silent until Yvonne closed the door and walked to the edge of the porch.

"Hello, Cal. If you're looking for Rachel, I'm afraid you're going to be disappointed. She left some time ago with Tom. Some problem at one of the camps. Her father isn't here, so she went to solve it herself."

"I'll bet she has no doubt she can do just that."

Yvonne tilted her head in a questioning look. His reply had surprised her. Yvonne would never admit that she had found the time spent with Cal so exciting. As far as she was concerned, it was Cal who had to speak first. In fact, Yvonne was a little surprised at herself. She had never intended to feel this way, had fought this sort of thing all her life. She had enjoyed flitting from one man to another.

"No, I don't think she has any doubt. Rachel takes running the Rocking W very seriously."

"Were you going for a ride?"

"Yes. It's a beautiful day. Will you join me?"

"With pleasure. Where shall we go?"

"Actually, I was thinking I'd like to see the Bar D. I'm sure it's as beautiful as the Rocking W."

Cal smiled. His pride in the Bar D was obvious. "I'd like to show it to you. Do you want to let them know where you're going?"

"Mr. Walker rode out early this morning, and Mrs. Walker has gone into town. I'm afraid I've been left to my own devices for today."

"Then let's go. There's a lot to see."

Yvonne took obvious delight in her tour of the ranch, and Cal was surprised to find he had never enjoyed himself so much in his life. He had ridden over his land all his life, and now found a new pleasure in seeing it through Yvonne's eyes.

It was large, but she made it appear larger. It was beautiful, and she made it seem more beautiful. It was his . . . and she made him feel more grateful for that than he ever had before.

When they arrived back at the Rocking W, it was past supper time, but none of the others were at home.

"Cal, won't you come in and have something to drink? I'm sure you must be hungry too. I know I'm famished."

"I'm very hungry," he laughed, "and I don't need to be asked twice about something cold to drink." He dismounted and walked up on the porch to stand beside her.

"Then come on in."

The two entered the house and went directly to the kitchen, where Yvonne prepared sandwiches of leftover slices of beef and poured tall, cool drinks of lemonade. Then she sat opposite him. Cal felt a sudden sense of rightness.

"You're not planning on going home for a while, are you?"

"No, I'm staying for a few months. All of my family is in Europe and I didn't want to go, so I asked Rachel if she would mind if I spent the time with her."

"Then you're really enjoying it out here? I mean . . . it's not lonely for you?"

"Lonely? Cal, it's quite possible to be lonely in the biggest of cities. I've already found that out. I'm not lonely here because I'm surrounded by people who are caring and generous. No, I don't think I would ever find it lonely here. Why did you ask that?"

"I don't really know. I guess it's just because I'd like to think you could find something here that you couldn't find anywhere else."

"I can. It's . . . satisfying. Yes, I think that's the right word. It satisfies something deep inside. I never thought I would feel that way, but I do."

"I'd like—" Cal shrugged away what he was going to say and began again. "I'm looking forward to the barbecue. It should be a lot of fun."

Yvonne was quite aware that he hadn't said what he'd intended to say . . . what she already knew he wanted to say. She was not one to let matters lie, nor to be anything but honest. Besides, she already knew there would be no future between him and Rachel. If she was not mistaken, and she hardly ever was, Steve McKean would fill that place in her friend's life and would take it when he finally put away his own ghosts.

"It will be fun. Rachel has promised me all kinds of enjoyment. I take it these things last for hours."

"You'll be lucky if you see your bed before dawn."

"It does sound like fun." Yvonne rose and walked to look out the kitchen window. Cal watched her, enjoying the picture she made standing against the light. She was remarkably beautiful. When she turned, their gazes met and there was a silence that was heavy with the realization that they were being drawn to each other by a force neither could control. Cal rose and came to stand beside her.

"Yvonne, there's something I want to say to you."

"Cal—"

"No, just hear me out. Then, if you want me to go, I will."

"Consider Rachel before you say something you might regret."

"I guess, for the first time, I am considering Rachel. I have pushed Rachel to marry me, simply because my father planted the seed of an idea in my mind a long time ago: that our two ranches would prosper if they were combined. I guess the seed grew and I wanted to marry her, but I wanted it for all the wrong reasons. She was smart enough to see that long ago. I would have made her a terrible husband, for I would have wanted her to just be my wife and leave everything else to me."

"And you don't think just being your wife is a good future?"

"For the right woman, it would be, I hope. But Rachel never would have been able to live like that. She's too . . . too . . . I don't know."

"Rachel is a very strong person."

"Yes, she is. And no one admires her more than I do. But the two of us would have been like fire and water. I never could have made her happy."

"And you think she never could have made you happy

either. What a terrible thing that would have been.''

''Yes,'' Cal laughed, ''she would have shot me, or maybe found something worse. We would have been at each other's throats the first time a decision came up and we disagreed.''

''Cal, you make Rachel sound like an ogre.''

''Hardly. She's a lovely, strong, ambitious and generous person. I think Rachel is definitely a special person. But I don't think she ever would have married me, and I give her credit for understanding it before I did.''

''So do you intend to tell her at the barbecue?''

''No, I intend to tell her the moment I see her. I need that cleared up.''

''Why so fast?''

''Because . . . I want to tell you so much. Look . . . ah . . . Yvonne, I know this is coming out of the blue. But the last days we've spent together, I've felt completely different than I've ever felt before.'' He reached to take both her hands in his. ''I don't think I realized what being in love . . . truly loving someone was all about until you came into my life.''

''And now?''

''And now, I want to ask you to consider staying here, letting me be part of your life. One day, maybe you'll consider staying permanently.''

''I think I know you reasonably well, Cal. I know that you are a good man, and honest. That's not too easy to find nowadays. I will consider you, and yes . . . I'll stay and enjoy getting to know you better. Much better.''

Her voice had grown soft, and her slightly parted lips were too much of an invitation for Cal to resist. He bent toward her and covered her soft mouth with his. What happened then was as far beyond their control as the moon and stars. She was in his arms, melting against him, filling him with a breathless heat such as he had never felt before.

Yvonne felt his strong arms pull her to him, and did not resist. She had no desire to resist, for she wanted his kiss, and the feel of his arms as they held her. This was not what she'd expected: still, it was something she welcomed. Yvonne had played at love, but had not expected to find it in this wilderness. Now she embraced it.

Her security was the knowledge that Rachel would be happy for her.

When Cal released her, his face was a study of wonder, surprise and a touch of worry.

"Yvonne." He breathed her name like a prayer. "I can't believe this."

"Just what is it you can't believe, Cal?" Rachel's voice came from the doorway. Both Yvonne and Cal spun around to face her. Rachel's face seemed cold to Cal, whose face registered first shock, then grim determination. He didn't completely release Yvonne, he simply turned to face Rachel and inhaled a deep breath, certain he was about to experience the tongue lashing of his life.

A few days later Steve was still considering Rachel's invitation. He knelt with the descending sun at his back, took the coffee pot from the heat of the fire and poured a cup. Across the fire from him, Apach sat smiling at the conversation between Mikah and Carlos, who had been taunting each other for the past few minutes.

They were waiting for Marshal Wade. All four were anxious to be gone; it would be dangerous if they were spotted by any casual passerby. There would hardly be a way to explain it.

"You sure we have the right place, Apach?" Mikah asked facetiously. It was unthinkable that Apach was lost. To make this clear, Apach just smiled and ignored the remark.

"The marshal will be here," Apach said. He smiled at Steve to acknowledge the humor of the situation. "He's almost as good at finding the right path as I am."

"We sure don't have a hell of a lot to tell him," Mikah said. "I hope he doesn't think this is a hopeless case and send us back to Yuma."

"He'd have a very hard time doing that, don't you think, amigo?" Carlos said to Steve.

"You're right, Carlos. If the marshal doesn't think we're doing the job, we'll just have to convince him that we'll find his answers as fast as we can. I don't intend to go back . . . not under any circumstances."

"I understand that," Mikah said softly. He had been watching Steve closely and he was certain there was more on his mind than what they would say to the marshal. Besides that, he was reasonably certain the marshal was going to play along with them as long as he could. "Say, are any of you going to the barbecue the Walkers are having?"

"It might come as a surprise," Apach said, "but I think everyone in the territory is invited. It appears I am going as well."

"And I," Carlos said. "Mikah?"

"Yep, I was invited personally by Mrs. Walker. She says no one goes without tasting her barbecue and gets away with it." He laughed. "There's no getting away with any excuses. Not even for our friend here who seems to have a distaste for parties. You are going, aren't you, Steve?''

Steve didn't answer: instead he stood and looked out over Mikah's shoulder. ''Wade's coming.''

Mikah smiled, but remained silent while Wade rode up and dismounted. He wondered if Wade was a little surprised to see all of them there.

''Evening, boys. Nice to see you all again. I hope there's fresh coffee in that pot.''

''Fresh if you can stand it,'' Steve chuckled. ''Mikah thinks you should slice coffee and suck on it all day.''

Wade laughed at Mikah's scowl, but he poured himself a cup of the coffee anyway. ''Now, how does the situation stand?''

''We've talked it over, compared our thoughts, and we've all come up with the same answers,'' Steve began. ''No matter which way you look at it, you have to admit they've been careful.''

''That means you've found out nothing.''

''No, it doesn't. It means they've been so careful that they've out-foxed themselves.''

''How so?''

''By making the mistake of not attacking themselves.''

Wade looked at him with a puzzled frown. Apach stood up and said, ''Steve is right. There are only a few ranches that have not been sold or threatened.''

''Right,'' Carlos said.

''Look, Marshal,'' Steve said, ''the Rocking W is big but it doesn't seem to be grabbing for more . . . at least not in land. There's the Bar D, and their main thought is joining with the Rocking W. There's no doubt in our minds about the pressure that was put on Macquen, Niles, Gibson and Travors. The deaths weren't accidental. Neither were the fires. Jessup was under the same pressure. The Parker ranch has already gone under, Otis Quantrell has been attacked and threatened. Jane Crenshaw has been too, and so has Martin Bradley. Doesn't it seem strange to you that Silas Holmes of the Triple Cross and Charles Morrison of the Circle M have never had a problem yet?''

"It is kind of strange, but it's sure no proof. I have to have more to go on than that."

"We know that. That's why Apach has gone to work for Quantrell, and Carlos for Mrs. Crenshaw. Any further attack will be made against one of those places, and I wouldn't doubt if it's soon. Maybe then we can find some real evidence on who's behind this."

"All right. We have to use what we have. I know you need more time." He could see the relief on their faces, and he smiled a grim smile. "Gentlemen, the last thing I want is to send you back to that place, and I know you feel the same. Trust me that I won't send you there if there's even a remote chance that we can solve this. As far as I am concerned, you're free men . . . and we're in this together."

"You don't know what a relief that is," Steve said. "We were contemplating what might happen if—"

"Don't. I'll swing a pardon one way or the other."

"You won't regret it. We'll find your answers, and I have a feeling it's going to be sooner than we think. Someone took a shot at me. I don't think they would have taken such a chance if they weren't just a little afraid. We could be on to something."

"I have to go up to Comstock for a few days. What do you say we meet back here in two weeks? Maybe something will have broken by then." All four nodded their assent. "Good. Then we'd better break this up. If any of you are seen together or with me, this whole undercover operation is for nothing."

The four watched him walk away, mount his horse, wave a farewell and ride off. For several minutes they were silent, then Apach put into words what all of them were thinking.

"The marshal is a fair and honest man. I for one would not want to disappoint him."

"You're right, Apach," Steve said. "Suppose we get down to work and find his answers?"

There was nothing left to talk about, and Steve left Apach and Carlos with only a reminder that they were to get word to him if anything looked suspicious. They separated, with Apach and Carlos going back separately, and Steve and Mikah riding toward the Rocking W.

They rode in silence. Mikah was trying to think of something to say to open a path for the question he was longing to ask. It was as if Steve knew what he was thinking.

"What's on your mind, Mikah? Something's been eating at you ever since we all met up."

"I don't know exactly. It's just . . . you've changed somehow, and I was wondering if something was wrong."

"Changed? I haven't changed."

"You're on the inside lookin' out. Me, I'm on the outside lookin' in. I've been with you going on four years. You've changed."

"Is that good or bad?" Steve had to smile.

"Good, I think. I just don't know what's happened. I have a feeling, though. I asked you a question before, and the marshal came before you could answer."

"I heard you."

"Yeah, well, that ain't no answer."

"Yes, I'm going."

"Good."

"Why good?"

"Because we need the rest."

"We?"

"Me and the boys. I have a feeling you can be as mean as a wildcat if whatever load you're carrying gets too heavy. Steve . . . why don't you make it lighter by telling someone? It will make it easier for you. Wash it out of your mind."

"You think you know a lot."

"No. All the time you were in prison with us, I never asked because I thought the wounds were too sore. But we're out, and I don't see you giving them a chance to heal."

"Mother hen," Steve muttered.

"No, friend . . . I hope."

"You are a friend, Mikah, but . . ."

"Boy, you're something. You got a thorn in your side, and you just can't let go of it. You got an idea that you can put people just where you think they ought to be and keep them there. Everyone in his own place. You know what's the matter with you?"

"No," Steve said with resignation, "but I have a feeling you're going to tell me, and there's nothing I can do about it."

"You're right. Your problem is that someone has just made it clear she isn't what you expect all women to be."

"Rachel?"

"Why not admit she isn't what you planned for her to be?"

"You're barking up the wrong tree."

"You can't tell me much about women, 'cause I've had a few myself, God bless 'em, and you can't tell me much about you, 'cause I've been with you too long. I think you're just too stubborn now to admit you been wrong. If that's true, you're sure going to miss the best part of livin'."

"Mikah, just for argument's sake, let's suppose you're right. Now think of how well you know Carter Walker, and tell me if there's one chance in hell he'd let something like this happen."

"I don't think he'd have anything to say about it. Miss Rachel's too much like him. I also have a feeling he has a lot of respect for her common sense. Maybe it's because you're afraid to take a chance again."

"Again?"

"You going to lie to me and say you ain't been burnt and you don't want to take that chance again?"

"Mikah, it would be a mistake, and she might be the one getting hurt."

"Why?"

"Because I don't think I can stay here when this is finished."

"Why not?"

"I have to finish some business."

"I have it in my mind that you're looking to settle a score of some sort."

"Yes, I have to clear my name. I don't want to be labeled a pardoned murderer."

"Maybe you never will be able to find out what you want."

"I will."

"Is it proof you're after . . . or is it a little revenge?"

"You don't think I have a little revenge coming?"

"Maybe it just isn't worth it. What do you really have to gain? What do you have to go home to that you can't find here?"

"Look, Mikah, there's not much point in all this. I know what has to be done, and I know what I need to do when this is over."

"You gonna leave without asking the three of us if we want to go along?"

"It's not your fight. You'll have your freedom."

"That's gonna be as much of an insult to Apach and Carlos as it is to me. We're in this with you for the long haul. I'm just trying to say—"

"Rachel has the right man, and when she marries him she'll have all she wants. Like I told you before, let it go at that."

"Maybe I could if you trusted me enough to tell me what got you in the fix you were in."

"I trust you, but now is not the time. Let's get a move on. I have a lot of work to do and so do you."

Steve kicked his horse into a faster pace, and Mikah grew silent as he followed. He wished with his whole heart he knew what it would take to get Steve to let go of the past and look to the future. He was also curious to see the woman who could twist a man's heart and soul the way Steve's was twisted.

There was no doubt in Mikah's mind that Rachel was no longer interested in Cal Davis, if she ever had been. He wondered if it would help if he spoke to Rachel on the subject.

"Yes, sir," he said to himself. "I might just do that . . . I might just."

Chapter Eleven

Rachel had been surprised when she walked into the kitchen and found Yvonne in Cal's arms. Surprised, first, that she felt no anger, and second, that Yvonne didn't speak or laugh it off. It was the first time she had seen Yvonne with such a serious look in her eyes. The whole situation was clear to her at one glance, and it was as if a heavy burden had been lifted. Then her eyes went to Cal.

Pure mischief held her silent for a long moment, long enough for Cal's face to grow worried.

"Rachel," he said as he came to her side. "I have to explain this to you."

"Do you?" Rachel had meant to say he didn't, but the words just slipped out.

"God, Rachel, I never meant to deceive you. I know if you'll think this through rationally you'll see it's for the best. You never really wanted me."

"Cal—"

"No, listen, please. I know I am not what you wanted. I was a damn fool, allowing my father's dream to become mine. I can't believe now that I said what I did to you."

"You mean about merging our two ranches? Think of what you're giving up, Cal."

Cal was silent for a minute until he noticed that the words she spoke were contradicted by the glow of laughter in her eyes. It was only then that he realized she wasn't angry.

He turned to look at Yvonne, who had no sign of worry or regret on her face. Yvonne was looking at Rachel; then slowly her gaze turned to Cal and she smiled.

"I think Rachel is giving us her blessing, Cal," Yvonne said.

Cal felt a wave of relief wash over him that left him weak. He smiled now. "I should have known how you would be, after I remembered that you've been holding me at arm's length for so long. I'm sorry, Rachel."

"You have nothing to be sorry for, Cal. I hope you and Yvonne are happy together. You see, it was just as I said, you didn't really want to marry me anyway. Besides," she laughed, "I never had any intention of merging the Rocking W with anyone."

Yvonne came to Cal's side and smiled at Rachel. "I suppose you'll have the last laugh at my expense."

"I certainly will," Rachel replied with a laugh.

"I don't understand," Cal interrupted.

"Yvonne has played at love ever since I've known her, swearing there was no man who could clip her wings. Now she's going to settle down and be a rancher's wife. Good Lord, would the girls at school love to see this. Yvonne

Avery, the most popular girl in the state, planning to keep house and raise babies. This is too rich to ever be kept a secret.''

''Who wants to keep it a secret?'' Yvonne smiled up at Cal. ''I think it would be nice to tell the whole world. What do you say we announce it at the barbecue?''

''Sounds like a great idea to me,'' Cal responded. Then he looked at Rachel and laughed. ''Who do you think is going to be more disappointed or shocked, your father or mine?''

''I think it's going to be a close contest. I know someone who's not going to be surprised.''

''Oh? Who?''

''I think my mother has seen this coming.''

They laughed together in a strange kind of release. It seemed to clear the atmosphere, and lend a sense of quiet, comfortable ease to all three.

It was over two hours before Yvonne walked with Cal to the porch to say goodbye. She made a promise that they would make their announcement at the barbecue, and to keep the whole thing a secret until then.

When Cal was gone, Yvonne returned to the kitchen. She sat down opposite Rachel. ''Thanks, Rachel. I know this was a shock to you. The fact is, I think it was a shock to the both of us as well. It just seemed to happen.''

''It was a surprise, I'll admit. You don't think I'm angry about anything, do you?''

''I just didn't want you to think I deliberately did something behind your back.''

''Yvonne, I know you too well for that. If you really thought in your heart that I loved Cal, you wouldn't have done anything about—''

"No, I wouldn't. Rachel?"

"What?"

"I think the reason you didn't get angry is that you're looking for a way out of this . . . and a way to someone else."

"You mean Steve?"

"Yes."

"I don't think—"

"That's the trouble with you, you know."

"What?"

"You make too many decisions with logic and not enough with your heart. Be honest, Rachel, you're in love with Steve McKean."

"To you I'll admit it. Much good it will do me. Steve doesn't know I'm alive. To him I'm a 'boss,' a distraction or just . . ."

"Sounds like you need to open his eyes."

"Yvonne, come on. What do you want me to do?"

"Why not be honest and tell him how you feel? You might get a surprise."

"Yeah, I might. He might just laugh in my face. He thinks I'm a spoiled little rich girl anyway."

"Oh my, is pride getting in your way?"

Rachel lifted her chin in stubborn defiance. "I do have some, you know. I'm not just the local saloon girl. I don't have to beg a man to love me."

"I never said you did. In fact, that might be part of the problem. You think he should have fallen at your feet like all the others in this territory."

"No . . . I don't!"

"No?"

"Damn," Rachel muttered. Then she looked into

Yvonne's eyes, and the two of them laughed. When they finally grew silent, Rachel sighed. "Oh, Yvonne, this is impossible. I can't just . . . just throw myself at him."

"Even though you'd like to?"

Rachel laughed softly. "Yes, even then."

"Then suppose you just . . . trip him a little?"

"Yvonne, you're incorrigible. I'll let things take whatever course they will. If it's meant to be, it will be. I for one don't think anything will come of it."

"Why?"

"Because he doesn't want to let go of his shields, and there's nothing I can do about that. He's a man set on some . . . some goal no one will ever know, and I don't think he's the kind to let much stand between him and what he wants."

"If the man is half the man I think he is, he'll come around."

"For now, let's get bathed and changed. We can start dinner before mother gets back. Maybe that will make her feel good."

"That's called charming someone," Yvonne giggled. "But I think it's a good idea. Tomorrow night is the barbecue, and I think your parents had better be well charmed by then."

The two laughed, but inside, Rachel wasn't too sure she wasn't presenting her parents with a big disappointment. No matter how much she had claimed that she would never marry Cal, she still felt they were counting on just that.

The day of the barbecue boasted a brilliant sun and a blue sky filled with puffs of soft white clouds. Preparations had been under way since the first light of dawn. A large wooden platform had been put together for dancing later, and its border was strung with lanterns. Pits had been dug for the fires, and two sides of beef were being prepared for the spits.

Long tables were set up and covered with white cloth. By suppertime they would be laden with delicious dishes brought from every ranch around.

Lori Walker was in total command of what looked to Rachel like mass confusion. Still, Rachel knew from experience that when the guests arrived, everything would be in order and running smoothly. She only wished her confused emotions could be similarly organized.

Her feelings seemed to have escaped her usual control. At one moment she was expectant and excited, and in the next she felt as if she wanted to run and hide somewhere. She found herself wondering if Steve would come at all, and then hoping he wouldn't. It was aggravating. And Yvonne was not helping matters. She hadn't said a word when Rachel went through her entire wardrobe, claiming she couldn't find anything fit to wear. Yvonne could still remember the Rachel who hadn't cared at all.

Rachel's final choice of a dress delighted Yvonne, and utterly surprised Lori. It was a lavender creation so feminine that Lori determinedly remained silent lest she break the moment and cause Rachel to reconsider.

For the first time in her life Rachel found pleasure in the reflection she saw in her mirror. She looked as she intended to look, like a woman. She had taken a great deal of time with her hair, and had even sampled some of Yvonne's best perfume.

By the time she and Yvonne were ready to join the celebration, the sun was nearing the horizon, and the tempting scent of roasting meat and other foods wafted through the open windows.

"Lord, does that smell good. Rachel, do hurry, I'm famished," Yvonne said.

"I'll be ready in a minute." Rachel spun from her mirror and faced Yvonne. "How do I look?"

"Like a lady intending to knock a man off his feet."

"Is it that obvious?"

"You'll have every man in the territory baying at the moon."

"Yvonne, please be serious. I . . . I think I'm about to make a fool of myself."

"Rachel, don't do this to yourself. Where's the girl with all the confidence? The one who could meet any man on her own terms and hold her own. You don't need me or anyone else to tell you anything. You just listen to your own heart and do what you think is right. You look wonderful. I think you're going to surprise everyone."

"Including my parents. How have you and Cal decided to announce your plans?"

"Well, I don't think we can keep it a secret too long. Everyone who has eyes will be able to see. I think we'll make our announcement just before the dancing starts. After everyone is well fed, full of drinks and in a mellow mood."

"Yvonne, I think you're a little scared yourself."

"Rachel . . . I'm a stranger around here, and I'm a city girl. I wonder how everyone is going to take the news that I'll be the wife of one of the biggest ranchers around. How about his family?"

"I'm sorry. I've been so tied up with myself, I've been unfeeling. You don't need to be scared. When they see how

Cal feels about you and you about him, you'll be as much a part of everything as I am. These people are big-hearted and ready to love you, so don't worry. You might find some jealous ladies, though.''

"Those I can handle.'' Yvonne breathed a deep sigh, and the old confident smile reappeared. "Well, so be it. I have Cal, and that's all I'll need tonight.''

"Good, that's the old Yvonne. What do you say we go and eat?''

Cal met them just outside the door, and Rachel knew he'd stationed himself there to wait for them. He smiled at Rachel, but the warmth of his gaze was for Yvonne. He offered each an arm.

"I get to escort the two most beautiful ladies in the territory. I'm a very lucky man.''

"Cal, are your parents here yet?'' Yvonne asked.

"Yes, they just came. I thought we could get them aside and tell them, so this won't come as so much of a shock. It seems a little unfair to make them wait until we tell all the others. What do you say, Yvonne?''

"Of course.'' Yvonne smiled, but Rachel could see she was nervous.

"Good, then if Rachel will excuse us, we can do that now. I want to make a public announcement as soon as I can. I don't want any other cowboy with a roaming eye thinking he can move in. Tonight, you're all mine.''

Rachel watched them leave and silently wished the best for both of them. She stood quietly for a while just enjoying the gathering of all the people she had known all her life. Her gaze roamed the area, then paused as her eyes met a silver gray gaze. She inhaled softly as he began to make his way slowly to her side.

Steve had firmly decided that he would find an excuse not to go to the celebration . . . he had been determined not to go . . . he had fought the desire to see Rachel again, fought it and lost. He was angry with himself, and yet there was a knot of excitement deep in his body that refused to go away.

He damn well refused to think that it was because Rachel was so near. He didn't like what was happening. He had things to do when this business was over, and those things didn't include a woman who was practically engaged to another man. He was grateful that Cal Davis stood between him and Rachel. Their relationship would protect him.

The gathering of people had grown larger and larger, and there was a lot of happy laughter. The scents and sounds of the barbecue filled him with a longing for things that had been, and might never be again.

He made his way through the crowd to find the host and hostess. He watched them, and felt once again that Carter was innocent of wrong doing. He had too much of a good thing here; Carter didn't strike Steve as the kind of man who would be behind this scheme. He knew that kind of man well, had dealt with him and lost. He would meet him again if he had his way, and this time he would come out of their confrontation with his name cleared and the truth known.

He watched the gathering crowd, and realized how many influential people were in attendance. There were a number of politicians who must have come great distances to be here. This assured Steve that he had been right about one thing. Carter Walker had his eye on a political career . . . perhaps he hoped to be the first governor of a new state.

Judges and lawyers, a senator or two, doctors and other

prominent businessmen were all there, rubbing shoulders with the cowboys from every ranch around. It was a strange gathering of assorted people, yet everyone seemed to feel comfortable.

He continued to look the crowd over, and finally realized that he was looking for one particular person. He would admit that only to himself, and only because he knew she was safe from him . . . or he was safe from her. That thought jolted him.

Walls he had so neatly built, and on whose permanence he had depended for so long, had cracks. He decided it would be best to get this business over with and get on to his own as soon as possible.

He was handed a drink of something cool, and was grateful for it, until he started to raise it to his lips. His hand froze as his gaze met hers. He had not been prepared for the vision before him. He struggled to recall Ann and her incredible beauty, to remind himself of her terrible betrayal. But for the life of him he couldn't keep her face before him, and the old emotions of hate and fury seemed to melt into something he couldn't name.

This Rachel was not the tomboy he was used to, but more woman than he could ever remember. She was dressed in lavender that seemed to flow about her and soften her. Her hair, caught in the rays of the dying sun, was like a live flame. Beneath the same light her skin was like rose petals. He could not only see her, he could feel her as if she had stepped within the circle of his arms. He could even taste her soft mouth, sweet as it had tasted when they shared a forbidden kiss.

He suddenly found he was moving toward her without his own volition. It was as if she were drawing him to her.

217

He saw her smile softening the corners of her mouth as he approached.

"Steve"—her voice was warm and smooth as if it were melting—"I'm glad you came. You would have missed the best party of the season if you'd stayed away."

"I wouldn't think of missing it . . . boss," he replied, and was annoyed at himself for sounding defensive. But she turned her face up to him and smiled, and he suddenly forgot the anger he was trying to hold on to so desperately. When she moved, the scent of her perfume reached him.

"I'm not 'boss' tonight. This is a time for us all to celebrate together. Why can't you just relax and enjoy yourself?"

"Don't I look like I'm enjoying myself?" Before she could answer, he went on. "It surprises me that there are so many big shots here."

"Why? They're all friends we've known for as many years as I can remember. They come to the barbecue every year."

The sun was just disappearing, and the lanterns had been lit. Steve was aware that Rachel looked even more beautiful in their golden light. The musicians who were to lend their talents to the festivities were gathering near the platform. Steve fought to maintain a casual conversation. His awareness of Rachel was driving his senses crazy.

"Where's Cal? I didn't think he'd be so foolish as to leave you free with all these coyotes loose around here."

"He's standing over there, by the musicians . . . with Yvonne. I think he's talking them into letting him make an announcement before they start to play."

Steve's breath caught in his chest, threatening to shut off his ability to speak. He fought the realization that he wanted

218

Rachel to stop Cal before he pronounced their wedding date
for all to hear.

"An announcement? You mean he's ready to let you set
the date?" He smiled, expecting her anger. Instead she
laughed softly.

"Oh, you know Cal likes to think for himself, and I
wouldn't be surprised if a wedding date is just what he has
in mind."

Steve was struck into silence. Rachel was taking Cal's
commanding way so casually. It surprised him, for Mikah
had assured him she had been fighting their union for a
long time. Mikah must be wrong. He forced himself not to
answer, because he wasn't too sure that he wouldn't tell
her she was making a big mistake. This was not his right,
so he willed himself to silence. He didn't notice that the
hand that held his glass was white-knuckled, and that the
muscle in his jaw was jerking . . . he didn't notice, but for
the first time Rachel did.

There was a drawn-out chord of music, and all eyes were
drawn to where Cal and Yvonne stood. Cal stood on a box
and raised both arms in a gesture of silence. He was smiling. The entire place quieted down.

"Ladies and gentlemen, may I ask your indulgence for
a moment? I have an announcement to make, and I want
the whole territory to share in my good fortune." To
Steve's annoyance, several smiling faces turned to look at
Rachel, who just smiled benignly. "I want to announce that
the most beautiful lady in this territory has done me the
honor of agreeing to be my wife. Ladies and gentlemen,
may I present the future Mrs. Davis." He reached a hand
down to help Yvonne up beside him. "Miss Yvonne Avery
and I will be married after the first of the year at the Bar

D, and you are all invited to share that special day with us.''

For one long-drawn-out moment there was utter silence. Eyes furtively leapt to Rachel and then away as if afraid to see how she was taking this. Even Steve felt a wave of protective anger wash over him. How dare Cal hurt her, dismiss her in front of all her friends! He turned to Rachel, seeking the right words to say, and saw her smiling. Then she raised her hands and began to applaud. It was as if a dam broke. If Rachel was going to take it this way, so were the rest of them. The applause and hearty congratulations followed Yvonne and Cal as they moved to the plank floor and the music began.

Steve still stood looking at Rachel. When finally she turned to face him, he could see that her pleasure in the announcement was sincere. He felt an unwelcome sense of both relief and disbelief.

"I thought . . .'' he began.

"I know, so did everybody else . . . except me. I never intended to marry Cal, and I didn't want to hurt him. Inviting Yvonne here was the smartest thing I've ever done. Come on, Steve, dance with me. If you keep standing there with that look on your face, everyone will think something is drastically wrong.''

They were on the floor and he had his arm about her before logic reared it's head. This was the kind of thing he was trying to keep away from. Close proximity to Rachel just muddied his thoughts and made it damn difficult to hang onto his control. Still, she felt so good in his arms, so warm and soft.

They moved together easily, and neither spoke for a while. Steve fought to find casual words that would make what he was feeling a lie, but none came. Instead he found himself drawing her closer, inhaling the scent of her, the woman smell of her. There was a growing wanting uncoiling deep inside of him and he struggled to subdue it.

The music stopped for a minute so the musicians could catch their breath. Rachel moved from his arms, and he felt the sudden emptiness. As if they had agreed, they walked together into the surrounding darkness.

It was a cool, magical night, with a soft breeze and a moon so big and gold that it seemed to Rachel she could reach up and touch it. The black velvet of the night sky was touched with millions of brilliant stars. From behind them the music had started again, and the faraway sound was making the night even more enchanting.

Their silence wasn't a nervous or strained kind of silence. It was as if each just took enjoyment from the presence of the other. That was true enough to surprise Steve, who found he didn't want to do anything to break the mood of the moment.

When they stopped walking, they stood in the shadows of the trees that bordered the long, sloping lawn of the ranch. Beyond them was the bunkhouse, which was totally dark. To all intents and purposes they were as alone as if they existed in a world of their own.

"You weren't surprised tonight," Steve said.

"About Yvonne and Cal? No, I wasn't."

"It doesn't bother you?"

"No, why should it? I'm happy for both of them."

"I thought it was settled between you and Cal."

"It was never settled except in our parents' minds," Rachel laughed. "I still don't know what Dad and Mother are going to say." She looked up at him, and the moonlight

221

turned her green eyes to emerald. "I never intended to marry Cal. I never loved him. We're friends, very good and very close friends, but that has always been all that was between us."

"I never thought he realized that," Steve said.

"But you did?" Her question was spoken in a half whisper.

"Yes, I did."

"How?"

"I don't know . . . maybe it was just your pride in the way you spoke of your ranch, and the way you said you helped run the Rocking W. I knew you weren't about to hand that over to Cal. Maybe it was the look in your eyes when you talk about what you have here."

"Maybe," she repeated in the same tone as his, "it's the way you felt at one time and you understood."

Steve let the walls between them crack a little more. "Yes, maybe."

"You did have a place of your own."

"Yes, a small place. It sat on the bend of a wide river, and it was the most beautiful spot you've ever seen. It took every last dime I could scrape together to buy the land." His guard down, Steve forgot to fight the old memories. It had been a place he had loved as much as Rachel loved hers. "It took me two summers to build the house, but it was good and tight. Then getting enough cattle to call the place a ranch was another near impossible job. I roamed the range, gathered all the strays I could, bought when I could save money, traded, and worked for other ranchers until I had a respectable herd of my own."

"It must have been hard. I remember the stories Dad used to tell me about how he built the Rocking W."

"It's hard, but there's something special about having something that you built with your own sweat."

"And you loved it."

"Yes, I loved it."

"What did you call it?"

"Stillwaters."

"What a lovely name for a ranch."

"It was just right. The river that ran past it had the deepest, bluest, calmest water I've ever seen."

"Steve . . . why did you leave it?" He grew quiet, and she could feel him withdraw from her. She suddenly felt as if she would never have this chance again. "Was . . . was there a woman there? Did you leave because you loved her?"

He spun to face her, but she didn't see pain on his face; she saw fury. "Oh, yes, a woman." He laughed a short, ragged laugh. "There was a woman all right, but not to help me build the ranch, to help me lose it."

"You lost it?" she gasped.

"It was stolen from me because I was stupid enough to trust a beautiful face. She and her father, damn his soul to hell, took all there was to take from me, and when I fought . . . when I fought back, they set me up for murder and sent me to Yuma Prison."

"Steve! Yuma Prison."

"You've heard of it, I'm sure. But you don't know what hell is until you get shoved inside of it."

"Did you do it?"

"Do what?"

"Kill a man?"

"Yes," he said shortly. "That does make a difference, doesn't it, Miss Rachel Walker?"

She heard the derision in his voice, and knew with every instinct she had that it was a cover for the other emotions that were tearing at him. Instead of backing away, as he expected her to do, she stepped closer, and laid her hand gently on his cheek.

"I said I was sorry once, and I'm sorry now, but not for the reason you think. I'm sorry for the hurt you must have felt, and for all you must have gone through in prison. I think there was more to this killing business, and I wish you could tell me. But if you can't . . . well, I understand that too. You're free now, Steve, and there's always a chance to begin again."

He wanted to shout at her that she didn't understand, that he wasn't free. He wanted to tell her what he had been brought here to do, that there was a possibility he could send her father to that same prison. He wanted to say so much, and he couldn't. What stopped him was the look in her eyes, and the sudden burst of raw need that filled him. Would Rachel understand that need? Would she run?

He took hold of her shoulders and drew her close to him. He had half expected her to suddenly come to her senses and push him away. Instead there was instant fire. It flared from her to him. Her body strained against his with a kind of certainty that said, This is right, this has always been right. With his head spinning and his body humming, it no longer seemed to matter that he had vowed this could not happen. She touched off sparks that incinerated all the secrets lingering within him. Above all the other thoughts whirling in his head was one simple demand: more.

She was heated, melting, hungry. He wanted her, too much for comfort. Too much for sanity. Perhaps she was all he had ever wanted.

Forever

Was this what she had wanted, waited for all her life? Yes, her whole soul replied. He was enough, more than she had dreamed of, more than she had ever understood.

Rachel felt as if she had been swimming underwater and had come up much too quickly. She was drunk with sheer pleasure.

For Steve it was a revelation. Nothing seemed to matter. Not the past, the future. Now was all that was important. But Rachel wasn't a woman for just now. She was the kind that planned for the future, that needed the security of tomorrow and all the tomorrows to follow. He couldn't offer her that.

When he reluctantly left the sweetness of her mouth, he looked into eyes aglow with an emotion he could hardly handle.

"You're not going to let me in, are you? Oh Steve, don't you know . . ."

"I know that this is a moment that tomorrow you might be sorry for."

"No."

"Rachel, I'm not a man with a future that I can plan. You, you're different. I'm not going to stay. You knew that from the start."

She did know. She knew he was good at falling back on coldness to conceal his inner thoughts and feelings. It was one of his best weapons and personal defenses. If he harbored frustrating, near-violent urges to take her to some private place and make love to her until everything was forgotten, he didn't show it. But all her senses told her this was true. His kiss, and the urgency of it told her more than he would ever know.

She could feel the tension humming through him like a

225

current, and she knew her own tension was just as strong. He needed her, but he fought it, by keeping her at arm's length.

But Rachel knew the time was now . . . or it would never be. She remained silent, but moved into his arms. When they closed about her it was with a small, tortured sound from him.

She did not speak, and he could not seem to. She simply stood with her arms about him and her head resting on his chest. His body was so firm, his heartbeat so steady and strong.

Then he looked down into her eyes again, and she felt a surge of pleasure. He lifted his hands to cup her face, then again took her mouth with his.

No light, gentle kiss this time. She tasted frustration and didn't understand it. But she also tasted desire, simmering, waiting, and couldn't resist it. Her body went fluid, every bone, every muscle. The need was there, and she did not want to deny it any longer.

Every instinct told Steve of her innocence, and he wanted to make this time worth her giving. In truth he would have liked to court her with candlelight and gentleness, but his desire was already raging beyond his control. He hoped he had the control he was going to need.

He held her, letting his lips taste the softness of her cheeks and throat. "Are you afraid, Rachel, or will you come with me?"

He heard the soft sigh of contentment before she answered quietly.

"I'll come with you." She didn't care where he might take her now, only that the magic of the wild call of her body to his be completed. He took her hand and led her further into the shadows.

Chapter Twelve

With her hand in his, she followed as he led her to the deserted bunkhouse. No one would be there for hours, and he would have this time with her, even if he never had another moment on this earth. Recriminations and guilt might follow, but this would be worth everything.

Within the bunkhouse, with its rows of bunks, golden moonlight streamed through the windows. Steve cautiously bolted the door before he returned to Rachel's side. He didn't know whether she would change her mind or be afraid. He was ready to back away, even though it would be the most difficult thing he had ever done. Still, he would never take a woman without her wanting him.

He stood close to her, but didn't touch her. Then she smiled and reached for him. He enclosed her in his arms with a sigh that resembled a prayer. She felt so soft and fragile pressed against him, and he buried his face in her hair and just savored the scent of her for a moment.

Then his trembling fingers reached for the buttons at the back of her dress. Gently he unbuttoned it, and the dress whispered down her body and lay in a pile at her feet. He slid the straps of her chemise off her shoulders, brushing his lips across her skin as he did. But his need to taste wasn't any stronger than her need to experience. She wanted all there was to have of him, everything he meant to give her. She wanted the secrets that lay within him, and she wanted to learn what his desire had to teach her.

She felt the coolness of the night air on her body when the last of her clothes followed her dress. He gazed at her, profoundly aware of her rare beauty. She was perfect, and he found his breath growing short just looking at her.

"God, Rachel, I need you." It was a soft cry, but she heard with all her heart. She reached to help him remove his clothes. She, too, enjoyed seeing him, touching him.

Then his mouth crushed hers again, and she was held against his firm body fiercely, as if she might fade away. He forgot patience, and she the need for it. He forgot gentleness, and she the need for it. His tongue delved deep into her mouth as if there were some taste, some hint of flavor he might be denied. But she would not deny him anything. Her passion changed from tingling arousal to raging desire, and her mouth was greedy, as insistent as his. She didn't mean to be swept along, but to take as much as she gave.

She hadn't known that passion would strip every remnant of civilization away, but she learned. Glorying in the sense of abandon, she touched and tasted where she would with hands and lips that moved quickly, and with no more patience than he.

He murmured against her ear, only her name, but the

sound of it drifted through her softly. They were on the bunk, and she didn't even know how they got there, only that they were tangled together, flesh to burning flesh. The slow liquefying pleasure made everything she'd ever felt before seem hollow. Then his tongue dipped inside her mouth.

A long, lingering stroke, a whispering caress. There was no need to hurry, he refused to hurry, even though his body was raging with the desire to be within her. Passion was mixed with wonder. She felt the power of a new emotion flow deep within her. She could feel it pouring from him too—contentment.

His lips moved over her shoulders, down, lazily down to linger on the pulse point at the inside of her elbow. She felt an answering heat from every other place. Her hand ran through his hair, the curling thickness of it, before she let her fingers stroke his face. He looked at her, a long look, and then their mouths fused again.

The sensations built slowly, not yet urgent, not yet desperate, but growing sharper. Gradually, quiet sighs became moans. With his mouth at her breast he heard her breathing grow more ragged. He was aware of her scent, her taste, the satin that was her skin. Hunger seeped into him, and the excitement that came from knowing the hunger would be satisfied. His hands journeyed down.

His hands were magic.

He let his fingers linger, stroke, excite until her body throbbed with anticipation. Grimly he clung to his own control, refusing to let his need get ahead of hers.

Her mind was filled with him. Head whirling, she moved sensuously beneath him. How warm his flesh was, how firm his body. Her hands wandered down to his hips, skimmed over his thighs. She felt the quiver of muscle beneath her hands.

She was floating, but the air was thick and syrupy. Her limbs were weighted, but her head was light and spinning. She felt him grasp her, heard him hoarsely groan her name. Then he was inside her and the explosion went on and on and on. She had only enough sanity left to pray it would never stop.

He watched her. He struggled to hold back that seductive darkness so that he would have this image of her to carry forever. The moonlight washed her in gold and shadows. With her head thrown back and her hair gloriously spread about her, she knew only pleasure. He held her there for an instant of perfect clarity. Then the darkness and all its savage delights overcame him.

They lay together, naked and warm as careless children. It was a pleasant thing that swirled in Steve's mind, the thought that they could stay this way forever. He knew it was an impossibility, but he clung to the illusion for this one forbidden moment. He knew it had to end too soon.

Slowly the sounds of the world came to them. Music and voices in the distance. Rachel searched her mind for some regret, but found none. Surely, after what they had just shared he would confide in her what troubled him so much. Surely they could chase all his ghosts away together.

Steve raised himself on one elbow and looked down into her eyes. With a gentle hand he brushed the hair away from her cheek, and then bent to kiss her with a touch so light she shivered.

Rachel reached up and took his face between her hands. She wanted to say so much to him, but the words tangled in her mind, mixed with the fear that the words would not be enough.

"Steve . . ."

"Shh, let's hold this moment for as long as we can."

"Is this all there will be?"

"What can we have, Rachel? There are too many differences between us for us to look ahead."

"What differences? There are none we can't overcome if we talk to each other, and don't let outside influences come between us."

"Some things just can't be settled as easily as that."

"What stands between us?"

"Rachel." He laughed bitterly, knowing he could not tell her of his reasons for being here, or his need for vengeance. "You're probably one of the richest women in the territory. I'm a roaming cowboy. Can't you see the impossibility of our situation?"

Instinctively she knew that money was not what stood between them, and she also knew he was still unable to open his heart to her. That knowledge hurt worst of all. They had been together, mind, heart, body and soul, and still there was a place inside of him that he kept locked away.

She struggled to hold back the tears. He knew she was fighting a battle, and it was all he could do to keep from comforting her. He longed to tell her all that he felt inside. Steve had promised himself he would not open his heart to love again. But suddenly it crashed down upon him that he did indeed love Rachel. The realization only made things more impossible.

He felt her searching gaze, but still he was unprepared for her question. "It's another woman, the one you can't talk about. Does she still mean so much to you, Steve? Even after her betrayal, you're not free to love someone else?'' Rachel was too new at loving not to be fiercely jealous of the woman Steve had held before her.

Should he let her go on believing a lie, or tell her she was wrong? If he did, there would be questions following that he had no answers for. He was silent a moment too long. He heard the soft protesting sound she made; then she seemed to withdraw from him, and the emptiness she left behind was devastating.

He closed his eyes when he felt her resistance grow, and she moved out of his arms. In the half-light he watched her dress.

Rachel couldn't speak. She could find no recriminating words for Steve, for their passion was something she had wanted as badly as he.

Steve was just as bereft of words. There was no way to explain himself to Rachel, and certainly no way to tell her he loved her. He had to let her go on believing that what had happened between them was caused by passion alone; then he had to gather the courage to ride away from her when the time came. The latter would be much harder to do than anything he had ever done before.

''Rachel—''

''Don't, Steve.'' She slid the dress over her body and came to him. With hands that trembled, he buttoned the dress, wondering if she was as cool as she sounded. She looked at him, then knelt beside the bunk. ''I wish I could wash away all the bad memories that keep you from me. I won't ever be able to forget what happened between us tonight, but I won't settle for something less than it should be. You won't let go of your dark thoughts, and I can't fight that. I just want you to know I care enough to help you fight . . . If you want me. But it's going to be when you can put all the darkness aside and let me into your life. Until then . . . remember . . ." She bent to him and kissed him until his head swam. Then she was gone.

He lay stunned, feeling as if the light had left his life and he didn't know how to get it back. Of course he knew. All he had to do was tell her the truth.

But the truth would drive her farther from him than she already was. He knew quite well that her father was too important in her life for her to believe anything negative anyone might say about him. And even though he believed Carter to be innocent, he couldn't prove to Wade that the man wasn't involved. He wished something would happen to bring things out into the open. Reluctantly, he rose and dressed. He had no intention of rejoining the party. It had lost its luster when Rachel left his side. Instead he went to the stable, saddled his horse and rode into the night.

The sound of a whistle cut the night air as the train came to a stop. When Nathan and Ann disembarked, it was to a nearly silent town. They questioned the stationmaster about the scarcity of people.

"Oh, it ain't usually like this, but there's a big whoop-de-do over to the Carter ranch, and just about every man, woman and child is over there. The town will be back to normal by tomorrow."

"Normal." Ann smiled. Nathan read her thoughts and had to smile too. This was not a town to compare with what they were used to. Ann would find this rural community stifling.

The stationmaster missed her point completely. "It's a

grand town, isn't it? Why, when we're goin' good, this place is buzzing.''

"I'm sure it is." Ann smiled at him, causing him to turn beet red.

"Tell me . . . ?"

"John, John Keetch."

"Tell me, John, do you know Thaddius Blake?"

"Thaddius? Sure, I know him. He's the owner of the biggest bank in the town."

"Biggest? You mean there's more than one?"

"Sure, we got two banks. Of course, the Blake bank is the best. Thaddius has a mortgage on most of the places in this territory."

"Does he now?" Nathan replied softly. "How about Mr. Raymond?"

"Robert Raymond?"

"Yes."

"I know him. He's a pretty good lawyer."

"How about telling us the best hotel so we can get settled?"

"No question, it's the Harbor House. Run by a good hard-working widow, good meals and clean bedding, and a good price."

"Thank you. Can you see that our luggage is taken over?"

"Sure, I'll see to it. You all here on business?"

"I'm actually here to see a friend of mine. Thank you for your help, good evening." Nathan cut him off before he could ask any more questions. He took Ann's elbow and started down the street. The stationmaster watched with unashamed curiosity as the two walked toward the hotel.

"Just a humming town," Ann laughed. "Are you sure

Steve is here? I can't see him tied down to a place like this."

"Perhaps Steve is not the fun-loving boy you used to know. I would think a few years in Yuma Prison would bring about some changes."

"Yes," she said, "I imagine so."

"In the morning we're going to look up Thaddius and Robert. If there's something going on in this territory that's going to bring a profit, those two will have a hand in it."

"And you want in on whatever is going on."

"You can count on that. I want that, but not as much as I want Steve McKean back in the hole he belongs in. Martin is waiting for him, and I intend to see to it that his wait is short."

"How do you intend to do that?"

"Any way I can, little girl," he chuckled, "any way I can. No matter what I have to do. I can't afford to have McKean loose."

"I don't see what he can do to you now. His ranch is safely in your hands. He can't do you any harm."

"Not getting soft-hearted, are you?"

"No. I just don't see the reason for going after him this way."

"Perhaps there are more reasons than you know," he said softly, almost to himself.

Ann was too alert for him to say more. In fact, he was sorry for saying that much. He could see her eyes narrowing and growing thoughtful.

"You aren't considering seeing or talking to him, are you?" he asked. "I don't think that would be wise. From the way he looked at you the last time he saw you, I don't think you would be quite safe in his hands. In fact, he might wring that pretty neck of yours.''

"I suppose he might. But then, Steve didn't always do what was expected of him . . . did he?''

"He did when I sentenced him, he did exactly what I expected him to do. He finally came to the full realization that it had been very foolhardy to have fought me the way he did. He should have sold me his ranch when I asked him to.'' Nathan smiled at Ann, a feral smile of smug satisfaction. "Of course, I will give you credit. You played him and Sam against each other with finesse. He used the gun, but in reality you pulled the trigger.''

"And we gained two ranches instead of one. A good profit.''

Nathan watched her closely, sensing some emotion behind her words that he was uncertain of.

"Yes, a good profit. And I think we can make an even better one here. I have a feeling these men are robbing the ranchers around here on a grand scale. It should be interesting. Ann, what are you going to do if you come face to face with him? He's not going to be forgiving. He might try to even the score with you.''

"I handled Steve McKean before, and I can handle him again. He's a gentle man who thinks with his heart too often.''

"Are you sure prison hasn't changed him?''

"Oh, I'm sure it has. It has probably made him harder . . . more savage.'' This thought was pleasing to Ann. She had a thoughtful look in her eyes, and licked her lips like a cat anticipating something tasty to eat. She fascinated Nathan more every day. He wondered, if she wanted to play with Steve again, whether she might not do it successfully.

"Well, get some rest. Tomorrow we look into a situation that promises to be profitable for us both."

"It sounds to me like that marshal had something he wanted from Steve. Why else would he go so far to see him . . . and why him? I never did trust that sheriff at home. I always thought he felt Steve was innocent. Maybe he had something to do with it."

"That's quite possible. In fact, it makes sense when you put it together with what is going on around here. Steve was always smart, and he was damn good with that gun. At least he was smart most of the time. He just never saw you coming."

"It may be that we'll have to get rid of Steve again. This time, if he interferes, we'll get rid of him permanently."

"Well, I'm tired. I think I'll go to bed."

Nathan left, and Ann locked her door behind him. Then she walked to the bed and sat down, her mind spinning with thoughts that would not have made Nathan comfortable. She let her mind drift to the nights she and Steve had spent together, the hot, unbridled passion they had shared.

Yes, she remembered. Much more than Nathan would have desired her to remember. She had had other lovers since Steve, but none had matched the heated lovemaking they had shared, and she had had a deep desire to know it again. Besides, she wanted to find out if she still had the power over him that she had wielded before.

She rose and took off her traveling clothes, then stood naked before the mirror. It told her that she still possessed the soft, firm body and smooth, creamy skin Steve had worshiped. She could almost feel his strong hands on her again, and the warmth of need coiled up within her.

Tomorrow she would find her own answers about Steve,

and she would see if she could turn his anger to passion again. The thought of it gave her a satisfying feeling of power.

"Steve," she whispered softly. "You belonged to me once, and you'll belong to me again. We can share all we had before and more. Tomorrow . . . tomorrow."

The moon was high, full and gold, and the celebration went on. To Rachel it seemed interminable.

She refused to try to answer the questions she saw in Yvonne's eyes. Her mother had also asked about Steve's disappearance, but finally retreated before Rachel's clipped denials that she knew anything about where he had gone.

Carter had not approached Rachel at all, but he had watched her closely, and knew something was drastically wrong. It did not take him long to link it to the fact that he had not seen Steve for hours . . . in fact, since the announcement.

He had his questions, and he had his way of finding his own answers. He was certain of one thing. Steve McKean would be gone fast if he had done anything to hurt Rachel.

He could see Lori watching both Rachel and him. He didn't have an answer yet, and he wasn't in the mood to exchange words with Lori.

Of course, both he and Lori had been somewhat shocked when Cal and Yvonne announced the fact that they intended to marry. But neither had been worried about Rachel, for they already knew her resistance to the idea of marrying Cal. In fact, they had watched Rachel embrace Yvonne and kiss Cal, and knew her display of pleasure was genuine.

Why, then, had she seemed so preoccupied and quiet for

the past few hours? Lori promised herself she would be asking Carter a lot of questions later, and Carter was promising himself to dodge the questions he knew were coming until he found out a few things on his own. First, where had Steve McKean disappeared to and why? Carter had begun to believe some time ago that it was a lot more than coincidence that had brought Steve to the Rocking W. Tomorrow . . . tomorrow.

Apach had left the party sometime after midnight, following a strong feeling that he should be back at Quantrell's. He almost always followed his instincts, and most times they proved true. Now he lay on his makeshift bed and listened to the night sounds.

He knew the sound of every night animal in the West, and that was the reason he was alert when he heard a sound that could not be attributed to any night animal he knew. He rose silently from his bed and stealthily found his way to the open barn door.

He stood out of the moonlight and scanned the area around him, but there was no sign of anyone. Still, his senses told him that something or someone was about, and at this time of night that boded nothing but trouble.

It came again, that whisper of sound, and Apach knew he wasn't alone. When the voice came to him from out of the darkness, he was prepared for it. He'd had a feeling he might be warned . . . once.

"Injun, you're making a big mistake."

"Coward, come out in the open and talk," Apach answered calmly.

"I ain't no coward, I just came here to make you an offer. It ain't my idea. I could have shot you just as easy."

"An offer?"

"Yeah. We know damn well you're busting your bones to work here for practically nothing. You can make a hell of a lot more with less work if you back off and come with us."

"Who do you work for?"

The laugh was quick and derisive. "Don't be a fool."

Apach was trying to reach the nearby wall where his rifle leaned. He knew quite well that those who attacked at night weren't above cutting him down at the least provocation. He felt immeasurably comforted when he had his rifle in hand.

"What do you want?"

"To make you an offer and to give you a warning."

"I don't take well to warnings or offers from people who can't stand in the light."

"Well, you better take well to this one. You'll only get one."

"Good, I hate to have my sleep disturbed. Go back and tell your boss to make me an offer face to face, and I might consider it."

"You're asking for more trouble than you know. You might just find yourself dead."

"I'll take that chance," Apach laughed softly. "I don't think you have the guts to take me on. Step out into the open and let's see." Apach waited, then he laughed again. "I thought not. Go back and tell your boss to stay away from me and this ranch. The next one of you that shows up here I'll send back slung over his saddle."

Apach was so involved with his nocturnal visitor that for once his instincts failed him. He heard a sound from behind him and spun around. But he was too late. Two of them were upon him before he could swing the rifle into play.

Their attack was quick and brutal, and within five minutes the men left him on the barn floor and faded into the night again. Apach lay for some time before he could gather the strength to crawl to a mound of hay and collapse upon it. He was beaten but not really injured, and he knew this was just a warning. He could be dead instead. He was furious at himself for being caught in such a way. He vowed his own personal revenge on the men who had done it.

He lay still, gathering his thoughts, trying to put a face to the voice he had heard. He was nearly certain he had heard it somewhere before. This attack made him reasonably sure there would be another, stronger one against the ranch. This must be the place they wanted next. He meant to ask Otis Quantrell a lot of pointed questions when he got home, and this time he wasn't going to take denial for an answer.

In the meantime he had to get himself together. He felt as if he had been run over by a stampede. He crawled to the watering trough outside, and dipped his head several times into the cold water. His ribs were beginning to ache, and he would certainly have some nasty bruises in the morning . . . if he could even walk then.

He struggled to his feet and made his way to the house. Pushing open the door, he found a chair and sat down to wait. Otis was going to answer some questions tonight, even if he had to force the answers out of him. He laughed to himself. He'd be lucky if he could just stay awake until Otis came home. He folded his arms, rested his head upon them and gave way to the rest he needed.

It seemed as if he had just closed his eyes when someone

was roughly shaking him awake. He forced himself to sit up, and heard Otis's voice as if from a distance.

"What the hell are you doin' in here, and what happened to you?" Apach raised his head, and Otis swore softly. "What the hell went on here?"

"I think you know better than I," Apach replied.

"They goin' to run you off?" The question was asked with the knowledge that that would be the best thing for Apach to do.

"No one runs me off of any place I choose to be. But I need you to give me a reason not to want to go. Don't you think it's time to tell me just why you're so scared, and why someone is trying to tear your place from your hands?"

Otis walked away from Apach, and stood looking out the still open door. Apach let him remain silent. This was not an easy thing to consider. Then he turned to look at Apach again.

"Maybe . . . maybe it would be better for you if you just rode on."

"Is that what you really want, or is it your fear talking?"

"Fear. What the hell do you know about fear? It appears to me you ain't got the common sense to be afraid of anything. Look at you. They beat you up and I could guess they tossed in a threat or two."

"Yes, they did."

"And here you sit, asking me to tell you things it isn't safe for you to know."

"It looks to me like it isn't safe for me not to know. I don't run from cowards like that, and they will never catch me that way again. I'm willing to stand with you and protect this place . . . once you give me one good reason why I should.''

''Damn it!''

Apach grinned. ''Indian or not, try trusting me. It might just be the smartest thing you've ever done.''

''Or I might just find both of us dead.''

''I'm ready for them. What about you?''

''You're a damn stubborn one, ain't you?''

''No, I just don't like to be told what to do by cowards.''

''Cowards! You ain't been here when—''

''When they attack your home at night, most likely wearing masks. You don't call that cowardly?''

''I guess.''

''Those kind don't think for themselves. I think it would be wise to tell me''—Apach held Quantrell's gaze—''just who it is that wants your ranch . . . and why.''

Otis breathed a ragged sigh and sank onto a chair. ''All right. I've been asked to sell.''

''Asked?''

''Well, at the beginning; then the askin' got pretty rough. I found myself like you are now, but I keep telling them I don't intend to sell.''

''Who does the asking?''

''A man comes around, usually at night, and he's real smooth and polite. He says he knows who can buy if the price is right. Says he really wants to protect me from this ever happening again. Says he'll be back.''

''But he never names names?''

''No.''

''Then how are you to know who is buying?''

''When I agree, he'll bring papers, and I'll be selling to some group. I'll never know.'' He looked closely at Apach.

"Is this the reason you came here to work?"

"I thought you might need help. I've heard a lot of stories." Apach avoided his question. "You'll have to fight them one night, you know that. I mean really fight. Kill a couple of the attackers. Teach them you mean what you say."

"I don't know . . ." Otis paused. He wasn't ready to go along with Apach. "You look tuckered out. Why don't you get some sleep? You can move your gear and sleep here," he said. He didn't acknowledge Apach's surprised look, and Apach didn't want to say anything. This was such a positive move that he didn't want to anger Otis.

Apach regarded him silently. Quantrell had come a long way in the time Apach had been working for him and tonight must have decided him.

"Thanks. I am pretty beat. But," he said firmly, "we talk in the morning, then we decide if I stay or if I ride away and let you 'sell' your place to strangers."

With these words Apach went into the next room. To his pleasure he found a bed with what looked like a comfortable mattress. He dropped down on it with a sigh, and within minutes he was asleep.

Sleep was something Steve couldn't find no matter how hard he struggled. He lay beside his low-burning fire and gazed up at the stars. His thoughts went to Rachel and refused to leave.

Rachel. He had never known anything like her and the magic that they had shared. Deliberately he dredged up the memory of Ann, a memory he had fought to suppress for so long. In his mind he compared, and realized that what he and Ann had shared had been more hot lust than any-thing permanent.

He recalled their trysts as heated mating, with Ann as much the aggressor as he. He had lost himself in her, com-ing close to losing his soul as well. He had sensed more than knew that she was part of the force that had brought the gun to his hand and death to his door. He could never prove it, but he wished there was a way he could.

He knew, just before he was dragged from the court-room, that his ranch was gone. Taken by the bank to be sold to the highest bidder. He knew this as well as he knew the highest bidder had been Judge Nathan Graham.

As he compared the past to the present, he wondered if the same thing wasn't going on here. There was no group of investors. There were one or two men who lusted for more and more. Men who might have a secret political goal as well. Was Carter Walker involved, after all?

One thing followed another. If he was guilty, what about Rachel? Was Rachel more like Ann than he'd thought? He considered this deeply, and found nothing but disbelief. No, there was no way to compare Rachel and Ann. Rachel had surrounded him with warmth, and had given him far more than he had given her. Ann had only taken and taken until he was drained and left hollow. No, there was no compar-ison.

This inner debate drained him of strength and resolve, and he fought to remind himself that if he failed Wade, prison awaited him. He had been betrayed before, and found it hard to believe that Wade would be able to get him a pardon if things did not go right here. Hell, he had some doubts of getting a full pardon even if things went exactly as planned.

He realized by now that sleep was impossible, and tossing his blanket aside, he stood to extinguish the fire. Quantrell's ranch was not that far away: Apach was close enough to talk to, if he was back from the barbecue.

He saddled his horse and rode slowly toward Quantrell's place. When he neared the house, he tried to make as little noise as possible. As far as he knew, Apach slept in the barn. He tied his horse behind it and crept into the dark building.

"Apach," he called softly. There was no answer. "Apach," he tried a little louder. Still no answer. He knew Apach too well. No one would be able to come in as he did and not find Apach ready and waiting.

He wondered whether Apach had not yet returned; it seemed unlikely.

He found a comfortable place to sit, and rolled and lit a cigarette, prepared to wait until Apach returned. He didn't wait long, but the voice that startled him did not belong to Apach.

"Put your hands on your head, real careful or this gun might just go off."

Steve jerked erect. When he looked around, he came face to face with Otis Quantrell. He rose cautiously and lifted his hands in the air at once. He had an idea Otis was nervous, and he didn't want to be shot by accident.

"Come to make an offer, did you? Well, you can go back and tell your boss that he can beat up on every cowboy in the territory and I still ain't selling."

"I didn't come to make you any offers, Mr. Quantrell. I came to see Apach. We have some business to talk about. Hasn't he come back from the barbecue yet? And who got beat up?"

Steve had a sinking feeling in the pit of his stomach. Was Apach hurt? Where was he?

"As if you didn't know. Did you come back to check on how well you did?"

"Has Apach been hurt?" Steve's voice was harder and growing angrier by the minute. "I need to see him. Where is he?"

"Up to the house, where you can't get your hands on him again."

Steve was relieved. Slowly he lowered his hands. "Mr. Quantrell, I have a lot to say to you, and I think it's time you listened."

247

Chapter Thirteen

Lori was unusually quiet, and it was a while before Carter noticed it. She was undressing for bed when it came to him that she hadn't spoken much since the party had ended. He sat on the edge of the bed they had shared for over twenty years and watched her.

He loved Lori with a singular passion that had never faltered. All he had done, he had done for her. Now there was something on her mind she had not shared with him, and that was rare in itself.

He watched her put on her nightgown, and as always the urge came to him to remove it and make love to her. But he had a feeling this was not the time. Something was preying on Lori's mind.

"Lori?"

She turned from her mirror, where she had been brushing her hair, and looked at him questioningly. "Yes, Carter?"

"What is it, girl? What's been eating at you all night?"

Any other time, she might have laughed, come into his arms, and all would soon be forgotten. This time she just looked at him for a long minute, as if she were trying to see whether there was something in him she had not noticed before.

"Have I done something to upset you, Lori?"

"Not really. It's just that . . ."

"Just what?" he went to her and sat beside her. Taking the brush from her hand, he laid it aside and took hold of her shoulders, forcing her to look at him. "There have never been any secrets between us, Lori, and I don't want any to come between us now. You tell me what's bothering you. Is it something I've done?"

"I . . . I don't know."

"What's that supposed to mean? Either I did or I didn't."

"Carter, I heard a lot of talk tonight, and I need you to reassure me that what I heard isn't so."

"If I can, I will. Tell me what you've been hearing."

"Are you trying to get powerful enough to run for the first governor of the state of Montana?"

"Would it upset you that much if I were?"

"If you were doing it the way some people are implying."

"How?"

"I've asked you this before, and I was always satisfied with your answer. I'm going to ask you one more time, and I know you have never told me a lie. Do you want to own more of the smaller ranches to get this power, or is the Rocking W enough?"

"I can be governor without another acre of land, and no,

I am not on the receiving end of the land that's being grabbed out here. I know what's going on, but you have to trust me, I would never step on the necks of my neighbors to go to the capital. I have always been open to buying any land that's up for sale, but I don't force it.''

Lori smiled and linked her arms about his neck. He kissed her lightly and returned her smile. "Is that enough to satisfy you?"

"I love you, Carter Walker. You satisfy me always."

"Good." He grinned wickedly as he drew her closer. "What do you say to a little satisfaction of my own?"

"I say wonderful, what have you been waiting for?"

He rose, and with ease lifted her in his arms and carried her to their bed. Their lovemaking had long ago lost the frantic hurry of first love, becoming a deeper, easier thing. They were comfortable with each other, and knew everything that would please each other. Afterward they lay together in the same comfortable silence.

"Lori, what is going on with Rachel? Sometimes I don't think I understand her the way I used to."

"Sometimes, my love, I don't think you know your daughter at all. Even though she is exactly like you."

"If she were exactly like me, she wouldn't have let Cal get away."

"You mean she should have brought all that land into the Rocking W?"

"No, not that, but . . ."

"Just like that, and just like a man. Carter, why did you marry me?"

"Now, what has that to do with anything?"

"Just tell me why."

"Because I loved you the first time I saw you, and I

knew I couldn't build anything worthwhile without you."

"There were a lot of pretty girls with their caps set for you. Some with a lot of wealth behind them."

"What does that have to do with anything? None of them made me feel the way you do. Money has . . ." He paused abruptly as if a thought he could hardly recognize had just presented itself.

"Ah, so now you see. Rachel tried to tell you before. She didn't love Cal, and all the land in the world would not have made her go to him."

"What is it Rachel wants?"

"I would say she wants a man like you, someone to love her for the same reasons you chose to love. I think she feels the same about the ranch as you do and she wouldn't share it with anyone but a man she loved."

"She may have a long wait."

"Well, I'm not too sure about that."

"What are you talking about? Or should I say, who are you talking about?"

"I don't know anything for certain, but if I had to take a wild guess, I'd say Rachel is in love with a man who doesn't quite fit the mold of the others she has tamed."

"For God's sake, Lori, who?"

"Steve McKean."

Carter was as quiet as if she had struck him. He struggled to control his words before he spoke again. "Steve is a fine hand, but he hasn't got a dime to his name except what I pay him."

"He's good at his job?"

"Better than any other hand I've ever had."

"You like him?"

"As a hired hand, yes, but . . ."

"But?"

"Hell, I don't know. This has taken me off stride. How do you know anyway?"

"Rachel has told me, in passing, that she has always looked for a man exactly like her father."

"And you think this penniless, roaming—"

"Before you say any more, let's think back a few years. Back to the time you asked me to marry you. Do you remember what my father said?"

Carter considered her words in silence for a few moments, then threw back his head and laughed. "He said I would never amount to a hill of beans, and if you married me you'd live a hard and unhappy life. I think I swore I'd make you the richest woman in the territory just to aggravate the old buzzard."

"So, how can we judge Steve?"

"By God, you are right. I'll just—"

"You'll just do nothing."

"Why? I can help."

"That's the last thing you can do. I think there are problems we know nothing about."

"What kind of problems?"

"I saw them together tonight, and for a while I thought they had really found each other. They wandered away alone. Then when I saw Rachel again she had returned to the party alone, and Steve was gone altogether. Rachel wasn't the same girl all the rest of the evening."

"You think . . . If he's hurt her in any way, I'll—"

"I don't know what to think right now, and you would be wise to keep quiet and do nothing. Rachel can handle this on her own. She'll talk to me about it eventually.

Maybe then we'll know just how deep her feelings for Steve are.''

"Damn, that makes me feel kind of helpless.''

"In this case, we're both helpless. We have to let Rachel decide her own future.''

Carter drew her close to him, wrapping his arms tight about her. "God, Lori, what would I ever do without you?''

"You'd muddle through like a bull in a china shop, and come nose to nose with your daughter. I, for one, would not like to see an explosion like that.''

Carter laughed again, and soon was pursuing much more interesting thoughts.

"I don't see what a rider from the Rocking W would have to say to me.''

"You might be surprised. Can we go in the house? I'd like to see Apach.''

"You might be in for another surprise. Apach was here in the barn tonight when some of my 'friends' came visiting. I guess they didn't like the idea of someone working for me. They pounded on him pretty good.''

"Is he hurt bad?''

"No, but he sure looks like hell warmed over. Come on.'' The rifle was lowered, to Steve's relief, and Otis motioned for him to follow. It surprised Steve as much as it had Apach that Otis had brought an Indian into his home. But he realized that Otis was an honorable man and considered Apach's beating a debt he owed the Indian. It was a bridge between the two men, and Steve knew Apach was smart enough to build on it.

Inside, Apach was asleep on a narrow bed in the corner. At the sound of the door opening, he sat up and reached for the gun that lay within reach of his hand. When he saw Steve, he tried to smile, and winced when his cracked lip forbade it.

"Apach, are you all right?"

"Yeah, I think I probably look worse than I feel. I'm afraid I got careless."

"You're lucky," Otis said. "I think you were supposed to carry a message."

"Well, you're right about that. Someone doesn't want you to have any help."

"Are they that sure of you?" Steve questioned.

"I guess they have an idea I can't last too long if they drive every rider off and I can't get my cattle ready for the trail drive. I stand to lose everything."

"And who stands to gain?"

"Why should I answer questions for you?"

"Because Steve and I are here to find out about this, and to stop it," Apach said half in anger.

"You ride for the biggest place around," Carter said to Steve. "I don't see why you concern yourself with me when the place you ride for has something to gain if you let well enough alone."

"Then you think Carter Walker has the most to gain?"

"I ain't pointing the finger at someone when I can't prove it. Worst is, I like Carter, but he would have a lot to gain if he was to get hold of all this land."

"But if we put our minds to it, we might be able to prove there's another snake in the woodpile," Apach inserted.

"You have some ideas, Apach?" Steve asked.

"I'm sure I've met one of the men who came tonight, I just can't remember where. But it wasn't on the Rocking W. Maybe if I scout around, I could find out which ranch he calls home. I'd like to get my hands on him when it's just me and him."

"Mr. Quantrell, can you keep this a secret and help us? We'll find out who is behind this one way or the other."

"What if it turns out to be Carter?"

"Then so be it," Steve said. "We have to put a stop to this. People like you and Mrs. Crenshaw deserve to hold on to whatever they've honestly built."

"What do you want me to do?"

"Not much yet, but let Apach stay here. That way you have some defense in case they come again. When someone does come and make you an offer, let Apach know. He can trail a snake over a hot rock. We'll find out where they come from."

"That's all right with me." Otis smiled. "He's pretty good . . . for an Injun." Even Apach laughed. Otis had taken another step toward trust.

"I'm going to ride into town this morning," Steve said. "While I'm gone, the two of you might just ride over to the Crenshaws', and you can convince her that we're all in this together."

"Fine, we'll go as soon as it's light."

Steve left and rode slowly toward town. He had lost sleep, but was surprised to find he wasn't tired. He'd gotten one rancher to stand up, and hoped he would soon have another. If that didn't force someone out into the open, he'd find another method of pressure.

Otis made a hasty breakfast for them both while Apach washed outside. He hoped the sight of his face wouldn't frighten Mrs. Crenshaw too much.

By the time he was finished and he and Otis had eaten,

it was past dawn, and the sun was already warming the air. They rode to Jane's ranch without much conversation, each caught up in his own thoughts. It was nearing eleven before they reached Crenshaw property.

When they stopped in front of Jane's porch, it was obvious to both men that a number of repairs had been done on the place recently. When the door opened and Jane walked out, she seemed surprisingly confident for a woman alone.

She smiled at Otis, but he could read the surprise in her eyes when she looked at Apach. She had known Otis for many years, and seeing him with an Indian was a bit of a shock. She diplomatically said nothing.

"Otis, what are you doing here so early?"

"Morning, Jane." Otis smiled. "This is my new hand, Apach." He paused, then spoke more seriously. "Jane, we'd like to talk to you."

"Certainly. Step down and come in. I'll make you some coffee."

He nodded and followed Jane into the house, with Apach right behind him. Inside Otis noticed a change, but couldn't put his finger on what it was.

"Mrs. Crenshaw, is there any way you can send for Carlos and the boys?" It was Apach who asked her, and she was aware that there was a subtle urgency about him. She was also surprised that he knew Carlos. Still, there were a lot of things surprising her lately and Carlos and Otis's Indian knowing each other was the least of them. She had seen the condition of his face and registered the fact that he rode and walked stiffly. She believed she knew what had happened, but held off asking questions.

"Yes, I can send for them. Carlos has made a signal in

case I might need him. Sit down, and I'll get them."

She stepped out on the porch and lifted a piece of metal in one hand. This she clanged against another that had been hung from the porch roof. The sound echoed for a great distance. Then she came back inside.

"They should be coming in a few minutes."

In the distance, Apach could soon hear the sound of rapidly approaching horses. They stopped before the house, and the door swung open to admit Carlos, gun in hand.

His worried face broke into a smile when he recognized Apach. He called back over his shoulder. "It's all right, come on in." In seconds the two boys came to the door. That they had been frightened for their mother was obvious in the relief on their faces.

But much more was displayed there, and Apach didn't miss that either. Both boys looked from Jane to Carlos, waiting to see what he would tell them to do next.

"Carlos, me and Mr. Quantrell have to talk some things over here. Don't you think the boys—?"

"No," Carlos said at once. "The boys work like men and they have as much at stake here as the rest of us. I think they should hear whatever is said."

Both boys looked at Carlos in silence, but their looks were full of hero worship. They found seats and remained silent and attentive. Otis turned to Apach, prepared for him to do the talking. Slowly and carefully Apach began.

Rachel was exasperated with herself. She fought her longing to go to Steve and be with him no matter what the situation. Leaving him the night before had been the most difficult thing she had ever done. Before she had closed the door between them, she had almost run back and thrown herself into his arms. But she couldn't afford to do that.

She knew that Steve would never be free of whatever plagued him if he couldn't tell her the truth. She thought of the woman who had created the damage, and wondered if he still didn't love her in a perverse kind of way.

She went into the kitchen and found her mother there, busily making several pies. Lori smiled when Rachel came in. She was hoping Rachel would talk of what was bothering her. Lori longed to find out what had happened between her and Steve, and had to bite her lip to keep from asking.

"Morning, Mother."

"Good morning, dear. Did you sleep well?"

"Actually, I didn't sleep much at all."

"Oh? Something wrong, or were you just keyed up after all the festivities last night?"

"A little of both, I suppose."

"Usually you're out of the house by this time. Rachel, how long have you known about Cal and Yvonne?"

"Not for very long. Why?"

"I just wondered. It didn't seem to upset you at all."

"Actually, I couldn't be happier," Rachel laughed. "It will keep you and Dad off my back about marrying Cal. Was Dad very upset?"

"No. After the first shock, and seeing your response, or lack of it, he came around. Rachel, he just wants you to be happy."

"Happy," Rachel said. "I wonder what that really means."

"My, we are philosophical today. What's wrong?"

"Oh, Mother, I have a feeling that just about everything is wrong."

"Do you want to tell me?"

"I wouldn't know how."

"Why not begin by telling me what happened between you and Steve McKean?" Lori said.

Rachel was silent for so long, Lori thought she might have gone too far. She had tried never to interfere in Rachel's private thoughts, and Rachel had always been open and honest with her. This was the first time she had stepped over the boundary.

"Everything, and nothing."

"That makes no sense at all."

"I know."

Lori walked to Rachel and laid her hand against her daughter's cheek. She smiled. "Do you love him?"

Rachel held her mother's gaze for a silent moment. "Yes, I do. Will that upset you and Dad?"

"Good heavens, child. Why would it upset us? It's your choices that are important here, not ours. Your father and I want to see you happy."

"What do you think about Steve?"

"I like him," Lori said at once. In fact, she spoke so quickly, Rachel had to laugh.

"Well, I guess there's nothing wishy-washy about you. But I don't think it's going to be so easy with Dad."

"You might be surprised. Why don't you just tell him?"

"I can't."

"Why?"

"Because I can't even tell Steve."

"That makes no sense at all. I thought—"

"You thought wrong. Steve is running away from something, and he won't even talk to me about it. I think . . . there was another woman, and I think she might have broken his heart, and he can't get her out of his mind. I . . . I'm afraid he still feels something for her, and he can't let go. Mother, does Dad know that Steve was in prison once?''

''Good Lord! No, I'm sure he doesn't. Did Steve tell you this?''

''Yes, why?''

''It seems like it would be a very difficult thing to confide in someone unless you cared about that person.''

''I hadn't thought of it that way.''

''Consider how you would feel. Why was he in prison?''

Reluctantly, Rachel answered, ''For killing a man.''

''Oh, Rachel.''

''I just can't see Steve committing murder.''

''Nor can I. I think you are right. Judgment shouldn't be made unless we know the whole story. Did he tell you why he did such a thing?''

''Mother, that's the problem that stands between us. He won't talk to me, and I know . . . I know in my heart there are secrets, maybe terrible secrets, he just won't talk about. How can I be with him if he won't let me inside, and trust me with the truth?''

''I think you are right, Rachel. But maybe it is difficult for him to talk about. Maybe you need to give him time.''

''I'm afraid,'' Rachel said softly. This alone was a surprise to Lori. She had never known Rachel to be as vulnerable as she was now. It hurt her that she couldn't help.

''Afraid of what, Rachel?'' Yvonne's voice startled both Lori and Rachel. Yvonne came into the room and paused by Rachel. ''Afraid of what?'' she repeated. ''I don't know this Rachel. What happened last night?''

Rachel looked at Yvonne in surprise.

"Oh, I saw you with Steve," Yvonne explained. "I think it's wonderful. What should you be afraid of?"

"It's not as simple as you think. I just wish it were."

"Oh, fiddle. Come and tell me what's going on."

Rachel told Yvonne her dilemma, and Yvonne listened in total silence, and without displaying her thoughts. When Rachel was finished, Yvonne sighed.

"Yes, there is only one thing to consider."

"One thing?" Rachel protested.

"Yes, one thing. You, and how you feel. Steve has been here for some time. Your father has learned to trust him, and if I'm not mistaken, so have all the other hands on the ranch. So the question is really how much you trust him."

"There . . . there was another woman, and I don't think he can forget her."

"Is that all? Just a little bit of jealousy? You can handle that. Wipe that other woman right out of his thoughts."

"I suppose you know just how to do that," Rachel said sarcastically.

Yvonne laughed a wicked laugh. "If you don't know, then you're not as smart as I always thought you were."

"Yvonne!"

It wasn't Lori who was shocked. Silently she was grateful to Yvonne for saying something she wanted to say herself.

"Come on, let's go into town and buy something extravagant. It's always what I do if I'm depressed. You'd be surprised what a new hat can do for your spirits. Come on, Rachel. I won't take no for an answer."

"All right, all right. Let's go."

When the two girls left, Lori sat and quietly gave thanks

for Yvonne's presence. If anyone could open Rachel's eyes, it would be her outgoing friend.

Steve reached town by early morning and went at once to the town hall. He wanted to find out how the Parker ranch had changed hands without anyone knowing who the real owner was. Someone's name had to be on the deed.

Inside it was cooler and he moved slowly, savoring the change from the heat outside. When he came to the front desk, a short, bald man with a round, almost cherubic face looked up.

"Is there something I can do for you, sir?"

"Yes, I heard there was a small ranch for sale in the valley, and I thought to inquire what the price was."

The man's eyes skimmed over Steve. His gaze said he was certain Steve couldn't afford whatever the price was.

"And what ranch is that? I haven't heard of anything for sale lately."

"The name was Parker, and I think the brand was the Lazy P."

There was a flicker of something in the man's eyes, but it was so elusive that Steve couldn't define it.

"Hmm, the Lazy P. If I'm not mistaken, and I hardly ever am about the records here, I think that ranch was sold some time ago."

"I see. Can you tell me who bought it?"

"I'm afraid not." The man made no effort to go to the records.

"Someone in the valley bought it?"

"I'm afraid, unless you have some business with the owners, that that is private business, and I cannot let the records be opened by just any passing cowboy."

"I see," Steve said. The man's smile was short-lived when Steve reached across the desk, grasped a handful of his shirt and dragged him halfway across. "I've asked you politely, and I'm sure you wouldn't want to aggravate me. Who owns the Lazy P now?"

The man wheezed through clenched teeth. His face was wet with sweat, and Steve could feel him tremble. "You can't do this! It's against the law!"

"I'm doing it. And I'm afraid if you don't answer me, I might just see how well you can bounce."

"No one! No one! It's being held by Robert Raymond and Thaddius Blake for someone else. I don't know who, I swear. It will change hands one day soon."

"How did the funds change hands?"

"There were no funds, it was a private agreement."

"I'll bet it was." Steve released him, gave him a half salute with two fingers, and left. Outside, he found the first alley and stepped inside to watch. Within minutes the clerk came out of the town hall, looked around, then skittered across the street. Directly to the bank.

"Well, that answers one question." He was about to step out into the street when he saw Rachel and Yvonne walk down the sidewalk and go into the dress shop.

Rachel wasn't really interested in hats, dresses, or anything else for that matter. Her mind kept going to Steve, and what Yvonne and her mother had said. What did she really believe? she asked herself.

That Steve killed a man and spent time in prison for it? Yes, she believed that, just as she believed there was a reason for it that she didn't know. That Steve had loved and could not forget another woman? Yes, she believed that too. She had to be honest with herself. The other woman, and the fact that he wouldn't talk about her, hurt worse than anything else.

She wanted him, and she would not lie to herself about that. But it was just as obvious that he was turning his back on all they could share just to keep from revealing . . . something . . . something . . . what?

"Rachel. Look!" Yvonne held up a parasol, white with pink flowers. "Isn't it darling?"

"Yes, I could just see myself riding out to roundup carrying that over my head."

"Maybe you won't always want to ride out to roundup," Yvonne laughed. "You might find an interest you never knew you had."

"I don't think there's a good chance of that in the near future."

"One never knows what the good Lord has planned for us."

"Yvonne, does anything ever dampen your enthusiasm?"

"Yes, you're coming close to it. Now, I insist. You have frowned enough, and I demand that you smile for the rest of the afternoon."

"All right, I agree. If you'll agree to stop this nonsense shopping. Let's go to the mercantile. I need some new things."

"With a smile?"

"With a smile," Rachel agreed. The two started toward the door.

Yvonne froze, and Rachel, a step behind her, could not see why. She looked over Yvonne's shoulder, and could clearly see Steve's broad-shouldered form . . . his, and the woman's he was talking to.

Forever

* * *

Steve had decided at once to try to get Rachel alone some-how and talk to her. He knew there was a chasm between them, just as he knew he was helpless to close the distance until he'd fulfilled his promise to Wade. He would not be dragged off to prison with Rachel looking on. It would be the final straw that would break him.

Besides this, he now felt he was making progress, and might have some results for Wade the next time they met.

He crossed the street to the dress shop, and was about to open the door when a sweet, and very familiar, voice came from behind him.

"Steve."

For a minute, he could not turn around. Intense sensa-tions curled up from the depths of him. Anger, pain, a crav-ing for vengeance.

But then reason and a million questions followed. Ann was here, and he wondered if her father could be far behind. If Judge Graham was here, then why?

He turned slowly and looked into the cornflower blue of her eyes. Eyes that could have melted his soul at one time. Now, to his delight, he felt nothing. Nothing but suspicion.

"Ann." He could hear the coldness in his voice. "What is the belle of Colorado doing in a place like Chambers-burg?"

"I might ask you the same thing." Her voice was the same mellow purr he remembered so well. "The last time—"

"Yes, the last time you saw me was when you testified at my trial."

"I spoke only the truth. I didn't think . . ."

265.

She sounded so hurt, so innocent. But he again felt nothing. Could he finally put her and her traitorous ways out of his life? Had Rachel finally wiped out the memories? She stepped closer, and the familiar scent of her perfume came to him. But this time it elicited only memories of pain and cruelty.

Ann knew she would have to maneuver carefully to bring Steve to heel again. He was no longer the young fool he had been, and she intended to be careful. She would let him vent his disappointment, but in the end she meant to bring him around. She was just laying her hand gently on his when another voice came from behind them.

"Hello, Steve." The voice dripped honey and was so unlike Rachel's that he had to turn to see if he was mistaken. But he wasn't. Rachel and Yvonne stood in the doorway, their eyes on Ann. "What are you doing in town? And where did you disappear to after the party?"

Chapter Fourteen

Steve was momentarily without words. His mind was caught up in controlling the rage he'd first felt when he had recognized Ann.

He started to speak, but Rachel beat him to it.

"Steve." Her voice was almost sultry. "You haven't introduced us."

"I'm sorry," he said, forcing himself to speak the correct words. "Ann Graham, Rachel Walker and Yvonne Avery. Rachel and her parents own the Rocking W."

"Yes"—Rachel smiled—"Steve has worked for me since he arrived in Chambersburg."

"How interesting," Ann replied. "I can remember when Steve said he would never work for someone else." She looked up at Steve. "I see you've changed your mind."

"I've changed my mind about a lot of things. But if

you're wondering whether Rachel knows about my past, the answer is yes.''

"What a thing to say! Did you imagine I intended—''

"Yes, I imagined just that. Tell me, Ann, is your father here?''

"He had some business here, and I thought the trip might be interesting. This is a quaint little town. Rather primitive, though, isn't it?''

"It suits me,'' Steve said bluntly.

Both Rachel and Yvonne could sense an undercurrent beneath the exchange. It was not difficult for Rachel to surmise that Ann Graham had something to do with Steve's past. Was she . . . ? The thought shook her for a minute.

She looked closely at Ann. She was so beautiful it was easy to see why Steve had found her so enchanting. Visions Rachel didn't want to see flickered through her mind. Steve in Ann's arms. Making love to Ann as he had to her. The thought was so bitter that she pushed it from her mind with angry force. She didn't want to feel the emotions that swept over her, nor did she want to acknowledge the brutal pang of jealousy.

She guessed that this woman had had something to do with sending Steve to prison, and she could not understand Steve's polite responses. Had he really gotten over her? Was last night . . . she shook the thought away.

She had no idea that Steve was already plotting how to find out just why Judge Graham had come to Chambersburg.

Something had drawn him here, and Steve wanted to know what it was. He was pleased that the emotions he had expected did not come. None of the old hunger and obsession with Ann's beauty. None of the old jealousy that had once put a gun in his hand at the wrong time.

"Steve, unless you have business in town, I think it's time for us to go back to the ranch," Rachel said.

"Actually, I do have some business in town and it has been a long time since I've seen Ann." Ann looked at him with surprise flickering in her eyes, but it was soon concealed. "I think, if you don't mind, Ann, that I'd like to catch up on old times."

Ann was completely unprepared for this. She had thought it might be fun to seduce Steve again. She had not taken into consideration that this Steve was a different man than the one who had once fallen under her spell. She smiled at Rachel with a smile that was filled with satisfaction. Her conceit would not let her think that a woman like Rachel could take any man from her if she wanted to keep him.

Rachel felt something twist deep inside her, but she would have died before she'd let Ann Graham, or Steve, see it. But Steve could read her eyes, and he hated the idea that he'd hurt her. Still, this was one chance he had to take.

He watched pride burn in Rachel's eyes, saw the lift of her chin, and realized just how much she had come to mean to him. How much he had come to love her. If the end justified the means, he was doing the right thing. He just hoped he would be able to reach Rachel once he learned the truth.

"All right, just remember, you're working for the Rocking W. Don't waste our time." Rachel spun about and walked away, but Yvonne stood for a minute, watching Steve's face as he followed Rachel's progress across the street. When Steve became conscious of her gaze, he turned to look at her.

She smiled. "I'm sure I'll see you later, Steve. In the

meantime, be careful.'' Ignoring Ann's sharp look, she turned and followed Rachel.

When Steve turned to face Ann, his expression was closed to her, and all she saw was the half-smile on his face. A smile that did not reach his eyes.

"Would you like to go to the restaurant and talk over coffee, or"—he held her gaze—"someplace more private?"

"Someplace more private," Ann responded quickly. "Come back to my hotel room with me." This was going to prove easier than she had expected. She might just enjoy herself for a while, before she reported to her father about meeting Steve. She knew that her father would suspect that Steve's presence in Chambersburg was not coincidental.

"All right."

They walked together to the hotel and said little until Ann closed the door to her room behind them. Ann never did care what anyone thought of her activities, but Steve had been amused at the clerk's face when they passed him and went upstairs together. News of their rendezvous was already making the rounds, and would, most likely, reach the Rocking W before he did. He was digging a grave for himself with Rachel, but he had to have some answers.

Ann stood with her back to him, removing her hat. He knew she was considering the situation. He could almost hear her calculating mind at work. Finally she turned to him.

"Steve, will you let me explain about . . . about that terrible day in court?"

"I don't see what good rehashing all that will do. I had hoped to talk of more pleasant things."

"But I think you blame me, and maybe hate me a little.

I was frightened, and my father and that lawyer—''

"I know, Ann." His voice was smooth and cool as if it no longer mattered. "You must have been confused."

"Yes, yes. That's right. I was confused. Questions and questions and questions, until my poor head was swirling. I . . . I guess I said what they wanted to hear and they twisted what I said."

Oh, she was so cold and so clever, he thought. All the blame was going to be someone else's, as it usually was with Ann. He wondered more and more how he could have ever thought he loved her. And why he had let her poison his mind.

"As I said, Ann, let's not talk of things past." Or I might just strangle you right here, he added mentally. "I'm surprised to see you here. You said your father had some business in town?"

"No, not really. He's just visiting some old friends."

"Oh, who?"

"Some lawyer and a banker he's known for a number of years."

He wondered if Nathan might just be visiting either Robert Raymond or Thaddius Blake. He would need more than that, but it was a beginning.

"He might be a little surprised to find me here," Steve suggested.

"Yes, I suppose he will. I must say I was shocked."

Steve remembered how she had reacted when he had turned to look at her, and realized that shock was not what she had been feeling. She had known he would be there, and if she had known, so had Nathan.

That meant only one thing. Nathan had come because he knew what was happening here, probably wanted or had some connection to it. No doubt, he wanted to make sure Steve didn't interfere in his plans.

Steve knew better than to put anything past Nathan or his daughter, and he certainly knew better than to fall into the depths of those beautiful cornflower blue eyes and drown as he had once before.

Instead, he recalled Rachel's green eyes, languid with passion, and her soft smile and tender touch. He would cling to those memories.

Ann came to him and put both hands on his folded arms. When she looked up into his eyes it was with innocence and gentleness, but it was a look he remembered well. It meant Ann wanted something. He could remember when he'd been happy to try to fulfill whatever wish or dream would make Ann smile. Now he remembered. He remembered a smile, not Ann's but Rachel's, open and honest. She'd had no guile and had asked for nothing.

"I know you must blame me, possibly even hate me, but try to understand. I felt so alone when they took you. My father kept saying over and over that your guilt was proven, that I had to say what he wanted me to say. They kept pushing and pushing until I didn't know what I was doing. Finally I couldn't fight him and that terrible lawyer any longer." She saw what she thought was uncertainty in Steve's eyes. Would he believe her? "I had to tell them the truth, but they had a way of twisting it until I was confused. I said what they wanted me to say. Oh, Steve, I have regretted it from that day on, but there was little I could do. Can you understand? Can you see how terrible it was for me too? Can you forget?" Her eyes welled with tears, and if he hadn't known how well she could use those tears, he might have believed her.

He continued looking at her, washing himself clean of the need to hold onto the anger that had been his companion for so long. He didn't need it anymore. He felt nothing, nothing but a sense of release, and it brought a deep peace that flowed through him with a welcome warmth.

"I don't think your father would approve of our renewing our . . . friendship. Not after what has happened. He never did relish my being part of his life."

"I don't care what my father thinks. I wish all that happened before had never been."

"So do I," Steve replied. How badly he wanted to grasp her and tell her about the hell where she had helped send him. But there was no point in doing that. He knew it wouldn't register with her. Darkness and ugliness were never admitted in Ann Graham's life.

"Does your father know any of the ranchers around here?"

"I don't know. He never spoke of any on our trip here." She put her arms about his neck and pressed her body intimately to his. "What does it matter? Here and now there is no reason to speak of others."

As gently as he could without making her aware of his distaste, he put his hands at her waist and held her away from him. "I don't think this is the time or the place. What if your father should come to the door? And the people of this town certainly enjoy gossip. If your father has business here, it might make things a bit uncomfortable."

Ann sighed, and stood on tiptoe to kiss him lightly. "I guess you're right. Besides, I think I should explain your presence here to my father. But . . . there will be a time . . . soon?"

"You can trust me, Ann. There will come a time for me

to make things clear to your father about us. In fact, we'll make it clear to the whole town."

"You've forgiven me," she said, enjoying the fact that it had been so easy to capture Steve again.

"I've forgotten all about it," Steve replied honestly. For now, it was easy to wipe every memory of every kiss and touch they'd shared from his heart. "Ann, I have to go now. As my boss reminded me, I can't be lingering on her time."

"I don't understand why you would let a creature like that run your life. She's so . . . so boyish. Doesn't she know women wear dresses? I imagine she rides with the rest of the men. I wonder what other things about her presence they enjoy."

Steve felt a wave of rage so deep it took all he could do to contain it. There would be time to express his fury later. But for now, he wanted to find out what her father was doing, and who he was doing it with. He smiled through clenched teeth and realized he had to get away from Ann soon, or he would say and do something that would ruin everything.

"Maybe we can get together soon, but it would be a good thing to keep it from your father. You could meet me somewhere."

"Anywhere, just tell me."

"Can I leave you a note somewhere?"

"Just leave it at the front desk."

Steve didn't like that idea, because the word would surely spread. "How about I slip it under your door?"

"All right. Make it soon, Steve. You have no idea how much I've missed you."

This was something Steve didn't believe for a minute.

He had a suspicion the cell door had not locked behind him before Ann had found solace for her loneliness in someone else's arms.

"It will be soon," Steve replied. He moved her away from him again and walked to the door. There he turned to look at her, and she smiled a seductive smile.

For the first time Steve thanked all the powers that be for his escape from her. Even though he'd paid for the escape with three horrible years in Yuma. With Ann, he realized now, he would have had a lifetime of misery.

When Steve closed the door behind him, he had already decided to get to Rachel as fast as he could. Rachel . . . Rachel, his heart sang her name. He had exorcised the past, and now he was determined he would not let her slip from his life.

Steve had hardly left Ann's room before she grabbed her cloak and left as well. She knew where to find her father, and she felt it would be a good thing to find out what he had planned for Steve, and to make sure his plans did not ruin hers.

She found him in Thaddius Blake's office with a third man. She was introduced and offered a seat, but she listened to the end of the conversation before she spoke.

"And so, Thaddius—" Nathan was smiling at Thaddius's darkened countenance. "I think being part of your little game could silence what I know about your past."

"This is blackmail."

"Yes, of course. A tactic you are well used to. Come, man, I have only a wish to help in your little scheme."

"And share the profits."

"Of course. But there will be more than enough profit

if you add my expertise to your plan. Besides, I'll take a small profit if I can have one thing I want."

"Which is?"

"Steve McKean sent back to prison."

"I guess we have a bargain."

"Good."

Thaddius turned to Ann. "I'm afraid your father and I haven't finished our business, but we could continue it over lunch tomorrow."

"There are no deals my father is involved in that do not concern me. Don't be under the illusion that I don't know where our profit comes from. Now, what is going on?"

For a moment Thaddius was taken aback. Nathan chuckled. "Ann has, uh, shall I say, developed some of our most rewarding prospects, and I know she will be as beneficial to whatever you plan as I will."

Robert smiled. Here was a woman he could admire. He looked deep into her eyes, and felt there could be much more to their relationship than monetary profit. Yes, Ann Graham might prove very interesting.

Ann smiled. She knew the look well, and her interest flared. Robert was a handsome man. He was tall, and his hair was thick and silver, although he didn't look a day over forty. He was tanned and smiled easily. His broad shoulders fit snugly in the best broadcloth, and she could see he was used to money and what it could buy. She licked her lips . . . she placed Steve aside as someone to enjoy, while she contemplated how to get control of Robert.

"You haven't told me how you found out about us, Nathan. What brought you here?"

"I didn't know about you, Robert, until I learned that an old enemy had been brought here by a U.S. marshal. I felt''—Nathan grinned—''that you might like to know about him . . . and might like to tell me just what could have drawn the marshal's interest around to you.''

''And the enemy is?''

''Steve McKean.''

''Ah, yes, the Steve McKean you want to handle personally.''

''You know the name, don't you?''

''Yes, I do. We've been watching him. He is much too smart, and much too nosy. It has now become necessary for us to move against some of our most difficult ranchers because of him.''

''It's not just him. He has three friends he brought with him. I have a feeling they might be on your trail.''

''Then we will just have to eliminate them, and speed up our plans so the marshal will be ineffectual.''

''Perhaps, if you tell me your plans, I can be of some help.''

Thaddius proceeded to inform them of what was planned and how far along those plans were.

''Why do you proceed so delicately?'' Ann asked. ''Why not burn the ranchers out or send enough force to make them submit? I think you are being too careful, considering how much is at stake.''

''My colleagues can't seem to muster the same . . . intensity, Miss Graham, and I do not have the benefit of a judge's power to push any harder.''

''We'll have to see about that,'' Nathan said.

''In the meantime, what is your next step?'' Ann asked.

''We have set the men to attack, and finally rid us of Mr. Quantrell. Once the others see that we are no longer playing a game with them, they'll surrender. Quantrell and

Jane Crenshaw are the only two who will give us trouble.''

"But from what I've heard, they aren't the biggest ranches in the territory. How do you plan to get to the other two?''

"Water.''

"Water?''

"The water that serves the two big ranches originates on Quantrell land. We intend to dam that river and change its course. This will effectively destroy their ranches. Once they have given in and sold to us, we will open the dam. We will also have control of the largest acreage in the territory. Statehood will see us in power. Completely.''

"When do you burn the Crenshaws out?''

"It's only her, one man, and her two small boys. It won't be a problem to get them out of our hair. My men intend to attack tonight.''

"Excellent.''

"Now, I think we had better ride out and introduce you to the two men who are aiding me in this.''

Robert stood and came around the desk to stand before Ann. "Would you like to ride along?'' His words had a deeper meaning than was obvious, and Ann didn't miss it.

"I would be delighted.'' She rose and they left the office together.

Rachel was silent, so silent Yvonne could have screamed, for she felt the tension and anger humming through her.

"It might be better if you cussed him out . . . or her.''

"I could kill him,'' Rachel grated.

"Oh? I have a feeling it would have been better to scratch her eyes out. There was more to his going with her than we knew.''

"She was so . . . so sure of him, and he just . . . God, I hate him."

"Rachel, don't be foolish. You're in love with the man, and you're about as jealous as you can be."

"I thought you were on my side," Rachel complained.

"I am, and I don't want to see you lose something you want just because you can't make use of your jealousy."

"Make use?"

"Rachel, this girl is a spider, and I think Steve is well aware of it."

"Then why would he go with her?"

"I don't know. But I watched his eyes when you walked away, and if his heart wasn't following you, I'll eat my hat. I would say the man has a motive we don't know anything about . . . or do you?"

"I . . . I know it was a woman whose testimony helped put him in prison. Yuma Prison to be exact. For killing a man. He said . . . he said it was self-defense."

"Oh my, Yuma Prison. I've heard about it. It must have been terrible. Rachel," Yvonne said hesitantly, "perhaps you had better reconsider your . . . attachment to Steve."

"Reconsider? Why?"

"Do you really know enough about why he was in prison? Do . . . do you trust him enough?"

"Yvonne, you either trust or you don't. Either way it has to be a commitment. I've thought about it, and I've watched and listened to Steve and made my own decision. I trust him, and I believe him."

"But—"

"If I'm making a mistake, well then, I guess I'm the one who has to pay for it."

Yvonne became quiet for a moment, for she could see

Rachel was firm and wasn't about to change her mind.

Rachel's thoughts at that moment would have made Steve feel much better. She had always had a feeling there was more to Steve than she knew, that he was not just a roaming rider but a man with some shadow pursuing him. She had to find out for certain, and the only way to do that was to ask Steve outright.

She would no longer deny that her feelings for Steve could not be argued away; nor would anger and jealousy dissipate them. Yvonne was right. She did love Steve, and she was not about to let a beautiful specter from the past take him from her. She would fight . . . any way she could.

By the time dinner was over, Rachel was on pins and needles. There had been no sign of Steve, and she was envisioning things that were driving her to distraction.

Carter and Lori had been invited to dinner at a nearby ranch, and Cal had come for Yvonne just after Rachel and Yvonne had shared a light meal. Now Rachel was alone with the plaguing thoughts that refused to go away.

She wanted him to come, and she didn't. She wanted to hear what he would say, and she didn't. She was so nervous that when she heard a knock on the door, she almost jumped out of her skin.

Steve had tied his horse near the stable. All the way back to the ranch he had considered what he would say to Rachel. He knew the truth was the best, but he wondered if he was going to be able to tell her before she shut the door in his face.

He was just about to walk to the house when he heard Mikah's voice behind him.

"Steve, what you doin' out here? I thought you were up at the camp."

"I came here from town. I have a lot of news to tell you, Mikah."

"Sure"—Mikah grinned—"and you was on your way into the house to tell me."

Steve had to smile. "I have to talk to Rachel."

"Well, you're in luck. The lady is home alone."

"Where is everyone?"

"Mr. Walker and his wife are over to the neighbors. Miss Yvonne, she's gone out courtin' with Cal Davis. So, I guess you came at the right time."

"Yes, I guess I did," Steve replied. But he didn't move, just stood considering the house for a while, until Mikah knew that something had drastically changed.

"What's eatin' you, Steve?"

"Damned if I know. I should go and meet Carlos and Apach at Jane Crenshaw's."

"Well, you're sure a long ride from there."

"Mikah, truth is, I'm scared to death and I don't exactly know what to do about it."

"I don't think I heard you right."

"You heard. I need to talk to Rachel."

"Now your walkin' the right path."

"Yeah, but she might just take a shot at me before I get a chance to say what I have to say."

"Must be a damn good reason for that. Miss Rachel strikes me as a pretty level-headed girl. What'd you do?"

"It's a long story."

"Well, if you ain't going to tell me, maybe you'd better get up on that porch and tell her," Mikah said patiently.

"I guess I'd better." Steve started to walk away.

"Steve?" He turned to look at Mikah. "We all don't get second chances in this life. If you got one, maybe you'd better do whatever it takes to hang on to it. That Miss Rachel, she's one fine girl. I think she could wipe out old memories real easy, given half the chance."

"I won't argue with you on that, Mikah, but it's me that needs the chance."

"Good luck."

"When I come out, ride with me to Mrs. Crenshaw's. I have some news, and I think it would be best if we were all together when I say it."

"I'll ride with you"—Mikah grinned—"long as you come out of there before morning."

"Just get ready," Steve replied. Again he turned toward the house. He was still struggling for words, but nothing seemed adequate. He walked up on the porch, removed his hat and knocked.

When the door opened, whatever words he was about to say died on his lips. She stood framed in the golden lamplight behind her. Her hair was loose and fell about her in a thick, glorious mass. She wore a soft gown of green, the exact color of her eyes.

It was as if she had reached out somehow and touched him. He could feel the gentle caress of her hands, and the silken softness of her skin. God, how much he wanted her.

"Steve." Even her voice wrapped itself about him and reached a place he had thought could never be reached again.

"Rachel, I have to talk to you. Don't slam the door until you give me a chance to explain."

"I had no intention of shutting the door. Come in. I have to talk to you, too." She turned and walked back into the house, and for a minute Steve was so surprised he didn't follow. Then he moved quickly. If she was in a mood to listen and talk to him, maybe he could make her understand. When he closed the door, he turned to find her waiting for him, her hands folded before her.

Rachel was thinking about how right she thought Yvonne was, and how wonderfully handsome Steve was. She wasn't going to let some wicked creature from Steve's past take him from her, and it didn't matter how beautiful she was. Rachel meant to use everything in her power to keep Steve here where she thought he belonged.

"Do you want to go first, or do you want me to?" she asked.

"I'd better," he replied. "I want to get this cleared up and I want to get the truth out in the open."

"The truth?" Rachel sounded frightened, and she was. She was certain Steve meant to tell her that he was leaving.

"Yes, the truth. Let me start from the beginning. I'm not here by accident, and I'm not just passing through. I've been sent here by the marshal of this territory to find out what and who is behind the attempt to grab all the land here.

"It's true I was in Yuma Prison, and it was for murder. It was Ann's father, Judge Graham, who sent me there, and it was Ann who testified against me at my sham of a trial."

"And you could still love her!" Rachel said in shock.

"Love her? The last person in the world I love is Ann."

"Then I don't understand."

Quick as he could, while he was struggling to keep from grabbing her up in his arms, he explained. She stood in silence as he finished his explanation.

"Rachel, for God's sake, say something. I know I've told

you a pack of lies, but I couldn't do anything about it. I didn't plan on falling in love with you and wanting to stay so bad I could taste it. I thought it would be a simple way to gain my freedom.''

"My father?"

"I honestly don't know. I hope . . . hell, I want to prove he's innocent. If he is, he has nothing to worry about.''

"What did you go with her for?"

"With Ann? Because her father is in town with her. I'm guessing he's found out what is going on here and wants to be part of it . . . or he knows I'm here and he wants to finish what he started. Maybe it's both. I had to find out for sure. I needed to find out from her what he was doing here, and who he was meeting.''

"Did you get a name?"

"Not directly from her. Do you know Thaddius Blake pretty well?"

"Thaddius Blake . . . the banker?"

"Yes. Him and a lawyer named Robert Raymond. I have a feeling there's one or more ranchers in this with them, and I'm just as sure that they're expendable when this is over.''

"Are you finished?"

"No, I'm not. Rachel, I love you, and I don't want to lose you. I made a big mistake three years ago, and I kind of closed myself off from feeling anything for anyone. I remember the first night, when you said you were sorry. Now, I know what you were sorry for. I was closed in a cell of my own making, and you had the key to unlock it. I'll beg if I have to, I'll do anything, but I don't want to lose you.''

"Now are you finished?"

"Yes, I guess I am."

"Then it's time for me to say something."

Steve steeled himself to hear her tell him to leave her house, her ranch and her life. He was prepared to do battle.

"When you first came here, I thought you were running from something. I didn't want to get near you because I was afraid."

"Afraid? Of me?"

"No, afraid of myself. I fought the way I felt for you because I couldn't find a way to handle it. Then . . . that night . . . the night we were together, I realized I was running from myself."

She stepped closer to him, and his senses took in everything about her, from the soft, vulnerable look in her eyes to the scent of her perfume.

"I love you too, Steve McKean. I think I have from the first moment we met. Now I'll tell you how I feel about your Ann Graham. I think she's the biggest fool in the world. I wouldn't have given you up for every ranch in your state. I meant to come after you if you hadn't come here tonight. I meant to fight those bad memories with everything I had."

Steve was finding it hard to believe what he was hearing. His heart was pounding as if he'd run for miles, and he could feel every nerve begin to sing. She loved him! The battle was over. He must have said her name, for she moved willingly into his arms when he reached for her.

Her mouth was soft, giving and warm as he tasted it deeply. He wanted to drown in her, in the feelings that flooded his whole being. A raging hunger filled him, and he knew it would never go away. If they shared a million years, he would still need her love as he did now.

Rachel knew she had been right, that Yvonne and her mother had been right. She had wanted that elusive thing that her mother and father shared, and now she knew the name to put to it. Steve, Steve! Her heart filled with his name and his strength. She knew this would be forever.

Steve knew he had to think, but logical thought escaped him completely when he enclosed her in his arms and felt her pressed against him, leaning into him as if she would become part of him.

Her mouth was ripe with passion. Muttering promises and pleas, he pressed his lips to the pulse at her throat, and heard the thunder that matched his erratic heartbeat.

When she was pressed against him like this there was no past, no future, only now. Now would be enough to last for a lifetime. A lifetime he hoped they would share.

With a little moan, she clung to him, giving as much as she was taking, and she was taking all, for Steve had never felt as madly in need of anything as did now. He held her away from him for a moment. But the moment was too long for her. She smiled up into his eyes with a look that spoke what his heart was feeling.

Chapter Fifteen

Rachel wanted to be lost in that soft velvet darkness he had first taken her to. Just to know he wanted her in the same way was exciting. To know that he loved her was glory. Words, there were so many words she wanted to say. But they would have to wait, for there was an overriding need that called to be satisfied. As she felt her bones melting, she drew him with her to her room.

Quickly, quickly. Neither spoke but each knew the other's mind. Hurry. Just to feel one another's flesh. Clothes tangled and untangled, then were discarded. Oh, the sweetness that came only from a touch.

Now they were shadows on the bed, and it was their passion that had substance and form. They were both driven by the need to take, and take hungrily, all that could be found between man and woman.

Damp skin, thundering pulses, breathless moans. For

both of them it was this moment, the heady present, that mattered. Yesterday and tomorrow were forgotten.

He knew he was rough, but all his control had vanished. Heat seemed to pour out of her, drawing him deeper and deeper into his own passion. Her body was sleek, smooth and agile.

His lips brushed over her, running low on her stomach with hungry kisses. She arched, stunned and only more desperate at the play of his tongue. He was relentless as she shuddered and her nails dug into his shoulders.

Wave after wave of molten pleasure swept her, but he continued the sweet torment as if he would keep her, them both, on the very edge of fulfillment. There couldn't be so much. But even as that thought raced through her mind there was more, and still more. She pulsed with energy, and as passion poured out of her it was replenished.

"Oh, God, Rachel. You can't know how much I need you."

"I do know, I do. I need you too." She gasped out his name as the thunderous release conquered them both.

The room was semidark, and Steve had no idea of the time. They were snuggled close in Rachel's bed, naked and warm. He wished this moment had found them in their own home where they could remain like careless children and enjoy this moment to the fullest, making love again, saturating themselves with each other.

But it couldn't be. Carter and Lori might come home at any time. And, he thought, there were things that had to be completed before he and Rachel could reach for their own happiness.

He grimaced to himself at the thoughts that must be going through Mikah's mind. Rachel must have sensed it, for she stirred and turned in his arms. Looking up at him, Rachel savored the knowledge that one day soon he would belong to her, and moments like this would not have to end.

She thought of the beautiful Ann with a kind of pity. Ann had seemed so in control, but now Rachel knew that Ann no longer had any control over Steve at all, and all her wiles would never bring him back. Ann was the loser.

Steve raised himself on one elbow and looked down on her. With a deep sigh, she lifted a hand languorously and brushed his hair back from his forehead. He took her hand and pressed a kiss in the palm of it, and then kissed her wrist.

"I love you, Rachel. Have I mentioned that before?"

"I shall never get tired of hearing you say it."

"Spend the rest of your life with me, love, and I'll say it often enough to make you tire of it."

"I doubt that. Is what I just heard a proposal?"

"It most certainly was, and I think I might just keep you here until I can make up your mind."

"Such a threat. I might call your bluff."

"I would, but I'm afraid if your father comes home before I'm out of here, he might grab his shotgun and do me in before I can explain my honorable intentions."

"Then, to protect you, I accept your proposal. And now I think we'd better get out of this bed."

"I can't seem to move." He laughed as he gathered her closer and kissed her deeply. "Rachel, this is like a miracle. I never thought I would love again."

"I know. But this is just the beginning for us. I want years and years with you to convince you our love will grow for a lifetime."

"A lifetime," he said. "I can remember a few months ago, when I thought there wouldn't even be a tomorrow let alone a lifetime."

"Then," she said softly, "give me the time to show you." She drew his head down to her and kissed him with enough promise to make his head swim.

It couldn't be possible that he could be so hungry for her so soon after they had shared such hot passion, but he was. At least this time the urgency had been mellowed. They made love with a soft and gentle fulfillment that could have made him weep. He had found a haven, a haven that could withstand anything the world had to offer.

Only after they were sated did they acknowledge that it was dangerous for them to linger any longer. Reluctantly they rose, found and untangled their clothes and dressed. It was then that he explained he had to go to Jane's ranch as soon as he could.

"I intend to go with you."

"Rachel—"

"Don't say it, Steve. I know my father isn't guilty, and from what you have said, I don't think you believe he is. I want to be there when the truth is discovered."

He couldn't deny she had every right to be with him if he found any answers at all, but he didn't want her hurt. She knew what he was thinking.

"It's all right, Steve. I know what to expect, and I won't give up on my father any more than I would give up on you."

He had to smile.

"All right, come along."

Rachel scribbled a hasty note to her parents. When they

went out of the house, Mikah was seated on the front porch, and three horses stood saddled and waiting.

"Three horses, Mikah?" Steve questioned.

"I had a feeling this little lady wasn't going to be left behind. I also have a feeling we'd better get on our way. Time is passing quick."

If this was a reference to how long it had taken before Steve had come out, Mikah's bland face displayed no sign of it.

Whether either of them knew it or not, there was a warm glow about them both that answered any questions Mikah might have asked. They had found something special, and he wished them well.

Steve said nothing more, because he didn't want to tempt Mikah into being more explicit. He didn't see Mikah wink at Rachel, nor her blush and smile of satisfaction that Steve's friend had accepted her so openly.

The three mounted and rode toward Jane Crenshaw's ranch. When they arrived, all the windows were ablaze with light. They walked up on the porch, and Steve knocked. The door was opened by Carlos, and Steve did not miss the fact that he carried his gun close to his side. Carlos smiled; then he caught sight of Rachel and Mikah. Apach remained the silent observer as was his usual way, while Otis listened avidly.

"What is happening, compadre?"

"A whole lot, Carlos. We have to do a lot of talking and planning."

"Something new has come to light?"

"Yes, something that might just give us all the answers we need."

"Come in," Jane invited. "Joey, go and unsaddle their horses and take them to the stable."

"Bring our rifles back in with you. I don't think it would be too wise for us to be anywhere unarmed until this is over," Steve said.

"Have you eaten?" Jane asked.

"Ah, no," Steve said.

"Then sit down and let me get you something. We've had our supper, but there's plenty of leftovers." Rachel moved to help her while Steve and the others found seats about the table. Joey returned so quickly from caring for the horses that it was obvious he didn't want to miss anything that might be said. Joey and David were awed by what was going on, and desired nothing more than to be part of the protection of their home.

"Mr. McKean," David asked, "why are they trying to make us get off our land?"

"Because someone else wants it."

"We don't want to sell it. My pa built this place with just Ma, me and Joey to help him. Ma wouldn't sell it. This is our home," he added.

"I know, but there are people who don't respect the rights of others. They feel that if you are stronger you ought to be able to take what you want."

"Well, I'm stronger than David, and Ma whooped me for taking anything from him," Joey said.

Everyone laughed at this, and Joey grinned. "I guess I got off easy, didn't I?"

"I guess you did," Mikah said. "When I was your age my pa gave me a lesson in takin' what didn't belong to me. It took a good week before I could sit down."

Rachel watched the group in conversation, and noticed

how Otis seemed to be silently agreeing with what was said. She was caught with the idea that she would like to know what kind of a boy Steve had been, and where he had learned his fine sense of honor.

Her gaze drew his, and for a minute she and Steve were the only ones in the room.

There were serious things to discuss, and Steve soon brought their attention back to it. "Mrs. Crenshaw—"

"Jane, please."

"Jane. What do you know about Thaddius Blake, Robert Raymond or a rancher near here called Morrison?"

"I'm acquainted with Mr. Morrison. I don't really know much about him, since his land is so far away from mine. But he seems like a good person. I've not dealt much with the bank, and have had no use for a lawyer. Why do you ask?"

"Because, from what I have gathered, it's the Morrison and the Holmes ranches that have never been touched by these raiders."

"I don't understand what either would have to gain by taking my ranch."

"And we won't ever know if we can't connect them to a few others in town whom I suspect."

"How do you plan on doing that?" asked Carlos.

"I don't know yet. I do know we have to have Wade do some checking on our local banker and this lawyer. There are only a few reasons why someone would want to drive people off their land. There has to be something of value in this for them."

"How soon are we going to get word to Wade?" Apach asked.

"I think you ought to carry it tomorrow, Apach. We need

293

that information as fast as we can get it. Something has to be done as soon as possible. I wish I had . . ."

"Had what?" Carlos questioned.

"A map of this territory."

"I have one from when my husband and I first came out here. He made his own. It's kind of rough, but—"

"Rough or not, it might give us some kind of a clue."

"Clue to what?" Rachel asked.

Steve held her gaze and spoke quietly. "A clue to how they could get control of the Rocking W or the Bar D, if complete control is what they're after. It just doesn't make any sense any other way. They can't want only the small ranches; they must have their eye on all the places. There has to be a way for them to get complete control."

"There is only one reason they can't touch us," Rachel said. "We're larger and stronger than the rest."

"I don't think that makes a difference to these men. If they wanted all the others, they'd want the Rocking W and the Bar D as well."

"I'll get the map," Jane said quickly.

Steve remained silent while she was gone. He had no intention of letting this grow into an argument with Rachel.

When the map was laid flat on the table, all gathered around to see it. It was rough, but after the riding and checking Steve and Apach had done, both thought the map was fairly accurate.

There was a long silence while the men studied the map.

"Carlos?" Steve asked.

"I don't see anything that would make it possible."

"Mikah?"

"I don't see nothing."

"Apach?" Steve turned to Apach, who was looking intently at the map. "Something, Apach?"

"Water," Apach said bluntly. Everyone's gaze returned to the map. No one spoke for a long time; then Rachel gasped.

"Of course, water. My God, they actually intend to take our source of water."

"You mean the Rocking W isn't independent when it comes to water?"

"We depend on the river, and the branches to it." She turned to Steve. "Look where the river comes from: Otis's ranch. If it were to be dammed, it—"

"It appears," Jane said angrily, "that they intend to cut us all off from the water. That would ruin us all."

"Why haven't they thought to do that before now?" Otis said.

"It wasn't the right time. They had to get rid of some of the others first. The ones who didn't depend on the water," Steve replied.

It was obvious to everyone now. The river flowed from the Quantrell property, across the Bar D, where it branched down to the Rocking W. A curve brought it directly across the Jessup property as well. The branch that crossed Rocking W land continued on through the Crenshaws' C Bar C.

"It's pretty clear. If they had the five ranches north of the Bar D, which they do, and the Lazy 8, all they would have to do is dam the river and cut off the water to the rest. In no time those sections of the river would dry up and would be almost worthless."

"I cannot believe anyone could be so heartless as to dry up this section of the territory and leave all these helpless people without water," Rachel said.

"They're not the kind of men you understand, Rachel," Steve replied. "They're the kind that take what they want no matter who or what stands in their way. There has to be more to gain than just property as well. I just can't decide . . ."

"Maybe politics has something to do with it," Jane said.

"If you think my father—" Rachel began.

"No, I didn't mean your father exactly," Jane said. "But he is favored and strong enough to run for the first governor of the territory."

"He wouldn't do it over the graves of his friends and neighbors."

"I don't think he would either," Steve said, "but if we look around, we might find someone else who has the same goals in mind."

"Steve"—Jane met his gaze—"I don't understand how you know so much, and why you care. You have no interest in what happens here. You can just ride on."

There was silence, while all eyes turned to Steve.

"I have a deep interest in what happens here, because I intend to stay here and make this place my home. I don't want to see the people in this valley robbed of their homes and land. To have them taken by relentless and deceptive men who have put nothing into building this territory. I know firsthand how hard it is to build a ranch like this, and I know the pain of losing it."

"I still—"

"What's happening here is not a secret. Marshal Thomas Wade is the man who brought me . . . us here, and we're going to find his answers no matter what our opponents try to throw in our path."

"Sí." Carlos smiled. "Steve, Mikah, Apach and I are

compatriots. We have been trying to put an end to the problem here. I just don't know what put Steve on the trail.''

"I guess it was the arrival of some old friends from Colorado. It seems the judge who sentenced me is here in Chambersburg. His being here to meet with Raymond and Blake was enough to tell me just who the shady folks in this operation are.''

"The judge who sentenced you . . . I don't—''

"Jane, it's a long story and we have a lot more important things to settle. When this is over, I'll do my best to clear things up for you all. In the meantime, I'd like you to trust me.''

Before Jane could answer, there was a crash of glass, and a bullet ricocheted off the table, inches from where Rachel had been standing. The two boys leapt from their seats, Jane cried out in shock, and Steve grasped Rachel's arm and jerked her to him. Then he reached for the lamp to blow it out so they wouldn't make a target for whoever was out there.

The room was darkened, except for the moonlight, which reflected their faces. Whoever had threatened Jane before was back.

"They don't know we're here. They think Jane's alone with the boys, or there's only one man here to protect them. We have an advantage,'' Steve said. "Apach, see if you can slip out the back and cross behind them. We'll give them a surprise they aren't counting on.''

"Good thing I brought your rifles inside,'' Joey said.

"How about more ammunition, Jane? Do you have some?''

"I have all you need. Ever since they attacked me, I've

297

made sure there was plenty of everything inside where I can get my hands on it.''

"Good, now why don't you and Rachel take the boys in the back bedroom and—''

"Not on your life, Steve McKean," Rachel said. "This is my fight too.''

"And mine," Jane seconded Rachel. "Besides that, I've made sure my boys know how to shoot. We're defending our home. We'll stay right here.''

Carlos chuckled, Mikah laughed outright, and even Apach turned so Steve would not see the laughter in his eyes. But the laughter died when three more shots echoed through the room.

"Jane Crenshaw!" The voice that called out to Jane was a familiar one to Apach. When a man is beaten, it's hard to forget the voice of the one responsible.

"That's the same man who came to 'advise' me to sell," Jane said.

"Then he knows what we want to know," Steve said. "I want to get hold of him . . . alive if I can. He might have the answers we want.''

"Fine," Carlos said. "Shall I go out and invite him in for a chat?''

"No," Steve replied, "I think that little job is for me. He might just decline your invitation and shoot you.''

"And he won't shoot you?" Rachel asked with a worried frown.

"I'm not going to give him that chance. Apach, I'll go out with you. Jane, call out to him. Keep his attention. Give him an argument or whatever, but just keep his attention on you.''

Apach and Steve headed for the back room and the window that faced away from the front of the house. Rachel watched them go with trepidation.

"Go away!" Jane shouted from near the front door. "I don't intend to sell, now or ever!"

"Mrs. Crenshaw, there's no more time for you to argue with me. I've brought the papers along. Now, you don't want to see those two boys of yours get hurt, do you? Your place will burn real easy, and I don't want to do that. Come on out and sign this paper and we'll give you a fair price."

"A fair price," Jane called. "Like the others got a fair price? You'll probably lie about that like you do about everything else."

"I don't like being called a liar, Mrs. Crenshaw. You're not making the situation easier for either of us. Why don't you just come out now so we can put an end to this problem?"

Jane and Rachel had watched Steve motion to the others to move silently from the room and disappear. There was no other sound from them, and Rachel desired nothing more than to follow and find out what was happening.

"No problem if you change your mind and go out and sign his papers," Rachel said angrily. "I wonder if he really thinks you're stupid enough to believe that."

"Well, I'm not. I know there wouldn't be any money changing hands, only more threats until I left with nothing."

"Is that the way it was with Parker's Lazy P? I heard there was no money exchanged. I wonder if Thaddius is one of the people behind this."

"I wouldn't put it past him," Jane replied.

"What I can't understand is how?"

"By intimidation. The same way this man is trying to

run me off. None of the real people make their presence known. They just send this riffraff to do their dirty work. That way nothing can be traced to them."

"Mrs. Crenshaw! I'm running out of patience with you. Are you coming out or not?"

Rachel and Jane exchanged glances. Neither knew if the men were prepared to make their presence known yet.

"You'd better try to hold him a little bit longer," Rachel advised. "We have to give them time to do whatever they plan."

Jane continued to shout at the harassing man, holding his full attention while Apach and Steve separated. She was growing desperate, for she could hear the annoyance and impatience in the man's voice.

Both Apach and Steve could hear the same, and they were sure he was about to shoot again. Steve had cautioned Mikah and Carlos to keep quiet and not to shoot. He had also fought and won the battle to keep Otis from attacking. The older man held himself in check, but it was an effort.

The man's voice halted abruptly, and Steve was sure he had caught a glimpse of Apach. He looked around the corner and found he was right. The attacker was turned from him just enough for Steve to move.

Steve fairly leapt from cover, crossed the distance between them in a few strides and threw his body at the man, dragging him from his horse to the ground.

Steve fell upon him, knocking the breath from him. The fight seemed to be knocked from him as well. He lay, gasping for air, and beginning to sweat when he looked up into Steve's relentlessly angry eyes.

"Where did you come from?" the man gasped.

"You're so used to preying on people who are defenseless. I thought I might give you a lesson in fighting people your own size.'' Steve rose, dragging his captive up with him, and toward the house.

The rest were just behind them, and when the door closed, the man was stunned by the number of people there. Worse, the men looked as if they meant to kill him at any second. He began to sweat as he looked from one hard face to another. Brave only when he had the upper hand, he was a coward in the face of superior force. He was a man small in stature. Thin and pasty-faced, he had a short beard to camouflage his receding chin, and narrow ferret eyes.

''Who . . . who are you?'' he blustered, but everyone present could clearly see he was shaken, and growing more scared by the minute. His true cowardice was becoming obvious.

''We'll ask the questions,'' Steve said as he forced the man down in a chair. ''And you,'' he said coldly, ''are going to answer them.'' He turned to Otis. ''Take the boys, Jane and Rachel and go into the bedroom. This is not going to be a sight for any of them to see.'' He winked at Rachel, and knew she would help Jane comfort the boys with the truth that he didn't intend to do serious harm to the intruder.

''I don't know what you're talking about! I'm just a messenger, I don't know nothing!''

''I want to have some answers,'' Steve said, ''and I'm not too particular how I have to go about getting them.''

''Wha . . . what are you talking about?''

Steve was silent for so long that the man began to tremble. Then Steve turned to a particularly fierce looking Apach, whose clenched teeth and dark, scowling countenance would have made stronger men tremble.

"Apach? I think your people have some effective methods of making people talk?"

"Oh, yes," Apach hissed. He bent close to the man in the chair and smiled the smile of a feral, hungry wolf. "There is a method of taking the skin off a man without killing him, peeling him like a ripe plum, then putting him out in the sun to roast, like a side of beef. Very, very painful. Shall I begin now?"

"I would like to think he wouldn't prey on any more women when we're done," Steve said.

"How about taking small parts of his body . . . one piece at a time. You know, first a finger, then a toe . . . then his arms, his nose, his tongue—"

"Not his tongue, I want him able to talk. But the idea of other parts is interesting."

"No! No! You can't do that!" the man screeched.

"No?" Apach grinned. "I assure you I not only can . . . I will."

"What do you want from me? I'm not the one who did this! I don't know nothing."

"Oh, I think you do," Carlos said, "and I take exception to you threatening the person I work for. It makes me irritable. When I get irritable there is no telling how far I might go to remove the irritant."

"Yes," Mikah agreed, "I have seen you before when you were annoyed. Didn't you slice the lips off the man who argued with you once?"

"Oh, sí," Carlos said with a deep and seemingly regretful sigh. "I sometimes lose control along with my temper."

While Carlos spoke, Apach removed a knife from the sheath at his waist, a knife that made the man's eyes bug from his head. Its blade was eight inches long, and three wide. It looked as lethal as the threats he was hearing as it glittered in the lamplight.

"Nooo," the man groaned. Sweat beaded his face and head, and he was trembling so badly Steve thought he might collapse at any moment.

Apach bent nearer the man and laid the blade of the knife along his cheek. "I think I shall begin with his ears. There are two, and he only needs one to hear our questions."

"I don't know what you want. I was only sent here to make an offer to Mrs. Crenshaw. There's nothing wrong with that."

"There is if your offer is made with a gun," Apach replied.

"And if your offer has been refused time and time again," Steve added. "Now, as to our questions. The first one is easy. Who do you work for?"

"He'll kill me," the man whimpered.

"That's a possibility," Steve said angrily. "We're a certainty. You tell us what we want to know, or begin to pray."

"You wouldn't dare. When this is found out, you'll be hanged."

"You can't think that we'd let your body be found? If your boss should come asking about you, and it would show his guilt if he did, we'd only claim we haven't seen you. He might be so angry with you for involving him that he'll just forget you ever existed."

There was a prolonged silence while the victim digested this truth. If he was missing, no one would come looking for him. He was at the mercy of men who appeared to have no mercy at all.

Apach seemed to become agitated and impatient, and this only made the victim more upset and nervous. Apach let the knife slip a bit, and a stinging burn along his cheek struck real terror into the victim. He was certain now that Apach meant just what he said.

It did him no good to look at the others, for their faces were frozen masks. He was going to get no reprieve. He finally acknowledged to himself that he had not been paid enough to allow himself to be butchered for the men who hired him.

"All right . . . all right. I'll tell you what you want to know. But you have to promise me something."

"We do not have to promise you anything," Carlos said. "You will tell us or we will see that you suffer mightily before you die."

"I only need a way to leave here. I can trust you, can't I? If I do what you say, you have to let me get away from here. I'm a dead man if you don't, and if that's going to be what happens, you may as well kill me now."

"How do we know you won't go back to your boss?" Mikah asked.

"And tell him what happened here? No, mister, I think I'll put a lot of distance between me and this territory. I don't want to see Montana again, I don't care if statehood is this close."

"How close?" Steve said. "Is there someone in your organization that has a tie to Washington?"

"Are you crazy? Of course. You don't think they're just doing this on the chance, do you?"

"Who? Who's their connection to Washington?" Steve demanded.

"You remember when Senator Charles from Minnesota

was here for the . . . no, you weren't around here then." Jane came into the room at that moment and he turned to look at her. "Mrs. Crenshaw, maybe you'll remember. It was last year, when we got started on all this. Senator Charles has a big interest in this territory, and he damn well wants the first governor to be one whose strings he can pull."

"Just who is this paragon of virtue going to be?" Steve asked.

"Who else but the most prominent lawyer in town? Robert Raymond is panting to get that position. Him and Blake have a real good scheme going, and all they had to do was convince a couple of the ranchers here to be their tools. You know, use them until they get what they want, then have the law find them guilty of everything and ship them off to prison."

"Yuma," Steve said. "I think that would be a good place all right, but for all of them and not just the fools they're using."

"And they were planning to take over the Rocking W and the Bar D too, weren't they? Carter Walker and Joe Davis had no part in this?"

"Carter Walker," the man snorted. "Hell, man, he's the one they want to get rid of most. He's the only man that could take the governorship, if the election was held today. No, him and Davis would have had to go."

"They were going to cut off the water supply, and drive the Walkers and Davises out by drying them up."

"How did you know that?"

"It's the only way to get Walker or Davis. They had too many men to fight with, and they would have fought right down to the bitter end."

"Yeah, the water was going to go . . . temporarily. When the biggest ranches sold, and everything was in their hands, all they would have to do was divert the river and open the dam."

"I think that's all we need to know," Apach said. The sound of his voice brought renewed fear to the man, who looked from face to face.

"I told you everything you wanted to know. You aren't going to go back on your word? You said I could go."

The four men looked at each other as if surprised.

"Apach, Mikah, Carlos, do any of you remember making any promises?" Steve said innocently.

"Me? No," Carlos said. "This man burnt Jane's bunkhouse down. I think he should pay."

"I agree," Mikah said.

"I do too," Apach added.

"No . . . no, you can't do this. I swear! I swear! I won't go near town. I'll go over to Selby, that's the next town. I'll take the first train out. I'll never be seen in this territory again. I swear. Please . . . I swear."

"Do any of you think we should trust him?" Steve presented the question as if he doubted it himself.

"Well, maybe if I rode over to Selby with him and made sure he took the train . . ." Carlos said.

"Remember," Steve cautioned the man, "within days they're going to know it was you who talked. I don't think they'll be forgiving."

"I don't want nothing to do with this anymore. They didn't tell me I'd have to face men like you. How was I to know the places around here had hired guns to defend them? I ain't going against you."

Steve smiled, "I served time in Yuma Prison for killing a man."

"Look, I did what you wanted. I told you what you wanted to know. I deserve something for that. Let me go."

"All right, Steve. I'll see he gets to Selby. If he jumps out of line on the way, do you want me to kill him?" Carlos said calmly, as if that would be an ordinary thing for him to do.

"Yes," Steve answered just as coldly. There was no doubt that the man believed exactly what was said.

When Carlos left, Mikah laughed and cursed. "We ought to have given him to Wade."

"He's a small frog, but you're right. Wade would have a lot of questions for him. We want the big fish, though. Apach, can you get to Wade? Tell him to come here. He should be near the line cabin at Pine Bluff. Right now all we have is that coward's word, and that won't hold up in court here, let alone Washington. We need more powerful help, and Wade is our best bet."

"I shall find him and return with him as soon as I can," Apach replied. In moments he was gone.

"Well, I guess all we can do is wait," Otis said, having come out of the bedroom.

"I'm going to have to convince Rachel to go home. I think Mikah ought to ride with her, just in case."

"I want—" Otis protested.

"This is a matter of what's needed," Steve said. "You go on to your place just in case. We don't want another fire." Otis considered this, then reluctantly agreed.

"Okay then, let's see what the ladies have to say," Steve concluded and walked over to open the bedroom door.

Chapter Sixteen

When Steve opened the door of the bedroom, Rachel was standing on the other side. There was no doubt in his mind that she had heard everything that had gone on in the room. He could see it in her eyes. There was a glow of wicked humor.

"I do believe you frightened that man out of years. What would you have done if he had developed a little courage and called your bluff?"

"I would have done what was necessary to get the answers we needed. You're not sympathizing with him? Guns and force are all his kind understand."

"No, I don't have any sympathy for a man who will terrorize children, or try to steal from people who have worked so hard to acquire a good life. It's just that I know you better than that. That gun might be worn by you, but I don't think you have any desire to use it."

"I guess you're right about that. I don't relish the thought of using a gun, or any other means of force, for that matter. The unthinking use of a gun lost me a good chunk of my life, and I don't intend to be stupid this time. If I have to use my gun, I'll make sure it's for the right reasons. Sometimes you have to fight fire with fire."

"I think what you said is right, Steve," Jane said. "I don't like the idea of guns either, but if I have to defend my home and my children, I'll use one. I think I would like my boys to think like you, that a gun is a last and most unwelcome choice."

"I'm trying to get us all out of this situation without using guns," Steve replied. "If Apach can get Marshal Wade back here soon, we can put our heads together and maybe find an answer."

"At least we know who is behind it and why," Rachel said. "I . . . I'm so glad you all see now that my father just wouldn't have done any of this."

"I see it." Steve smiled at her. "I should have known from the beginning. Your father was your model, and there isn't an ounce of dishonor or viciousness in your whole body." His gaze warmed her, and again she had the peaceful and satisfying feeling that she had found the other half of herself, the man who would make her life whole and complete.

"I'm hungry." David's voice cut into their thoughts. All three of them laughed.

"Leave it to a child to get to the important things," Jane laughed as she turned to David. "You're always hungry. I baked fresh bread yesterday. Make yourself a sandwich."

"Okay."

Steve laughed and Rachel enjoyed the light-hearted moment. David went to make his sandwich and Jane and Mi-kah left the room, purposely giving Steve and Rachel some time alone.

When the door closed, Rachel didn't speak. Instead she stepped into the circle of Steve's arms and felt them close about her. Both had the same desire, just to hold each other and enjoy the sense of peace and promise that didn't need words.

Steve closed his eyes and savored the feel of her in his arms. The kiss they shared was one of such tenderness that Rachel wrapped her spirit in it and surrendered to the pure pleasure.

When at last, and most reluctantly, he held her a little away from him, he was warmed by the look in her eyes that spoke of the future they would have together. There would be many tomorrows for them, but none quite like this one. Today, they had the chance to wipe every barrier away.

"The sun will be coming up soon," he said quietly.

"Yes. A new day."

"Would you consider going for a walk to the top of that hill out there, and watching the sun come up with me?"

"You sure you're not hungry?" Rachel teased.

"Trust me, darling, I'm hungry all right," he chuckled wickedly.

"I meant for food."

"Well, there's food for the stomach and food for the spirit. Right now, food for the stomach is running second . . . and not a close second at that. Come with me."

"My spirit feels in need of a little nourishment as well. I would love to walk out and see the sun rise . . . and be with you."

When they came into the next room, Jane was busy at work. She smiled at Steve and Rachel.

"If you don't mind, Jane," Steve said at once, "Rachel and I are going out for a while. The sun is coming up, and you seem to have a place for a good view of it."

"The best. From the top of that hill, you can see for a long way. Walter and I made that our favorite place. I've seen the sun come up there many times. It's only one of the million reasons why I can't give this place up."

"I'll go with you," David said. His voice was filled with enthusiasm, and both Steve and Rachel wondered at the resilience of people his age.

"No, David." Jane smiled at her son. "You have plenty of time to watch the sunrise. Besides, you've seen the sun come up before. You stay here, and let our guests enjoy themselves."

"Okay," David replied, and sagged back down on his chair reluctantly.

Neither Steve nor Rachel allowed themselves to laugh until they were some distance from the house.

"What would you have done if Jane had not been so . . . observant?" Rachel laughed.

"I don't know, but trust me, I would have thought of something. I hadn't thought we'd have company. I was sure that a boy his age would think of his stomach first."

"Which is what you would have done?" Rachel laughed. "Your face did look rather strange when David said he was coming. I thought Mikah was going to burst, trying to keep from laughing."

"Well, I was desperate. Thank God for Jane."

They stopped at the crest of the hill, beneath a large tree with limbs that spread wide. The ground beneath was carpeted with soft grass. Steve drew Rachel down with him, and sat with his back against the tree. Rachel sat at his side, her head resting on his shoulder.

Nature took this moment to display her most brilliant and beautiful portrait. The sky turned crimson, with vivid streaks of lavender and gold. White clouds and a slowly bluing sky created a breathless scene, and both lay still, captured by the beauty around them and the joy of having each other to share it with.

When the rim of the sun began to form into an amazingly bright sphere of molten gold, it washed the whole world in light.

"I could build a house right here and enjoy this for as many years as I have left," Steve said contentedly.

"I'm afraid this particular part of the world doesn't belong to us," Rachel sighed. "But I do know a place almost as pretty on our range that we could build on."

"Rachel?" Steve spoke so quietly and hesitantly that Rachel could feel something growing tense within him.

"What?"

"There's a lot we have to talk about."

"Now?" Rachel was reluctant to face any problems at this moment. "Can't it wait until this problem is over?"

"Maybe this is the best time. It's just that I don't know what my future is. Wade is trying for a full pardon, but it depends on a lot of uncertain things that might be out of his control."

"Like what?" She turned in his arms so she could look up at him.

"Like the presence of Judge Graham. He's here for more than one reason. I'm sure he knew I was here. I know him too well, and I can't see him not putting every block in my way that he can. He's the kind of man who would relish putting me back in prison. He still holds the power and knows it. He'd take great pleasure in forcing me to finish my sentence. I don't know what Wade could do about it if the judge decided to challenge the pardon. The truth is, I don't know how Wade swung this at all.''

''Steve can't this judge be reasoned with?''

''Not for a minute. He's a man who has no idea what mercy is. I can see him enjoying the fact that he still has the power to send me back. I have a feeling old Martin Swope is waiting.''

''Steve, my father has some contacts as well. He'll help you fight.''

''Are you sure of that? I'm not exactly a prime subject for his son-in-law. I'm sure he wants much better for you. I don't have a dime, except what he has paid me. No land, and no prospects. Besides . . . I don't think I could stay on the Rocking W and just be.''

''I hadn't thought you would,'' Rachel protested before Steve could voice his thoughts on their future.

''Then what did you think we were going to do? What kind of a future do you think it's possible for us to have?''

''Shall I tell you that I have been thinking about this from the first time we were together?''

''Were you now? After that night in the bunkhouse, I thought you wouldn't ever be in my arms again. I was really stupid that night for not holding you close to me and never letting you go.''

''I would have stayed if you had given me a chance. But I understand,'' she said. Holding his gaze, she added, ''I've seen Ann Graham, and I can see how hard it would be for you to wipe her from your mind so easily.''

"It wasn't that I held onto her memory, but that I couldn't get the hatred for what I let her do to me out of my mind. There wasn't room for someone as sweet and gentle as you."

"Well, I'm here now, and there's no more room for old memories. Do you want to know what my answers are?"

"Just what answers did you come up with?"

"You know where Otis's land is?"

"Yes."

"And you know where the borders of Martin Bradley's are?"

"Yes, but—"

"Let me finish."

Steve kissed her, a quick, feather-light kiss. "All right, finish."

"Between those two there's a nice piece of land. It's been unclaimed, just lying there for as many years as I can remember. Sometimes we've grazed our cattle on it, but it doesn't belong to us. As far as I know, it doesn't belong to anyone. We could lay claim to it, and work it for ourselves. The river branches right across it, and it's really pretty. It's not big, but how much room do we need?"

"Do you realize what you would be giving up?"

"What?"

"What! Just about everything."

"Oh, no, Steve." Rachel rose on one elbow and smiled down on him. "I realize what I am getting. I would rather build and grow with you than live out my life without you, no matter what luxuries the Rocking W has. It's still my father's and my mother's. This would be ours, yours and mine. We could build our own private world."

Steve caught his breath at the wonder of his love for her,

and the fact that she loved him. He reached up and caught her face between his hands.

"Rachel"—he breathed her name—"I will never be able to tell you if I have a million years how precious you are to me and how much I love you. You're like the beginning of my life. We could have a future."

"Yes, we could. I love you too, Steve, with my whole heart. When this is over, we'll begin together. We'll make it work."

"Yes . . . we'll make it work. When this is over." He murmured the last words softly as their lips met in a deep kiss of promise.

He could not deny to himself that his body was ablaze with his desire to take her now, at this wondrous moment. But he contained his need. One day soon, if all went well, they would have their time together. Time in their own home, in their own bed, and time to spend leisurely exploring each other without the need to hurry. The thought of it swirled in his mind and filled him with intense pleasure.

He could feel the melting warmth of her pressed against him, and worried that he didn't have the strength of resolve not to fulfill his need if this exquisite torture continued. It took every ounce of will he could muster to let her go and sit up.

"I think we had better get back," he said.

"Are you in such a hurry?"

"Only to get this problem over with. I want you in my arms when you don't have to leave them." He drew her to him and kissed her so possessively that there was no doubt in her mind. It drained away every thought but one. Steve . . . Steve.

For Steve there were no doubts either. He knew that Rachel was his strength, his pride and his courage, and would be for as long as they lived.

"Come, love." His voice was hoarse with suppressed desire. He was certain that if they didn't leave this place now, it would be a long time before he would let her go. "I think we'd better get back. There are a lot of things to accomplish today. You have to go home and speak to your father. Don't let him take action on his own. If we move too soon and without enough proof, we'll be defeated. The people we're dealing with are clever."

"What are you going to do?"

"Stay here until Apach and Carlos get back. If Wade gets here soon, we'll be able to make some plans."

"I don't see how you are going to get any proof."

"It might surprise you how many contacts Wade has. Any man who can open the doors of Yuma Prison and take four convicted men out for his own purposes has a lot of power. I'm counting on it."

"I hope his power extends to keeping you safe. But if it doesn't, my family and I will move heaven and earth to get you free."

Steve laughed, "Ah, Rachel, how lucky I am." He kissed her again, then rose quickly and drew her up beside him. With his arm about her waist they walked back to Jane's small house.

When they arrived back at the house, it was to find that Jane had cooked a large breakfast. Steve ate hungrily, much to Rachel's amusement.

"So much for food for the spirit," she murmured. Steve grinned, acknowledging the reference.

"First things first, love," he replied just loud enough for her to hear. "Since I can't have the meal I want, I'll take second best."

David did overhear and couldn't understand why someone would think his mother's cooking was second-rate. He thought she was the best cook in the territory.

After the meal, Mikah and Rachel went back to the Rocking W. Steve had insisted that Mikah go with her.

Mikah and Rachel didn't speak at first. Mikah knew Rachel was deep in thought, and didn't want to disturb her. Finally she spoke.

"Mikah, you were in prison with Steve?"

"Yes, I was."

"Can you tell me what he went through there? I think I have a right to know if I'm going to be able to bring him any peace. Was it so terrible?"

Under any other circumstances Mikah never would have spoken. But he had watched Steve closely, and he felt certain that Rachel was not only the one person who could salve Steve's wounds, but that she did have a right to know.

He began to speak, and throughout the whole story he didn't look at her. He sensed rather than knew that she was crying. Most likely crying the last tears she would shed for Steve. From this time on she would not let tears control her.

"Oh, Mikah, how can one man be so cruel as to almost bury a man alive?"

"I don't know. I guess there's lots of men like the warden. Swope is filled with some kind of sickness that no doctor could cure. I know one thing for certain. Swope is less to blame than that Judge Graham."

"He's here . . . in town. Did Steve tell you?"

Sylvie Sommerfield

"Yes, and I don't like it," Mikah said, his voice filled with worry.

"Do you think he's come here because of Steve?"

"I don't know. I'd bet my life if there's a chance to cause Steve some harm, he's going to do it."

"But why? Why after the marshal gained his freedom?"

"Because . . . I have a feeling," he said, "that the judge is afraid of something. Maybe there's more we should know about him. Maybe he has a few secrets of his own."

"But what could Steve do? He doesn't know anything about the judge that would threaten him."

"He says not, but sometimes we know something and don't realize it."

"How would we ever find out?"

"I don't know. It's something we have to throw in Wade's lap."

"I can't wait to meet this marshal. He sounds . . ."

"Honest and strong? He is. I think he's got a fine sense of justice that's pretty hard to find."

"I . . . I wish Steve were free."

Mikah looked closely at Rachel, and discovered she was clinging to hope in a kind of fearful desperation. She was afraid, and this was a rare thing for a woman like her.

Mikah brought his horse to a halt, and Rachel, surprised at his stopping, reined in too. "Mikah?"

"Look, Miss Rachel, I know how much Steve loves you. You two just keep hold of that and don't give up no matter how bad it looks. In that prison, hope was all any of us ever had, and it brought Steve through something most men would have died from. He's a strong man, and he needs you and your strength to keep him that way."

"Oh, Mikah, I would never give up on us. I want to

build a life with him, and I don't intend to let that dream go, no matter how hard it gets."

"You worried Judge Graham might send him back?"

"Yes."

"I think that's the only thing that would break him. I don't think they would let him live if he went back there."

Rachel held Mikah's gaze with a firm, determined look. "I would run with him, no matter how far or for how long, if it would keep him safe."

Mikah smiled. "I guess I know how lucky one man can get. Maybe everything will work out. If it doesn't . . . we'll all run."

"I hope it doesn't come to that. I think the judge is in for the battle of his life, before he makes us run."

"Then let's get going. I been spoiling for a fight with the judge when the ground is even. It should prove interesting . . . real interesting."

The two rode on, both determined to keep the nagging fear at the back of their minds. When they arrived at the Rocking W they found Carter and Tom saddling their horses.

A few minutes earlier, Carter had gone to the bunkhouse and discovered that Mikah had not been there all night.

"No, boss," Tom had said, "I haven't seen Mikah for a spell, and I haven't seen Miss Rachel either."

"Ride with me, Tom," Carter had said. "Rachel hasn't been home all night. There's too much going on around here that I don't know about." Carter and Tom were preparing to go on a search when Mikah and Rachel rode into the yard.

"Where in tarnation have you been? Your note didn't say a hell of a lot. Just that you'd be back soon. I hope you have a good explanation for worrying your mother like that," Carter growled.

"I do, and trust me, it's the best explanation you've ever heard. Come in the house. I have to tell you and Mother a lot of things. And I need your help."

"My help?" Carter was taken off stride and forgot his fatherly admonitions. "What's wrong, girl?"

"Come in, Dad. This is a long and very involved story. I think you're in for a lot of surprises."

Inside, they were met by an anxious Yvonne and Lori, who were calmed by the same words Rachel had said to her father. Gathered around the table, they waited impatiently for Rachel to explain, which she did as succinctly as she could.

"Rachel!" Lori said in shock. "This is unbelievable. Thaddius and Robert, why? I don't think anyone would believe such upstanding citizens could do such a thing."

"I agree, Mother, but it is the truth. They would not only have owned this valley, but for all intents and purposes, they would have owned the town as well."

"But you have no proof?" Carter said.

"We don't have any now," Mikah said, "but we will. Just as soon as we get together with the marshal, we'll do what's necessary to gather all the proof needed."

"Just how does Steve intend to go about this?" Carter asked calmly. "I think he needs more help if what you say of his past is true."

"Steve has some plans, and if you give me a chance, I'll explain as much as I can," Rachel said, matching Carter in calmness.

"You love him," Lori said, stating a fact.

"Yes, I love him. More than that, I trust him."

Yvonne smiled. "I guess that's the answer to most everything."

For a while there was silence; then Carter spoke. "If what you say is true, and I think it is, your man needs some help. Maybe a little more than he, his friends or his marshal can provide." He rose from the chair and smiled at a questioning Rachel. Walking to her, he embraced her with a possessive bear hug.

It had just occurred to Carter that his daughter would one day soon belong to another man. It was a disquieting thought. That, combined with the idea of someone disrupting the entire valley and trying to destroy what he had so lovingly built, had stirred his anger.

"What are you going to do, Dad?"

"It may surprise you, my dear, but I have a few contacts of my own. It might surprise a lot of people. I don't take well to someone trying to grab my land, nor the land of my friends. The kind of person who would destroy the source of the water that feeds just about every ranch around is someone without conscience. He should be shown the same mercy as he would show us. Besides, if your heart's set on this roving cowboy, I think it's time we started working together." He turned to Lori. "Come on, let's take a ride into town. I have a few telegrams to send, and some people to see."

"Dad?"

"There's not a lot of time for questions. You try and stay put for a while. When I get back we'll talk this out and tomorrow we'll ride to the Crenshaws' and talk to Steve and maybe his friend, the marshal. Together we might just be able to rope and throw our friends."

Rachel went to her parents and embraced her father and

then her mother. "Thank you both for being so understanding."

When her parents and Mikah had left, Yvonne and Rachel sat together. It was the ever observant Yvonne who realized Rachel's problems were deeper than she had said.

"You're worried?"

"Yes."

"There's something more than you've said."

"Yvonne, I didn't tell Dad that Steve still has years in prison hanging over his head if that judge can't be persuaded to let the marshal get him a pardon."

"But—"

"The judge still has the power, and Steve says he has no mercy for anyone, and especially not for him. For some reason, he has a particular hatred for Steve. No matter what Dad does to save the ranches around here, if Steve . . ." Her voice caught on a sob.

"What will you do?"

Rachel told Yvonne of the land they wanted and how futile it might be for them to dream. "If there's no escaping the judge's vindictiveness, Steve and I will have to run from here."

"And leave all you've worked for with your family?"

"Steve will be my family, and I'm sure both Dad and Mother will understand."

"But where will you go? Steve will be a wanted man for as long as you live. Where can you hide? It will destroy both of your lives."

"And what is my life without Steve? I . . . I don't think he would come out of Yuma alive. Mikah feels the same way. It seems, or so Mikah says, that the warden was doing his best to kill Steve when the marshal came for him. He'll succeed this time. I can see the fear of it in Steve's eyes, no matter what he says."

"And still he stays here to help keep this valley and your ranch safe."

"Yes." Rachel smiled. "That's the kind of man he is. Oh, Yvonne, I love him so much. I can't bear the thought of losing him now."

"Maybe there's a way. We have a lot of people on our side. I wouldn't be surprised if your judge doesn't get the surprise of his life. Steve has made a lot of friends here, and with what we now know, most everyone affected by these ugly men will be gathering together. You know Cal and his family carry a lot of weight around here as well."

"I know. I know how wonderful everyone is. But this judge uses the law like a sword, and the law, in the hands of a man like that, is hard to fight."

"Maybe, if he is as you say he is, he is also a coward."

"A coward?"

"Men who have to use the methods he does are often cowards. We just have to find out what he is afraid of. He also has a daughter."

"Yes," Rachel said reluctantly.

"I take it that she and Steve—"

"Yes," Rachel repeated. "I think it was her betrayal that made Steve so wary. I think he is a man to whom trust and loyalty mean a lot."

"Those qualities are rather rare. I think you and I are very lucky women."

"Yes, lucky. If—"

"*If* is a word I don't want to consider, and *if* is a word you should put from your mind as well. You have a lot to fight for, and you have a lot of friends to fight with you."

Rachel smiled, and the two embraced. Still, in the depths of Rachel's heart there was cold doubt. She had looked into Steve's eyes and seen the fear he had tried to hide. She meant to do whatever she had to do to see that he didn't return to die in that place. There had to be something . . . something.

Lori and Carter rode in silence for a while, each caught in his own thoughts. It was Lori who interrupted Carter's contemplations.

"Carter?"

"Yes?"

"What do you plan to do?"

"I need to send some telegrams, and to find out what I can about what is going on."

"Telegrams to whom?"

Carter smiled. "I have a few more contacts than I think our friends counted on. We have to put a stop to this. The possibility of someone taking over the land around here from people like us and our neighbors, who worked our whole lives to make our ranches what they are, has made me angrier than I've ever been. Steve and his friends need all the help we can give them. I'm still shocked at the idea that they might have come here because they thought I was behind all this. I'm sure glad they found out different."

"And how do you feel about Steve?"

"Did you think I was angry about that? No, I'm pleased, to tell you the truth. I've worked with him, and listened to the men. He's a good man, who knows what he's doing. He and Rachel will make a team that will be hard to beat."

"So you see him as someone to take over the Rocking W one day?"

Carter laughed. "I don't think even he will be able to do that, no matter how much Rachel loves him. No, he'll help her run the place . . . if he's smart. After all, many a man in this territory would be more than willing to be in his shoes, married to the owner of such a place."

"Carter," Lori laughed, "I think you are in for a surprise."

"About what?"

"I don't think you or I can work this little problem out for Rachel. It's something they have to decide for themselves."

"I know Rachel. She'll never leave, or give up the reins of the Rocking W. He'll just have to learn to adjust."

"Like you would?"

"What does that mean?"

"Do you remember before we were married, and my father offered you a place in his business? He said you were a footloose fool when you refused. You said you'd be your own boss, and make a fortune out of it as well, and you did."

Carter considered this. "That was different."

"How?"

Carter was annoyed with this thought. Rachel was his only child, his heir, and the Rocking W would be hers. He knew she loved the place and she would never give it up. But what about the man she had come to love? Would he take her from it, from him? No, Rachel would never leave . . . he knew that . . . he was certain of that.

"Your father ran a bank. Good Lord, Lori, do you think I was cut out to run a bank? But Steve, he can run the ranch, and be a big help to Rachel."

"I hope it works out that way."

"I don't see—"

"We don't have to see, Carter. This is a decision for Rachel when the time comes. For once, you will have nothing to say about it."

"Lori, have I been so demanding, such an ogre that I would drive my daughter from us?"

"No, my love. You've been just the opposite. There's been nothing Rachel or I have ever wanted that you haven't found a way to give us. I know how you feel, helpless, like I do. We can't make decisions for Rachel, and we have to give her the right to decide her future, no matter whether it fits our plans or not."

"There's noplace for them to go, and nothing better for them than the Rocking W."

"What if Steve wants to go back to his own home?"

"We," Carter said with a determined jut of his jaw, "will put up every argument in the book, and we'll pray a lot."

They continued into town and went directly to the telegraph office, where Carter sent several telegrams to people whose names surprised the operator, and Lori as well. When they left the office, Carter suggested they cross the street to the bank. There was a look in his eyes that Lori recognized well. Carter was going to enjoy himself.

Chapter Seventeen

It was late evening before Apach returned to Jane Crenshaw's house with Wade and two men Wade had enlisted to help. When they rode up to the house, Steve was already walking out on the porch. He'd heard riders and carried his rifle for safety's sake. Wade didn't miss this fact.

"You had some trouble, or so Apach has told me."

"Yes, you might say we had a little trouble," Steve replied, smiling at Apach's snort of derision at the understatement. "But we've had some good luck as well."

When they'd all gathered in the house, Steve explained the situation. At the conclusion of his report, he turned to Wade. "What's our next move?"

"We need to make sure Quantrell is well protected," Wade replied.

"If we all gather there, the cat's out of the bag."

"What do you suggest?"

"I do have one idea."

"I'm interested in anything that might bring an end to this. What's your plan?"

Steve explained, and there was a silent regard while they considered his idea.

"It sounds like a good plan to me," Jane said. "I'd be willing to go along with it. I do think it will take a lot of convincing and trust on the part of the other ranchers, but I'll be happy to go and explain to them how good this will be for us all in the end." Jane smiled. "Rachel trusts you, and the marshal trusts you. Besides, I can't see Carlos trusting you if you were dishonest. I'll go along."

"Thanks, Jane. I hope this works." Steve said.

Steve turned to Wade. "I think it's time for you and Apach to ride over to the Lazy 8 with your men. There's no time like the present to get things moving. I'll be along as soon as I tie things up here."

It had not occurred to Apach or Wade and his two men how late it would be before they reached Otis's ranch. They approached the house without trying to silence their coming. They had not quite reached the porch when Otis's voice came out of the darkness.

"Apach? That you?"

"Yes, Mr. Quantrell, it is me. Come out, there is something important I have to speak to you about."

Without hesitation, Otis walked out onto the porch. It was a clear statement of how much he had come to trust Apach, who dismounted and walked up the steps to stand beside him.

"I'm glad you're back. What's happening?"

"Nothing you don't already know about. Things are going to come to a head, and we might be in the way of some trouble.''

''There's nothing different about that,'' Otis laughed.

''I would like to bring my friends into your house.''

Otis hesitated for a minute. Inviting people he didn't know into his house this late at night could be asking for trouble. But since it was Apach . . .

''Bring them in . . . but I don't see what good it will do.''

''Maybe more good than you think,'' Apach said. He gave a sharp whistle, and the others rode up to the house.

It was clear to everyone that Otis was nervous, so Wade explained at once that they were U.S. marshals.

''U.S. marshals,'' Otis said. ''It's going to take more than three of you to stop what's going on here.''

''I don't think so,'' Apach said. ''It will take a lot of trust, but Steve's ready to do something drastic. He has no intention of you losing your ranch.''

''Well, I ain't anxious to lose it either, but I don't think I can hold out much longer. They been playing with me for a while, but I think they're losing their patience.''

''Then let's sit down and talk. I think you'll see just how good this idea is, and how we can rid ourselves of these vultures finally.''

''Come on in. I guess I want to hear what you have to say.''

Inside, after Otis had offered some of his best whiskey, they sat around the table and Apach came to the point.

''These men know they can drive you small landowners out if they come at you one at a time. It's time to join forces and meet them head on.''

''I can't see the Rocking W or the Bar D jumping on

the bandwagon for my benefit. I ain't too sure that one of them's not behind all this."

"They're not," Apach assured him quickly. "Mr. Quantrell, last night we realized that you're one of the most important people in this territory."

"I'm only one man."

"You're the one man who controls the water."

"Yeah, I've been thinking about that. I guess that was the reason they wanted my land so bad they'd send men to beat me. I ain't a man to back away, but I been pretty scared that I'd have to. Apach has made a difference." Apach smiled his acknowledgment of this, and Otis continued. "What is it you want me to do?"

"I want you to make out a bill of sale for your ranch to Steve," Wade said.

"What!"

"All the small places will do the same," Apach said.

"I'm supposed to just hand over my place to him? I don't even know him. He might be as bad as the others and grab the whole kit and kaboodle," Otis replied.

"He will not," Apach said firmly. "He is a man whose word means a great deal. He will return your ranch to you as soon as this thing is brought out into the open.

"Jane Crenshaw made her bill of sale out right away and she's doing her best to convince the others. No matter what the outcome, the ranch will be returned to you as soon as this is resolved."

"You really have that much trust in McKean?" Otis asked Apach.

"I do. Steve, Carlos, Mikah and I have been working to resolve this problem ever since we arrived."

There was a long silence, and everyone held his breath.

Forever

Otis was the key, and they couldn't go on with the plan if he didn't agree to it.

Otis was a cautious man, and not one given to trust easily. But he had learned to trust Apach, and now that was what he depended upon.

"All right. I'll get me something to write on. I'll sign it over . . . to him." He pointed to Apach, who was more shocked than any of the others.

"To me?" Apach questioned, stunned.

"Yes, to you. I want you to hold my land until we settle this. Then consider coming to work for me permanent when this is over. I think we'd make a good pair. I don't have family, and I ain't seen a man can handle horses like you do. When my time comes, if you help me build, it will all be yours. You can protect the water for this territory for the rest of your life."

No one was more dumbfounded than Apach, but he knew better than to accept the offer.

"Mr. Quantrell," Apach said, "under your white law I cannot own land. I will stand behind Steve's honor if you will grant me the favor of signing the ranch to him. And I would be honored to continue to work for you."

Otis quietly nodded, and Apach took his outstretched hand. He vowed to himself that Otis would never regret his generosity.

It was growing too late to go on with their plans tonight, and Apach knew Steve wanted to return to the Rocking W.

"You have given me great honor, Mr. Quantrell. I will work very hard to help you."

Otis nodded, then rose to find pen and paper. At the table, he wrote what Wade dictated. All of them signed it.

It was then that Steve rode up. Otis said he'd agreed to

the plan, and handed the papers to Steve. He remained quiet when Otis told him he had first chosen Apach. Steve agreed with the sentiment.

"All right, we have a start," Wade said. "Who's next?"

"We can cover the other places tomorrow," Steve suggested. "Right now I'm going back to the Rocking W. I think it's time to talk to Carter, and to Joe Davis. With all of us united, Judge Graham and his gang have to give up their plans." Steve rose and stretched. It had been a long day, and the ride home was long. He suspected he might have to help Rachel convince Carter . . . if Carter hadn't closed the door between him and Rachel by the time he got there.

"I'm going to look into a few things, then head back to Pine Bluff. You two stay here with Mr. Quantrell," Wade said to his two men. "Steve, this is going to work. I would like to see their faces when they find out you own half the land in the territory."

"It's going to cause a reaction, that's for sure," Steve agreed.

They left, leaving Otis, Apach and the two marshals to guard the Lazy 8.

Apach wasn't sure what he could say to make Otis understand just how important Otis's sacrifice had been to him. He had never owned anything in his life except the horse he had caught and the clothes on his back. The idea of having a home was a new concept to him; it gave him a feeling of belonging. He would stay with Otis until the end . . . and keep his ranch growing.

"Sacrifice? Hell, boy, that wouldn't have been no sacrifice. I have no one to leave this place to. I wish I could give it to you."

"Mr. Quantrell," Apach said, "there is little you know of me. Why do you trust me so much?"

"I know men. You understand horses, and that's what this place is built on."

Apach went to where Otis was sitting and knelt on one knee before the older man. "I have no family. They were killed long ago. I have lived by my wits, and by what I could gather. Many times I have been hungry, and there were times I have done things I am ashamed of. But I swear to you, I will work as I have never worked before to make this place the best in the territory. I am your servant from this day forward."

"No, young man," Otis said quietly. "You are not my servant . . . you will be a son. Let's see what the two of us can do together."

"For a white father you are a very good man." Apach smiled.

"Well, for an Indian you're going to make a pretty good rancher."

The two said no more, for the commitment was fully accepted by both.

Steve rode through the darkness, his mind on Rachel and the dreams he still could not accept as being possible. He wondered if Rachel had been able to explain everything to Carter, and if he had understood.

It could be that Carter would greet him with a shotgun in hand and order him off the ranch. No matter, he had to do all he could to protect what would one day be Rachel's. She had a right to her inheritance . . . and he had no right to anything.

This time he would allow himself the dreams that had

been snatched from him. How he longed to have his own place again, a home . . . a family. The thought of having children with Rachel made his breath catch in his throat. He wanted that so badly, he had to push the thought from his mind.

There were no lights burning in the windows when he arrived, but as he dismounted before the porch, someone moved in the shadows and he realized it was Rachel.

The house had been dark when he approached, and he'd assumed that Rachel and her family had gone to bed. She must have been sitting on the porch, waiting for him.

When she came down the steps, he gathered her into his arms and held her close to him. His mind spun with the sweet pleasure that holding her always gave him. Each time might be the last time, and that made it all the more precious.

"I thought you would be in bed," he whispered.

"I knew you would come home sometime tonight. Besides, I couldn't sleep. Come, sit down and tell me what you've decided to do. Did the marshal have any answers for you?"

"We came up with a plan," Steve replied. They sat together on the porch swing. He put his arm about her, and she rested against him. "What did your father and mother have to say about the situation . . . about us?"

"My mother is all for us. In fact, I have a suspicion she has expected this from the moment you first rode into our yard."

"Oh, really?" Steve laughed.

"Really. She said you reminded her of Dad when he was your age. I thought at the time she was blind"—Rachel turned to look up at him—''but she isn't. You're a lot like Dad.''

''I don't see the resemblance, but I'm grateful she feels that way. I suspect he feels differently than your mother.''

''No, he doesn't. Does that surprise you?''

''It sure does. You don't mean he approves?''

''I think he trusts you, and he likes you. There might be one problem—''

''What's that?''

''He thinks we're going to make our home here, and you are going to go on working for him.''

''You told him different?''

''No, that's for us to tell him. When this is all over. Steve, what did you decide to do?''

''As of tonight, I'm the new owner of the Lazy 8 and Jane Crenshaw's place. With some cooperation I hope to face those men with enough control to stop them. Actually, the Lazy 8 is the prime place. I will control the water, and they'll have to come to me.''

Rachel sat up and looked at him. ''I don't understand . . . Steve, you want them to come after you!''

''They will,'' he said, ''if I let them. But I'm not going to wait. I'm going after them. I want them to know their game is over, and they stand no chance of getting control of this territory.''

''Steve, they'll kill you.''

''They might try, but they'll never succeed. Rachel, I don't want to use my guns for this fight, but I will if I have to. We have to stop them now, or they'll never be stopped.''

''There's something more bothering you, isn't there?''

''I talked with Wade privately. I don't think he's as sure

as he once was that he can get that pardon for me. If that happens . . .''

''If that happens, where will we go?'' she said softly.

''We?''

''Oh, yes. We. You don't think I'm going to let you get away, do you? You're mine, Steve McKean, and whatever it takes, we'll remain together.''

Steve said nothing; his heart was too full for speech. Instead he gathered her into his arms and kissed her until he felt close to losing control. He prayed that fate would let him keep this brilliant bit of heaven. But he also swore that if he didn't get his pardon, he would not drag Rachel from her safe, protected life to one of running from the law. Living with fear was not what he wanted for her. No, if that time came, he would disappear from her life even if it tore the heart from him.

He tasted her willing mouth, tenderly caressing her lips with his until he felt as if he were drowning. God, how he wanted her. He knew that if she were his for a million years he would never have enough of her.

Rachel's giving warmth was driving him wild with desire. Her arms were about him, and her body was pressed so intimately to his that he could feel every sweet curve and valley. Desire played havoc with his body until he could hardly cling to any semblance of control. Only then did he reluctantly hold her away from him.

''Rachel, I love you. More than anything in this world I want you to be happy and to have the best of everything. I don't know how all this is going to work out. But—''

''Oh, no. Steve, I know what you are going to say. I won't let you get away with that. Where you go, I go. I won't let you run alone, if it comes to that. I couldn't bear the thought of you alone, needing someone . . . afraid. I would die a little every day, too. I would rather be with you no matter where you had to go, than to be left here worrying . . . wanting you . . . needing you. I could bear anything but that. You want me to be happy, but I never will be if you take from my life the one thing that would make me happiest of all.''

Steve felt the sting of tears in his eyes. He was unable to speak. He clung to her, thanking God that she was part of his life. Let it be, he prayed, let it be. If there is any hope for me, let it be in Rachel's arms.

For one magical moment he pushed all reality away and simply surrendered to his love. He kissed her deeply and drank in her sweetness as a drowning man gasps for air.

Rachel sensed his desperation, and held him close. She reached for him, mind, body and soul, and promised herself that she would hold him in spite of all, and in the face of fate. She would fight, for her life would be empty without him.

Steve knew quite well he was spinning rapidly past the point of having any control at all. But he also knew this was not the time or place to complete what his body was demanding. If fate decreed it, they would have their time. For now, he had to see that her family and her friends were kept safe from the threats that surrounded them. He held her away from him.

Looking into her languid, heavy-lidded eyes, he knew she was as caught up in desire as he was. That realization was almost enough to batter what control he had left.

''You had better go in,'' he said. ''We have a long, hard battle on our hands. We're going to fight for our love, Rachel. I swear, I am going to fight like I have never fought for anything in my life. Go in, get some rest. If we're lucky, we'll have all the tomorrows in the world. I love you.''

"And I love you," she whispered. "I will fight with you . . . tomorrow, and tomorrow and tomorrow. Good night, my love.''

He wanted to kiss her again, but one more kiss would destroy what little control he had. Instead, gently he released her. He felt the emptiness of his arms immediately and knew the hell he would suffer if he never held her again.

"Good night.''

He sat on the porch for a few minutes after she had left him, then decided he'd better tell Mikah what was transpiring. He rose and, leading his horse, walked to the barn. Inside, he unsaddled the horse, gave him some feed, and put away his gear. He was about to leave the barn and walk to the bunkhouse when a voice from nearby broke into his thoughts.

"Where the hell you been? I been waiting for you for hours.''

"Mikah, I was just on my way to see you. I have a lot to tell you. I think it's time to set some plans into motion.''

"We better talk here. There's too many ears in the bunkhouse.''

"Fine . . . now listen . . .''

Chapter Eighteen

"You mean you set yourself up as a target?" Mikah's voice was heavy with shock and disapproval. "They're going to wipe you out first chance they get. What the hell were you thinking to put yourself in such a position?"

Steve knew it was worry for him that made Mikah's voice sharp. But there was no way to undo what he had done, and he wouldn't even if he could.

"It has to be brought to a head, Mikah, and this is the best way. They can't intimidate me, and going after Quantrell or Jane will be useless now."

"No, they can't intimidate you. They can gun you down when you least expect it. You know that kind doesn't fight straight. They must have a lot of hard cases they can call on who are good with their guns. Did it occur to you that you have a weakness?"

"Weakness?"

"How do you think they'll try to get to you?"

"They can't."

"No? What about through Rachel? You think I'm the only one who knows about how you feel about her? In this place word travels fast, and nobody likes a little gossip more than a lonesome cowboy. There's not a man in the bunkhouse who ain't betting on who the future boss of the Rocking W might be. Especially since Cal Davis and Miss Yvonne are planning to get married."

"I'm not going to be the next boss of the Rocking W, and you can pass that word along."

"You and Miss Rachel . . . ?"

"Oh, me and Rachel will be together, all right . . . if I'm not behind bars," Steve laughed. "But I intend to have a place of my own." He proceeded to tell Mikah about the strip of unclaimed land and his plans to take it.

"It sounds good to me. I expect you'll need the best blacksmith in the territory."

"I don't see how I could do it without you." Steve grinned. "I think Apach is going to stay on with Quantrell, and, if I'm not mistaken, Carlos has gotten real attached to the Crenshaw place and the family that owns it. Those two boys follow him around like he's the answer to all they need . . . I wouldn't be surprised if he is. So, it might just be you, me, and if my luck holds, Rachel."

"And if it doesn't?" Mikah asked.

"Then Rachel would be better off finding someone else. There would be no future at all with me."

"I'll bet she doesn't see it that way."

"It doesn't matter if she does or doesn't. I won't ruin the rest of her life."

"Steve—"

"Mikah, drop it. We both need some sleep. I have a feeling that in a few days all hell is going to break loose around here."

Mikah knew he would not change Steve's thinking, but he also knew that Rachel was not the kind of woman to let him go. The two walked back to the bunkhouse in silence, each caught in his own thoughts.

Within half an hour Mikah was asleep. But Steve found sleep elusive. It was nearing dawn before he drifted off.

Steve struggled up from a heavy sleep long before he was rested. It was daybreak, and the men about him were preparing for work. He lay for a while with his eyes closed, considering what to do first.

He was the last to leave the bunkhouse, and as he started toward the barn, a voice from the porch of the house stopped him.

"McKean!"

He turned to see Carter standing on the porch. For a second he could only wonder if Rachel had been mistaken about how her father felt. He walked slowly toward the house, trying to read Carter's face. But it was as if Carter had no emotions at all. His face was closed and bland.

"Morning, Mr. Walker."

"Morning. Come on in the house. I think you and I have a lot of things to talk over and get straight."

"Yes, sir." Steve spoke to Carter's back, for he was already entering the house. Steve had a feeling this might not be an enjoyable conversation.

Inside, he found Carter waiting for him. "Come into the kitchen and have some breakfast with me. Lori's got flapjacks, and she makes the best in the world."

Steve followed Carter into the large, homey kitchen and was greeted with a warm smile from Lori. "Good morning, Steve. You're just in time to share breakfast with us. I'm sure Rachel will be down very shortly. She's not one to sleep late."

When their plates were full, and Lori had seated herself across the table from Steve, Carter spoke.

"Steve, Rachel had a long talk with us yesterday. It seems you two plan on a future together."

"You have something against that?"

"Don't get defensive. Actually, neither her mother nor I are opposed to it. In fact, we both think she's chosen well."

Steve was silenced for a minute. This was hardly what he had expected. It was just as obvious that Carter and Lori both read his response accurately.

"Did you think otherwise?" Lori asked.

"Frankly, yes," Steve said. "You don't know much about me. Besides, I don't add up to a Cal Davis. I have a lot less to offer Rachel."

"I wouldn't say that," Carter said. "I have a pretty good eye for people. I've hired a lot of men. Some have worked out and some haven't. You are a cut above most of them, and I think that's because you've run a place of your own and you appreciate how hard it is. You work like a man who's working his own land. That's rare. Most do what is asked of them and no more. You continually give that extra bit, even though you have nothing to gain by it."

"I like what I do, and I don't believe responsibility stops with the clock."

"So I see."

"Mr. Walker—"

"Just a minute. I want to say one thing more. We have

no problem with Rachel's choice. I know the two of you won't have much. But the Rocking W is big, and if you're going to help run—"

"Before you go any further," Steve interrupted. "I think I have to make a couple of things clear."

Neither man saw the amusement in Lori's eyes, or the half smile she hid behind her coffee cup. Carter, as far as she could see, was running up against a will as firm as his own. She decided it would be interesting to see the outcome.

"Like what?" Carter asked in true surprise. He had felt he was being magnanimous.

"If Rachel does agree to be with me, we're not going to be living here. I've worked for you out of necessity, but I don't intend to work for you or for any other man in the future. I'm going to work for myself. My future and Rachel's."

Carter sat back in his chair and gazed at Steve for some time. He was not used to having his generosity thrown back in his face as if it were charity.

"This is stupid," he finally said. "You would be cheating Rachel."

"Isn't it up to Rachel to decide that?"

"But . . . you would have to go away, and that isn't fair to us either."

"Why do we have to go away?"

"Where could you settle around here? Unless one of the smaller ranchers has already decided to give up and sell to you."

"Matter of fact"—Steve grinned devilishly—"I now own the C Bar C and the Lazy 8. We're working on the others."

Carter was stunned into silence. "You'll own all of them?"

"Yes. There's a great deal I need to explain to you. But ... first there is something important I have to say. If I don't get my pardon, I won't expect Rachel ... I'll go away and leave her her life."

"Is it that simple?"

"God, do you think it would be simple for me? I would rather die than leave Rachel. But I won't ruin her life, and I won't let her waste the best years of her life waiting for me or running with me."

"You don't intend to go back to Yuma, do you?" Lori said.

"No, I don't."

"You'll become an outlaw?" Carter questioned.

"If that's what it takes."

"I see," Carter said quietly, as if he were considering some possibility that only he knew of.

"Look, the question isn't my freedom, it's not even Rachel and me. It's whether we can save these small ranchers from being gobbled up by some pretty ruthless people."

"Rachel says you're well versed on these people."

"I am. I know how merciless Judge Graham can be." Steve went on to explain the entire situation as concisely as he could. As each man's name was mentioned, Carter grew more and more angry. His face and eyes reflected cold fury at the betrayal he felt.

"What are we going to do?" Carter bent slightly toward Steve as if he had the ultimate answer.

"We?"

"Hell, yes, we. This territory means a lot to me, and Rachel means even more. I'll do whatever is necessary to protect both. I've spent the better part of my life here. Soaked my sweat and blood into this ground. I won't give all that up without a fight. Besides"—his voice grew hard and cold—"these are men I knew and trusted for years. If there is anything I can't abide, it's a liar and a cheat. Now, let's hear these plans you have to . . ."

"To what?" Rachel's voice came from the doorway, and all three turned to look at her.

Steve stood slowly, his eyes locked on her. She looked fresh from sleep, warm and inviting. He found himself hungry for the time when they would waken in their own home and he could take her in his arms.

As he had been watching Rachel, Lori had been watching him. In her heart she felt this was all Rachel needed. This tall, strong man loved her daughter deeply. It was so obvious that anyone who looked at him would know.

"What are the three of you conspiring about?"

"Not conspiring," Steve said. "I've just been filling your parents in on what we were planning to do."

Rachel smiled at Steve so invitingly that it took all his resolve not to gather her in his arms and carry her back to her bed.

"What do you say, Dad? Think we have a chance?"

"Who, you two against those marauders, or you and Steve?"

Rachel flushed, but met her father's laughing gaze. "Both."

"I think *we* have a chance of defeating these charlatans, and I think you and Steve will make the best neighbors we've ever had. I'll tell you both that I will give you all the help you need."

"Is this a special gathering or can anyone join?"

Everyone turned to see a curious Yvonne entering the room. She had heard their voices and had remained still until she could see how the conversation was going. Happy at what she'd heard, she had come into the kitchen.

"It's open to all my family," Rachel said happily, "and since you're the closest thing to a sister I have, come in and help us celebrate."

"What are we celebrating?"

"Beginnings and endings," Steve said.

"Do you want to elaborate on that?"

"Sure do. If all our plans go as well as we hope, we can have a double wedding."

"Well, congratulations. But you said *if* everything goes well. What else are you up to?"

"Saving this territory from scavengers who would strip it of everything worthwhile."

"You have a plan, Steve," Carter said, "and I'd like to discuss it with you. This is a big chance that you're taking. You're making yourself the target, and if I'm not mistaken, these men don't have a lot of pity on anyone who gets in their way."

"They don't. But they're mostly cowards who find their strength in preying on old men or helpless women. I'm a different story. They're not going to play their game of force with me."

"And if they resort to gunfighters? I remember a range war in Texas. There was a lot of shooting before it was all over," Carter said. Rachel made a small, inarticulate sound.

"If it comes to that . . . then I have to fight for what I want. I'll resort to guns if need be."

"You're that good?"

"I'm afraid I'm too good. It's caused me nothing but

grief so far. Maybe it's time for me to gain something from it.''

"I guess all I can say is you won't be standing alone. My men aren't gunfighters, but they can defend the land you hold in your name."

"Mr. Walker"—Steve's voice was rock steady—"I have to have your land and the Bar D as well, or this won't work."

For a stunned minute Carter could only look at Steve. His faith in his daughter's choice of men was going to be tested in the most severe way. If he did sign a deed, Steve could own the entire territory, and perhaps that was what he really had in mind. Had courting Rachel been a means to that end? Carter had to make a choice. His gaze met Lori's; what passed between them was unintelligible to anyone else, but it caused Carter to smile and reply to Steve's words.

"All right, it's yours . . . temporarily. I offered it to you completely and you refused it. I don't suspect you'd take it under these circumstances."

"Thank you," was the only thing Steve could reply. "I'll need something more from you as well."

"Good God, man. You've ridden in here and taken my daughter and my ranch. What more could you possibly need?"

"I need you to ride to the Bar D with me so I can convince Joe Davis to put his ranch on the line as well. Then, if you agree, I'll need your influence to convince the others to do the same."

"You sure don't do things halfway, do you?"

"I can't afford to."

"I don't think I would want to walk in your shoes for the next few weeks. But I'll ride with you."

"Thanks."

"Steve?" It was Yvonne who interrupted.

"What?"

"What if you can't prove what they're up to? What if they just find you and murder you?"

"I can't let them," Steve replied with grim determination.

"You're going to stay right here where we can be with you," Rachel said.

"Don't be foolish, Rachel. They won't move if they don't think I'm easy to get to."

"What are you going to do?" she asked, worriedly.

"First, go into town and let the word out that I now own practically every place in the territory, and that I'm laying claim to that prime piece of land between Morrison's and Bradley's." His gaze held hers. "I have some plans for that land. It's a perfect place to build a ranch and a life."

Rachel couldn't deny that he held her dreams in his hands. She was just frightened that he would give up his life to make sure the rest of them were safe. "And then what?"

"Wait. And that might be the hardest thing about all of this."

"All right. Let's get to the Bar D." Carter laughed. "I think I'm looking forward to seeing old Joe's face when we ask him to hand over everything he owns."

"He'll hand it over," Yvonne said positively.

"Then let's get a move on," Steve said.

It had taken some time for Carter to convince the others, but in the end he was successful. When he and Steve rode into town, it was rather quiet as they tied their horses at the rail. They walked across the wooden sidewalk to the steps that led to Robert Raymond's office.

"Carter, I think I'd better go it alone from here."

"You might need help."

"I don't think so, not today. Men like this don't do their own dirty work. Most are cowards who have to hire their guns. He won't do anything now. I just want to break the news to him."

"I'll be across the street at the restaurant."

"Fine. I'll be there as soon as this little meeting is over."

"Steve, do you intend to go to the judge also?"

"No."

"Why not?"

"I can't prove that the judge and these skunks are connected yet. But I intend to see he goes down with the rest of them."

"And his daughter?" Carter held Steve's gaze.

"She made her choices a long time ago. She's riding the same horse as her father and the rest. You can't change horses in midstream."

Carter nodded, smiled, clapped Steve on the shoulder and turned to walk across the street to the restaurant.

Steve mounted the steps and opened the door to Robert's outer office, where he was met by a thin, rather arrogant young man who had been Robert's secretary for a number of years.

"I'm sorry, sir. Mr. Raymond only sees people by appointment."

"You go in and tell Mr. Raymond that the new owner of the Rocking W would like to talk some business over with him. If that doesn't get his attention, tell him there are a few other ranches in the territory I now own as well.''

There was a sneer on the young man's face as he turned to enter the office.

But when he returned, his pinched face was flushed, and he could not meet Steve's amused look. It was obvious Robert had reprimanded the man severely, and that gave Steve a good idea that Robert Raymond had gotten a shock.

When Steve walked into his office, Robert rose from behind his desk with a broad smile. He extended his hand.

''Mr. McKean, what can I do for you?'' Steve realized the shock had rattled Robert, for he had not given his name when he had come in. Clearly Robert knew quite well who Steve was and was worried about the message he had sent in.

''I didn't know we had met before, Mr. Raymond. I guess you have heard of my recent purchases.''

''Ah . . . no, I mean, I know only the message you sent. You said you now own the Rocking W.''

''No,'' Steve said casually, ''I said I now own most of the territory. The Rocking W, the Bar D, Otis Quantrell have sold out to me, as well as Jane Crenshaw and Jim Jessup. In effect''—Steve grinned—''I own just about everything around here.''

Robert's face had grown whiter, and his eyes more angry with each word. Steve could see that his hands were clenched, even though he tried valiantly to hang onto his smile.

''That should make you a very wealthy man. I don't think beating about the bush is going to do much good between us.''

''No, it isn't.''

''Where the hell did a man who has so recently been a

convicted killer find the money to buy like this?"

"I don't see that my finances are any of your concern, and I didn't realize you knew so much about my past. Who is your informant?"

Robert smiled and ignored the question. "The money isn't my concern. The ranches are. I had made a lucrative offer for those places."

"Lucrative? For whom?"

"For all concerned."

"I don't think so. Strong-arm tactics aren't what I consider 'lucrative offers.' "

"What do you want, McKean? A bigger offer? More profit for you? What?"

"I don't want a thing from you, Mr. Raymond. In fact, I think it would be best if you left the territory altogether."

Robert laughed. "Leave the territory? Don't be a fool. Name your price, McKean."

"How do you know who I am? Was it one of your guns who took a shot at me?"

"I don't know what you're talking about, and I know all the riders in this territory."

"And all about their past history?"

"Sometimes."

"I don't think so. Would you like to know what I think?"

"I suppose you intend to tell me anyway."

"I do." Steve's voice lowered, and he bent toward Robert. "I think you've been able to push around a lot of helpless people. You've scared them. But I don't scare, and I don't run. You can give up and leave them alone, or I can prove to you that all your plans for this territory are over. That includes being the first governor."

If this shook Robert further, he had gained enough control not to let it show on his face. His eyes glinted dangerously, and the fake smile had disappeared. "You are interfering in something beyond you, McKean. I would advise you to sell me that land here and now, and get out of this territory as fast as you can. A man with your reputation might find himself in a lot of trouble, maybe more than you can handle. I hear a man with a fast gun just draws men willing to try him."

"Is that a threat by any chance?"

"Hardly. I do not threaten. I am merely advising you for your own good."

"I appreciate your advice." Steve's voice matched his opponent's in coolness. "But I have too much at stake. I think I'll stick around and see what unfolds when Montana becomes a state."

"Then I don't think we have anything more to discuss."

"I know. I hope you have it straight in your mind. It will do you no good to go after any of the other ranches. They couldn't sell to you if they wanted to." Steve rose. "And I wouldn't sell to you if you had the last dollar in the world."

With these words, Steve strode from the office, closing the door quietly behind him. Robert sat immobile for a minute, then slammed his fist on his desk. "Henry!"

"Yes, Mr. Raymond?"

"Go to the bank. Tell Thaddius to get over here as fast as he can. Tell him to send for that Judge Graham too. Tell him we have a little problem to work out."

Henry scurried away. From across the street Steve watched him leave the office. He stood out of sight, waiting to see what Henry's urgent errand was. It made him feel good to see Henry returning with the banker. What made him feel even better was to see Judge Graham follow within minutes.

"Gathering of vultures," Steve said to himself. He opened the restaurant door and walked inside to explain to Carter just how right he had been.

Chapter Nineteen

When Steve and Carter returned to the ranch, each could read the relief on the faces of the three women. It was clear they had been waiting on pins and needles for their return. Mikah, too, was waiting impatiently for Steve's explanation of all that had happened.

The midday meal had been prepared, and they all sat down to eat while Steve related what had been said in Raymond's office.

"There is no longer any doubt in my mind that Judge Graham is involved in this little plan. He's in it up to his neck."

"Is that the most important thing to you, Steve?" Rachel asked.

"No, Rachel." Steve smiled at her. "I think you know what's most important to me. If the judge wasn't in on it, I think I would just forget him. But in this case, it'll kill two birds with one stone. He can go down with them.''

"Well," Lori said, "I'm sure nothing's going to happen today. Can't we put this aside for a while?"

"You're right, Lori," Carter said. "The sharks are going to gather and make plans. It's time for us to do the same. What do you say, Steve?"

"You're right. I think we ought to send Mikah for Carlos and Apach. Otis and Jane are reasonably safe now. If our enemies come, they'll come where they think they can find me."

"How . . . how soon?" Rachel struggled to keep her worry under control.

"That's something I don't know. No matter when it is, I'm going to be ready for them."

"Will they come here, do you think?" Mikah questioned as he looked from Steve to Carter.

"I doubt it. The Rocking W has too many riders. It's best if I'm seen in town and going about my work the way I always do."

"They'll catch you alone," Rachel protested.

"I have no intention of being alone. That's why I want Mikah to go for Apach and Carlos. The four of us can handle this better than an army."

"For the rest of today, we're not going anywhere or seeing anybody," Rachel said. "You and I have a lot to talk about. This day is mine." She said the words like a statement, but Steve knew she was pleading for this time so the two of them could be together.

"I think you're right, Rachel. We're safe for today. Besides, it will take a while for Mikah to get Apach and Carlos here. Why don't we ride over and look at that land you've been talking about? We might just decide where you want the house."

He could see the relief and gratitude in her eyes.

"I'd like that."

"How about I pack you some food?" Lori said. "You might be longer than you plan."

"Good idea," Steve replied. "How soon can you be ready?"

"I'm ready right now. Come on, Mother, I'll help with that food."

"And I have some work to get done," Carter said. "I'll see you all at supper."

Mikah left, and when Carter, Steve and Rachel had gone, Yvonne and Lori sat together.

"Rachel is scared to death," Lori observed.

Yvonne agreed. "It's rather a new feeling for her, and I don't think she knows quite how to handle it. I hope Steve is right, and nothing happens to him. Rachel's not one to love easily but now that she does, she'd find it very hard to get over it."

"Well, let's talk about something positive . . . like a double wedding."

"Yes," Yvonne said. Both women tried . . . and both knew they weren't fooling each other for a minute.

Steve and Rachel rode together toward the piece of land they hoped would be their home one day. It was small, as ranches go. Certainly nothing like the Rocking W. But to Rachel it held the promise of the future she and Steve would share.

They found the perfect place for the house, on a raised curve of land that had a breathtaking view. There they sat beneath a tree and planned the house. The strain of her worry was making Rachel tense. But she vowed she would not make it harder on Steve by crying the tears she wanted to cry.

Steve was not unaware of her feelings, and after they had eaten, he drew Rachel down on the blanket. They lay holding each other, feeling the peace of being together.

Slowly Steve's kisses coaxed her, until passion took the place of fear, and until, for the moment, he wiped all thoughts of tomorrow from her mind. It was very late when they returned.

For the first three days there was no sign of any trouble. Steve was growing tense as well. Apach had come and so had Carlos. Mikah had made it clear that the three of them, along with Carter and what men he could spare from necessary work, could keep the Rocking W safe.

After four days Steve decided he could wait no longer. The tension was worse than action. He questioned Carter about supplies before breakfast, and Carter told him he was about to send a hand into town for some.

"I'll go and order the supplies. Let them see me in town unprotected."

"You want me to go along?"

"No. I want them to make a move."

"You just be damn careful," Carter said. "Remember, I'm the one who has to live with Rachel if anything happens to you."

"I'll keep that in mind. I wouldn't want to be in that place. I should be back before supper."

Carter nodded and watched Steve walk to the barn to saddle his horse. He was well aware of the gun that hung low on Steve's hip, and the fact that he had spent several hours a day practicing with it. Carter had watched in fascination one day; if there was a man faster than Steve, he had never seen him.

Steve was saddling his horse when Rachel entered the barn. She stood watching him for a minute without his knowing she was there. She knew where he was going.

"Morning, Steve."

He turned to look at her. "Rachel, good morning. I didn't know you were up yet."

"So you were going to slip out and go into town without telling me where you were going."

"I didn't—"

"Don't bother," she said, smiling. "I know you too well by now, and I don't want to hear any sweet talk while you ride off to get yourself killed."

"Now come on."

"I'm going with you."

"No."

"Yes, and you're not going to be able to stop me without hog-tying me, and you'd have a pretty hard time doing that."

"Rachel, this is no time for joking around."

"Who's joking?" she replied as she walked to the stall where her horse stood, led him out and began to saddle him. Steve had a feeling none of his arguments were going to work.

He continued to saddle his horse, waited for her to finish, and the two rode from the ranch.

In town, they tied their horses before the general store and went inside. Once the supplies were purchased, and the owner had declared they would be delivered that morning,

Steve tried to find a way to temporarily separate from Rachel.

"I'd better take a walk over to the saloon and see if I can hear any news."

"You want to get rid of me. All right. I'm going to the mercantile. Steve, don't look for trouble."

"I never have."

"It just always seems to find you."

"If something is started, Rachel, it's a good thing to see it ends right."

"Yes, ends right. Not with you dead."

"I'll be careful."

Rachel knew she could push it no further. Steve had to do what he was doing, and she had to let him . . . even if it crushed her spirit to let him walk back out onto the street.

She stood and watched him go, wishing with all her heart the two of them were a million miles from here. Then she walked inside the mercantile . . . and came face to face with Ann Graham.

Steve had just started across the street, unaware that Robert, Thaddius, Nathan, Silas and Charles stood in a quiet group in Robert's office watching from the window. They had carefully arranged for the sheriff to be called from town for a week on trumped-up business, and the deputy, in their pay, was to remain absent until everything was over. If the gunfighter they had hired won, Steve would be out of their way. If he lost, the deputy would be after Steve.

Steve had crossed halfway when a rough voice called out his name.

"McKean!"

He paused, knowing that if he turned around he would

be committing himself. He knew what was to come, and he knew who was behind it. He looked up, and through the curtains he could see the shadowed forms of the men watching.

"McKean! You afraid to turn around?"

Steve turned and looked across twenty feet at the man who had called him.

"I have no fight with you."

"I was told you'd run." The voice was taunting.

"I have no intention of running," Steve said. "I was only giving you the opportunity to get some sense . . . before I kill you."

The man was tall and lean, and Steve knew from experience that he knew how to use the gun he wore. His face carried the hungry look of a man paid to kill. Small, narrow eyes regarded Steve with little emotion.

"You think you're fast? I think you're afraid."

"You talk too much," Steve replied in a bored voice. "If you're going to try it . . . then try."

The two stood, poised, expectant . . . waiting for the first blink, the first move.

Inside the mercantile Rachel and Ann heard the voices from outside before they could speak to each other. To Rachel it was chilling. She could feel a cold hand squeeze her heart. Her fears were coming true.

She didn't care to speak to Ann, and Ann, who had heard as well, didn't care to confront her either, not now, not when Steve was there on the street facing death. Both of them were drawn to the window. Rachel muffled the sound of fear that bubbled up inside her. She would never give Ann Graham that kind of satisfaction.

She glanced at Ann only for a second, but she was surprised by the look in the other woman's eyes. She was afraid too. It seemed Ann didn't want to see Steve gunned down either. For a second a surge of hot jealousy coursed through Rachel. This woman was partly responsible for Steve's being in prison in the first place, and despite everything, she still loved Steve in her confused and twisted way.

Rachel wanted to rush out and call Steve's name, but she knew that anything that distracted him now might cost him his life.

Steve remained still as stone as he waited for the other man to move. He was surprised that he felt no fear, and was steady. He had to stop this man or everything they'd planned would be for nothing.

"What's the matter?" he taunted. "Second thoughts? Who's afraid now?"

"I heard you was fast, but I can take you."

"You're a lot of wind. You talk a good game, but you're not man enough to follow it up." Steve watched with satisfaction as the man's eyes lit with rage. It was what he wanted. An angry man was often too quick and not accurate.

"You're wasting my time," he continued. "Go and practice on some wild boys. They're more your class."

There was a deep growl from the man, then two hands moved with lightning speed. Two shots rang out: one splattered into the ground between Steve's feet; the other found its mark in the gunfighter's heart.

There was an explosive silence, then Steve turned to walk away. A few steps and he was met by Rachel, who threw herself into his arms. Ann stood inside the mercantile, and did nothing to stop the tears that slid down her cheeks.

The window at Robert's office was empty now. The men stood inside the room and considered their next move. It was the judge who found their answer.

Steve and Rachel rode back to the ranch in a strange kind of silence. She would have given anything to erase the look of death from his stark face. She knew that what he had just done had torn a part of him away, and she hoped her love would be enough to heal the wound.

After they returned, Rachel answered her family's questions while Steve sought a moment of solitude. She didn't try to do anything more than to be there when he reached for her, and he did. They spent the night in each other's arms, forcing all reality away except the love they shared.

The next day Steve found it easier to answer questions, and to make it clear that he thought this just the beginning. Mikah, Apach and Carlos were silent. They knew what needed to be done.

"My God," Lori breathed. "How can this be? Men who just kill for the love of killing."

"They kill for the love of profit and power," Steve said. "There's a fortune to be made here, not to mention the power they could hold. Montana Territory is rich in fertile land. They want to control that. To do it, they have to own everything you've worked for all these years. We have to stop them one way or the other."

"And the other is a gun," Lori said.

"It was inevitable. When there's an intruder in your home, and he wants to destroy you, your best bet is to destroy him first. In this territory that takes a gun."

"They are going to keep throwing gunfighters against you until one of them is faster and kills you," Carter said. "We have to find a way to stop all this."

"They want what they think I have. I am just afraid they will find another way."

"Another way?" Rachel frowned.

"Another way," Steve said grimly. "And that means none of you three women leaves this ranch without us. All they need is for one of you to fall into their hands. They know that we would give them anything to keep you safe."

Rachel smiled. "I promise I'll not leave your side until you get tired of me."

"That will be a lifetime." Steve smiled for the first time since he'd returned from town.

"We have to find another answer," Carter said. "We can't go on being prisoners in our own home."

"Oh, I don't think it will take so long," Steve said with more certainty and calmness than he felt. "They don't want to waste more time eliminating us than they have to. You're the backbone of resistance, Carter, and you upset all their plans. First when you hired me, and second when you sold to me. They have to break us first. I have a feeling we'll be getting a visit from someone soon. Until then, we have to keep our eyes open for their next move."

"We need someone in authority."

"What good would that do? They will simply deny everything, and you can't prove a thing. Besides, when we need him, Marshal Wade will be here. I just hope he can bring in enough force to stop them. How is the judge around here?"

"Judge Montgomery? He's a fair and just man. I think if we bring some proof to him, he'll act on it."

"I certainly hope he's stronger and more honest than Graham. I wish there was a way to tie Graham to this."

"I just hope you never have to cross his path again," Rachel added fervently.

Rachel wakened just before dawn with a feeling that something was either drastically wrong or that something was about to happen. She rose silently and made her way to the kitchen. Perhaps if she made some coffee and had a cup or two it would help.

She didn't light a lamp, for the sun was on the horizon and there was enough light to brighten the kitchen. She prepared the coffee and walked out onto the porch, holding the warmth of the cup between her hands.

She sat on the front porch steps and listened to the peaceful chatter of birds, enjoying the moment. It was a shadow . . . or a movement near the barn that drew her attention. Who could be up already?

She set the cup aside and rose. Slowly she walked to the barn. But when she opened the barn door there was no sound.

"Steve?" she half whispered.

"Over here." The sound of his voice was muffled, and came from the dark interior. She followed the sound of his voice.

She was not prepared for the rough arm that caught her about the waist, or the hard hand that covered her mouth and stopped the scream. She struggled and fought with two men with every ounce of strength she had, but it was ineffectual. Within seconds she was bound and gagged and thrown up on a horse before one of her captors.

Soon they were in motion and riding away from the

ranch. She had heard no sound from her captors, nor had she recognized either of them. She cursed herself for being so careless, and began to consider how she could escape.

The farther they rode, the more furious she felt. She was being taken to lure Steve, and to make him surrender what they wanted. She also knew Steve would give up all he had . . . even his life for her. She willed him to use his head and not his heart.

Steve jerked awake as if he'd been shocked. He sat upright, wondering what had wakened him. Had he been dreaming? If so, he couldn't remember what about. Still he felt an uncomfortable nagging in his mind, as if he should be up and about doing something.

Unable to sleep any longer, he rose, washed and dressed. Then he left the bunkhouse quietly. The men had at least another half hour of sleep, and he didn't want to cheat them of it.

When he crossed the yard to the house, he was surprised to find a cup of still warm coffee on the top step of the porch. For some reason it sent a current of warning through him.

He opened the front door and was greeted with silence. Again the alarms jangled. Who had been out drinking coffee on the porch? He walked into the kitchen and smelled the aroma of freshly brewed coffee. Nothing made sense.

He was about to rouse someone when Lori appeared in the doorway.

"Steve, good morning. Thanks for making the coffee. I thought I would be the first one up. I usually am."

"I didn't make the coffee. I guess someone else is up early."

"Carter is still in bed, and when I passed Yvonne's room, the door was ajar, and she was still asleep."

"Then it has to be Rachel."

"I'll go and see." Lori left the room, and was back in seconds. "She's not in bed. Perhaps she's in the barn."

"I'll check." Steve moved quickly, for a terrible thought was eating at him. In the barn Steve searched, but there was no sign of Rachel, and her horse still stood in its stall. He returned to the house, and when Lori saw his face, her smile faded.

"Go and wake up Carter," he said abruptly. "I'll get the men up. Rachel isn't here."

"Oh, God." Lori's voice shook with fear.

"Her horse is still here, and I don't think she is foolish enough to go for a walk. Hurry."

They had to admit the bitter truth. Rachel was gone. Steve sent for Apach, who came swiftly.

"Apach, if anyone can follow their trail, it's you. We have to find her, and I don't think we have a whole lot of time to do it."

Apach agreed. "They will not harm her, at least not now. But they will only give her back to you on one condition."

"I know."

"If they harm a hair on her head . . ." Carter said.

"Our prime worry is to find her before they approach us," Steve said. "In that case . . . we would have to give them what they want. Do you know what a thing like that would do to Rachel, and to every person who put his or her trust in us?"

"It would kill her," Lori said.

"We can't let that happen."

Carlos came in along with Mikah, and Steve made short

work of explaining the situation to them. "We have to get going. Time won't wait for us."

Within the hour, the men rode away from the ranch, letting Apach's expertise guide them.

Rachel was growing more angry and desperate every moment. She saw the sun climbing higher in the sky and knew she had been missed by now. She had to get free.

Carefully she studied her captors and the area around her.

She had no idea where they planned on taking her, but she did know every inch of the land surrounding her ranch.

She had roamed this land from the time she was a child and could sit before her father on his horse. It took some time, but after a while she figured out where they were going.

Quite a distance from her home, the river tumbled down a cliffside. Behind the waterfall was a place she had played as a child, a hideaway where she could think on her own. She had thought she was the only person in the world who knew about her secret sanctuary. It startled her that these strange men seemed to share her secret. It was also clear to her that neither her father nor Steve would think of looking for her here. It was up to her, she felt, to find her way to freedom.

Under the waterfall there was an indentation in the rock that created a small cave. She was half dragged, half thrust inside. Then, to her surprise, without a word either of warning or of threat, she was left alone. Immediately she peered outside the veil of water and could see the shadowed shapes of the two men guarding her. She sat down and considered her next move.

The day wore on, and the men still sat outside. She wondered if they were waiting for something or someone. There had to be a way to get out of this . . . there had to. But the sun began to die, and she had thought of nothing. She refused to lose faith. Steve would be searching for her. He would not give up easily. She wondered what he was doing and thinking right now. After a while only the glisten of reflected moonlight broke the shadows within the cave. Outside, darkness kissed the land.

Steve had grown more silent and more frantic with each passing moment. As the day wore on, his fear for Rachel began to grow. His fear for her, and his disbelief that Apach couldn't find any trail. The men who had taken her were clever enough to know how to hide their trail. Steve knew that eventually Apach would hunt them down, but time was a luxury they didn't have.

It was two in the morning before anyone could convince Steve that no trail would be discernible when it was this dark. They headed back to the ranch.

"We will begin again at dawn," Apach said. "I am sorry to have failed you, my brother."

"You haven't failed me, Apach. I know you're doing your best. This kidnapping was well planned. Get some rest; dawn comes early."

Steve couldn't sleep; he was tormented by thoughts of Rachel and what might have happened. He wouldn't put anything past his enemies. They were deadly, and Rachel might be paying the price for his interference.

Time, which had flown by so fast before, began to crawl so slowly that Steve found it hard to keep from rushing to his horse and continuing the search alone. Even though he knew it would do little good. He could hardly stand the deep loneliness he suddenly felt, knowing he could not reach out and touch the woman who had given him back his life and a new belief in himself.

He dressed and went outside, and watched the sky go from black to gray and then develop strands of pink and red. He felt a kind of relief that a new day was dawning. When he went back into the house, he found a sleepless Lori, Carter and Yvonne sitting at the table, drinking coffee.

"There's a light on in the barn," Steve said. "I think Mikah is saddling up, and Apach and Carlos will be with him. We had better go."

Carter spoke just before he stood. "I've drawn in as many men as I can get hold of. I've worked out a pattern for them to cover, just so we don't waste time covering the same ground."

"Good idea," Steve replied.

"Steve, don't you want something to eat, or at least some coffee before you go?" Lori asked.

"No, no thanks, Mrs. Walker. There's no time. One minute might be the minute we need most."

"I understand." She fought not to cry. "You must find my daughter . . . you must."

"We'll find her." Carter went to Lori and put his arm about her shoulders. "We'll find her." Carter had never felt so helpless in his life, and he could see the same fear and frustration written on Steve's face.

Neither man spoke again . . . there was nothing more to say. Footsteps on the porch told them the others had arrived. When Apach, Mikah and Carlos came in, their faces were grim. Every man was containing himself with great control. But thoughts of violence ran rampant in all five men.

"Everyone ready?" Carter asked.

They nodded. Guns belts were slung around their hips, and rifles were held in steady hands. Their eyes were cold as death. They had little respect for people who preyed on women.

Steve picked up his rifle. "I think we'd better be on our way. Carter, what area do you have covered?"

"Three men are searching west of here, five up on the north ridge, and two between here and the river."

"That leaves a lot of territory for us to cover."

"We've been over some of it before."

"We'll go over it again until we find some sign," Steve said determinedly. "Let's go." They had started for the door when the sound of footsteps came to them. They looked at each other in surprise.

Steve was closer to the door than the others. Rifle in hand, he reached out and opened it. He had thought he was prepared for anything . . . anything but the sight of Rachel standing in the doorway.

For a minute they were so shocked that no one could speak. Rachel smiled.

"Were you all waiting up for me?"

Steve gave a ragged sound of relief and snatched Rachel into his arms. When she was crushed against Steve's chest, she could feel that he was shaking.

"Rachel, Rachel, I thought . . . Are you all right? Where have you been? What happened?" While he was questioning her, he was touching her hair, her cheeks, and taking her hands in his. She could see his almost painful relief.

Quickly she tried to answer their questions, and to assure them she was fine. She told them of the abduction, and where she had been all night.

"I don't understand how you got away from them." Steve's voice was still a bit out of control.

"Well, it is strange. Once they put me there, they didn't even bother to check to see what I was doing. I would look out occasionally and see them there, seated around their fire. When I looked out at dawn this morning, they were both gone. I found an unsaddled horse outside and here I am."

"This doesn't make sense." Steve was as puzzled as the rest of them. "They knew they had the advantage. If they had kept you . . ."

"You would have given them whatever they demanded," Rachel finished, reaching out to touch him.

"Yes, anything," Steve replied quietly, his gaze warming her through and through.

"Now it's not necessary."

"This still doesn't make any sense. It's as if they just decided to let you go."

"Or let her escape," Apach said.

"Let her escape," Steve repeated. "But why?"

"The only thing I can think of is that they wanted a distraction . . . something to hold our interest for a day or so."

"A distraction," Steve said. "Of course, they're planning something, and they needed another day to get it done. But what?"

As if to answer their questions, again they heard the sound of footsteps on the porch, only this time it sounded like more than one person, and they were the heavy footsteps of men.

It was Carter who went to the door. When he opened it, three men stood before him. He recognized them all.

"Deputy Taylor, what can we do for you?"

"I've come here officially, Mr. Walker. Can I come in?"

"Yes, of course. What official business?"

The deputy didn't answer him. Instead, he looked at Steve.

"Steve McKean?"

"Yes?"

"I have to bring you in. You're under arrest."

There were several mutters and gasps.

"Under arrest for what?"

"For murder. I hope you won't force me to handcuff you. I hate to do this, Mr. Walker," he said to Carter, "but I have my orders."

"Orders from Sheriff Manson?"

"No sir. Seems the sheriff had some business that took him out of town temporarily."

"This happened pretty sudden, didn't it?"

"Oh, yes sir, you might say that. But Simon Franklin is sitting in for him. He's the one who wants you brought in. Says he got word you have an old sentence hanging over your head and he's gotten orders to hold you here for both running from prison and for shooting a man. You come along with no trouble now. I don't want you causing a fuss in this house."

"I'll go," Steve replied.

But both Carter and Rachel were gazing at the deputy with looks on their faces that shook Steve.

Chapter Twenty

"He's not going to jail!" Rachel declared. "He's not guilty of anything. I was there, and I saw the whole thing. That man attacked him first."

"Ma'am, I don't care how it happened," the deputy responded. Then he motioned to the two men with him and they drew their guns. "I have orders to bring him in, and I expect to do just that . . . one way or the other. I hope you don't decide to do something foolish."

Steve understood now why Rachel had been taken, and what they planned. The chances were very high that he would never complete the trip into town. He wondered if he would even get off of Rocking W range alive.

"He'll go with you peacefully," Carter said firmly.

"Dad!" Rachel looked at Carter in disbelief.

"It's all right, Rachel. Mikah and I will ride with them." He spoke to Rachel, but his eyes were on the deputy.

"Apach and Carlos have other things to do." He looked at Apach, who understood at once what he wanted. He was to find Wade as fast as possible. It was a good thing Wade was camping not too far away. He turned to Steve. "I know Judge Montgomery. He's not the kind to put up with railroading in his court."

Steve was relieved to hear Carter's confidence, and to believe that once Wade arrived the problem could be solved. Rachel was silent, for she knew Carter meant to keep Steve from being shot "trying to get away."

"You're right, Dad, and I'm riding with you."

Steve started to protest until his gaze met Rachel's and he saw the determination in her look.

"Good," Carter said in approval. "That way we can all talk to the judge when we get there."

The deputy smiled again. "Judge Montgomery is out of town. He got another judge to sit in for him while he was gone. It seems he and the sheriff had some business elsewhere."

"Another judge?" Steve felt the hand of brutal fate tapping his shoulder. He knew without asking, but he wanted to hear the words. "This other judge, what's his name?"

"Graham, Judge Nathan Graham." It was obvious that the deputy wasn't aware of the association between Steve and Graham. It would be days, Steve suspected, before Judge Montgomery would be back. Long enough to see him hanged, or returned to Yuma Prison. He feared the latter more.

"Do not let them make you lose control," Apach said. He turned to the deputy, who took a step away from him when he saw the look in Apach's eyes. "If anything should happen to my friend on your way to town, I would leave this territory in a hurry. Otherwise you might not leave it at all.''

The deputy was flustered. He had begun to dislike what was happening. He had not been warned that there would be so many people interested in protecting this man. In fact, he had been told nothing.

''Nothing is going to happen to him,'' he said in a calm and positive voice. ''I'm just gonna do my job and bring him in.''

''See that he arrives safely.''

''He'll get there safe all right. That I promise.'' He frowned. ''I gotta get him there for the hanging.''

''You're so sure of the outcome?'' Carter asked softly. His tone held the same threat as Apach's words.

The deputy shook his head. ''No, sir. It isn't my job to judge. I just do as I'm told. The law is up to the judge.'' He turned to Steve again. ''We'd better get going.''

Steve, Mikah, Carter and Rachel left with the deputy. Apach and Carlos left right after them. They had work to do.

When the cell door closed behind Steve, he felt overwhelmed by anger and a fierce claustrophobia, as if he were being smothered. He was afraid, and he refused to let those around him know it.

Rachel stayed with him as long as she was allowed, and the deputy had to force her and her family away in the end. Steve felt the emptiness when she was gone. He wondered what the future might hold for him . . . or if he was going to have a future at all.

It was late at night. Through the cell window he could hear the town grow quiet. Still, he couldn't sleep. He clung to the sweet memories of Rachel and their love. He knew he had little in the world to carry him through this but Rachel's love.

The hours drifted into each other. Steve wondered what Wade could do when he arrived . . . if he arrived in time.

Near midnight he heard the door between the sheriff's office and the cells open. He was prepared for some hired killer to come finish him off but he hadn't expected to see Nathan Graham enter and approach his cell. He was even more surprised when Graham took the cell key from his pocket and opened the door. Steve backed away to lean against the wall. Then he folded his arms and waited for what he knew was coming.

"Well, well, well," Steve said with a smile, "to what do I owe this late night visit?"

"Don't be foolish, Steve." Nathan smiled. "We have a great deal to talk about."

"Oh? And what might that be?"

"I want you to sign over the ranches you own to some friends of mine."

Steve laughed. "When hell freezes over."

"You know I will see that you don't wind up with that land. I will find the best way to stop you. You have been a constant problem to me, with all your interfering in my plans."

"Even if you kill me, the land you and your friends want will still belong to me. Tell me something. The kidnapping of Rachel Walker was just a way to stall for time, wasn't it?"

"That's right. We needed your attention on anything but what was going on in town. It was not easy to rid ourselves of Judge Montgomery. It took some doing to convince him that I was most willing to sit in his place.

"I also needed to prove a point to you, and I think I've done that efficiently. You are no longer free to protect Rachel. Should you disagree with me tonight, well"—he shrugged eloquently—"there is no imagining what might happen if we are forced to take her again."

"You are a bastard."

"There is no need to get personal. This is just a little business deal."

"Let me tell you something, I'll hang before you or your friends get your hands on that land. Why don't you just end it, and tell your friends there will be no dealings?"

"I think there is one thing you have overlooked."

"Oh, what's that?"

"Do you remember how you lost your ranch before?"

"Did you think I would forget?"

"You have no legal heirs, my friend," Nathan said. He smiled a vicious smile. "So if we see you hanged, we can acquire your land with ease, and there is nothing you or your friends can do about it. The land will be ours. What you have to decide is whether you want to live or not."

"It seems we had this battle before."

"And if you remember correctly, I won then. I will win now. If you want to stay alive, why not capitulate and sign the papers?"

"You're not going to be so lucky this time."

"You consider it luck? I am surprised at your continued stubbornness, and your continued stupidity."

"I wouldn't give you the satisfaction if I were standing on the gallows right now. There has to be a trial. I'll shout my head off about what you and your friends are doing."

Nathan chuckled. "I'm afraid not. You see, Swope is coming here with the papers that committed you to prison. In fact, I expect him in on the morning train. He is truly anxious to resume your acquaintance. You were such an amusing guest. We have 'arranged' your leaving Yuma to look like an escape. I am afraid I will just have to accommodate him. There will be no trial. You have forty-eight hours to make a decision. Send the deputy for me when you decide to be smart and sell."

Nathan again laughed his satisfied laugh. "Oh, by the way. If you are waiting for your friend the marshal, don't. He was the first thing we took care of. He won't be coming to your aid. There is no one else who can verify that you didn't escape from prison. You sell . . . or take the consequences. What do you say?"

"Marshal . . . how did you know about Wade?"

"The Pinkertons are able and useful. They've served me well."

"I see."

"Now, have you thought everything over?"

"Like I said before, go to hell," Steve replied calmly, his calmness covering his reaction to Graham's revelations.

"Then I will say good night. Remember, forty-eight hours. No more." Nathan turned and walked away, locking the door behind him.

Steve sat slowly down on his bunk. He needed to think. There had to be some way to stop this, but for the life of him, he couldn't think of anything. His mind was in a turmoil.

Wade. What had happened to Wade? Wade was the only one who could keep him from Yuma. And Nathan was right, he had no heirs.

For the first time since he had run across Nathan Graham again, he felt desperation creeping into his thoughts. It was debilitating, and he knew he couldn't afford it.

He forced the thoughts of prison out of his mind and began to consider some kind of plan . . . any kind of plan, no matter how desperate, would be acceptable now.

But nothing came . . . nothing but visions of Rachel, and the bitter thought that he had failed her and the other land owners. He had been the one to convince them to go along with his plan.

Emotionally drained, he finally lay on his bunk and drifted into an uneasy sleep. He forced everything from his mind but Rachel, Rachel and his dreams of the future. How close, and yet how far away they were.

He didn't hear the outer door open again, and didn't sense anyone there until his name was spoken softly.

"Steve . . . Steve."

He nearly leapt from the bunk. "Rachel! How did you get in here? I thought the outside door was locked."

"It was. I . . . found a way . . ."

"You went to Nathan!"

"I had to see you." Her voice broke on a sob.

"He is so clever. I'll bet he was pleased that you came to him. He probably hopes you'll persuade me to do what I have refused him. Aren't you supposed to convince me to give the land up?"

"Do it, Steve. I couldn't stand to see you hang."

"I won't hang."

"They said—"

"They're liars, and he doesn't intend to see me hang. He has something better in mind."

"What?"

Sylvie Sommerfield

"Nathan will make sure I go back to prison," he said.

"No!" she gasped. "No, you can't."

"Listen to me, Rachel. If we give in to them, everybody loses. People who trusted me will lose everything they have. You . . . I can stand anything but having you lose your ranch, your dreams."

Rachel reached between the bars and put her arms as far about him as she could. She looked up at him with tears in her eyes. "I don't think you realize how big a part you play in my dreams. I don't care about anything else. I want you to live. Oh, Steve, I love you so much."

Steve cupped her face between his hands and bent to kiss her, treasuring what might be the last time he could touch her. "I love you too, Rachel, with my whole heart," he whispered against her lips. "I wish—"

"I know." She was crying now. "Steve, there has to be something we can do."

"Go back to the ranch and see if Apach and Carlos have returned. I wouldn't put it past Nathan to lie about Wade."

"Lie. Why, did he say Wade couldn't help you?"

"He said something had happened to Wade, and he couldn't make it here before everything was already over."

"I feel so helpless. There has to be something more I can do."

"You can have faith in us. It can't end like this, I won't let it. There has to be a way. I just need time to find an answer. If Nathan came to me tonight, then he must want to hurry this thing up."

"Dad said almost the same thing. He also said he didn't understand why he got no answers from the telegrams he sent."

"Telegrams to whom?"

"As far as I know, to Colorado, Arizona and Washington."

"What for?"

"I don't know. Maybe he doesn't want to get my hopes up. I know Dad. If he can do anything, he will."

"He'll have to move mountains, and worse, he'll have to move them fast. I have forty-eight hours to make some kind of move."

"Forty-eight hours," she said. "It seems we have had so little time together."

"I know, love." The bars between them kept Steve from holding and comforting her. But they touched, and the kisses they shared held the promise both wanted to believe in. "Go, Rachel. This is hard enough for me, but seeing you with tears in your eyes is more than I can take."

She clung to him, and they kissed again and again. Then firmly he held her away from him.

"Go now, please. And try to keep your mind on the fact that we are all going to fight as hard as we can."

"I love you," she whispered.

He smiled tenderly. "I know. It's what's been holding me together."

Rachel backed reluctantly away from the cell, then turned and left. Steve could still feel her presence, and taste the sweetness of her lips.

"Rachel . . . Rachel . . ."

"Forty-eight hours," Carter repeated. "How clever they are not to try to bring him to trial. There are too many who have come to like him. It would be hard to find a jury to convict him. So they want to send him back to Yuma. Well, one way or the other we have to find a way to stop them."

"Can you think of something?" Rachel said. "I know Steve is struggling, but there seems to be nothing." She went on to tell about Wade, and that Steve was anxious to know if Apach had returned. "He has been gone for hours. Wade and Apach should have returned by now."

"And I can't understand why we have had no replies to the telegrams you sent, Carter." Lori sounded truly upset and puzzled.

"I know. Perhaps I should go to town. You know Hank at the telegraph. He might just not have gotten around to delivering."

"I want to go back to the jail, even though I was told last night that Steve isn't allowed any more visitors."

"Keeping him out of contact with everyone who supports him is a tactic to break his resistance. Steve will be all right, Rachel. He's smart enough to know what their strategy is. Let's concentrate on getting him out, not on visiting."

Rachel started to answer when a harsh sound came from outside. Carter looked out the window and smiled. "It's Apach, and he's driving a wagon. I have a feeling the marshal has found a way to get here. I wonder who the rest of them are."

"Rest of them?" Rachel questioned as she came to the window. As Carter had said, a wagon was pulling to a stop before the porch. Everyone hurried out onto the porch and watched as the new arrivals climbed down.

Forty-eight hours, Steve thought. Time was passing, and he had come up with no solution. He knew that everyone was being kept away from him just to weaken him, but he had no intention of weakening. He was going to find a way to transfer the land to someone safe, no matter how he had to do it.

It was midday of the second day of his incarceration, and aside from Rachel the only person he had seen had been Nathan. He had a feeling Nathan would be back for his answer soon.

He had hardly formed the thought when the door opened, and Robert and Nathan came in. They were accompanied by Simon, who was the poorest excuse for a sheriff that Steve had ever seen. Simon stood aside and waited for Robert or Nathan to speak. Not once did he meet Steve's gaze.

"Well, Mr. McKean," Robert said, "have you considered your decision?"

"Of course I've considered it," Steve said.

"Excellent. I thought you would see reason. I have papers all made up, you can just—"

"I said I considered it . . . for about one minute. Let's not fool each other. You don't intend for me to last long after I give you what you want, and I don't intend to let you rob these people of their livelihood. I know you can't allow your dirty ambitions to become public . . . so I sent Apach and Mikah to some friends of mine." He smiled at Nathan. "Did you think he went for the marshal?" Steve laughed. "It seems you have a habit of underestimating me.

"You're lying," Nathan said, anger flushing his face.

"Am I?" One dark eyebrow rose challengingly. "Are you willing to test that?" Steve hoped none of the men were good poker players, because his bluff wouldn't stand too long if they decided to call it.

"You're sealing your own fate," Robert said, his voice as calm as Steve's. "Nathan met the morning train. It seems a good friend of yours is most anxious to see you. He has hand and ankle shackles, and two tickets back to Yuma. Have a nice trip.'' Robert smiled, and turned to call out to someone in the outer office. Two men walked in, and stood waiting for orders.

''Nathan, we have two witnesses, and you have the authority to bring an escaped criminal to justice,'' Robert said. ''I don't see why we don't take care of this little problem right now. Your friend Swope can be on the next train back, prisoner in tow.''

''What about . . . the land?'' the judge said.

Robert laughed. ''Nathan, did you really believe what he said? It was a good bluff, but a bluff nonetheless. Mr. McKean, when we are rid of you, do you think it will take us long to get what we want?''

''I don't believe these people will give up even if I'm not here. I'll find a way to return their land to them. They have seen your game, and they have learned they can stick together. They'll do just that.''

''Never. They are all a bunch of sheep. Once we own Quantrell's place and cut off the water, they will come crying to sell. And I will buy . . . at my own price,'' Robert said with a gleam of malicious humor in his eyes.

Nathan took a folded paper from his breast pocket, unfolded it and scrawled his name on the bottom. ''You are a retrieved criminal, and this paper makes it official. You remember that an escaped convict has an additional sentence. You will be in Mr. Swope's care for a long, long time. We had a little talk, Swope and I. He feels as I do. It would be terrible for you to die in prison. So he will keep you alive . . . just alive. But you will wish a million times over that you could die.''

''You will be taken from here tonight to a safer place.''

Robert smiled. "I have a feeling your friends might try to do something stupid, so we will take you out of their reach. Who knows, for your safe return they might surrender and stop trying to fight the inevitable."

At these words the two men Robert had called in drew their guns and started toward Steve. Steve backed away. If he was going back to Yuma, he wasn't going without a fight.

"Carter Walker knows better than to give in to people like you. With or without me, he will fight you all the way."

"Carter Walker will surrender like the rest of the sheep, once you and his water are gone," Robert replied. He motioned to the two men. "Get him. Drag him out of here. Let's give him a taste of shackles again."

"I wouldn't do that if I were you." The voice came from the open doorway behind the group.

Steve jerked his head in the direction of the door. Robert and Nathan spun around in surprise. Apach, Mikah, Carlos and Carter stood in the doorway . . . with Marshal Thomas P. Wade beside them! Behind them stood a very relieved Rachel, who couldn't take her eyes from Steve.

Wade's arm was in a sling, and he looked pale and a bit weak. Still, his smile was strong and his eyes cold as glass.

"Trying to kill a U.S. Marshal is likely the biggest mistake you've ever made," he said. "It was a mistake that is going to be very costly for you when Steve testifies in court, and is backed up by every rancher in this territory."

It was Nathan who recovered first. He matched Wade's smile. "I'm afraid it won't do your friend much good. I am the judge who sentenced him, and I claim he is an escapee. I have the right and the power to send him back to Yuma, no matter what you think or do.''

"Is that so?'' Wade said quietly.

"Mitchell,'' he called.

In another moment, Mitchell Charles walked into the room. Nathan's face turned gray, but he remained soundless. "You remember Sheriff Charles, from Brandt? He and I have done a whole lot of investigating since you sentenced Steve. An undeserved sentence, by the way. When you and your men weren't around to intimidate them, a lot of people had a lot of things to say. Best of all, a friend of Sheriff Charles's looked into your credentials. It seems you were disbarred a long time ago. No wonder you fled to a small town. It was the only place you could pass yourself off as a judge and get away with it. No, Steve won't be going back to prison . . . but you and your friends will. I think you're right about one thing. Old Martin Swope is going to have a grand time with you. I think he has resented you and your power for a long time. Now it will be his turn.''

"You can't do this!'' Nathan gasped.

"Can't I? Just watch. I've had my fill of you leeches, grabbing and stealing other people's lives. The ranch Steve owned back in Colorado is his again. As for you and your friends, Swope will be taking you back as soon as we can get this trial over and your sentence pronounced.''

They were defeated, and both Robert and Nathan knew it. Nathan was in a total panic, but the lawyer's mind was already spinning. He would find a way out of this for himself if he had to name every person in the plot and define his part in it. He didn't intend to be Swope's victim.

They were forced into the cell Steve had occupied, and

the door was firmly locked before Wade turned to Steve.

"As for you," he said scowling, "I told you to find out who was behind all this. I didn't tell you to take on the whole territory by yourself."

"I didn't plan it that way." Steve smiled. "It just seemed to happen. I sure am grateful you showed up when you did."

"Had no choice." He pointed to Steve's three friends, who grinned in response. "This group would have dragged me here if they had to, and me near death's door."

"Death's door," Carlos laughed. "We found him curled up in bed in a bordello house. Convalescing, I suppose. And don't let him lie to you, he shouted at us to go faster all the way back."

Steve extended his hand to Wade, who took it in a firm grip. "I thank you anyway. You saved me from the worst thing I could imagine."

"And I thank you. We couldn't have resolved this problem without you."

"You're welcome. But I don't think I'll be handy for any more problems you might have."

"Have some plans, do you?"

Steve turned to Rachel, who came to his side. He put his arm about her waist and drew her close to him. "I have a lot of plans. The first is to invite you to a wedding."

"I'd be right pleased. I suppose you're going to take your bride home to Colorado. Your ranch is there."

"No, I'm going to sell it. It will give Rachel and me a good start here. Like you said, this territory will be a state soon. I kind of like the idea of being the son-in-law of the first governor."

"That's not a definite thing yet, son." Carter laughed.

"Why, Carter"—Steve grinned—"I thought Mrs. Walker and Rachel had decided it already."

"You prepared to put yourself in their harness?" Carter chuckled.

"I couldn't be happier about the prospect." Steve looked down into Rachel's eyes and grinned at the bright new future they would share.

Epilogue

The house was small, but it was filled with so much warmth and happiness that it seemed a mansion. Moonlight came in through the window and fell across the man who was standing there looking out.

Steve could still hardly believe the wonderful life he shared with Rachel. He considered himself the luckiest man in the world. The house he had built with his own hands when they had married had already had another room added for the child they were expecting any day now.

He took this quiet moment to thank the powers that be for his good fortune. There had been a time when he had looked at the future with doubt and despair.

He turned at a slight sound and saw Rachel getting up from the bed. She came to his side and he slid his arm about her.

''Are you all right?'' he questioned. He was still afraid

the woman who lit his life could be taken from it. That was a nightmare he couldn't stand to contemplate.

"I think you had better send Mikah for Mother."

"Now?" He felt the sweat begin to pop on his forehead.

"Now, my love. I think your son or daughter has decided to come and see what this world is all about."

"I think it is a little girl, and if she has decided to come in the middle of the night, she's just as obstinate as her mother."

"Perhaps." Rachel giggled.

"I'll send Mikah right away." He swept her up in his arms and carried her back to the bed they shared.

"Steve, I'm fine. This is going to take a long time. Why don't I go to the kitchen and make some coffee? I'm sure Dad will come with Mother."

"I wouldn't doubt it. But I'll make the coffee, and you just stay put." He laid her gently on the bed and bent close. "Rachel, please, don't be stubborn this time. My heart just can't take it. Be careful with yourself. You're my life. Have I told you recently how much I love you?"

"It is always good to hear, even though you manage it a few times a day." She laughed, but she could see the fear in his eyes. Steve was always prepared for something to snatch his happiness away. In the two years they had been married, she had not yet wiped that fear away. "Please"—she tensed with a pain in her back—"send for Mother."

Steve rose and raced from the room, and within minutes an excited Mikah was riding toward the Rocking W.

The balance of the night went faster than Lori, Carter or Rachel expected, yet it seemed to be a thousand years long to Steve, who died with every cry from Rachel. Finally Mikah returned with the doctor.

When Steve heard the baby's first soft cry, he could have wept. He hurried into the room and found Rachel smiling and holding the child in her arms.

"Look, Steve," she whispered, "our daughter. You were right."

For a moment Steve could only see that Rachel was fine and happy. He went to sit beside her. Taking her hand in his, he kissed it, then bent to kiss her.

"Thank you," he whispered against her lips. "I didn't think I would ever be this happy. We have everything in the world. I love you, Rachel."

"And I love you." At that moment the child gave a sighing sound. "I think your daughter just said she loves you too."

"My daughter," he said wondrously. He was captivated by the tiny perfect features, and the small hands that waved about until he caught one in his. He felt a surge of love so profound that he laughed shakily. "She's as beautiful as her mother."

"And as stubborn?" Rachel teased.

"Maybe I can stand that," he laughed. "What will we name her?"

"I think I'm going to let you have that pleasure."

"How about Elizabeth? Do you like it? It was my mother's name."

"Elizabeth is lovely." Rachel looked at the child in her arms. "Welcome to the world, Elizabeth McKean. I'm going to spend a lot of time telling you what a wonderful father you have." She looked up at Steve. "And how much he has filled my world with love and happiness."

For Steve this moment was one of perfection and beauty. There was nothing more he needed in his life but what he could hold here in his arms. The woman who made his life complete, and the child they had created with the profound love they had for each other. The world and his life were full, and he intended to see that in the future he filled their lives with all the love and happiness he could give.

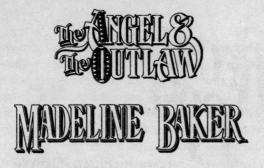

THE ANGEL & THE OUTLAW

MADELINE BAKER

Bestselling Author Of *Lakota Renegade*

An outlaw, a horse thief, a man killer, J.T. Cutter isn't surprised when he is strung up for his crimes. What amazes him is the heavenly being who grants him one year to change his wicked ways. Yet when he returns to his old life, he hopes to cram a whole lot of hell-raising into those twelve months no matter what the future holds.

But even as J.T. heads back down the trail to damnation, a sharp-tongued beauty is making other plans for him. With the body of a temptress and the heart of a saint, Brandy is the only woman who can save J.T. And no matter what it takes, she'll prove to him that the road to redemption can lead to rapturous bliss.

_3931-1 $5.99 US/$7.99 CAN

BAD COMPANY

CAROL CARSON

Trixianna Lawless is furious when the ruggedly handsome sheriff arrests her for bank robbery. But when she finds herself in Chance's house instead of jail, she begins to wish that he would look at her with his piercing blue eyes . . . and take her into his well-muscled arms.

___4448-X $4.99 US/$5.99 CAN

Dorchester Publishing Co., Inc.
P.O. Box 6640
Wayne, PA 19087-8640

Please add $1.75 for shipping and handling for the first book and $.50 for each book thereafter. NY, NYC, and PA residents, please add appropriate sales tax. No cash, stamps, or C.O.D.s. All orders shipped within 6 weeks via postal service book rate. Canadian orders require $2.00 extra postage and must be paid in U.S. dollars through a U.S. banking facility.

Name_____
Address_____
City_____State_____Zip_____
I have enclosed $_____ in payment for the checked book(s).
Payment <u>must</u> accompany all orders. ❑ Please send a free catalog.

GOLDEN DREAMS

ANNA DeFOREST

After her father's sudden death leaves her penniless, Boston-bred Kate Holden arrives in Cripple Creek anxious to start a new life, her elegant upbringing a distant memory and her dream of going to college and becoming a history professor long-forgotten. But the golden-haired Kate soon finds that the Colorado mining town is no place for a young, single woman to make a living. Then desperate circumstances force her to strike a deal with the only man who was ever able to turn her nose from a book—the dark and brooding Justin Talbott.

As skilled at passion as he is at staking a valuable claim, Justin vows he'll taste the feisty scholar's sweet lips—and teach her unschooled body the meaning of desire. But bitter from past betrayals, the wealthy claimholder wants no part of her heart. He has sworn never to let another woman close enough to hurt him—until the lonely beauty awakens a romantic side he thinks has died along with his ideals. For though bedding her has its pleasures, Justin is soon to realize that only claiming Kate's heart will fulfill their golden dreams.

_4179-0 $4.99 US/$5.99 CAN

SIERRA
Connie Mason

Bestselling Author Of *Wind Rider*

Fresh from finishing school, Sierra Alden is the toast of the Barbary Coast. And everybody knows a proper lady doesn't go traipsing through untamed lands with a perfect stranger, especially one as devilishly handsome as Ramsey Hunter. But Sierra believes the rumors that say that her long-lost brother and sister are living in Denver, and she will imperil her reputation and her heart to find them.

Ram isn't the type of man to let a woman boss him around. Yet from the instant he spies Sierra on the muddy streets of San Francisco, she turns his life upside down. Before long, he is her unwilling guide across the wilderness and her more-than-willing tutor in the ways of love. But sweet words and gentle kisses aren't enough to claim the love of the delicious temptation called Sierra.

_3815-3   **$5.99 US/$6.99 CAN**

DEBRA DIER
LORD SAVAGE
Author of *Scoundrel*

Lady Elizabeth Barrington is sent to Colorado to find the Marquess of Angelstone, the grandson of an English duke who disappeared during an attack by renegade Indians. But the only thing she discovers is Ash MacGregor, a bounty-hunting rogue who takes great pleasure residing in the back of a bawdy house. Convinced that his rugged good looks resemble those of the noble family, Elizabeth vows she will prove to him that aristocratic blood does pulse through his veins. And in six month's time, she will make him into a proper man. But the more she tries to show him which fork to use or how to help a lady into her carriage, the more she yearns to be caressed by this virile stranger, touched by this beautiful barbarian, embraced by Lord Savage.

___4119-7 $4.99 US/$5.99 CAN

Dorchester Publishing Co., Inc.
P.O. Box 6640
Wayne, PA 19087-8640

Please add $1.75 for shipping and handling for the first book and $.50 for each book thereafter. NY, NYC, and PA residents, please add appropriate sales tax. No cash, stamps, or C.O.D.s. All orders shipped within 6 weeks via postal service book rate. Canadian orders require $2.00 extra postage and must be paid in U.S. dollars through a U.S. banking facility.

Name_____
Address_____
City_____ State_____ Zip_____
I have enclosed $_____ in payment for the checked book(s).
Payment <u>must</u> accompany all orders. ☐ Please send a free catalog.

PASSION'S TIMELESS HOUR

VIVIAN KNIGHT-JENKINS

Bestselling Author Of *The Outlaw Heart*

Propelled by a freak accident from the killing fields of Vietnam to a Civil War battlefield, army nurse Rebecca Ann Warren discovers long-buried desires in the arms of Confederate leader Alexander Random. But when Alex begins to suspect she may be a Yankee spy, the only way Rebecca can prove her innocence is to convince him of the impossible...that she is from another time, another place.

__52079-6 $4.99 US/$6.99 CAN